Birds of a Feather

A Maisie Dobbs Mystery

JACQUELINE WINSPEAR

JOHN MURRAY

© Jacqueline Winspear 2004

First published by Soho Press, Inc. in the United States of America

First published in Great Britain in 2005 by John Murray (Publishers)
A division of Hodder Headline

Paperback edition 2005

11

A CIP catalogue record for this title is available from the British Library

ISBN 978-0-7195-6624-0

Typeset in Bembo
Printed and bound by Clays Ltd, St Ives plc

John Murray (Publishers)
338 Euston Road
London NW1 3BH

Wakefield Libraries
& Information Services

This book should be returned by the last date stamped above. You may renew the loan personally, by post or telephone for a further period if the book is not required by another reader.

D
adventure
Image

'A terrific mystery . . . Both intriguing and full of suspense, it makes for an absorbing read'
Observer

'A heroine to cherish . . . . Always open-minded, she bobs her hair, drives a red MG and by the end of this story has acquired two suitors. Let's see if they can appreciate how special she is'
New York Times

'*Birds of a Feather* succeeds both as a suspenseful mystery and as a picture of a time and place. Maisie's liveliness of mind, good sense, and kind nature make her a heroine a reader can enjoy spending time with'
Boston Globe

'Jacqueline Winspear has produced one of the most promising characters of the decade with Maisie Dobbs'
Brisbane Courier Mail

'Strongly recommended for fans of good historical writing'
Canberra Times

Birds of a Feather

To Kenneth Leech
1919–2002

During my childhood I was lucky to have Ken Leech as my teacher. In the years of my growing up and into adulthood, I was privileged to count him among my friends.

How will you fare, sonny, how will you fare
In the far off winter night
When you sit by the fire in the old man's chair
And your neighbours talk of the fight?
Will you slink away, as it were from a blow,
Your old head shamed and bent?
Or say, "I was not the first to go,
But I went, thank God, I went"?

– from the song "Fall In" by Harold Begbie, 1914

MAISIE DOBBS shuffled the papers on her desk into a neat pile and placed them in a plain manila folder. She took up a green marble-patterned W.H. Smith fountain pen and inscribed the cover with the name of her new clients: Mr and Mrs Herbert Johnson, who were concerned that their son's fiancée might have misled them regarding her past. It was the sort of case that was easily attended to, that would provide a useful reference, and that could be closed with presentation of a timely report and accompanying account for her services. But for Maisie the case notes would not be filed away until those whose lives were touched by her investigation had reached a certain peace with her findings, with themselves, and with one another – as far as that might be possible. As she wrote, a tendril of jet black hair tumbled down into her eyes. Sighing, she quickly pushed it back into the chignon at the nape of her neck. Suddenly, Maisie set her pen on the blotting pad, pulled the troublesome wisp of hair free so that it hung down again, and walked to the large mirror hanging on the wall above the fireplace. She unpinned her long hair and tucked it inside the collar of her white silk blouse, pulling out just an inch or so around her chin-line. Would shorter hair suit her?

"Perhaps Lady Rowan is right," said Maisie to her reflection in the mirror. "Perhaps it *would* look better in a bob."

She turned from side to side several times, and lifted her hair just slightly. Shorter hair might save a few minutes of precious time each morning, and it would no longer come free of the chignon and fall into her eyes. But one thing held her back. She lifted her hair and turned her head. Was the scar visible? Would shorter hair fall in such a way as to reveal the purple weal that etched a line from her neck into the sensitive flesh of her scalp? If her hair were cut, would she lean forward over her notes one day and unwittingly allow a client to see the damage inflicted by the German shell that had ripped into the casualty clearing station where she was working, in France, in 1917?

Looking at the room reflected in the mirror, Maisie considered how far she had come – not only from the dark dingy office in Warren Street that was all she had been able to afford just over a year ago, but from that first meeting with Maurice Blanche, her mentor and teacher, when she had been a maid in the household of Lord Julian Compton and his wife, Lady Rowan. It was Maurice and Lady Rowan who had noted Maisie's intellect and ensured that she had every opportunity to pursue her hunger for education. They had made it possible for the former tweeny maid to gain admission to Girton College, Cambridge.

Maisie quickly pulled her hair into a neat chignon again, and as she pinned the twist into place, she glanced out of the floor-to-ceiling window that overlooked Fitzroy Square. Her assistant, Billy Beale, had just turned in to the square and was crossing the rain-damp grey flagstones toward the office. Her scar began to throb. As she watched Billy, Maisie began to assume his posture. She moved toward the window with shoulders dropped, hands thrust into imaginary pockets, and her gait mimicking the awkwardness caused by Billy's still-troublesome war wounds. Her disposition began to change, and she realized that the occasional malaise she had sensed several weeks ago was now a constant in Billy's life.

As she looked down at him from what had once been the drawing room window of the Georgian building, he stretched the cuff of his overcoat over the palm of his hand and polished the brass nameplate informing visitors that the office of M. Dobbs, Psychologist and Investigator, was situated within. Satisfied, Billy straightened, drew back his shoulders, stretched his spine, ran his fingers through his tousled shock of wheaten hair, and took out his key to the main door. Maisie watched as he corrected his posture. *You can't fool me, Billy Beale*, she said to herself. The front door closed with a heavy thud, and the stairs creaked as Billy ascended to the office.

"Morning, Miss. I picked up the records you wanted." Billy placed a plain brown envelope on Maisie's desk. "Oh, and another thing, Miss, I bought a *Daily Express* for you to 'ave a butcher's at." He took a newspaper from the inside pocket of his overcoat. "That woman what was found murdered in 'er own 'ome a week or two ago down in Surrey – you remember, in Coulsden – well, there's more details 'ere, of who she was, and the state she was in when she was found."

"Thank you, Billy," said Maisie, taking the newspaper.

"She was only your age, Miss. Terrible, innit?"

"It certainly is."

"I wonder if our friend . . . well, your friend, really – Detective Inspector Stratton – is involved?"

"Most likely. Seeing as the murder took place outside London, it's a Murder Squad case."

Billy looked thoughtful. "Fancy 'avin' to say you work for the Murder Squad, eh, Miss? Don't exactly warm folk to you, does it?"

Maisie scanned the article quickly. "Oh, that's a newspaper invention to sell more papers. I think they started to use it when the Crippen case became big news. It used to be called the Reserve Squad, but that didn't sound ominous enough. And Criminal Investigation Department *is* a bit of a mouthful." Maisie looked up at Billy, "And by the way, Billy, what do you mean by my 'friend,' eh?"

"Aw, nuffin' really, Miss. It's just that –"

Billy was interrupted by the ringing of the black telephone on Maisie's desk. He raised his eyebrows and reached for the receiver.

"Fitzroy five six double o. Good afternoon, Detective Inspector Stratton. Yes, she's 'ere. I'll put her on." He smiled broadly, covering the receiver with his palm as Maisie, blushing slightly, held out her hand to take it. "Now, Miss, what was it that Doctor Blanche used to say about coincidence being a – what was it? Oh yes, a messenger of truth?"

"That's enough, Billy." Maisie took the receiver and waved him away. "Inspector Stratton, how very nice to hear from you. I expect you're busy with the murder case in Coulsden."

"And how did you know that, Miss Dobbs? No, don't tell me. It's probably best that I don't know."

Maisie laughed. "To what do I owe this call, Inspector?"

"Purely social, Miss Dobbs. I thought I'd ask if you might care to dine with me."

Maisie hesitated, tapped the desk with her pen, and then replied, "Thank you for the invitation, Inspector Stratton. It really is most kind of you . . . but perhaps we can lunch together instead."

There was a pause. "Certainly, Miss Dobbs. Will you be free on Friday?"

"Yes, Friday would be excellent."

"Good. I'll meet you at your office at noon, and we can go from there to Bertorelli's."

Maisie hesitated. "May I meet you *at* Bertorelli's? At noon?"

Again the line was quiet. Why does this have to be so difficult? Maisie thought.

"Of course. Friday, noon at Bertorelli's."

"I'll see you then. Good-bye." She replaced the receiver thoughtfully.

"Aye-oop, 'ere's a nice cuppa for you, Miss." Billy placed the tea tray on his desk, poured milk and tea into a large enamel mug for Maisie, and placed it in front of her.

"Don't mind me askin', Miss – and I know it ain't none of my business, like – but why don't you take 'im up on the offer of a dinner? I mean, gettin' the odd dinner fer nuffin' ain't such a bad thing."

"Lunch and dinner are two entirely different things, and going out for luncheon with a gentleman is definitely not the same as going out to dine in the evening."

"You get more grub at dinner, for a start –"

4

Billy was interrupted by the doorbell. As he moved to the window to see who might be calling, Maisie noticed him rub his thigh and wince. The war wound, suffered almost thirteen years before, during the Battle of Messines in 1917, was nipping at him again. Billy left to answer the doorbell, and as he did so, Maisie heard him negotiate the stairs with difficulty as he descended to the front door.

"Message for M. Dobbs. Urgent. Sign 'ere, please."

"Thanks, mate." As Billy signed for the envelope he reached into his pocket for some change to hand the messenger. He closed the door and sighed before mounting the stairs again. As he returned to the office he held out the envelope to Maisie.

"That leg giving you trouble?" she asked.

"Just a bit more than usual. Mind you, I'm not as young as I was."

"Have you been back to the doctor?"

"Not lately. There ain't much they can do, is there? I'm a lucky feller – got a nice job when there's 'undreds and 'undreds of blokes linin' up fer work. Can't be feelin' sorry for meself, can I?"

"We're fortunate, Billy. There seems to be more business for us, what with people going missing after losing all their money, and others getting up to no good at all." She turned the envelope in her hands. "Well, well, well . . ."

"What is it, Miss?"

"Did you notice the return address on the envelope? This letter's from Joseph Waite."

"You mean the Joseph Waite? Moneybags Joseph Waite? The one they call the Banker's Butcher?"

"He's requested that I come to his residence – 'soonest,' he says – to receive instructions for an investigation."

"I suppose 'e's used to orderin' folk around and gettin' 'is own way –" Billy was interrupted once more by the ringing telephone. "Gawd, Miss, there goes the dog-and-bone again!"

Maisie reached for the receiver.

"Fitzroy five six double o."

"May I speak to Miss Maisie Dobbs, please?"

"Speaking. How may I help you?"

"This is Miss Arthur, secretary to Joseph Waite. Mr Waite is expecting you."

"Good morning, Miss Arthur. I have only just received his letter by personal messenger."

"Good. Can you come today at three? Mr Waite will see you then, for half an hour."

The woman's voice trembled slightly. Was Miss Arthur so much in awe of her employer?

"Right you are, Miss Arthur. My assistant and I will arrive at three. Now, may I have directions?"

"Yes, this is the address: do you know Dulwich?"

"Ready when you are, Miss."

Maisie looked at the silver nurse's watch pinned to her jacket as if it were a brooch. The watch had been a gift from Lady Rowan when Maisie took leave from Girton College and became a VAD at the London Hospital, a member of the wartime Voluntary Aid Detachment of nursing staff during the Great War. It had kept perfect time since the very first moment she pinned it to her uniform, serving her well while she tended injured men at a casualty clearing station in France, and again when she nursed shell-shocked patients upon her return. And since completing her studies at Girton the watch had been synchronized many times with the pocket watch belonging to Maurice Blanche, when she worked as his assistant. It would serve her for a few more years yet.

"Just time to complete one more small task, Billy; then we'll be on our way. It's the first week of the month, and I have some accounts to do."

Maisie took a key from her purse, opened the middle drawer on the right-hand side of her large desk, and selected one small ledger from the six bound notebooks in the drawer. The ledger was labelled MOTOR CAR.

Maisie had been given use of the smart MG 14/40 sports roadster belonging to Lady Rowan the year before. Recurring hip pain suffered as the result of a hunting accident rendered driving difficult for Lady Rowan, and she insisted that Maisie borrow the motor car whenever she wanted. After using the vehicle constantly for some months, Maisie had offered to purchase the MG. Lady Rowan teased that it must have been the only transaction involving a motor car in which the buyer insisted upon paying more than the owner had stipulated. A small percentage for interest had been added at Maisie's insistence. Taking up her pen, Maisie pulled her cheque-book from the same drawer and wrote a cheque, payable to Lady Rowan Compton. The amount paid was entered in a ledger column and the new balance owed underlined in red.

"Right then, Billy, just about done. All secure?"

"Yes, Miss. Case maps are in my desk, and locked. Card file is locked. Tea is locked —"

"Billy!"

"Just pullin' yer leg, Miss!" Billy opened the door for Maisie, and they left the office, making sure that the door was locked behind them.

Maisie looked up at the leaden sky. "Looks like rain again, doesn't it?"

"It does at that. Better get on our way and 'ope it blows over."

The MG was parked at the edge of Fitzroy Street, its shining paintwork a splash of claret against the grey April afternoon.

Billy held the door for her, then lifted the bonnet to turn on the fuel pump, closing it again with a clatter that made Maisie wince. As he leaned over the engine, Maisie observed the dark smudges below his eyes. Banter was Billy's way of denying pain. He gave the thumbs-up sign, and Maisie set the ignition, throttle, and choke before pressing the starter button on the floor. The engine burst into life. He opened the passenger door and took his seat beside her.

"Off we go, then. Sure of your way?"

"Yes, I know Dulwich. The journey shouldn't take more than an hour, depending upon the traffic." Maisie slipped the MG into gear and eased out into Warren Street.

"Let's just go over what we already know about Waite. That Maurice had file cards on him is intriguing in itself."

"Well, according to this first card, Dr Blanche went to 'im askin' for money for a clinic. What's that about?" Billy glanced at Maisie, then looked ahead at the road. "It's starting to come down."

"I know. English weather, so fabulously predictable you never know what might happen," observed Maisie before answering Billy's question. "Maurice was a doctor, Billy, you know that. Before he specialized in medical jurisprudence, his patients had a bit more life in them."

"I should 'ope so."

"Anyway, years ago, long before I went to work at Ebury Place, Maurice was involved in a case that took him to the East End. While he was there, examining a murder victim, a man came rushing in shouting for help. Maurice followed the man to a neighbouring house, where he found a woman in great difficulty in labour with her first child. The long and the short of it is that he saved her life and the life of the child, and came away determined to do something about the lack of medical care available to the poor in London, especially women and children. So for one or two days a week, he became a doctor for the living again, working with patients in the East End and then across the water, in Lambeth and Bermondsey."

"Where does Waite come in?"

"Read the card and you'll see. I think it was just before I came to Ebury Place, in 1910, that Maurice took Lady Rowan on one of his rounds. She was appalled and determined to help. She set about tapping all her wealthy friends for money so that Maurice might have a proper clinic."

"I bet they gave her the money just to get her off their backs!"

"She has a reputation for getting what she wants and for not being afraid to ask. I think her example inspired Maurice. He probably met Waite socially and just asked. He knows immediately how to judge a person's mood, and to use that — I suppose you'd call it energy — to his advantage."

"Bit like you, Miss?"

Maisie did not reply but simply smiled. It had been her remarkable intuitive powers, along with a sharp intellect, that had led Maurice Blanche to accept her as his pupil and later as his assistant in the work he described as the forensic science of the whole person.

Billy continued. "Well, apparently old Dr Blanche tapped Waite for five 'undred quid."

"Look again, and you'll probably find that the five hundred was the first of several contributions." Maisie used the back of her hand to wipe away condensation accumulating inside the windscreen.

"Oh 'ere's another thing," said Billy, suddenly leaning back with his eyes closed.

"What is it?" Maisie looked at her passenger, whose complexion was now rather green.

"I don't know if I should read in the motor, Miss. Makes me go all queasy."

Maisie pulled over to the side of the road and instructed Billy to open the passenger door, put his feet on the ground and his head between his knees. She took the cards and then summed up the notes on Joseph Waite. "Wealthy, self-made man. Started off as a butcher's apprentice in Yorkshire – Harrogate – at age twelve. Quickly demonstrated a business mind. By the time he was twenty he'd bought his first shop. Cultivated the business, then outgrew it within two years. Started selling fruit and veg as well, dried goods and fancy foods, all high quality and good prices. Opened another shop, then another. Now has several Waite's International Stores in every city, and smaller Waite's Fancy Foods in regional towns. What they all have in common is first-class service, deliveries, good prices, and quality foods. Plus he pays a surprise visit to at least one store each day. He can turn up at any time."

"I bet they love that, them as works for 'im."

"Hmmm, you have a point. Miss Arthur sounded like a rabbit on the run when we spoke on the telephone this morning." Maisie flicked over the card she was holding. "Now this is interesting . . ."

she continued. "He called upon Maurice – yes, I remember this – to consult him about ten years ago. Oh heavens. . ."

"What is it? What does it say?" asked Billy, wiping his brow with a handkerchief.

"This is not like Maurice. It says only, 'I could not comply with his request. Discontinued communication.'"

"Charmin'. So where does that put us today?"

"Well, he must still have a high opinion of Maurice to be asking for my help." Maisie looked at Billy to check his pallor. "Oh dear. Your nose is bleeding! Quickly, lean back and press down on the bridge of your nose with this handkerchief." Maisie pulled a clean embroidered handkerchief from her pocket, and placed it on Billy's nose.

"Oh my Gawd, I'm sorry. First I 'ave to lean forward, then back. I dunno . . . I'm getting right in the way today, aren't I?"

"Nonsense, you're a great help to me. How's that nose?"

Billy looked down into the handkerchief, and dabbed at his nose. "I think it's better."

"Now then, we'd better get going."

Maisie parked outside the main gates leading to a red-brick neo-Georgian mansion that stood majestically in the landscaped grounds beyond an ornate wrought iron gate.

"D'you reckon someone'll come to open the gate?" asked Billy.

"Someone's coming now." Maisie pointed to a young man wearing plus fours, a tweed hacking jacket, wool shirt and spruce green tie. He hurriedly opened an umbrella as he ran toward the entrance, and nodded to Maisie as he unlatched the gates and opened them. Maisie drove forward, stopping alongside the man.

"You must be Miss Dobbs, to see Mr Waite at three o'clock."

"Yes, that's me."

"And this is . . .?" The man bent forward to look at Billy in the passenger seat.

"My assistant, Mr William Beale."

Billy was still dabbing his nose with Maisie's handkerchief.

"Right you are, Ma'am. Park in front of the main door please, and make sure you reverse into place, Ma'am, with the nose of your motor pointing toward the gate."

Maisie raised an eyebrow at the young man, who shrugged.

"It's how Mr Waite likes it done, Ma'am."

"Bit picky, if you ask me," said Billy as Maisie drove toward the house. "'Reverse in wiv the nose pointing out'. Perhaps that's 'ow I should walk in there, backwards, wiv me nose turned away! I wonder who 'e thinks 'e is?"

"One of the richest men in Britain, if not Europe." Maisie manoeuvered the car as instructed. "And as we know, he needs something from us, otherwise we wouldn't be here. Come on."

They strode quickly from the car toward the main door where a woman waited to greet them. She was about fifty-five, in Maisie's estimation, and wore a plain slate grey mid-calf length dress with white cuffs and a white Peter Pan collar. A cameo was pinned to the centre of her collar and her only other adornment was a silver wristwatch on a black leather strap. Her grey hair was drawn back so tightly that it pulled at her temples. Despite her austere appearance, when Maisie and Billy reached the top step she smiled warmly with a welcoming sparkle in her pale blue eyes.

"Come in quickly before you catch your death! What a morning! Mr Harris, the butler, has been taken poorly with a nasty cold. I'm Mrs Willis, the housekeeper. Let me take your coats." Mrs Willis took Maisie's mackintosh and Billy's overcoat, and passed them to a maid. "Hang them on the drier over the fireplace in the laundry room. Mr Waite's guests will be leaving in –" she looked at her watch "– approximately thirty-five minutes, so get the coats as dry as possible by then."

"Thank you very much, Mrs Willis," said Maisie.

"Mr Waite will join you in the library shortly."

Maisie sensed a mood of tension pervading the house. Mrs Willis's pace was hurried, urging them forward. At the library door she checked her watch as she reached for the brass door handle. A door opened behind them and another woman hurried to join the trio.

"Mrs Willis! Mrs Willis, I will take over from here and show Mr Waite's guests in to the library," she panted.

Mrs Willis relinquished them, frowning with annoyance, "Certainly, Miss Arthur. Please continue." She turned to Maisie and Billy. "Good morning," she said as she stepped away without looking at Miss Arthur again. Unfortunately she was prevented from making a dignified exit as the door opened once more and a rotund man strode towards them, consulting his watch as he approached.

"Right then, it's three o'clock. We'd better get on with it." Barely looking at Maisie and Billy, he strode into the library.

Billy leaned towards Maisie and whispered, "It's like a three-ring-circus in 'ere!"

She responded with a brief nod.

"Sit down, sit down," Joseph Waite pointed to two chairs on the long side of a rectangular polished mahogany table and immediately seated himself in a larger chair at its head. His girth made him seem short, though he was almost six feet tall and moved deceptively quickly. According to Maurice's notes, Waite had been born in 1865, which meant he was now sixty-five. His navy blue pinstripe suit was doubtless constructed at great expense by a Savile Row tailor. It was complemented by a white shirt, light grey silk tie, highly polished black shoes, and light grey silk socks that Maisie could just see as she glanced down at the floor. Expensive, very expensive, but then Joseph Waite reeked of new money and of the large Havana cigar that he moved from his right hand to his left in order to reach out first to Maisie, then to Billy.

"Joseph Waite."

Maisie took a breath and opened her mouth to reply but was prevented from doing so.

"I'll get directly to the point, Miss Dobbs. My daughter, Charlotte, is missing from home. I'm a busy man, so I will tell you straight, I do not want to involve the police because I don't for one

minute think that this is a police matter. And I don't
turning this place upside down while they waste time
about this and that, and drawing every bored press man
while they're about it."

Maisie once again drew breath and opened her mouth to speak,
but Waite held his hand up, his palm facing her. She noticed a large
gold ring on his little finger, and as he replaced his hand on the
table, she saw that it was encrusted with diamonds. She stole a sideways look at Billy, who raised an eyebrow.

"It's not a police matter because this is not the first time she's left
my house. You are to find her, Miss Dobbs, and bring her back
before word gets out. A man in my position can't have a daughter
running around and turning up in the newspapers. I don't 'ave to
tell you that these are difficult times for a man of commerce, but
Waite's is trimming its sails accordingly and doing very nicely, thank
you. It's got to stay that way. Now then." Waite consulted his watch
yet again. "You've got twenty minutes of my time, so ask any questions you want. I won't 'old back."

Maisie perceived that although Waite had worked hard to eliminate a strong Yorkshire accent, the occasional revealing long vowel
and the odd Northern dropped *h* broke through.

"I'd like some details about your daughter." Maisie reached for
the blank index cards that Billy handed her. "First of all, how old
is Charlotte?"

"Thirty-two. About your age."

"Quite."

"And with about half the gumption!"

"I beg your pardon, Mr Waite?"

"I'll make no bones about it; Charlotte is her mother's daughter.
A wilting lily, I call 'er. A good day's work wouldn't do her any
harm at all, but of course the daughter of a man in my position has
no need. More's the pity."

"Indeed. Perhaps you could tell us something about what happened on the day Charlotte disappeared. When was she last seen?"

"Two days ago. Saturday. Morning. At breakfast. I was down in

13

dining room, and Charlotte came in, full of the joys of spring, and sat down at the other end of the table. One minute she seemed as right as rain, eating a bit of toast, drinking a cup of tea, then all of a sudden she starts with the tears, sobs a bit, and runs from the room."

"Did you go after her?"

The man sighed and reached for an ashtray, into which he tapped the smouldering end of his cigar, leaving a circle of pungent ash. He drew deeply on the cigar again and exhaled.

"No, I didn't. I finished my breakfast. Charlotte is a bit of a Sarah Bernhardt, Miss Dobbs. An actress – should've been on the stage, like her mother. Nothing is ever good enough for her. I thought she'd've made a suitable marriage by now, but no, in fact – you should write it down there –" He waved his cigar toward Maisie's index card. "She was jilted by her fiancé a couple of months ago. Even with my money she can't get a husband!"

"Mr Waite, the behaviour you describe suggests that your daughter may have been in a state of despair."

"Despair? Despair? She's always had fine food in her belly, clothes – and very good clothes, I might add – on her back. I've given her a good education, in Switzerland, if you please. And she had a proper coming out ball. You could've fed a family for a year with what I spent on the frock alone. That girl's had the very best, so don't tell me about despair, Miss Dobbs. That girl's got no right to despair."

Maisie met his gaze firmly. *Here it comes*, she thought, *now he's going to tell me about his hard life.*

"Despair, Miss Dobbs, is when your father dies in a pit accident when you're ten years old and you're the eldest of six. That's what despair is. Despair is what gives you a right good kick in the rump and sets you off to provide for your family when you're nobbut a child."

Waite, who had slipped into broad Yorkshire, went on. "Despair, Miss Dobbs, is when you lose your mother and her youngest to consumption when you're fourteen. That, Miss Dobbs, is despair.

14

Despair is just when you think you've got everyone taken care of, because you're working night and day to make something of yourself, and you lose another brother down the same pit that killed your father, because he took any job he could get to help out. That, Miss Dobbs, is despair. But you know about that yourself, don't you?" Waite leaned forward and ground his cigar into the ashtray.

Maisie realized that somewhere in his office Joseph Waite had a dossier on her that held as much information as she had acquired about him, if not more.

"Mr Waite, I am well aware of life's challenges, but if I am to take on this case – and the choice is mine – I have a responsibility for the welfare of all parties. If this type of departure is something of a habit for your daughter and discord in the house is at the heart of her unsettled disposition, then clearly something must be done to alleviate the, let us say, *pressure* on all parties. I must have your commitment to further conversation with respect to the problem when we have found Charlotte."

Joseph Waite's lips became taut. He was not a man used to being challenged. Yet, as Maisie now knew, it was the similarity in their backgrounds that had led him to choose her for this task, and he would not draw back. He was a very intelligent as well as belligerent man and would appreciate that not a moment more could be lost.

"Mr Waite, even if Charlotte has disappeared of her own volition, news of her disappearance will soon attract the attention of the press, just as you fear. Given your financial situation and these difficult times, there is a risk that you may be subjected to attempts at extortion. And though you seem sure that Charlotte is safe and merely hiding from you, of that we cannot be certain until she is found. You speak of prior disappearances. May I have the details?"

Waite leaned back in his chair shaking his head. "She runs away, to my mind, anytime she can't get what she wants. The first time was after I refused to allow her a motor car." He looked across the lawns and waved the cigar in the direction of what Maisie expected were the garages. "She can be chauffeured anywhere she wants. I don't hold with women driving."

Maisie exchanged glances with Billy.

"So she ran to her mother's house, no doubt to complain about her terrible father. I tell you, where I come from, there's women who'd give their eye teeth to have someone to drive them instead of walking five miles to the shops pushing a pram with a baby inside, a couple of nippers on top, and the shopping bags hanging off the handle!"

"And the second time?"

"Oh, she was engaged to be married and wanted to get out of it. The one before this last one. Just upped and moved into the Ritz, if you please. Nice home here, and she wants to live at the Ritz. I went and got her back myself."

"I see." Maisie imagined the embarrassment of a woman being frog-marched out of the Ritz by her angry father. "So in your opinion Charlotte has a tendency to run away when she is faced with a confrontation."

"Aye, that's about the measure of it," replied Waite. "So what do you think now about your little 'further conversation' when Charlotte returns, eh, Miss Dobbs, considering the girl can't even look her own father in the eye?"

Maisie was quick to respond. "My terms remain, sir. Part of my work in bringing Charlotte home will be to listen to her and to *hear* what she has to say."

Waite scraped back his chair, pushed his hands into his trouser pockets, and walked to the window. He looked up at the sky for just a moment and took out a pocket-watch. "I agree to your terms. Send your contract to me by nine tomorrow morning. Miss Arthur will take care of any deposit required, and will settle your account and expenses upon receipt. If you need me to answer more questions, Miss Arthur will schedule an appointment. Otherwise I expect your progress report by Friday. In person and at this same time – that is, should you fail to have found her by then. I'm a busy man, as I've said, Miss Dobbs." He turned to leave.

"Mr Waite?"

"Yes?"

"May we see Charlotte's rooms, please?"

"Miss Arthur will call Mrs Willis to show you the rooms. Good afternoon."

———

Mrs Willis was instructed to show Maisie and Billy to Charlotte's suite. They were escorted up the wide staircase to the second floor, where they turned right along a spacious landing. Mrs Willis lifted her hand to knock at the door and then, remembering that there was no need, took a bunch of keys from her pocket, selected one, and unlocked the door to reveal a large sitting room with additional doors on either side that Maisie thought would lead to a bathroom and bedroom respectively. The sash windows were open to a broad view of the perfect lawns at the front of the house, with stripes of light and dark green where gardeners had worked with mowers and rollers to give an immaculate finish.

Mrs Willis beckoned them into the rooms, which were aired by a light breeze that seemed to dance with the cabbage-rose-printed curtains, flicking them back and forth. Though appointed with the most expensive furniture and linens, the rooms felt cold and spartan to Maisie. There was none of the ornamentation she had expected: no photographs in frames, no mementos, no books on the bedside table, no exotic perfume bottles set on top of the dressing table. Maisie walked through into the bedroom, and back into the sitting room. Like the Queen Anne chairs beside the fireplace, the rose-printed curtains were traditional, but the dressing table and wardrobe were modern, constructed of solid dark wood with geometric lines. The dressing table mirrors were triangular, a jagged icy triptych that unsettled Maisie. Her skin prickled as if pierced by tiny needles. The design of the dressing table itself was matched by that of the wardrobe, with its centre mirror set into the wood. It seemed to Maisie that no rest was to be had in this room, unless one stared out of the window or at the curtains.

"Lovely rooms, aren't they? We only changed the curtains last week – she has pale green velvets in winter. Lined with a special combed cotton, they are, to keep the rooms warmer. The dressing table suite was made 'specially to Mr Waite's specifications."

Maisie smiled and nodded. "Thank you, Mrs Willis. We may need to ask you some more questions in a while. At the moment we just need to look around."

Mrs Willis pursed her lips, hesitating. "Of course. I'll come back in about twenty minutes, but if you need me in the meantime, just press this button." She indicated one of three brass buttons on a panel beside the door.

Sensing that Waite had given instructions that they were to be escorted at all times, Maisie smiled and nodded. She suspected that Mrs Willis had enough on her plate to worry about in the house without chaperoning private investigators.

As the door closed, Billy turned to Maisie. "It looks as if nobody ever set foot in these rooms, dunnit?"

Maisie made no reply, but set her document case down on a chair with a cover that matched the curtains and, in the bedroom, even the counterpane on Charlotte's bed. Maisie's work with Maurice Blanche had taught her that a person speaks not only with the voice but with those objects she chooses to surround herself. That photographs tell a story is well accepted, but the way furniture is positioned in a room tells something about its occupant; the contents of a larder reveal desire and restraint, as most surely does the level of liquid in a decanter.

"What are we lookin' for, Miss?"

"I don't know, Billy, but I will when we find it."

They worked together, carefully and systematically searching through drawers, in the wardrobe, and in every nook and cranny of the room. Maisie asked Billy to search carefully under the bed and behind furniture, to pull out cushions from the chair, and to list all items in the medicine cabinet in the white-tiled bathroom. She, in turn, would investigate the contents of the dressing table, wardrobe and writing desk.

Though she was troubled by the design of the furniture, Maisie was even more intrigued by Charlotte's clothing. Instead of suits, dresses and gowns from the houses of Worth, Schiaparelli or Molyneux, as would befit a woman of Charlotte's station, there were just a few plain grey and brown skirts and jackets bought from Debenham & Freebody. A long black gown protected by a sheet of fine muslin was Charlotte's one concession to evening wear, and there was also a black afternoon dress in a style fashionable several years earlier, with a low waistband and below-the-knee hemline. Charlotte's blouses were equally plain and it seemed as if she had bought several of similar design at the same time. Had she taken more colourful and frivolous clothing with her, leaving behind a life that lacked colour in search of something more vibrant?

It was in the writing desk, to the right of the window, that Maisie found an address book. At first, she thought that she would find no other personal papers, no letters, nothing that gave away anything of Charlotte Waite's character or hinted at the cause of her distress, but as she opened the second drawer, underneath a collection of pens and stationery, Maisie found a prayer book along with a copy of *The Monastic Rule of Saint Benedict*, and several pamphlets on the life of a contemplative. Taking up the books, Maisie walked again to the wardrobe and touched the dark, drab fabrics of the clothes Charlotte had left behind.

"Miss, look what I've found." Billy came towards Maisie with a piece of paper in his hand.

"What is it, Billy?"

"Found it shoved down the side of that chair cushion. Could've been put there deliberately or fallen out of a pocket." Billy handed Maisie the small slip of paper.

"Looks like someone's jotted down train departures. See here –" Maisie pointed to the letters and read: "'Ch. X to App. Chg Ash'. Then there's a list of times. Hmmm. I'll keep it with these other things for now and we'll look at them later." She folded the paper and placed it inside the prayer book, then turned to Billy.

"Billy, I'd like to spend some time in here alone."

He was now used to Maisie's way of working and showed no

19

surprise at her request. "Right you are, Miss. Shall I interview Mrs Willis?"

"Yes, do that. Here's what we need to know: first, Charlotte – her behaviour over the past two or three months. Was there any change in her manner or appearance? Ask about even the slightest change in habits of dress, diet, recreation." Maisie looked around the room. "She doesn't have her own telephone, so find out who has called; the staff always know when a new name comes along. Speak to Miss Arthur about her allowance; how much, when it's paid and how it's paid. Does she have her own accounts – heaven knows, I hope the poor woman has some privacy – and are statements kept by Miss Arthur?"

Maisie paced back and forth, as Billy licked his pencil, ready to continue taking notes.

"Most important: find out about Charlotte's former fiancé, his name, profession – if he has one – and where he works. I'll need to see him. Speak to the chauffeur, Billy, and find out where she goes, whom she sees. You know the ropes. Oh, and a recent photograph, one that really looks like Charlotte; ask different staff if it's a good resemblance. See what you can get hold of. I want about fifteen minutes here, then I'd like to speak to Charlotte Waite's personal maid. Find out who she is and have her come up to this room."

"Awright, Miss, consider it all done."

"Oh, and Billy, tread very carefully on this one. We don't know where loyalties lie yet, though I must say, I can feel a certain chill when there's any mention of Charlotte."

"You know, I reckon I felt that meself."

"Well, keep it in mind. Leave no stone unturned."

Billy quietly shut the door behind him. Maisie sat in Charlotte's chair and closed her eyes. She took four deep breaths through her nose, as she had been taught so many years ago by Khan, the blind Ceylonese mystic to whom Maurice had introduced her, to learn that seeing is not necessarily a function of the eyes alone. From her days of sitting with Khan, and her instruction in deep meditation, Maisie was attuned to the risks inherent in using such a tool in her work, and knew that even her strong spirit was vulnerable to the auras of the troubled soul. Maisie concentrated on her breathing, stilling both her body and her mind, and she began to feel the strength of emotion that resided in the room. This was Charlotte's refuge while in the house and had become a receptacle for her every thought, feeling, inspiration, reflection and wish. And as she sat in meditation, Maisie felt that Charlotte had been deeply troubled and that her departure had had little to do with a broken engagement. Charlotte Waite had run away, but what was she running from? Or to? What had caused such an intense ache in her heart that even now in her room, Maisie felt Charlotte's lingering sorrow?

Maisie opened her eyes and continued to sit in silence for some moments. Then she began to inspect the books and pamphlets that Charlotte had collected. *The Monastic Rule of Saint Benedict* opened immediately at the place marked with a haphazardly torn envelope fragment. She inspected the scrap of vellum closely, for it seemed heavy, then turned it over. On the reverse side was a thick smudge of red sealing wax, about three-quarters of an inch in diameter, pressed into a rose-shaped seal with a cross in the centre. Maisie squinted to see the words etched into the seal above and below the cross. She shook her head, reached down into her document case and took out what initially looked like a powder compact but that, when opened, revealed a magnifying glass. Maisie leaned closer to the seal and, using the glass, read the words "Camden Abbey." *Camden Abbey*. The name sounded familiar.

There was a knock at the door. Maisie quickly placed the books, pamphlets and other items in her case, ensured they were secure, then rose, breathed deeply again, and opened the door. A young woman of about nineteen bobbed a half-curtsey in front of her. Her black dress was shorter than the one Maisie had worn when she was a servant at the home of Lord and Lady Compton; a small bibbed apron to protect her dress and a delicate white lace band on top of her tightly curled hair completed the maid's uniform.

"Miss Dobbs? I was told you wanted to see me, Ma'am. I'm Perkins, Miss Waite's personal maid."

"Oh, come in, Miss Perkins." Maisie stood to one side to allow the woman to enter the room.

"Would you like to sit down?"

The maid shook her head. "No, Ma'am."

"Well then, let's stand by the window. It's a blustery day now, but I do like to look out upon garden." Maisie knew that an enclosed area encouraged an enclosed mind. Maurice had taught her: always take the person to be questioned to a place where there's space, or where they can see few boundaries. Space broadens the mind and gives the voice room to be heard.

Maisie sat on the low, wide windowsill, the toe of one shoe touching the floor for balance. Perkins stood at the opposite end of the windowsill, facing Maisie.

"Tell me, Miss Perkins, how long have you worked for Miss Waite?"

"Mr Waite. I work for Mr Waite. Mr Waite pays my wages, so it's him I work for. Looking after Miss Waite is what I do in his house, and I've been her maid for a year."

"I see." Maisie noticed the speed with which she had been corrected, and thought that with just one question, she had discovered where Perkins' loyalties lay.

"And who was Miss Waite's maid before you?"

"Well, there were lots of them, Ma'am. Isabel Wright left last year, then six months before her there was Ethel Day – I remember them because I've worked for Mr Waite since I was twelve, Ma'am."

"And do you like working here, Miss Perkins?"

"I like working for Mr Waite. He's very good to us here, Ma'am."

Maisie nodded, and looked out of the window. She was aware that the maid had leaned forward to see the gardens.

"I'll bet you are too busy to look out of the windows, aren't you?"

"Oh yes, 'specially with the way Miss Waite keeps me running . . . Oh, begging your pardon, Ma'am."

Maisie smiled, encouraging Perkins into her confidence. "Tell me – what is it like working for Miss Waite? And I should add that everything you tell me will remain between the two of us." She leaned forward, and though the maid did not consciously discern any alteration in Maisie's speech, she had allowed her accent to change slightly so that she sounded just a little like the young woman in front of her. "I need to ask questions to get a sense of what has been happening in Miss Waite's life in the past two or three months, and especially in more recent weeks."

The young woman gazed into the distance again, chewed her inner lip, then moved closer to Maisie. She began to speak, at first tentatively, then with greater strength. "To tell you the truth, she's not the easiest person to work for. She'd have me running up and downstairs all day. Wash this, press that, cup of tea, not too hot, not too cold, lemon – oh no, changed my mind, cream instead. First she's going out, then she's staying in; then suddenly, just as I'm laying my head on the pillow, the bell rings, and I have to go down and dress her for a late dinner. No thank-you's or anything, no little something extra left on the sideboard for me, and I'm the one that has to clean up when she has a tantrum!"

"Oh dear."

"It's like being outside, you know: no climate but all weather. Hot and cold she is, never seems to know her own mind. One minute she's all happy, the next, you'd've thought the moon had crashed into the stars and set light to the sky outside her window." Perkins shrugged. "Well, that's what Miss Harding, the cook, says."

"And what about the past few weeks or so? More of the same behaviour?"

Perkins watched the clouds for a moment before answering. "I'd say she was quieter. More . . . more *distant*, I think you'd say. I mean, she always went through times like that. Miss Harding said she ought to be taken to see somebody about her moods. But this was different. It sort of went on and on, and she didn't go out much. Didn't seem to dress up as much either. In fact, she got rid of some lovely clothes, you know, from Paris and Bond Street. Very strange for a lady, to want to walk around in them drab clothes all day, and only have one evening dress, 'specially as she used to go to the collections, you know, and have mannequins walk up and down the room for her to pick and choose what she wanted. You should have seen it in here when the boxes arrived!"

"Have you any idea what might have caused her to withdraw?"

"Not really. None of my business. I was just glad there were no bells ringing at midnight."

"Do you think Mr Waite noticed?"

"Mr Waite works hard. We all know that. Far as I know, they don't see much of each other."

"Are you aware of discord between Miss Waite and her father?"

Perkins looked at her shoes and stepped away from the window just a little. Maisie noticed immediately. *She's closing her mind. Deliberately.*

"Not my business to pry, Ma'am. I just do my job. What they think of each other upstairs isn't any of my concern."

"Hmmm. Yes. Your work is demanding enough, Miss Perkins. No reason for you to keep tabs on people. One more question, though: do you know whom Miss Waite saw, or where she went, in the weeks preceding her departure from this house? Did you notice anything out of the ordinary?"

The maid sighed in a way that indicated that she had said all she wanted to say, but that she would try to answer the question. "She did go up to Town a few times. I'm not sure where she went, but she mainly sees a woman called Lydia Fisher, I think. She lives in Chelsea, somewhere around there. And I reckon she was going somewhere else as well, because she took a pair of walking shoes with her on a couple of occasions. But a lot of her time was spent just sitting up here."

"Doing what?"

"Not sure I know, Miss. Sort of in a daydream, looking out of the window."

"I see." The younger woman began to fidget with her hair, her lace headband, her apron, indicating to Maisie that no more valuable information would be forthcoming. As they moved toward the door, Maisie reached into her bag and took out a calling card.

"Miss Perkins, I am familiar with the workings of a house of this size, and also appreciate that the staff are usually the first to know when something is amiss. Please feel free to telephone me if you think of anything that might be useful. It's clear that you have had some difficulties with Miss Waite, but despite everything, her father – your employer – wants her home."

"Yes, Ma'am." Perkins took the card, placed it in her pinafore pocket, bobbed another half curtsey, and left the room.

Maisie watched the maid walk along the landing, stopping briefly to curtsey as Billy approached in the company of Mrs Willis, who was looking at her watch. It was time for them to leave.

"Have you got everything, Billy?"

"Yes, Miss. In fact, Mrs Willis knew where to find a recent photograph of Miss Waite. 'Ere." Billy opened his notebook and took out the photograph, which he handed to Maisie.

Charlotte was sitting on a white filigree cast-iron chair set in front of a rose garden, which Maisie suspected was at the rear of the house. She seemed to be what the gentlemen of the press might have termed a "flapper." Her hair, which framed her face, was waved and drawn back into a low chignon at the nape of her neck. She wore a knee-length dress that appeared rather flimsy; a breeze had caught the hem the moment before the shutter snapped. Charlotte had made no move to press the garment down, and laughed into the camera. Maisie held the photo closer to scrutinize the face. If eyes were windows to the soul, then Charlotte was indeed troubled, for the eyes that looked at the camera seemed to be filled not with joy or amusement as the pose suggested, but with sorrow.

Maisie looked up. "Thank you, Mrs Willis." She turned to Billy. "If you've completed everything, we can talk back at the office. I'm sure Mrs Willis has a lot to do."

Mrs Willis escorted them to the front door, where a maid waited with Maisie's mackintosh and Billy's overcoat. They were about to step outside when Maisie paused. "A quick question for you, Mrs Willis. I have a sense that Miss Waite commands little respect in the household. Why is that?"

"I'm sure I don't know what you mean, Ma'am," said Mrs Willis, who now seemed anxious to see Maisie and Billy inside their motor car, driving away.

"Mrs Willis, in confidence. Tell me what you think." Maisie inclined her head conspiratorially toward Mrs Willis.

"Mr Waite is respected by everyone who works for him. He gives back as much as he asks of those in his employ, and sometimes more. His loyalty to his staff earns loyalty in return. And that's all I can say."

Maisie and Billy thanked Mrs Willis, left the house, and climbed into the motor car.

"Didn't say much, did she?" said Billy, waving at the gatekeeper as they left.

"On the contrary, she told me a lot. It was an impertinent question, and, within the confines of what she *could* say, Mrs Willis was quite forthcoming."

Billy opened his notebook and began to speak, but Maisie silenced him with a hand gently placed on his arm and a finger to her lips. "No, not now. Allow the information we've gathered to sit and stew for a while. Just tell me one thing – the name and profession of the former fiancé."

2

BILLY WAS already at the office in Fitzroy Square when Maisie arrived at eight o'clock the next morning. The spring rain had at last subsided, and now the early morning sunshine was mirrored in puddles remaining from yesterday's downpour, casting dappled shadows across the square and playing upon fresh green leaves.

"Good morning, Billy." Maisie looked at her assistant as she came into the office. "You look a bit drawn – is everything all right?"

"Yes, Miss. Well, not really. Every day I look out as the bus passes the labour exchange and the line ain't gettin' any shorter. I can count my lucky stars getting this job wiv you. You know, I've got the missus and three nippers to think about – the eldest is in school now – and what wiv this ol' leg of mine –"

"You mustn't worry, Billy. Not only are we fortunate in getting new business, but Maurice's clients now know that they can trust his former assistant. If money's a problem, Billy –"

"Oh, no, no, my wages are better 'ere than they were round the corner with old Sharpie. I just –"

"What, Billy?"

"You're sure you need me?"

"Absolutely sure. Time and again you have proved that you are worth your weight in gold, which I would pay you if I could. If I have any criticism of your work, I will tell you."

Billy gave her a wary grin.

"Is that all that's bothering you, Billy?"

"That's all, Miss."

27

"Right then. Let's see where we are with the Waite case."

The sound of mail being pushed through the letterbox was a signal to Billy to get up from his desk. "Back in a minute, better see if there's anything for us."

Maisie frowned. She knew that even as he made his way downstairs, Billy was preparing to return to the room playing the part of the old Billy, the court jester with a heart of gold. It was Billy's loyalty to her, and the link between him and Captain Simon Lynch, that had won him the job as her assistant – as well as his willingness to help her by working all hours on some of the more tedious surveillance tasks.

In 1917 Corporal William Beale had been brought into the casualty clearing station where Maisie was assisting Captain Simon Lynch, the army doctor she had been introduced to by her friend Priscilla, while she was at Girton College. Simon had declared his love for her and proposed marriage, and now they were working alongside each other. Billy Beale never forgot the man who saved his leg – and his life. And he never forgot the young nurse who tended to his wounds, instantly recognizing her years later when Maisie Dobbs became a tenant at the Warren Street premises where he was caretaker. Both she and Simon had been wounded subsequently when the casualty clearing station came under heavy artillery fire. She had recovered; Simon had not.

Maisie sat down at the table by the window, opened the file she had taken from her briefcase, and gestured for Billy to join her. He sat down, taking a plain lead pencil from the jam jar, and a large sheet of paper for them to record evidence details, thoughts, possibilities, and projections, a diagram that they referred to as their "case map".

"First of all," said Maisie, "Waite will receive our contract and terms" – she consulted the watch pinned to the breast pocket of her new burgundy wool suit, and continued – "in about fifteen minutes."

"And we know 'e's got the money!" said Billy.

"That we do. Let's do three things this morning, then split up. I

28

want to map what our impressions were: of the house, the four people we met, and of Charlotte's room. We'll also look at the items we found while we were there."

"And the grounds, Miss. Don't forget all that 'nose pointing out' nonsense, and them lawns what look like they were clipped by a pair o' nail scissors."

"Good. You're right, mustn't forget that welcome! Anyway, after we've made a start, you can set to work on Charlotte's address book, just checking on who's where, and that it's all current."

"Yes, Miss. Just put some flesh on the bones, no need to knock on any doors yet. Where will you be going, Miss?"

"I am going to a branch of Waite's International Stores. I thought I'd go to the one on Oxford Street, close to Tottenham Court Road. It was his first shop in London, and it's his most important branch, next to the one in Harrogate, of course. The main offices of Waite's are above the premises. With a bit of luck, I'll see the man in his element."

"Why do you think it's called Waite's *International* Stores, Miss?"

"I looked up a file of Maurice's, which expanded on the information noted on the index card. I was actually looking for anything that would add to the comment about the severing of contact, but there was nothing there, so I'll have to speak to Maurice about it. Anyway, when he added fruit and vegetables, other dry goods, and more from abroad to his butchery business, he slipped 'International' in between 'Waite's' and 'Stores' and never looked back."

"It must've been 'ard work for 'im, eh?"

"Most certainly, and of course life wasn't easy at home, either. You heard his little monologue yesterday."

"And who's 'is wife?"

"According to Maurice's file, Charlotte's mother was a music-hall singer and small-time actress from Bradford. He met her there at the opening of his shop. Apparently Waite's shop openings were always big events. Charlotte was born just" – Maisie raised an eyebrow – "seven months after the marriage."

"Miss Arthur said that Mrs Waite spends most of 'er time up in Leeds, at the 'ouse up there. And I made a note to check on 'er information that Charlotte is not with 'er mother, even though Miss Arthur said she'd already made sure of that." Billy tapped at the points with his pencil.

"Good. I got the impression that Charlotte and her mother weren't close. What do you think, Billy?"

Billy scratched the top of his ear where his hair was in need of a trim. "Well, what I thought was that Charlotte didn't really fit in anywhere. There she was, living with that dad of 'ers, Mr Lord-High-and-Mighty running 'er life, and at thirty-two, mind you. Most of 'er friends are married by now, so they ain't got time to go out with the other girls like they used to. She's sort of been left be'ind, ain't she, Miss? Like so many, really. I mean, men they might've married are gone, killed in the war. What's she supposed to do with 'erself all day? That father of 'er's don't think much of 'er, not by the sound of it. She's really a spinster, all on her own."

Maisie winced at Billy's assessment of the situation. She was, after all, a spinster herself in those terms. "Good. Yes, good point," she replied, thought for a moment, then opened her document case and removed the books and pamphlets found in Charlotte Waite's room. She laid them out on the table.

"What do you make of it all, Miss?"

Maisie picked up the seal, then the scrap of paper. "Well, the 'Ch. X' is Charing Cross."

"And 'Ash' could be Ashford, couldn't it, Miss?"

Maisie nodded. "It's all fitting together now, Billy. Let's say this is in connection with the trains that go from Charing Cross to Ashford, where one has to change for the trains to –"

"Gawd, I don't know. Apples?" Billy grinned.

"Appledore!"

"*Appledore*?"

"Yes, I used to go there with my father sometimes. We'd go fishing on the canal near Iden Lock." Maisie reached for the seal. "And that makes sense of this."

"What's that?"

"The seal from an envelope. Charlotte had probably received a letter from Camden Abbey, perhaps sent to her with the books and pamphlets, and as she began to read, she tore the seal from the envelope to mark her place."

"So what do you think, Miss? Can you tell from this little lot where she's gone off to?"

"It tells us that Charlotte was curious about the contemplative life. There's something I need to look into. I may know someone who can help us." Maisie gathered the items together and looked at her watch. "Let's move on. We can't allow one possibility to cloud our vision. Charlotte could have left these things to dupe her father. Or she could have left with such urgency as to forget them." She stood up. "Right then. Charlotte's run away before, but she's always let her father know where she is, in one way or another. He's assumed that she's hiding from him this time. We have to question that assumption and consider other possibilities. Even if we take his account of her departure as truth, she may now be being held against her will, or she may have met with an accident. And of course we cannot rule out the possibility that she may have taken her own life. But let us begin by assuming that she has disappeared voluntarily, has been gone for several days and has deliberately covered her tracks. Why did she leave this time? Where is she? Has she run *from* something or *to* something – or *someone*? I want us to try to have a better feeling for what went on last Saturday, and how far we can believe Waite's version of events. No need to move anything on the table, but just help me shift it over there a bit, so it's in the middle of the room."

Billy took one end of the table while Maisie took the other, and they placed it where Maisie indicated.

"You can be Waite, so sit at this end." Maisie pointed out the place where Billy should set his chair.

"I'll need to shove me jacket up inside me cardigan, Miss, seeing as I ain't got quite the middle that 'e 'as."

"Pretend, Billy. Seriously, I want you to close your eyes, sit at the

31

table, and truly imagine that you are Joseph Waite. I'll go outside the door, give you a couple of minutes, then I'll come in and sit down as if I'm Charlotte. For the purposes of this experiment, I *am* Charlotte."

"Awright." Billy frowned. "I'll give it a go."

Maisie nodded, and walked towards the door, but before reaching for the handle she turned to her desk, took the *Times* from her briefcase, and dropped it on the table in front of him.

"You'll probably be reading this."

She left the room as Billy shifted uncomfortably in his seat. He closed his eyes, drew back his shoulders, tucked his legs underneath the chair so that his heels rode up and the balls of his feet supported the imaginary weight of his middle. His war wound nipped at his leg as he moved, but he ignored it. He puffed out his cheeks for just a few seconds, and imagined what it might be like to have built a successful enterprise to become a powerful man of commerce. Slowly he began to feel quite different, and realized he was getting just an inkling of the way in which Maisie used her knowledge of the body to gain an understanding of another person. He reached for the newspaper and snapped it open, feeling richer than he had felt in a good long while. And it surprised him that he felt a glimmer of an emotion that rarely surfaced in his being: anger.

"Good morning, Father," said Maisie, entering the room.

"Good morning, Charlotte." Billy reached for his pocket watch, noted the time, and placed the newspaper on the table between them. "What are you doing with yourself today?" He continued, checking his watch again, and taking a sip of tea.

"I thought I might go shopping and meet a friend for lunch."

"Nothing better to do today, Charlotte?"

There was an edge to Billy's voice that almost caused Maisie to slip out of character and look up, but she continued, defiantly. "What do you *want* me to do, Father?"

Billy consulted his watch again without responding, while Maisie – as Charlotte – reached for the newspaper. She turned to the front page, read barely two lines, then suddenly gasped and burst into tears. She threw down the paper, scraped back her chair and ran from the room with her hand covering her mouth. Billy sighed, wiped his brow and stretched out his legs, happy to be rid of his assumed character.

Maisie returned. "That was an interesting exercise, wasn't it?"

"It was really strange, Miss. I remembered watching 'im when 'e talked about Charlotte, so I copied his posture."

Maisie nodded for Billy to continue.

"And, well, it was right peculiar, it was, 'ow I started to feel different, like another person."

"Explain, Billy. I know this seems difficult, but it is most important and helpful."

"I was right touchy, like a piece of tinder ready to catch fire. I started to think about the father that died down the coal pit, 'is mother and 'ow she must've 'ad to work 'er fingers to the bone, and then all that 'e'd gone through, 'ard graft and all. Then I thought about the wife up in Yorkshire, sittin' on 'er behind, and by the time you walked in the door I felt all of what 'e'd felt – well, what I felt 'e'd felt – and, to be quite 'onest with you, I didn't even really 'ave patience with you. I mean Charlotte."

"Do you believe he was in the room when Charlotte ran out?"

"I reckon so, but it was as if I was *making* meself sit there, because I'm determined not to let 'er annoy me. I couldn't do any more reading of the newspaper, I was so . . . so angry! That's why I 'anded it to 'er, I mean you. What about you, Miss?"

"You know, after seeing Charlotte's room yesterday, in taking on her character I wasn't exactly full of the joys of spring. I didn't get that feeling at all when I was in her room. Instead, I had the sense of a troubled soul. But there must have been provocation of some sort to make her leave home. I have to say, I felt other emotions, though I confess I am now drawing upon the feelings I intuited when we went into her room and when I was alone for a while." Maisie picked up a pencil from the table and began to doodle along the bottom of the paper. She drew an eye with a single tear seeping from the corner.

"What did you 'sense,' then?" asked Billy.

"She was confused. As I acted her part at breakfast, I felt a conflict. I could not hate my father, though I dislike what he is and I am trying desperately not to be intimidated by him. I would like to leave his house, to live elsewhere, anywhere. But I'm stuck." Maisie looked out of the window, allowing her eyelids to close halfway and rest as she considered Charlotte Waite. "I felt defiant when I first picked up the newspaper which, according to Waite, was the last thing Charlotte did before bursting into tears and leaving the room."

Billy nodded as Maisie got up from her chair and walked to the window with her arms crossed.

"What this exercise suggests is that Waite's recounting of his daughter's departure has only a tenuous relationship to the truth. It serves to remind us that the story we heard yesterday was told through *his* eyes. To him, it may be exactly as it happened, but I think if you asked Charlotte, or a fly on the wall, you'd get a different account. One thing, though: we should go through Saturday's *Times* to see if anything in it caused Charlotte Waite's distress."

Maisie flicked a piece of lint from her new burgundy suit, which she was beginning to think had been purchased in error as it seemed to attract any white fluff that happened to be passing.

"I'll get a copy." Billy made a note in the cloth-bound palm-size book he carried with him.

"Let's put the table back and go over the rest of the visit carefully. Then I've some paperwork to do before we go our separate ways at noon. We should meet back here at about five to exchange notes."

"Right you are, Miss."

"By the way, I didn't know you could mimic a northern accent."

Billy looked surprised as he leafed through his notebook, pencil at the ready to work on the case map. "What d'yer mean, Miss? I ain't got no northern accent. I'm an East End boy. Shoreditch born and bred, that's me."

Billy left the office first, taking with him the address book found in Charlotte Waite's rooms. There were few names listed, all with London addresses except for a cousin and Charlotte's mother, both in Yorkshire. Billy had already confirmed that Charlotte had not sought refuge with either of them. As Joseph Waite supported both his wife and niece, it was unlikely that they would risk their future financial security by deceit. Billy's next task was to confirm each name listed and also find out more about Charlotte's former fiancé, Gerald Bartrup.

Maisie cast a final glance around the office, then departed after locking up. Once outside she made her way along Fitzroy Street, then Charlotte Street, taking a route parallel to Tottenham Court Road. As she walked towards her destination – the Waite's International Store on Oxford Street – she turned the contents of Charlotte's address book over in her mind, then mentally walked through Charlotte's rooms once more. Maisie always maintained that first impressions of a room or a person are akin to soup when it is fresh. One can appreciate the flavour, the heat and the ingredients that went into the pot that will merge together to provide sustenance. But it's on the second day that a soup really reveals itself and releases its blend of spices and aromas onto the tastebuds. In the same way, as Maisie walked through the rooms in her mind's eye, she was aware of the rigid control that pervaded the Waite household and must have enveloped Charlotte like a shroud.

In suggesting they recreate the scene at breakfast, when Charlotte Waite hurriedly left the room in a flood of tears, Maisie was using one of Maurice's training techniques that had become a standard part of their investigative procedure. She knew that, as her assistant, Billy had to be constantly aware of every single piece of information and evidence that emerged as their work on a case developed. His senses must be fine-tuned, and he had to think beyond what was seen, heard and read. Useful information might just as likely be derived from intuition. He must learn to question, she thought, not to take any evidence at face value. Maurice often quoted one of his former colleagues, the famous professor of forensic medicine, Alexandre Lacassagne, who had died some years earlier: *As my friend Lacassagne would say, Maisie, 'One must know how to doubt.'*

As Maisie walked purposefully towards the shop, a key question nagged at her: where would a person who carried such a heavy burden run to? Where could she go to find solace, compassion – and herself? As she considered the possibilities, Maisie cautioned herself not to jump to conclusions.

She walked along Charlotte Street, then crossed into Rathbone Place until she reached Oxford Street. Joseph Waite's conspicuous grocery shop was situated across the road, between Charing Cross Road and Soho Street. For a few moments Maisie stood looking at the shop. Blue-striped awnings matching the tiled exterior extended over the double doors through which customers entered. To the left of the door a showcase window held a presentation of fancy tinned foods and fruits and vegetables; to the right, a corresponding window held a display of meats. Whole carcasses were hooked to a brass bar that ran along the top and chickens hung from another brass bar halfway down. A selection of meats was displayed on an angled counter topped with a slab of marble to better exhibit the legs of lamb, pork chops, minced meats, stewing steaks and other cuts, strategically placed and garnished with bunches of parsley, sage, and thyme to tempt the customer.

Above the awnings was a tile mosaic that spelled out the words WAITE'S INTERNATIONAL STORES. In smaller letters underneath, the sign read: A FAMILY BUSINESS. EST. 1885.

As customers went in and out of the shop, a small group of children gathered by the window and held out their cupped hands, hoping for a coin or two from the shoppers. Such booty would not be spent on sweets or trinkets, for these children knew the stab of hunger from an empty belly and the smarting pain of a clip around the ear if they came home without a few precious pennies for the family's keep. Maisie knew that for each child waiting there was a mother who watered down a stew to make it go further, and a father who had walked all day from one employment line to another. Whatever else Joseph Waite might be, he was not completely without feeling. It had been reported in the newspapers that at the end of each day, any food that might spoil before the shops opened the next morning was delivered to soup kitchens in the poorest areas.

Maisie crossed the road and walked through the elegant doors. Counters ran along the walls on either side, with a third connecting them at the far end of the shop. Each was divided into sections, with one or two shop assistants working each section, depending upon the number of customers waiting. There was an ornate brass till in each section, to receive cash for the items weighed and purchased. Of course the wealthy had accounts that were settled monthly or weekly, with the maid personally presenting an order that would be filled and delivered to the house by a blue-and-gold Waite's delivery van.

The oak floor was polished to a shine. As she watched, Maisie noticed that a boy swept the floor every quarter of an hour. As soon as he had finished making his way, broom in hand, from one end to the other, it was time for him to start again, rhythmically directing sawdust and any debris into a large dustpan as he worked back and forth, back and forth. White-tiled walls reflected the bright glass lights that hung from cast-iron ceiling fixtures, and along the top of the walls a border of coloured tiles formed another mosaic, depicting the very best foods that money could buy. A marble-topped table stood in the centre of the floor, groaning with a tableau of vegetables and tinned goods. Maisie wondered if a visitor entering the store would believe that there were people in Britain wanting for a good meal.

She walked around the shop, looking first at the cheese counter, then the fruits and vegetables. Dry goods were displayed in barrels and wooden boxes, and as a customer asked for a half pound of currants or a pound of rice the assistant, dressed in a blue cotton dress and matching cap decorated with yellow piping, would measure the amount onto the scale, then tip the currants or rice into a blue paper bag which was then folded at the top and handed, with a smile, to the customer. Money was handed over, and as the assistant pressed the brass keys of the heavy till, the tally popped up in the glass panel. Yes, thought Maisie, listening to the tills ringing and willing assistants advising on the best way to cook this or that, Waite's was weathering the country's economic woes very well. She walked to the other side of the shop and stood alongside the fancy-goods counter. A woman had just pointed to the glass-topped tin of biscuits and asked for "a good half-pound of Sweet Maries, please" when Maisie became aware that the physical energy in the shop had suddenly changed. A deep blue Rolls Royce had drawn up outside the entrance, and a chauffeur was walking around to the front passenger door. As Maisie watched, the man silhouetted inside removed his Homburg and in its place set a flat cap on his head. Ah, she thought: Joseph Waite, the "everyman" of the grocery trade. The man who was so in touch with his origins that he would sit alongside his chauffeur in his grand motor car – at least when he was visiting one of his shops.

Waite dispatched the chauffeur to send the street urchins away from the store with a penny each for their trouble. Then he strode into his store, light of foot despite his extra weight. He stopped to speak to each customer on his way to the first counter, and Maisie felt the force of personality that had made him rich, famous, and loved by working-class folk and the privileged alike. Waite was the common man, in business *for* the people who made him what he had become, or so it seemed as he took over the cheese counter, asking the next customer what he could do for her on this bright day. As the woman gave her order, Waite made much of washing his hands at the sink situated on the wall behind the counter, then turned and took up a half wheel of English cheddar. Positioning the cheese on a marble slab, Waite drew the wire cutter across, placed the wedge of cheddar on a wafer of waxed paper, weighed it, then held the cheese out for her inspection in the palm of his hand. Maisie noticed that while washing his hands he had whispered to the assistant. Now as he said, "A nice half-pound for you *exactly*, Mrs Johnson," she realized that he had asked the customer's name.

Mrs Johnson blushed and nodded agreement, uttering a shy "thank you" to the famous Joseph Waite. As he placed the cheese in a paper bag and twisted the corners to secure the item, she turned to other customers and smiled, eager to be seen basking in these few moments of attention from the man himself.

Waite moved on, working at each counter before reaching the section where he was clearly in his element: the meat counter. It was the most decorated part of the shop, with the stuffed head of an Aberdeen Angus mounted on the wall behind the counter, complete with a ring through its nose and glassy eyes that betrayed the fury the beast must have felt upon being taken to the slaughterhouse. Whole carcasses hung from a horizontal brass rod near the ceiling, which could be lowered by a pulley secured on the left-hand wall. The tills had been ringing at a steady pace until Waite walked into his domain. Now they rang even more briskly.

Waving the assistants to one side, he snapped his fingers. An apprentice appeared bearing a freshly laundered white butcher's apron, which he unfolded and held ready. Taking off his jacket, Waite handed it to another assistant, turned and washed his hands again, drying them on a fresh white towel held at the ready by a young boy. He took the apron and placed the bib over his head, wrapping the strings around his waist, bringing them to the front, and tying a double knot. One of the apprentices had begun to operate the rope pulley, slowly inching the carcasses down to ground level, whereupon two others wearing butchers' white aprons, white shirts and blue-and-gold bow ties, lifted a pig carcass onto the marble slab.

Swiftly and deftly Waite wielded the cleaver and boning knife, his sausage-like fingers holding the meat steady while he separated legs, ribs, trotters, joints, and muscle. With a flourish he held up a leg of pork, explaining to the customers who had gathered to watch Joseph Waite, the famous butcher's boy who had done so very well, yet knew what it was to be poor – that even the cheapest cuts could be cooked to provide a succulent Sunday dinner, and the leftovers minced together with a few carrots, potatoes and a little bit of onion for a pie on Monday – which would, of course, last until Tuesday or Wednesday.

Waite finished preparing the carcass for display and sale and, as he removed his apron, his customers broke into applause. Waite waved an acknowledgment, then washed his hands once more and turned to the apprentice holding out his jacket. He slipped into it, nodded to his staff, and waved to the customers one last time before leaving by a side door that Maisie assumed led to the upstairs offices. The assistants exchanged glances and exhaled, blowing out their cheeks for added emphasis, relieved that the ritual was over.

Having seen all she had come to see, Maisie turned to leave. She had taken only one step when her eyes were drawn to the wall above the doorway and another mosaic crafted at great expense. It was not its beauty that caused Maisie to catch her breath, but the sad truth inscribed there. Upon each tile was the name of an employee of Waite's International Stores lost in the Great War. There were at least one hundred, each name accompanied by the town in which the man had worked. Above the names a banner of coloured tiles formed the words: IN LOVING REMEMBRANCE – LEST WE FORGET.

Maisie's eyes filled with tears as she was taken once again by the grief that still assailed her when she least expected it, when the sharp and dreadful memories came to her unbidden. Maisie knew the recollections were not hers exclusively. A shared grief often seemed to linger in the air, perhaps borne on a soft breeze carrying the name of one who was lost heard in conversation or remembered at a gathering, and the realization that one or two of that group were gone, their laughter never to be heard again. It was as if the sorrow of every single man and woman who had lived with the fear or reality of losing a loved one to war had formed an abyss to be negotiated anew every day.

Composing herself, Maisie approached an assistant at the cheese counter who had no customers to serve at the moment.

"Excuse me."

"Yes, Madam, how may I help you today?"

"I just wondered about the names on the wall."

"Oh, yes, Miss. Tragic, we lost so many. Joined up as pals, a lot of 'em. The Waite's Boys, they called themselves. Mr Waite had that memorial started as soon as the first were lost. There's one in every Waite's shop, all the same, all the names in every shop."

"You must all think a lot of him." Maisie inclined her head, seeking a response.

The assistant smiled. "Yes, we all think a lot of him, Madam. And he looks after all the families." He nodded towards the memorial tiles.

"You mean financially?"

"Yes, there's not one of those families wants for anything. They get their groceries every Christmas, and a Christmas box – money, you know – and they get a bit off their groceries if they shop at Waite's. Got special little cards, they have, to get the money back. And if anyone's taken poorly, well, Mr Waite's office is under orders to look after them."

"I see. Very generous, isn't he?"

"Very." The assistant moved to end the conversation as a customer approached, then continued. "Read through those names, Madam, and you'll see why Mr Waite has a personal interest in the families."

Maisie looked above the door and read: "Gough, Gould, Gowden, Haines, Jackson, Michaels, Richards" – her eyes focused on the bottom of one column, then rose to the top of the next – "Waite . . . Joseph Charles Waite, Jr, London." She could read no further.

3

O N TUESDAY afternoon, following her visit to the branch of
Waite's International Stores, Maisie telephoned the offices of
Carstairs & Clifton and requested an immediate appointment with
Mr Gerald Bartrup, to whom she had received a personal recom-
mendation. She had no doubt that her request would be granted,
for new customers seeking investment advice were thin on the
ground in such times. Maisie was curious about the relationship
between Bartrup and Charlotte. Had theirs been a love match that
had soured with time and deeper familiarity? Or had Charlotte
been pressured by her father to make a suitable marriage? The
engagement had ended, but was there still a connection? If so,
Charlotte might well have appealed to her former fiancé upon
fleeing her father's house.

She alighted at Bank underground station, and walked to the
red-brick building that housed the offices of Carstairs & Clifton. A
doorman directed her to the reception desk where her appointment
was confirmed, and she was directed to a staircase, at the top of
which she was met by another clerk who escorted her to Mr
Bartrup's office.

Bartrup, a man of medium height, about thirty-eight years old,
with a receding hairline and a rather florid complexion, came from
behind a large mahogany desk and extended a hand. "Ah, Miss
Dobbs. Delighted to meet you."

"And I you, Mr Bartrup."

"Do take a seat. Would you like some refreshment? Tea,
perhaps?"

"No thank you, Mr Bartrup."

Bartrup took his place behind the desk, and placed his hands together on the leather blotting pad in front of him.

"Now, then, you wish to discuss investment of a legacy I understand, Miss Dobbs?"

"Mr Bartrup. I must confess immediately that investment counsel is not my reason for coming to see you today."

"But, I thought . . ." The flustered man reached for a file on his desk.

"Mr Bartrup, I wanted to speak to you in confidence about a matter of urgency. I am working on behalf of Mr Joseph Waite, who is concerned about his daughter. She has recently left her father's home and has not since been in communication with her family."

Bartrup threw back his head and began to laugh. "Another bid for freedom until the old man locks her up again!"

"I beg your pardon?"

"Don't worry, I am speaking figuratively, not literally, Miss Dobbs. As you may have noticed, Mr Joseph Waite runs a very tight ship, and will not brook any wishes counter to his own." He leaned towards Maisie. "And I suppose I am the wicked man who caused Her Royal Waiteness to leave, am I not?"

"I'm not implying that, Mr Bartrup, though I had hoped you might be able to shed some light on her mood of late even if you do not know her whereabouts."

"I have no idea where she is. And Charlotte is *always* in a mood, Miss Dobbs. In fact, she was in quite the mood when she broke off our engagement some weeks ago."

"*She* broke off the engagement?"

"Oh yes. Without a 'by your leave' and with no explanation whatsoever. Didn't even look sorry about it. Was curt and to the point: 'I'm sorry, Gerald, we cannot marry. Our engagement is over.' And that was that."

"Do you have any idea –?"

"Why she did it?" Bartup stood up and walked to the window.

He turned to Maisie. "No, Miss Dobbs. No idea at all. But . . ." He looked down at his feet then back at Maisie. "I can't say I was surprised or completely sorry. Charlotte is an attractive girl and by any standards it was a good match, but our communications had been difficult for some time. It was as if she were receding into herself. She is an unhappy woman, Miss Dobbs."

Maisie looked at Bartrup intently. "Can you tell me anything about Miss Waite's previous disappearances?"

"Not really. All I can tell you is that they occurred before we met, and apparently – I heard this from friends – they never lasted long. Frankly, she knew which side her bread was buttered. We had been engaged for six months, with no date set for the wedding. Of course we'd come up with possibilities, but a reason was always found to exclude that date and go back to the drawing board. Sometimes Charlotte discovered the conflicting engagement, sometimes her father. She did not do the disappearing act while we were courting, or after we became engaged, though I had been warned by others about her previous forays into freedom away from the pressures of living in Waite-shire!"

Bartrup smiled, though Maisie suspected that he still felt the sting of being cast aside by Charlotte Waite.

"Mind you," he added, "our engagement ended some two months ago, so that couldn't have made her bolt." Bartrup looked thoughtful, then consulted his watch. "Good Lord! Miss Dobbs, I can manage one last question, then I must move on to my next appointment."

Maisie sensed that there was no other appointment, but one last question would be sufficient. "Thank you, Mr Bartrup. It's a simple question: where do you think Charlotte might be? Where would she run to?"

Bartrup sighed and leaned his chin on the fist he made with both hands, his elbows on the table in front of him. "I wish I could help you, Miss Dobbs, but I really don't know. She certainly didn't come to me, nor am I someone she would confide in."

"You must have been saddened by your engagement ending, Mr Bartrup."

"Frankly, at first I was taken aback but then, well, one has to just get on with it, doesn't one?"

"I have taken a good deal of your time, Mr Bartrup, and I must thank you." Maisie stood and held out her hand for Bartrup, who returned her handshake.

"If I can be of any help, Miss Dobbs, please do not hesitate to call again, though afternoon is always best, given the vagaries of work in the City."

"Of course. Thank you." Maisie bade him farewell and was escorted out of the offices of Carstairs & Clifton. She emerged into bright mid-afternoon sunshine and hurried to Bank station for the quick journey back to Fitzroy Square. Maisie knew that Billy would not return to the office before five o'clock, so she would have some time to review Maurice's notes again and gather her thoughts. Bartrup had been of almost no help, and recollection of the conversation led her to believe that Charlotte had probably done well to break off the engagement. Marriage to such a man would have provided no comfort except financial, and Charlotte had no urgent need for economic security. Perhaps Charlotte's curiosity about the contemplative life that the book and pamphlets in her room suggested, stemmed from a desire for a deeper, more intimate connection than that promised by marriage to the men in her circle.

Walking across Fitzroy Square, Maisie felt an ominous chill in the air and looked up to see heavy grey cumulus clouds which seemed to her like water-filled balloons ready to burst. She quickened her pace, keys at the ready to open the front door. She entered the room just in time to see long needles of rain slanting across the windows where sunlight had filtered in that morning.

Maisie removed her mackintosh, hung it on the hook behind the door and went to a filing cabinet that contained more extensive information than that in the card file. She was concerned; thus far she had made no progress, had perhaps wasted time. The various elements of information gathered indicated to Maisie that finding Charlotte Waite might be even more urgent than her overbearing, yet in some ways dismissive father believed. As Maisie unlocked the cabinet she reflected upon the memorial tiles in Joseph Waite's store and admonished herself: how had she missed the fact that Waite had a son?

Leafing through the manila folders, Maisie found the file she was looking for and took it to her desk. She began to remove notes and letters from it, fanning them out on the desk in front of her. Knowing that at that point Maurice might have cautioned her against anger directed at the self, Maisie quickly sat back in the chair with her eyes closed. She placed her left hand on her solar plexus to centre herself, and her right hand across her heart to denote kindness, as she had been taught by Khan. She took several deep breaths, opened her eyes, and looked at the documents in front of her, with the intention of studying carefully every detail of Joseph Waite's background. She read for some time, jotted notes and words on a sheet of paper that she would later add to the case map. The thud of the outer door being closed brought her contemplative silence to an end, followed by the unmistakable "dot-and-carry-one" footfall of Billy Beale climbing the stairs. The door opened and immediately Maisie felt the energy in the room change as Billy entered. Clearly he had news to impart.

"Afternoon, Miss. Nice to see the days starting to get longer, innit? Not that you'd notice this afternoon." Billy shook out his overcoat and hung it on the back of the door, while Maisie looked in dismay at the droplets of rainwater that now speckled the floor. "Didn't it come down, all of a sudden? I thought it'd 'old off, what wiv it clearin' up this mornin'."

"Indeed, Billy. Um, could you get a cloth and wipe up the water on the floor?"

"Aw, sorry, Miss." Billy took a rag from one of the drawers in his desk and slowly bent down to mop up the rainwater, taking care with his aching knee.

Having completed the task, Billy took his notebook, Charlotte Waite's address book and a newspaper from the inside pocket of his overcoat, and sat down beside Maisie at the table by the window.

"Well, I don't know about you, Miss, but I've 'ad a very interestin' day."

"I'm delighted to hear it."

Billy placed the address book in front of Maisie, inclined his head towards it and grinned. "Notice anything strange about this 'ere book?"

Maisie picked up the black leather-bound book, ran her fingers around the closed gilt-edged pages and flicked open a page or two.

"Go on."

"Well, I ain't never 'ad an address book meself. I might scratch down somethin' on the back of me *Daily Sketch*, but I've never gone in for addresses all written down in alphabetical order, like."

Maisie nodded.

"But what I reckon is that people like you, what 'ave address books because they know enough people to 'ave to write down all the names and addresses and telephone numbers and all, don't 'ave address books that look like this." Billy reached for the book, flapped it back and forth, and then set it down on the table again for effect. "I bet if we looked through your address book it'd be full of directions and notes and some telephone numbers, and some people would've moved so many times, you've 'ad to scribble out the address to put the new one in. Then no sooner've you done that, they've either moved again or gone and got themselves married and changed names, so you 'ave to move the 'ole thing."

"You've got a point there, Billy."

"Well, I looked at this book, and I thought to meself that she either don't know many people or this ain't 'er main address book."

"Do you think she deliberately left a bogus address book to fool people who searched for her?" Maisie tested Billy.

"Nah, I don't think she's that sort. 'Specially if she ran off a bit quick. No, 'ere's what I think 'appened: she 'ad a new book for a present or bought 'erself a new book because the old one's got a bit tatty. So she starts to put in the names and – course, I'm speculatin' 'ere, Miss – starts with the people she knows best *now*. They're the ones it's most important to 'ave in the book. But because it's not the most thrillin' job, she puts it off and still goes back to 'er old book because she's used to it, it's like an old friend in itself."

"Good thinking, Billy."

"Anyway, this is all well and good, because the people who're important *now* in 'er life are all 'ere – and by the way, I saw one of 'em today, I'll tell you about that next – but the ones from a long time ago, what she probably 'asn't seen for ages and only keeps the name in the book so she can send a card at Christmas, ain't 'ere . . . and Charlotte Waite took 'er old book with 'er to wherever she went off to."

"I am very impressed, Billy; you've put a lot of thought into this." Maisie smiled.

Billy sat up straighter and reached for his notebook. "So, I was standin' outside the 'ome of, let me see, 'ere we are – Lydia Fisher. Lives in Cheyne Mews – very nice, I'm sure. So, I was standin' outside, taking a dekko at the premises, when up she comes in 'er car. Very posh, I must say. She was dressed to the nines, bright red lips and that black stuff on 'er eyes, fur draped over 'er shoulder. Of course, I 'ad to say somethin' to 'er, didn't I?" Billy held out his upturned palms for effect. "Seein' as she'd almost knocked me into the wall with 'er drivin' and she'd see me again when we do our official inquiry. So I told 'er my name, and that I worked for you, and that what I 'ad to say was in confidence."

"And you had this conversation out in the street?"

"Well, the beginnin' of it, yes. I said that we was workin' for the Waite family, and she says, 'Do come in.' There was a maid who brought us tea in the upstairs drawin' room. Mind you, the lady knocked back a couple of quick ones, poured 'em 'erself from one of them fancy crystal decanters on the sideboard. She's only got a maid and a cook, is my guess. Probably no chauffeur because she seems to like 'avin' the car to 'erself." Billy cleared his throat and continued. "So I says that it's all confidential, that Charlotte Waite 'ad left 'er father's 'ome and that we'd been retained to look for 'er."

"Good."

"Well, she rolls 'er eyes, says, 'Again!' all snotty, like, then says, 'That's no surprise, she's run so many times, they should put that woman in the Olympics!' I knew what she meant, what wiv what we already know about Miss Waite. Then she says, 'Well, not to worry, she's finally run off to a convent, I expect,' to which, Miss, I said, 'Are you serious, Miss Fisher?' She says, all airs and all, '*Mrs* Fisher, if you please.' Anyway, it turns out that at their last two luncheons Miss Waite'd talked about the end of her engagement and 'ow she couldn't find someone she really loved, so she might as well go off to live in a nunnery where she could at least be useful."

"Did Fisher think she meant it?"

"The funny thing is, y'know, she said that at first she thought Charlotte was tryin' to shock 'em. Then she said she realized that Charlotte might be serious and that she'd been down to a place in Kent somewhere. 'Ow about that, then?"

"Well, that's interesting." Maisie understood how the serene image of a nun might appeal to a bored, unhappy young woman. She recalled wartime nurses being photographed in such a way as to evoke the purity and dedication of those in religious orders. Such romantic images subsequently encouraged more young women to enlist. "I wonder what Waite will have to say about that?" she added. "He didn't seem to be a religious man, and there's no reference to either his beliefs or Catholicism in Maurice's notes."

"Do you think Charlotte is trying to annoy 'er father?"

"Well, she's not a child, but she's clearly capable of such behaviour." Maisie was thoughtful. "You know, we could be awfully lucky here. I didn't say anything about it this morning because I didn't want to jump to conclusions and close our minds in the process, but I used to know an enclosed nun, Dame Constance Charteris. She was abbess of a community of Benedictines living close to Girton. She used to meet several students for tutorials on religious philosophy. Because they're an enclosed order, communication with outsiders takes place with a sort of barrier in between. I remember it was rather strange at first, being in a tutorial with someone who sat behind a grille."

"And 'ow's that lucky, Miss?"

"I can't remember all the details, but shortly after I left Girton to become a VAD nurse, the nuns had to find a new place to live. I think their abbey in Cambridgeshire was requisitioned for military use, and I could swear they went to Kent. I just need to make a couple of telephone calls to find out, and if that's so, I'll send word to Dame Constance, asking to see her as soon as possible."

Billy scratched his head and looked at the floor.

"What is it, Billy? Have you remembered something?"

"Nah, it's not that, it's . . . well, don't mind me sayin' so, but it does seem all a bit too, y'know, simple, like. You findin' a seal that seems to be from the place where your nuns went off to. It's a bit too . . ."

"Coincidental?"

"Yeah, that's it. Seems a bit too much of one for me."

Maisie smiled and nodded. "I used to think in that way, Billy, when I first began working officially for Dr Blanche. I confess I was intrigued by the apparent serendipity of our discoveries, links in the chain that led us to solve a case. Time and time again it appeared that we were exactly where we were supposed to be when a vital clue came to the surface."

"And what did Dr Blanche say about it then?"

"That coincidence is a messenger sent by truth. That there are no accidents of fate. And that we must trust such gifts in our work, rather than disregard them because they seem so obvious – the police files are full of such oversights."

Billy nodded. "So, that bein' the case, can't we just go down there, see if Miss Waite is with your Dame Constance, bring 'er back 'ome and put a tin lid on this job with a 'thank-you-very-much' for the fee?"

Maisie shook her head. "No, Billy. If Charlotte Waite has sought her out, Dame Constance will be very protective of her *and* what the Benedictines stand for."

"I bet old Waite would just march in, find out if Charlotte was there and – if she was – drag her out."

"He could try." Maisie smiled at her assistant. "But I wouldn't bet on his chances against Dame Constance. No, let's do this with an eye to protocol; it'll serve us well."

Billy nodded, and Maisie reached for her own notes.

She described Joseph Waite, the way in which his forceful personality filled the shop, drawing customers to him with his easy camaraderie while at the same time intimidating his staff. Maisie explained to Billy how such intimidation seemed at odds with the regard the assistants appeared to have for Waite, especially for the way he looked after the families of those fallen in the Great War.

Billy chimed in, "Y'know what my ol' father used to say, don't you? 'E used to say that if you 'ad workers, it wasn't so important to be liked as it was to be respected, and it was possible to respect someone without actually likin' them. P'r'aps Waite doesn't need to be liked."

"I think that's a fairly accurate assessment of the situation," Maisie nodded, and continued, "The other thing, and the most important: Joseph Waite lost a son in the war, a son who worked for him at the shop. He was probably being groomed to inherit the business."

Billy was surprised. "P'r'aps that's why 'e's so, y'know, miserable. After all, 'e would be, especially if that girl of 'is is a bit of a drooping flower."

"I think 'wilting lily' was the phrase he used. And yes, it could account for a lot, but might have nothing at all to do with Charlotte's disappearance, which must obviously be our focus."

"What 'appened to 'im, the son?"

"It appears that young Waite was killed along with many men employed by Waite's. They joined up together. Joseph was a product of Waite's first marriage. Waite married, quite literally, the girl next door, when he was twenty-four and she was twenty. Sadly, she died in childbirth a year later. By then Waite was doing quite well, but it must have been yet another heavy loss to add to his list."

"It's a wonder 'e didn't mention it the other day. Y'know, when 'e was going on about despair."

"Yes and no. Extreme emotions are strange forces, Billy. The loss of his son might be kept separate from his other griefs, his alone, shared with no one." Maisie stopped for a moment, then continued speaking: "One of Waite's sisters, who was unmarried at the time, came to live at his house to care for the child. As you can imagine, Waite kept his family employed, so they were well looked after, except the brother he spoke of yesterday who had gone to work at the pit. The son would have been about six when Waite remarried in haste and, as you know, Charlotte was born seven months later. So Joseph, the son, was seven when his sister was born. By the way, you'll notice young Joseph's middle name was Charles and the daughter was christened Charlotte. Joseph Waite's father was Charles. Thus he effectively named both children after their late grandfather."

Maisie reached for the coloured pencils and drew them towards Billy and herself. "Now then, let's map this out and see what we might have missed." They began working together, and after a few minutes Maisie continued. "I'll visit Lydia Fisher this week, Billy. Tomorrow morning, I think, so don't expect me in until lunch-time-ish. It's going to be a very busy week, I may not be able to keep my Friday luncheon appointment with Inspector Stratton."

"Oh, Miss –" Billy suddenly laid a red pencil down on the desk and hit his forehead smartly, as if to reprimand himself for his forgetfulness. "That reminds me, you mentionin' D. I. Stratton. I spoke to ol' Jack Barker – y'know, who sells the *Express* outside Warren Street station – and 'e spoke to 'is mate what sells *The Times*, who 'ad a copy or two left over from the weekend."

"What has that got to do with Inspector Stratton?"

"Remember we was talkin' about 'im bein' on that case of the woman who'd been murdered, in Coulsden?"

"Yes."

"I said I'd find out what Charlotte Waite was readin', y'know, when she did a runner out of the room where they 'ad breakfast."

Maisie drew breath sharply.

"Anyway, it turns out that *The Times* – and every other paper this last weekend, for that matter – printed the latest news about that woman who'd been found murdered in Coulsden. 'er name was Philippa Sedgewick. She was married, about your age – remember

52

I remarked on it? And she was a vicar's daughter. *The Times* listed it on the front page, wiv the main story on page two. It was right there wiv all the important news, about the deficit and unemployment and about Mr Gandhi's walk to the sea for salt. All the papers 'ad the murder story, wiv all the 'orrible details. Would've turned anyone off their breakfast."

Maisie tapped her pencil on the palm of her hand. Billy said nothing, knowing that Maisie was disengaging her mind from his. She looked out of the window at the evening sky. Perhaps it wasn't such a coincidence that Billy had mentioned Mr Gandhi. Khan had spoken of the man and his idea of *satyagraha*, which in Sanskrit meant "insistence on truth". Maisie shivered, remembering the emotions she had experienced while sitting in Charlotte Waite's rooms, the most powerful of which was the melancholy that seeped from every nook and cranny in the place where the missing woman had lived. Perhaps fear and not an overbearing father had been the true impetus for Charlotte's flight.

4

THE PREVIOUS September Lady Rowan had insisted that Maisie leave the rented bed-sitting room next to her Warren Street office and live in their Belgravia mansion's second-floor apartment. At first Maisie declined for she had been a resident of the house before, when she came to live in the servants' quarters at the age of thirteen. And though the veil of class distinction that separated Maisie and her employer had been lifted over the years – especially as Lady Rowan became more involved in sponsoring Maisie's education – the memory of those early days in their relationship lingered like a faint scent in the air. The offer was well meant, yet Maisie feared that the change in status might be difficult. Finally, however, she had allowed herself to be persuaded.

One evening just after taking up residence, Maisie had waited until the downstairs staff were having a cup of nighttime cocoa in the kitchen, then quietly slipped through the door on the landing that led to the back stairs. She made her way up to the servants' quarters, to the room she'd occupied when she first came to 15 Ebury Place. The furniture was covered in sheets, as the girls who usually slept in this room were currently at Chelstone, the Comptons' country estate in Kent. Maisie sat on the cast-iron-framed bed she had once wearily climbed into every night, with work-worn hands and an aching back. It was Enid she thought of, her friend and fellow servant who had left the Compton's employ to seek more lucrative work in a munitions factory in late 1914. Maisie had seen her for the last time in April 1915, just a few hours before she was killed in an explosion at the factory.

Maisie consulted her watch. She had to hurry. She wanted to look her best to gain an audience with the possibly indisposed Mrs Fisher, and to do that she must appear on a social par with her.

She had purchased several new items of clothing recently, an expenditure that nagged at her for she was not given to frivolous spending. But as Lady Rowan pointed out, "It's all very well wearing those plain clothes while you're snooping around London or tramping through a field, but you've important clients who will want to know they are dealing with someone successful!"

So Maisie had invested in the burgundy ensemble that subsequently seemed to pick up fluff all too quickly, a black dress suitable for day or early-evening wear, and the deep-plum-coloured suit she now laid out on the bed. The long-line jacket had a shawl collar that extended down to a single button set just below waist level and to one side. Maisie chose a plain cream silk blouse with a jewel neckline to wear under the jacket, and a string of pearls with matching earrings. The jacket cuffs bore only one button, and revealed just a half inch of silk at each wrist. The matching knife-pleated skirt fell to just below the knee. The cost of her silk stockings made her shudder as she put them on. She took care to lick her fingers quickly before running her hand through each stocking to prevent a hangnail catching and causing an unsightly pull.

Maisie drew the line at matching shoes for each outfit, instead selecting her best plain black pair with a single strap that extended across her instep and buttoned with a square black button. The heels were a modest one-and-a-half inches.

She collected her black shoulder bag, her document case, an umbrella – just in case – and her new plum-coloured hat with a black ribbon band gathered in a simple rosette at the side. The cloche she'd worn for some time now seemed tired, and though perfectly serviceable for an ordinary day's work, would not do today. This hat had a slightly broader, more fashionable brim, and revealed more of her face and midnight blue eyes. Maisie took care to pin back any tendrils of hair that looked as if they might creep out and go astray.

Maisie set off to walk to Cheyne Mews, exercise she enjoyed, for this morning the sky was robin's-egg blue, the sun was shining, and though she passed only a few people they smiled readily and wished her a good morning. Gradually the number of pedestrians thinned out until Maisie was the only person making her way along the avenue. A light breeze ran though the trees, causing newly unfolded leaves to rustle, and she was suddenly aware of a chill in the air, a chill so strong that it caused her to stop. She rubbed her arms and shivered. A sensation seemed to run across the back of her neck, as if an icy finger had been drawn from just below one earlobe across to the other, and Maisie was so sure someone was standing behind her that she turned quickly. But there was no one.

She was quite cold by the time she reached 9 Cheyne Mews, a typical mews house in which horses had once been stabled, facing onto a cobbled street. Now the only means of transportation evident to Maisie was a sleek new Lagonda parked outside the Fisher residence. She knew from George, the Comptons' chauffeur who regularly regaled her with news of the latest automobile inventions, that this was an exclusive motor car, capable of more than ninety miles per hour. The Lagonda had been parked without due care; one of the front wheels rested on the narrow pavement. Unlike the neighbouring houses, the three-storey house was plain, unadorned by windowboxes. There was just one step up to the front door. Maisie rang the bell and waited for the maid to answer. When no one came, Maisie rang the bell again and then a third time, at which point the door finally opened.

"Sorry Ma'am. Begging your pardon for keeping you waiting." The young maid was flushed and in tears.

"I'm here to see Mrs Fisher." Maisie inclined her head. "Are you all right?"

"Yes, Ma'am." Her bottom lip trembled. "Well, I don't know, I'm sure." She took a handkerchief from the pocket of her lace apron and dabbed her eyes.

"What is it?" Maisie placed a hand on the maid's shoulder, a move that caused the girl to break down completely.

"Let's get you inside, and then tell me what's wrong."

Standing in the narrow hallway, the maid blurted out her fears. "Well, the lady hasn't got up yet, and I'm new here, see, and the cook, who knows her better than me, doesn't get here till half past eleven. The lady told me yesterday afternoon that she didn't want to be disturbed until nine this morning, and look at the time now! I've knocked and knocked, and I know she had a drink or two yesterday afternoon, and I know she would've kept going – I've learned that already – and she's got a temper on her if she's crossed, but she did say –"

"Now then, calm down and show me to her room."

The maid looked doubtful, but when Maisie informed her that she had once been a nurse the maid nodded, rubbed her swollen eyes, and led Maisie up a flight of stairs to the first floor where the main reception and bedrooms were situated. She stopped outside a carved door that looked as if it might have been brought from an exotic overseas locale. Maisie knocked sharply.

"Mrs Fisher. Are you awake? Mrs Fisher!" Her voice was loud and clear, yet there was no answer. She tried opening the door, which was locked. Maisie knew that it was crucial that she gain entrance to the room.

"She may be indisposed, especially if she overindulged. I'll need to get into the room. Go downstairs and prepare a glass of water with liver salts for her."

The maid hurried downstairs. Maisie shook her head: she's so new she hasn't even asked my name.

Opening her document case, Maisie reached for a cloth bag with a drawstring top that contained several implements, similar to fishermen's needles, of varying size. She selected one. *That should do it.* She knelt, inserted the sharp point into the keyhole and manipulated the lock. *Yes!* Maisie stood up, closed her eyes for just a second to control the images rushing into her mind's eye, and opened the door.

Lydia Fisher's body lay on the floor between an elegant pale blue chaise longue and an overturned side table, the contents of a tea tray strewn across an Aubusson rug. Maisie was never shocked upon encountering a scene of death. Not since the war. She automatically reached under the woman's left ear with her fingertips, feeling for a pulse. Nothing. No sign of life. Mrs Fisher was dressed for an afternoon out. It appeared that she had not changed her clothes after arriving home yesterday.

The corridor floor creaked as the maid returned. Maisie moved quickly to the door to prevent the highly-strung young woman from seeing into the room. She stopped her just in time.

"You must do exactly as I say. Telephone Scotland Yard. Ask to speak to Detective Inspector Stratton and no one else. Say that you are acting on the instructions of Miss Maisie Dobbs and that he is to come to this address immediately."

"Is Mrs Fisher all right, Ma'am?"

"Just do as I say – now! When you've done that, come back to the room only if there is to be a delay or if you have not been able to speak personally to Inspector Stratton. When the police arrive, direct them to me straightaway."

Maisie estimated that she would have twenty minutes or so alone in the room. Not as much as she would have liked, but enough. Again she brought out the drawstring bag. She pulled out a folded pair of rubber gloves that were at least one size too small and pulled them onto her hands, pressing down between each finger for a snug fit. She turned to the body of Lydia Fisher.

The woman's clothing had been torn many times, though there was little blood from the multiple knife wounds to her chest. Kneeling, Maisie looked closely at each burnt umber-rimmed wound, taking care not to disturb the fabric of the victim's clothing or the position of her body. Next she turned her attention to the terror-filled dead eyes, then to the purple lips and mouth, and the fingers. *Ten minutes.*

The teapot had been smashed, but some of the dregs were caught in part of its base. Maisie reached into the drawstring bag and took out a small utensil similar to a salt spoon. She dipped it into the liquid and tasted. Then she moved closer and sniffed. Next she turned her attention to the room. Little time remained. Apparently Lydia Fisher had been killed while taking tea with a guest. Maisie suspected that the disarray in the room had been caused by Lydia herself. She walked around the body, noting the position of the chaise longue and of other furniture that had been disturbed. Ornaments had fallen from another side table, bottles had been knocked from the cocktail cabinet. Maisie nodded: morphine. The narcotic would have caused intense muscle spasms and hallucinations before death. The killer would have watched, perhaps avoiding ever weaker lunges by the victim for fifteen minutes or so before death occurred. And once Fisher was dead, the murderer, who had watched the woman die, had taken another portion of revenge with a knife. *Five minutes.*

Maisie closed her eyes and breathed deeply, trying to get a sense of what energies the events of the last twenty-four hours had left in their wake. Though death had surely accompanied him, Maisie felt that the visitor had been known to Lydia Fisher. Maisie had been to murder scenes on many occasions and had immediately felt the frenzy of attack. Fear and hatred, the emotions that led to such a terrible outcome, lingered and caused a constellation of violent jagged colours to blur her vision temporarily, as they had done this morning when she stood outside Lydia Fisher's carved door. *One more minute.*

Two motor cars screeched to a halt outside. Maisie deftly removed her gloves and returned them to the cloth bag, which she slipped into her case before moving to a position outside the door to wait for Stratton. She took one last look at Lydia Fisher's body and the terrible fear etched in the woman's wide-open eyes.

Maisie heard the maid answer the door, which was quickly followed by an introduction lacking any pleasantries by Stratton, and a terse "Good morning" from his sergeant, Caldwell. The maid informed them that Miss Dobbs was waiting upstairs.

Maisie greeted Stratton and Caldwell and led them into Lydia's drawing room.

"I came to the house hoping to talk to Mrs Fisher in connection with an assignment. The maid was distressed that Mrs Fisher had not answered her knock. She's new and I think somewhat intimidated by her employer. I informed her that I had been a nurse, and had her bring me here."

"Hmmm." Stratton, kneeling by the body, turned to Caldwell, who was inspecting the disarray in the room.

"Looks like she fought off the murderer, sir. Probably a big bloke, I'd say, what with all this mess."

Stratton met Maisie's eyes briefly. "I'll need the murder bag, Caldwell. And try to get hold of Sir Bernard Spilsbury. If you can't get him, then call out the duty man. Secure the property and place a cordon around the area."

Caldwell regarded Maisie with a smirk. "Will you be needing me when you question Miss Dobbs here, sir?"

Stratton sighed. "I will question Miss Dobbs later. This woman was murdered yesterday, probably late afternoon – as Miss Dobbs already knows." He glanced at Maisie. "For now I want to ensure that the body is inspected and removed for postmortem before the newspapermen arrive. And I have no doubt they'll arrive soon."

Maisie was asked to wait in the ground-floor reception room, where she was later questioned by Stratton, accompanied by Caldwell. Sir Bernard Spilsbury, the famous pathologist, arrived and Maisie was permitted to leave, though she knew there would be more questioning to come. As she departed the house she heard Caldwell voice his unsolicited opinion: "Well, sir, if you ask me, it's her old man. Nearly always is. Mind you, could be she had one on the side, woman like that, all furs and a big car of her own to gad about in. Who knows what she brought home!"

Maisie knew very well who Lydia Fisher had brought home yesterday afternoon. But who might have visited soon after – perhaps soon enough for the tea still to be warm in the pot? Had she answered the door herself? Billy had said the maid left the house on an errand after bringing tea, so he had seen himself out. Had Lydia poured another cup of tea in an effort to regain sobriety in the face of an unexpected caller? How had the visitor found an opportunity to introduce a narcotic into the tea? Had the caller seen that Lydia was intoxicated and offered to make fresh tea? Tea that could so easily be laced with poison? And could more of the drug have been administered while Lydia's muscles began to spasm after the first few sips? So many questions spun through Maisie's mind and the one person who could answer them was decidedly not available for questioning. Or was she?

Maisie wondered how she might gain access to Lydia Fisher's home once more. She wanted to know how Lydia Fisher lived and what had caused her grief, because of one thing she was sure: Lydia Fisher had grieved.

While she walked, Maisie remembered feeling a prickling of the skin on her neck while she stood in the upstairs hallway of Lydia Fisher's house, outside the room where her body lay. She had not shied away from the sensation but had instead silently asked, *What is it you want me to see?* Never before at the scene of a crime had Maisie felt such a duality of sensation, like a fabric that on one side is smooth as satin but on the other, rough with a raised pile. She knew that the last person who had come to the house came with a terrible burden. A burden that was no lighter for having taken Lydia Fisher's life.

Maisie walked quickly towards Victoria underground station. She planned to return to her office as quickly as possible. She would leave a message for Billy to the effect that she would be back at five o'clock. Not a moment was to be lost in the search for Charlotte Waite. If the Coulsden victim, Philippa Sedgewick, had been Charlotte's friend, as was Lydia Fisher, then Charlotte must be found. One dead friend was a tragedy. Two dead friends . . . a terrifying coincidence.

Just as Maisie reached Victoria, the black car she had already seen once that day drew alongside her. The door opened and Detective Inspector Richard Stratton emerged and tipped his hat.

"Miss Dobbs, I thought I might find you on your way to the station. I noticed that you didn't have your little red motor with you today. Look – you've had a horrible time this morning – would you care to join me for a quick cup of tea?"

Maisie looked at her watch. Lunchtime had passed and she had hardly noticed. "Yes, I do have time – just – but I must be back at my office by five."

"I would be delighted to escort you there in my car. Let's just nip across the road." Stratton indicated a small teashop and Maisie inclined her head in agreement.

Stratton took Maisie lightly by the elbow to steer her through the sparse traffic. Maisie knew he would probably be less solicitous when he questioned her again formally.

A waitress directed them to a corner table.

"Miss Dobbs, I'm curious about the fact that you visited Mrs Fisher today of all days. Is there anything else you can tell me about your presence at the scene?"

"I've told you all I can, I believe. The victim was once a friend of the young woman I am seeking on behalf of a client. I thought she might be able to assist me."

The waitress returned with a tray and proceeded to set a white china teapot on the table, followed by a hot-water jug, sugar bowl, milk jug, and two matching white china teacups and saucers. She bobbed a curtsey and left the table, returning a moment later with a plate containing sliced Hovis bread with butter and jam, several iced fancy-cakes and two Eccles cakes.

"Hmmm. Interesting. Mind you, this woman had lots of friends."

"Perhaps mere acquaintances, Inspector."

"Yes, possibly." Stratton looked thoughtful as Maisie began to pour tea.

"So you put the milk in *after* the tea," said Stratton.

"Never put the milk in first, Inspector Stratton, because you might waste some. If you put it in last, you can tell exactly how much you really need." Maisie handed the cup of tea to Stratton, pushed the sugar bowl towards him and filled her own cup.

As Stratton lifted the hot tea to his lips, Maisie pressed ahead with her own question. "I take it you agree that the murder at Cheyne Mews is linked to the Coulsden murder, Inspector?"

Stratton set his cup on the saucer so fiercely, the sound caused several people to look in their direction.

"Inspector, it really doesn't take much in the way of deduction." Maisie spoke softly.

Stratton regarded Maisie before answering. "In confidence . . ."

"Of course."

Stratton continued, "The scene was very much the same as the Coulsden murder, with very little bloodshed given the extent of the attack. Spilsbury suspects ingestion of a narcotic, most likely morphine, prior to an assault with a more violent weapon. The same method was used with the Coulsden victim. The body was cold, and rigor had set in."

"Has Spilsbury indicated the time of death yet?"

"Informally he confirmed it was yesterday, either in the late afternoon or in the evening. I'll have to wait until he submits his detailed report. He's usually more definite even at the scene of the murder. Apparently Lydia Fisher dismissed the maid after being served tea yesterday and neither she nor the cook had seen her since. But according to the staff, that wasn't unusual. She was frequently known to go out at night without first requesting the assistance of her maid. And she often took to her rooms for several days on end, demanding not to be disturbed and furious if she was. The murderer could have locked the door to the room behind him, let himself out, and no one the wiser for hours. The cook said that the previous maid wouldn't turn a hair if Mrs Fisher remained in her rooms for two or three days. If you hadn't arrived at the house and found the young maid in tears, the body could have lain there for a long time. The cook would have come along, told her not to fuss, and that would have been that."

"Thank heavens I called to see her."

"There's something else. The maid went out after tea on Wednesday, which the victim took with a man of about thirty to thirty-five. By the way, Miss Dobbs, I must underline again the need

63

for absolute confidence." Stratton sipped his tea and looked at Maisie intently.

"Of course, Inspector." Maisie wanted Stratton to continue.

"Anyway, he was of medium build, with a slight limp – possibly an old soldier – and he had hair 'like a stook of hay', according to the maid. He's our best suspect thus far, so we must identify and find him as soon as possible."

Maisie set her cup on the saucer, wondering whether she should pre-empt Stratton's discovery that Billy Beale had been an earlier visitor. She quickly decided against it. *Perhaps* there had been another caller whose description was similar.

"Inspector, I know you might find this somewhat irregular, but I wonder, might I revisit the room where the body was found? A woman's insight might be helpful."

"Well, it *is* most irregular, Miss Dobbs."

Stratton looked at his watch. "I will consider it. Now then, I should ensure that you are escorted to your office."

Maisie waited for Stratton to pull back her chair. They were met outside by Stratton's driver, who drove them swiftly across London and, arriving at Fitzroy Square, parked the motor car on the pedestrian area outside Maisie's office.

"Having a police car is handy at times," said Stratton.

The driver opened the door for Stratton and Maisie to alight and, just as Stratton held out his hand to bid Maisie good-bye, Billy Beale came round the corner. He was carrying his cap. At that moment the last ray of afternoon sun caught his unruly blond hair at the same time as a rogue breeze swept across the square, giving the impression of a wayward halo around his head.

"Evenin', Miss; evenin', Detective Inspector Stratton."

Stratton shook hands with Billy, who touched his forehead, nodded to Maisie, and turned towards the front door. His appearance was not lost on Stratton, who watched Billy walk up the steps, pull the sleeve of his coat down over his hand and polish Maisie's nameplate in his customary fashion before taking out his key, unlocking the outer door, and entering the Georgian building. As he closed the door behind him, Stratton turned to face Maisie.

"Miss Dobbs, I think perhaps that there is more to discuss regarding your presence in Cheyne Mews this afternoon. However, we can do so tomorrow. I will be here at nine o'clock to collect you so that we may visit Lydia Fisher's house together. As you said, a woman's perspective might be of use to the police in the investigation of this crime."

Maisie held out her hand to Stratton. "Very well, Inspector. However, I would prefer to meet you at Victoria at, say, a quarter past nine? Then we can go on from there. I have other engagements during the day, so I must be back at my office by half past ten."

"Right you are, Miss Dobbs." Stratton nodded, stepped into the police car, and was driven away.

5

MAISIE DOUBTED that Stratton would seriously consider Billy Beale a suspect. They had met before and Stratton seemed both impressed by Billy's devotion to his employer and amused by his enthusiastic approach to his new job. On the other hand, he might suspect that Maisie had gone to the house to cover up Billy's tracks. No, the Inspector was an intelligent man, he would not seri-ously consider such a thing, though he would want to question Billy to eliminate him from inquiries and to extract any useful observations.

Maisie reached the top step of the first flight of stairs and lin-gered over a concern: Joseph Waite's demand that the police not be notified of his daughter's disappearance despite the possible rele-vance of Charlotte's friendship with Lydia Fisher. The pursuit of the murderer might require that this information be disclosed. Maisie worried about the consequences of withholding evidence from Stratton. And she worried about something else: what if Waite was wrong? What if Charlotte had not disappeared of her own free will? What if she knew the murderer? Could she have become another victim? But then again, what if Charlotte had killed her friend – had killed two friends?

Before she could open the door to the office it swung open and Billy stood waiting, his jacket removed and shirtsleeves rolled up, ready for work. Maisie looked at her watch.

"Billy, let's sit down."

Billy's ready smile evaporated. "What's wrong, Miss?"

"Sit down first, Billy."

Billy became agitated, which accentuated his limp. Maisie understood, knowing that the unease of the moment would strike his leg, a point of physical vulnerability.

Maisie sat opposite him and deliberately relaxed her body to bring calm to the room and to communicate that she was in control of the situation. "Billy, this morning I went to the home of Lydia Fisher in Cheyne Mews and found her – dead."

"Oh my Gawd!" Billy rose from the chair, half stumbling, to stand by the window. "I knew she was drinking too much." Agitated, he ran his fingers repeatedly through his hair. "I should've taken away the bottle, got on the blower to you, got you over there. You would've known what to do. I could've stopped 'er, I knew she was downin' 'em too fast, I should –"

"Billy." Maisie left the table and stood in front of her assistant. "Lydia Fisher was murdered after you left her yesterday. There was nothing you could have done."

"Murdered? Topped by someone?"

"Yes. The exact time of death has yet to be determined, but when I quickly examined the body, I estimated that she had lain there since early yesterday evening."

Maisie recounted her visit to the Fisher home, finding the body, her subsequent initial questioning and the meeting with Stratton later. Billy was fearful of the police interrogation that would doubtless ensue. Maisie asked Billy to describe this meeting with Lydia Fisher again, and his departure from the mews house.

"Billy, you did a good job," she said when he had concluded shakily. "I will explain to Detective Inspector Stratton that you were working on behalf of a concerned father, and so on. The challenge will be to keep the Waite name out of the conversation." Maisie rubbed her neck, thought for a moment, and continued. "But the fact is, apart from the killer, you were possibly the last person to see Lydia Fisher alive."

"And she was pretty well oiled when I left, and that's a fact."

"What was the time again?"

"I got back 'ere at five, didn't I? For our meetin'." As he spoke,

Billy reached into his jacket, which was hanging over the back of the chair, and pulled out his notebook. "And I 'ad a couple of other errands to do, so it was about . . . 'ere we go, Miss, it was twenty-five past three in the afternoon."

"Was anyone else in the house at the time, other than the staff?"

"Now, it's funny that you should say that Miss, because although I didn't see anyone, I thought someone else might be about. In fact, now I come to think of it, I saw a suitcase – one of them big leather ones with the straps – on the landing."

"That's interesting. I don't remember seeing a large suitcase this morning."

"P'r'aps the maid moved it. It could've belonged to Mrs Fisher, couldn't it? Remember she corrected me, Miss? I noticed she 'ad a wedding ring on, but the 'ouse didn't 'ave that feelin' about it, y'know, like there was a man about."

"Why didn't you say anything about this, Billy?"

"Well, Miss, she wasn't dead then, was she? And I wasn't lookin' out for 'er . I was only there to find out about Miss Waite, wasn't I?"

Maisie sighed. "Fair enough. But remember –"

"Yeah, I know, 'Everything in its entirety must be written down.' Well, Miss, I did do that, I did write it down in my book, but I just didn't say nothin' because Mrs Fisher wasn't the one what'd run off, was she?"

Billy sat down awkwardly, though Maisie remained standing and looked out across the square. It was darker now. He had mentioned earlier that he wanted to be home in time to take his children to the recreation ground. It crossed Maisie's mind that he had been optimistic in thinking that he would get home while it was still light enough to play outdoors. She turned back to him.

"Yes, you're right Billy. Now then, recall one more time what happened when you left."

"When she'd told me about Miss Waite and the nuns, and all, she seemed to be lollin' all over the place, so I said my good-byes and thank-you-very-muches, and off I went."

Maisie sighed. "Oh dear. I do wish one of the household had let you out."

"So do I, come to think of it. But the maid wasn't there. Mind you, I think someone else went in after me."

"Well, I would hope so, Billy."

"Nah, Miss, you know what I mean. *Directly* after me."

"Explain."

"I was on the street, and you know 'ow narrow them mewses are, don't you? Well, it was that funny it was, because I came out of the 'ouse, 'ad to squeeze past that big car of 'ers, the way she'd parked it all over the pavement, then I turned right to go down towards Victoria. I 'adn't gone but a couple of yards when I 'eard steps behind me; then the door slammed. I thought it must've been Mr Fisher, comin' in from work or somethin' and I just 'adn't seen 'im."

"You're sure it was Number Nine's door that opened and closed?"

"As sure as I can be. It was the sound, Miss. I'm good wiv noises. It's 'avin the nippers what does it – always gotta know where the noise is comin' from, otherwise the little beggars'll be getting' up to no good at all. Anyway, if it'd been the next 'ouse along, it wouldn't 'ave sounded the same, in either direction. No, it was Number Nine." Billy looked at Maisie, his eyes revealing the shock of a sudden unwanted thought. "'Ere, Miss, you don't think it was the one what did 'er in, do you?"

"It's a possibility."

Maisie considered another possibility, that Lydia Fisher might have been lying to Billy throughout. The suitcase he noticed could have belonged to Charlotte Waite. It might have been Charlotte who – alone or aided by another – had slain her friend. Waite had referred to his daughter as a "wilting lily" but Maisie was beginning to consider her a dark horse.

"This is gettin' interestin', innit, Miss?"

"Intriguing is what it is. Intriguing. I've written to Dame Constance at Camden Abbey in Kent, and expect to hear from her by return. Whether Charlotte has run there for shelter or not, Dame Constance will be able to throw light on the mind of an aspiring nun. I'll visit her as soon as I can. And I want to consult with Dr Blanche, so I'll stop at the Dower House at Chelstone to see him first."

"Will you see your old dad while you're there?"

"Of course I will. Why do you ask?"

"Wonderful man, your dad. You just don't seem to see much of 'im, that's all, seein' as 'e's your only real family."

Maisie drew back, surprised. The simplicity of Billy's observation stung her, as if she had been attacked by an unseen insect. She knew that it was only the truth that could injure in such a manner, and her face reddened.

"I see my father as much as I can." Maisie leaned towards a pile of papers which she shuffled before consulting her watch. "Goodness me, Billy! You should be on your way. You won't be home in time to play with your children though, will you?"

"Oh yes I will, Miss. Never miss a play before they go up to bed. Nice to 'ave a bit of a romp around, although the missus moans about it, says it gets 'em all excited so they won't sleep."

"We might as well finish work for the day. I'm meeting Detective Inspector Stratton tomorrow morning to go to Lydia Fisher's house. Be prepared to hold the fort for a couple of days while I am down in Kent."

"You can count on me, Miss." Billy extended his wounded leg and rose from his chair.

"That leg giving you trouble again? You seemed to be in less pain this morning."

"It comes and goes, Miss. Comes and goes. I'll be off then."

"Very well, Billy."

Billy pulled on his overcoat and gave a final wave before clambering down the stairs in an ungainly fashion that could be heard with each receding footfall. The front door opened and closed with a thud. It was six o'clock.

Maisie was in no rush to leave. It had been a long day, and so much had happened. But far from being anxious to return to her rooms, Maisie felt a dragging at her heart as she contemplated the evening ahead. Perhaps she would go down to the kitchen and have a cup of cocoa with Sandra, one of several housemaids who remained at the Comptons' Belgravia mansion while the rest of the household were at Chelstone. Though Sandra, Valerie, and Teresa were all nice girls, they weren't quite sure about Maisie Dobbs, whom they knew had been one of them once upon a time but wasn't any more. So they were often uneasy about initiating conversation with her, though they were friendly enough.

Gathering up her notes, Maisie placed some outstanding correspondence in her document case, checked that her desk was secure, turned off the gaslights and left the office. Tomorrow was another working day, which, it was to be hoped, would reveal more about the death of Lydia Fisher and, perhaps, about the character, motives, and whereabouts of her client's daughter. She made a mental note to prepare some additional questions for Joseph Waite about his daughter's friends. She had not yet decided whether to ask him about his son.

The square was busy when she closed the outer door behind her. There were people wandering across to visit friends, art students from the Slade returning to their digs, and a few people going in and out of the corner grocery shop where Mrs Clark and her daughter, Phoebe, would be running back and forth to find even the most obscure items that the eclectic mix of customers in Fitzroy Square requested, despite the fact that the country was in the midst of a depression.

Maisie had turned right into Warren Street, pulling on her gloves as she walked, when she stopped suddenly to look at two men who were standing across the road. They had just left the Prince of Wales pub and stood for a moment under a street lamp, then moved into the shadows away from the illumination. Maisie also stepped into the shadows to avoid being seen. They spoke for a few moments, each nervously casting glances up and down the street. One man, the stranger, pulled an envelope from a pocket inside his coat while the other looked both ways, took the envelope, and placed something in the first man's waiting hand. Maisie suspected that it was several pound notes rolled together, payment for the first item. She continued to watch as the men departed. The one she did not know walked back into the pub, while the fair hair of the other man caught the faint light of the streetlamps burning through an evening smog, as he limped unsteadily on his way towards the Euston Road.

Maisie was deeply troubled as she sat in her rooms at 15 Ebury Place that evening. When Sandra came to inquire whether she would like "a nice cup of cocoa", Maisie declined the offer and continued to stare out of the window into the darkness. What was happening to Billy? One minute he seemed to be in the depths of a debilitating malaise, the next revitalized and energetic. He seemed to ricochet between forgetting the most basic rules of their work together – work that he had taken to so readily – and being so productive in his duties as to cause Maisie to consider an increase in wages at a time when most employers were making staff redundant. Billy's war wounds were still troubling him, no matter how strong his protestations. And perhaps she had completely underestimated his ability to cope with memories as they were brought in on the tide of pain that seemed to ebb and flow in such a disturbing manner.

Silence encroached, seeping into the very fabric of the rich linen furnishings. Maisie gathered her thoughts and sought to banish the sound of nothing at all by reviewing her notes on the Waite case once again. Lydia Fisher had been killed before she could ask her about Charlotte Waite. Had she been murdered to prevent Maisie from seeing her? But what about the Coulsden case? Had it really been the newspaper account of that murder that had caused Charlotte to bolt? Could the two murders be random and simply a coincidence that should have no bearing on Maisie's assignment? Maisie pondered more questions, then finally put her work aside for the night. She felt a lack of composure in her body, a sure sign of the turmoil in her mind, which must be stilled if she was to enjoy a good night's sleep and a fruitful morning.

Taking the pillows from her bed, Maisie placed them on the floor, loosened her dressing gown slightly for greater freedom of movement, and sat down with legs crossed. There was only one way to still her thoughts and racing heart, and that was to secure dominion over her body in meditation. She took four long breaths through her nose, placed her hands on her knees with the thumb and forefinger of each hand touching, and half closed her eyes. Allowing her gaze to rest on a barely discernible stain on the carpet in front of her, Maisie endeavoured to banish all thought. Slowly the stillness of the room embraced her being and the heartbeat that had been so frantic seemed to become one with her breath. As a consideration or worry struggled to enter her mind, Maisie relaxed and refused such thoughts an audience, instead imagining them leaving the range of her inner vision, like clouds that pass in the afternoon sky. She breathed deeply and was calm.

Later, as Maisie opened her eyes fully, she acknowledged the truth that had been revealed to her in the silence – the truth that had caused her to avoid visiting her father, for he would see it immediately. The truth that Maisie had been avoiding for so long was a simple one: she was lonely. And as she remained still for just a moment longer, she wondered if that, too, had been Charlotte Waite's sorrow.

6

M AISIE AWOKE as the sun forced its way through the crack where the curtains met, fingering at her leaden eyelids until they opened. She moved her head on the pillow to avoid the blade of light, reached out and pulled her bedside clock a little closer.

"Oh, lumme, a quarter past eight!"

She leaped from the bed, ran to the bathroom, turned on the bath taps and then pulled the lever to activate the shower that had only recently been installed. In addition to piping-hot water that pumped from the eight-inch-diameter showerhead, a series of sprays on the vertical pipe ensured that water reached not only the head but the whole body.

"Oh no!" said Maisie, as she stood under the streaming water and extended her arm to reach the soap, for she had realized that her long tresses, now completely drenched, would not be dry by the time she left the house. Leaving the shower, complaining aloud about the "newfangled thing", she dried herself quickly, wrapped a thick white towel around her head and put on a plain cotton robe. Sitting at her dressing table, she applied just a little cold cream to her face, rubbing the residue into her hands. She dabbed her cheeks, removing any excess cream with a corner of the towel. She applied only the smallest amount of rouge to her cheeks and lips, then hurried back into her bedroom, opened the wardrobe door and selected a plain midnight blue day dress with a dropped waist-line and sleeves that came to just below the elbow. Maisie had gen-erally chosen dresses and skirts that came to her mid-calf, and was glad that fashion was moving in her direction once again following a flirtation with shorter hemlines. Her trusty dark blue jacket, some years old now, would have to do, as would her old cloche and plain black shoes. In fact the cloche would come in very handy this morning.

She removed the towel from her head and consulted the clock: half past eight. It would take fifteen minutes walking at a brisk clip to reach Victoria, so she had only a quarter of an hour to dry her hair. Grabbing her jacket, hat, gloves and document case, she took six hairpins from a glass bowl on her dressing table and rushed out of her room, along the landing, then through a small disguised door to the left that led to the back stairs of the house.

As Maisie entered the kitchen, the three housemaids, who were talking, seemed to jump as she spoke. "Oh dear, I wonder if you can help, I need to dry my hair ever so quickly!"

Sandra was the first to step forward, followed by Teresa.

"Tess, take Miss Dobbs's things. Come over here, Miss. we won't be able to get it bone dry, but enough so's you can pin it up. Quick, Val, open the fire door."

Maisie noticed that now she was on downstairs territory, the staff called her "Miss" rather than the more formal upstairs "Ma'am". She towelled her head once more and was instructed to lean over in front of the fire door of the stove, so that the heat would begin to dry her hair.

"Now then, don't get too close, Miss. You don't want to singe that lovely hair, now, do you?"

"Singe it? I feel like burning the lot off, Sandra."

"I suppose we could always go and get Her Ladyship's new Hawkins Supreme, you know, that green hair-drying machine thing of hers. She only used it the once. Said it was like having a vacuum cleaner going over her head."

As Valerie flapped the morning newspaper so that heat would move around Maisie's black tresses, she began to giggle. Then Sandra lost the battle to hold back her own laughter, as did Teresa. Maisie looked up through a veil of ringlets of still-damp hair and, for the first time in a long time, she began to laugh too.

"Oh, don't, don't make me laugh like that!" As tears began to stream from her eyes, Maisie rubbed them away.

"Miss, Miss, I'm sorry, it's just that, well, we suddenly saw the funny side of it, I mean, we've all 'ad to do it, you know, I s'pose we never thought you'd ever rush in 'ere all of a fluster."

Maisie leaned back, took up her brush and began to sweep her hair into a manageable twist. "I'm only human! You know, Mrs Crawford would have boxed my ears for brushing my hair in the kitchen, and that's a fact!"

Valerie moved to close the stove door as Sandra wiped down the long kitchen table with a cloth. "Well, Miss, it's nice to see you laugh, it really is. It's good for a body, laughing. Puts a spring in your step, it does."

Maisie smiled. "I appreciate the help, and the company." Maisie looked at the silver watch pinned to her dress, "I had better get moving or I'll be late for my appointment."

Sandra put down the cloth she was holding. "I'll go to the door with you, Miss."

Maisie was about to insist that she need not be escorted, when it occurred to her that Sandra, the longest-serving housemaid and the oldest at twenty-six, might want to speak to her in confidence. At the top of the stone steps at the side of the mansion Maisie turned to Sandra in silence and smiled, encouraging her to speak.

"Miss, I hope this doesn't sound, you know, out of place." Sandra stood with her hands clasped behind her back and looked at her polished black shoes for a second, as if searching for the best way to deliver her words. She hesitated, and Maisie said nothing but moved just slightly closer. "Well, you work very hard, Miss, anyone can see that. Even late into the night. So, what I wanted to say was, that you're always welcome to come down for a chat if you want. You see —" she picked at a loose thread on her pinafore "— we know you can't do that when everyone's in residence, because it's not done, is it? But when you're alone at the house, we just want you to know that you don't have to be." Sandra looked at Maisie as if she had finished, then quickly added, "Mind you, we're probably all a bit boring for you, Miss."

Maisie smiled at Sandra, and said, "Not at all, Sandra. You are most kind. Some of my happiest times were spent downstairs in that kitchen. I'll take you up on the offer." Maisie looked at her watch. "Oh heavens, I must dash now. But Sandra . . ."

"Yes, Miss?"

"Thank you. Thank you for your understanding."

"Yes, Miss." Sandra bobbed a curtsey, nodded, and waved good-bye to Maisie.

Detective Inspector Stratton climbed out of the police car as soon as it came to a halt and opened the rear passenger door for Maisie. He took the seat next to her and, without any niceties of greeting, began immediately to speak of "the Fisher case".

"I'll get straight to the point, Miss Dobbs: what was your assistant doing at Lydia Fisher's house on the day she was murdered?"

"Inspector Stratton, you have not yet informed me as to whether, in fact, my assistant visited on the actual day of her death as she was not found until eleven yesterday morning."

"Please do not be obstructive, Miss Dobbs. I am allowing you to revisit the victim's home this morning in the hope that you might be able to assist us."

"Indeed, Inspector, I appreciate your trust, though I am only trying to point out that we do not know yet exactly when the deceased met her fate. Or do we?" Maisie smiled at Stratton with a warmth that remained from the laughter that had embraced her less than an hour before.

Stratton looked mildly put out. "Spilsbury has reported the time of death to have been at about six o'clock in the evening on the day *before* you found her. Now, what about Beale?"

"Mr Beale did indeed see Mrs Fisher at her home. However, he left Cheyne Mews before four o'clock to return to the office to meet me, and I can vouch for him."

"When did he leave you again?"

"Oh, Inspector –"

"Miss Dobbs."

"It was approximately six o'clock. No doubt his wife would be able to confirm his arrival at home by, say, half past six or so. He travels to and from work by either bus or underground, though I believe he prefers to go home by train as it's a bit quicker – from St Pancras on the Metropolitan Line to Whitechapel. Depending upon the trains, I suppose he might not get home until seven. I doubt if he'd be out much later, Inspector, as he likes to play with his children before they go to bed." Maisie thought for a moment, then added, "I know that occasionally he stops for a quick half pint at the Prince of Wales, but only at the end of the week."

"I'll have to question him, you know."

"Yes, of course, Inspector." Maisie looked out of the window.

The car slowed to make the turn into Cheyne Mews and drew alongside Number 9. A single police constable stood outside. Stratton made no move to leave the car but turned to Maisie again.

"Tell me again why you were coming to visit Mrs Fisher, Miss Dobbs?"

Maisie had prepared an answer to this question. "I have been clutching at straws, Inspector, and Mrs Fisher might have been able to throw light on a case I am working on concerning a daughter who has left the home of her parents. It was a tenuous connection. I believe they were acquainted at one point and I wanted to speak to her to see if she could illuminate aspects of the girl's character. I should add, Inspector, that the 'girl' is in her thirties and has a very overbearing father."

"And Beale?"

"He had been confirming the names and whereabouts of her acquaintances. Our subject's connection with Mrs Fisher had been so intermittent that we did not even know whether we had her correct address. He was checking our information when she came along and he took the opportunity to speak to her. They conversed and he left. I've told you the rest."

78

"And the name of the woman you are looking for?"

"As I said yesterday, I have signed a contract of confidentiality. Should it be absolutely necessary to divulge the name of my client, I will do so in the interests of public safety and justice. At this stage I request your respect for my professional obligation to my client."

Stratton frowned but nodded. "For now, Miss Dobbs, I will not press the point. We are looking for a male suspect, not a woman. However, have you any other information that might be pertinent to this case?"

"Only that Mr Beale commented upon the alcoholic beverages that Mrs Fisher enjoyed instead of tea."

Stratton rubbed his chin and looked at Maisie again, "Yes, that is in line with Spilsbury's findings."

Maisie pulled on her gloves and took up her bag in anticipation of leaving the car. "Inspector, did Spilsbury comment upon the poison theory?"

"Oh yes," said Stratton, reaching for the door handle. "She was definitely poisoned first. It was taken in tea – so she probably had a cup or two at some point after Beale left the house. Cuthbert is currently beavering away in his laboratory to identify the exact poison or combination of substances employed, though Sir Bernard Spilsbury has said that he suspects an opiate, probably morphia."

"What about the knife attack?"

"She was dead when the attack took place, hence – as you saw – there was little blood at the scene. But there are some lingering questions about the knife."

"Oh?"

"It seems that the stab wounds are very much like those inflicted by a bayonet. But you know Sir Bernard. We can expect a very precise description of the weapon soon."

Maisie drew breath quickly and asked one more question as Stratton opened the door for her. "And has he confirmed a connection to the Coulsden case?"

Stratton took her hand as she stepped from the motor car. "The means of murder is identical."

"Spoiled a nice piece of carpet, didn't he?" Stratton was looking out of the drawing room window to the street below.

Flippant comments were not unusual among those whose job it was to investigate the aftermath of violent crime. Maurice had told Maisie long ago that it was part of the unconscious effort to bring some normality to that which is far from usual. But it was the first time she had heard an Aubusson rug being referred to as a "nice piece of carpet".

"Inspector, may I have some time alone in the room, please?"

He paused, then shrugged before leaving the room and closing the door behind him. Though he had never liaised professionally with Maurice Blanche, he had heard of his methods from colleagues who had worked with the man, and knew his "strange" ways often led to a quick solution of the crime in question. Blanche's former assistant was indubitably using procedures learned from her employer. The room had been thoroughly investigated, so there was no risk to evidence. And Stratton knew that, had she wanted, Maisie Dobbs could have altered or removed evidence when she first found the corpse.

Maisie walked slowly around the room, touching the personal belongings of Lydia Fisher, and again she was assailed by the sense that this was a lonely woman. That she had yearned for conversation rather than talk; for heartfelt passion, not indulgence; and that she had ached for the intimate connection that came with true friendship rather than from a cadre of society sycophants.

She took careful stock of the contents of the drawing room: pale blue velvet curtains, the deeper lapis blue chaise with pale blue piping, an oak writing table in the art nouveau style, a set of side tables, now properly nested rather than tipped over, a mirror shaped like a huge butterfly on one wall, and a modernist painting on the other. The drinks cabinet in the corner to the right of the window had been "dusted" by the police, and there was a gramophone in the opposite corner. It had been a pleasing, airy room.

But it was the room of a person who lived alone, not a married woman.

She walked over to the chaise, knelt by the umber stain on the rug, and touched the place where Lydia Fisher had fallen. Maisie closed her eyes and breathed deeply, all the time keeping a light touch upon the place where the dead woman's blood had spilled grudgingly onto the carpet. As she did so a cold, clammy air seemed to descend and envelop her. The sensation was not unexpected, and she knew it would come as she reached out to the past in search of a reason, a word, a clue. Anything that would tell her why Lydia Fisher had died. Anything that might tell her why there was something so recognizable in a room she had never entered before coming to visit Mrs Fisher yesterday.

Seconds passed. Time was suspended. Instead of seeing the room in which she stood, she saw the one Charlotte Waite had left so hurriedly five days earlier. Some emotion was shared by the two women, and though she was quick to consider loneliness, which she would find so easy to understand, Maisie knew a more elusive feeling she was as yet unable to name linked them.

Maisie opened her eyes, and the connection with Lydia Fisher began to ebb. She heard Stratton's voice coming closer. He had obviously thought that she'd had time enough to commune with whatever Lydia Fisher had left behind. Maisie took one last look, but just before she opened the door she felt drawn towards the window where Stratton had stood earlier. Leaning on the sill, she wished she could raise the window for air. A sudden warmth in her hands caused her to look down. Perhaps the radiator underneath had heated the wood. She ran her hands along the sill, then knelt to see if she could turn down the heat. To her surprise the iron pipes were cold. Running her hands down the wall, then along the floorboards, Maisie searched with her fingertips. There was something here for her, something of consequence. Just as she heard Stratton's footfall outside the door, Maisie felt a hint of something both soft and prickly brush against her forefinger. She leaned closer. The item was tiny and white, so small, in fact, that it could have been swept up by the cleaners. It would be of no interest to the police. It might have fallen to the floor at any time, a small, stray wisp.

"Miss Dobbs," Stratton knocked at the door.

"Come in, Inspector."

As Stratton walked into the room, Maisie was folding a linen handkerchief.

"Finished, Miss Dobbs?"

"Yes, Inspector. I was rather saddened; do excuse me." Maisie sniffed as she placed the handkerchief in her pocket.

Stratton and Maisie left the house and continued their conversation in the car.

"Your thoughts?"

"I'd like to know more about Mr Fisher, wouldn't you, Inspector?"

"Absolutely – in fact, I've got my men on the job now."

"Where is he? What does he do?"

"Ah, well, it's what he does that directly affects where he is. He's some sort of traveller, an explorer if you like. According to the maid, he's rarely home. He spends most of his time going off to some far-flung locale with a group of interested individuals – all wealthy – who pay him handsomely to be dragged off into British East Africa, the Gobi Desert, or some such place to be photographed with animals that you could quite easily see at Regent's Park Zoo!"

"So that explains it."

"What?"

"Her loneliness."

"Hmmm." Stratton looked sideways at Maisie.

"Inspector, I wonder if I could ask a favour?" Maisie smiled.

"Miss Dobbs, I fear that your request may be for something else that will bring me near to losing my job."

"Not if it helps to find the murderer. I wonder if I could see any belongings taken from the Coulsden victim's home?"

"Look Miss Dobbs, though I am grateful for any interpretations

82

you can give me from your 'woman's perspective', I am intrigued as to why you are interested in that case. The Fisher woman is understandable, given the 'tenuous' link to one of your own private cases. But there can be no reason for you to examine Mrs Sedgewick's effects. It would be most irregular."

"I understand perfectly, Inspector."

They sat in silence for a moment.

"I can have my driver take us right to your door, if you wish."

"No, Inspector, that will be quite all right, I have other errands to complete before returning to my office."

The car drew up outside Victoria Station and once again Stratton alighted first to offer Maisie his hand.

"Thank you, Inspector."

"Miss Dobbs. While I am sure that your assistant's meeting with Mrs Fisher went exactly as you have described, I must question him tomorrow morning. You will appreciate that in normal circumstances the procedure would be more formal. However, in this case I will simply ask you to instruct him to present himself at the Yard for questioning at ten o'clock."

As he departed Stratton wondered what Maisie Dobbs might have gleaned from the minutes spent alone in Lydia Fisher's house. What could a nice young woman like Miss Dobbs possibly know about the life of an inebriate partygoer like Lydia Fisher?

It was eleven o'clock in the morning when Maisie left Stratton. Before making her way to Fitzroy Square, Maisie hurried back to 15 Ebury Place. She used the staff entrance at the side of the mansion, walked quickly through the kitchen, which was late-morning silent, and went directly to her rooms, using the back stairs. Once there, she took off her blue jacket, removed the white linen handkerchief from the pocket and, without looking at the wisp that was now secure within its folds, placed it in the left-hand drawer of her writing table. It would be safe there.

7

"Not bad for a Friday morning, is it Miss?" Billy took off his overcoat and set it on the hook behind the door. He rubbed his hands together and smiled at Maisie. "Missed seeing you for our little meeting at five yesterday, though I got your note that you was visiting Miss Waite's hairdresser and her seamstress in the afternoon, after your mornin' with D.I. Stratton. I've bin checkin' on more names in that address book, not that there's much else there to be gettin' on with."

"I thought that might be the case, but we must leave no stone unturned."

"Too right, Miss. Did the hairdresser say anything interesting?"

"No, not really. Only that Charlotte had changed in recent weeks. Apparently she used to have her hair set once a week, sometimes more often if she had parties to go to. But she's only been in for one cut in the past six weeks, and she wanted it very plain, so she could draw it back in a bun." Maisie reached for a folder on the desk. "And the seamstress hadn't seen her for some weeks, which was unusual, because apparently she was always having alterations made to her very expensive clothing."

"Well then, as we've got to see Mr Waite this afternoon, p'r'aps we can get some more information from 'im. Bet you're glad it's the weekend, ain't you?"

"My weekend is going to be taken up with the Waite case, and with driving down to Kent. And your weekend is a long way off, Billy; I hate to tell you this, but you've to be at Scotland Yard at ten sharp."

Billy's countenance changed immediately. "Scotland Yard, Miss?"

"Don't worry, Billy, it's in connection with the Fisher case." Maisie looked up from her desk, where she was removing papers from her document case and setting them on the blotting pad in front of her. "Why? You haven't done anything else they'd be interested in, have you?" She smiled but looked at him intently.

Billy turned towards the tea tray and replied with his back to Maisie, "Nah, not me, Miss. Tea?"

"Yes, that would be lovely Billy. We both have a busy day, especially as I'll be away early next week and we've to leave at two for our three o'clock appointment with Joseph Waite. I don't want to be late for him."

"Right you are, Miss."

"And before you ask, my lunch has been cancelled, so I won't be seeing the Detective Inspector today, which isn't surprising seeing as you will be with him for a couple of hours. We need to make faster progress in our work on the Waite case. Charlotte has absconded before, though we both think she's old enough to be off on her own anyway. But the fact is that our opinions don't count, and what goes on in the relationship between Joseph Waite and his daughter is for them to worry about – at this stage anyway." She held her hand up to silence Billy, who seemed about to comment. "Yes, I know we've gone as quickly as we could, but I'm concerned that Lydia Fisher might have been inadvertently or deliberately misleading you about Charlotte's desire to become a nun. We have to ensure that our client is satisfied, and satisfied as quickly as possible, but there are now more pressing reasons to locate Charlotte Waite quickly. We may be *compelled* to bring in the police."

"Yes, Miss."

"We cannot get away from the fact that we have identified a possible – and I must emphasize *possible* – link between the murders of two women and Charlotte Waite's disappearance."

Billy blew out his cheeks. "Gawd, Miss, when you put it like that . . ."

"Quite."

"Mind you," said Billy, changing position in the chair to stretch out his leg. "Mind you, I looked at the address book again, and that first woman, you know, the murder victim in Coulsden, well, she ain't in there. I checked under the *P*'s for Philippa, and under the *S*'s for Sedgewick. So if Miss Waite knew 'er, she's in the other address book."

"Good point. We need to find out more about Mrs Sedgewick. Look, if you've got time when you get out of the interview with Stratton and Caldwell, see what else you can dig up on the Sedgewick murder, go through the newspapers again. Oh, that reminds me – don't let Sergeant Caldwell annoy you, Billy. Rise above it, and remember it's his job to goad you a bit." Maisie was thoughtful, "I wish there was a way you could get chatty with Inspector Stratton while you're there."

Billy laughed. "I don't think it's me 'e wants to get chatty wiv, Miss."

Maisie blushed, and stood up to view the case map.

"So you 'aven't 'eard from your Dame Constance yet, Miss?"

"No, not yet. One cannot expect to hear from a cloistered nun by telephone. But I'm keeping my fingers crossed that I'll hear by this afternoon's post. Dame Constance will have replied immediately – if she's half as precise as she used to be. My letter to her would have arrived by yesterday morning, so assuming her reply went by the afternoon post, it should arrive today."

"And you'll be off to Kent on Monday, then?"

"Perhaps earlier. I've spoken to Dr Blanche and will see him first about Waite."

"You'll remember to say 'ello to Mr Dobbs for me, won't you?"

Maisie looked at her watch and nodded. "Yes, of course I will, Billy. You should be getting along now, you don't want to keep Inspector Stratton waiting."

Billy scraped his chair back and winced slightly as his foot dragged along the floor.

Maisie pretended not to notice, but as Billy pulled on his overcoat she voiced her concern. "Are you sure I'm not leaving you with too much on your plate? I should only be away for a couple of days, but I'll cut my journey short if you aren't feeling up to it."

"Nah, Miss. I told you last week, I'm much better now. Loads of energy, and the pain ain't as bad as it was. Tell you the truth, I reckon it was the weather rusting the shrapnel they left in me legs."

Maisie smiled. "Very well, Billy."

Maisie began to collect her papers, which she placed under lock and key in her desk drawer. She consulted her watch and had just gathered her mackintosh, hat, and gloves when the bell above the office door rang out as someone tugged the brass bell-pull by the outer door. Maisie wondered who could be summoning her at this inopportune moment. The thought crossed her mind that Dame Constance might have sent word via telegram. She ran downstairs.

"Why, Mrs Beale, what a surprise!" Maisie was amazed to see Billy's wife standing on the doorstep, holding one child by the hand and the other on her hip. She had met Doreen Beale only once before, at Christmas when she delivered gifts to the Beale's two-up-two-down terraced home in Whitechapel. Maisie had suspected then that this small, sturdy countrywoman did not quite fit into the close-knit neighbourhood, as she came from Sussex and did not share the rough-and-tumble language or raucous humour, of the people her Cockney husband had grown up with.

"Oh, I hope you don't mind, Miss Dobbs, me coming here without sending word first, but I wonder if you could spare me a moment. I know Mr Beale isn't here. I watched him leave. I didn't want him to know I'd come to see you."

"Of course. Do come up to the office." Maisie stood back to allow Doreen Beale to enter the building.

"Will the pram be all right, you know, left out here?"

"I'm sure it will, Mrs Beale. I confess, I've never seen children in these parts, but I think it's safe. Come in; let's go up to the office." Maisie smiled at the toddler, who hid his head in the folds of his mother's coat, and then at the baby, who copied her brother, turning her head into the coat's upper sleeve which, Maisie noticed, was already damp with dribble.

She pulled out a chair for Billy's wife, and then took some plain white paper from her desk, which she put on the floor with the jam jar of coloured pencils.

"There you are, you can draw me a train!" Maisie smiled again at the little boy with an elflike cap of white-blond hair, who looked up at his mother.

"Go on, Bobby, make a nice train."

With one child occupied and the other beginning to fall asleep in her mother's arms, Maisie smiled at Doreen Beale. "Now then Mrs Beale, what can I do for you? Is something wrong with Billy?"

The woman's eyes reddened, which accentuated her fair skin. Maisie noticed that the light blue veins at her temples had become swollen as she fought back tears.

"Oh, Mrs Beale, whatever is the matter? What is it?"

Maisie reached out to the woman, then came round the desk to place an arm around her shoulder. The baby began to whimper, and the little boy stopped drawing and seemed frozen on the floor with his thumb in his mouth. Tears began to well in his eyes as he mirrored his mother's countenance.

Doreen Beale composed herself and turned to her son with a smile.

"Come on, young Bobby, draw a nice picture for your daddy." She stood up from her chair, and with her head indicated for Maisie to walk to the window with her. "Little ears –" she whispered. "It's Billy, Miss Dobbs. I thought you might be able to tell me what's wrong with him."

"Whatever I can do –" Maisie began, but was cut off by Doreen Beale, who clearly needed to shed her burden.

"You see, my Billy used to be your solid sort. No tempers, no ups and downs. Even just after the war when we first started walking out together – we were both young then, of course – but even after all he went through, he was always so, you know, straight as a die. Like I said, no moods or tempers." She moved slightly to reposition the child on her hip. "Well, just lately, in the last few months, all that's changed. Now, I know his leg has been giving him trouble again – it never went away, really – and that got him down, you know. It wears you out, that sort of nagging pain."

Maisie nodded, but did not speak. Doreen Beale took a handkerchief from the pocket of her plain brown coat and rubbed a dewdrop of moisture that had accumulated at the end of her nose. She sniffed and rubbed again.

"One minute he's all over the place, doing jobs around the house, playing with the children, you know. He's like a bumblebee, off to work, home again, going over to our allotment to get some vegetables – hardly makes time even to eat. Then it seems that just as quickly he comes down like a lead balloon, and even his face looks grey. And I know it's his leg that's at the bottom of it all. And the – you know – the memories, I suppose." Doreen Beale sniffed and blew her nose again. "Oh, excuse me Miss Dobbs, for all this. My mother always said that whatever you do, you should never take on so in front of your children."

Maisie was quiet for a moment, then spoke. "I have to say, Mrs Beale, that I've noticed changes in Billy's behaviour too. I've also been worried, so I'm glad you felt able to speak to me about it. You must be very concerned."

Doreen Beale nodded. "Billy's a lovely dad to the children, and a good provider, always has been. And he's a diamond to me, you know, a real diamond. Not like some of them I see. But I just don't know what's wrong with him. And the terrible thing is that I'm afraid to ask again."

"What happened when you asked before?"

"Oh, he says, 'I'm alright, love,' and then goes off and does something. Then, of course, he used to stay after work for a half a pint with his friends of a Friday night. Like I said, he's not like some of them – just one half-pint a week, my Billy. But now he's home late two or three nights a week, sometimes full of beans, and sometimes with a face as long as a week. He was out Tuesday, Wednesday and Thursday, not back home until long after seven."

Maisie tried not to show alarm. "He was late Tuesday *and* Wednesday?"

"Yes, Miss, though I don't blame you, even though you'd asked him to work late."

Maisie did not reveal her surprise. She waited for a moment before asking, "Mrs Beale, would you like me to speak to Billy?"

"Oh, Miss Dobbs, I don't know. I mean, yes, I would – but there again, I feel like such a yellow belly. You know, my mother always said that you should never speak of your marriage outside the four walls and two people who are in the marriage, that it wasn't right."

Maisie thought for a moment, knowing how difficult it must have been for Doreen Beale to come to the office. "I believe your mother's advice was well meant, but sometimes speaking to someone else, someone trusted, helps. At the very least your load is lightened knowing that I have noticed the same behaviour. I'll have a word with Billy. And don't worry, I won't let on that we've spoken."

Doreen Beale dabbed her eyes with her handkerchief and nodded. "I'd best be getting on, Miss Dobbs. I've got a wedding dress to finish this week."

"Are you getting much work, Mrs Beale?" said Maisie, knowing that the income of a dressmaker was directly affected by the amount of money in people's pockets.

"Not as much as I was getting, but the jobs trickle in. And people do still appreciate fine work."

"Good. Now then, would you like to splash some cold water on your cheeks? I'll keep an eye on the children while you nip along the landing to the lavatory. There's a basin in there, and I put a fresh towel on the hook this morning."

When she returned Bobby was still very deliberately using the pencils to draw a train, and Maisie was standing by the table with the baby's head nestled into the curve of her neck. Doreen Beale collected her children and left the office. Maisie watched as she made her way towards Warren Street, pushing the pram with Lizzie asleep under a blanket and Bobby perched on the end, his stubby fingers clasped around the handlebar. And as she turned away, knowing that she now had to hurry to keep her appointment with Charlotte's milliner, Maisie touched the place on her neck where she could still feel the soft downy head of Lizzie Beale.

8

MAISIE SUSPECTED that Billy's interview with Stratton had been draining – especially now that she knew that Billy had not returned home immediately upon leaving the office on the evening that Lydia Fisher had been killed. Though Maisie could not believe that Billy had returned to Cheyne Mews, in light of the underhand transaction she had witnessed between Billy and another man on Wednesday outside the Prince of Wales pub in Warren Street, she was concerned.

The interview with Stratton and Caldwell at Scotland Yard had been a long one, and as soon as Billy arrived back at Fitzroy Square, they set off for the appointment with Joseph Waite at his home in Dulwich. On the way, Maisie hoped to discuss their position regarding the search for Charlotte Waite, and for Billy to recount details of the interview, but Billy seemed to have slipped into an abyss of fatigue. He stared out of the passenger window, offering none of the usual commentary upon the people he saw going about their daily business as the MG sped by, nor did he offer conversation peppered with quips and puns.

"I expect you're a bit tired after this morning's meeting with Stratton, aren't you?"

"Oh, no. Just thinking, Miss, just thinking."

"What about, Billy? Is there a matter of some concern to you?" Maisie was watchful as she spoke, both of the traffic and of Billy's demeanour.

Billy folded his arms, as if against the cold. "I've just been thinking about them two women, you know, Miss Waite and Mrs Fisher. Like two peas in a pod, they were."

"What do you mean?"

"They both seemed, you know, sort of cut off. I mean, they went out and all – well, at least they did before Miss Waite got all quiet. Right pair of social butterflies they were, but when all's said and done, they weren't, you know . . ." Billy crinkled his eyes as he searched for the right descriptive word. "Connected. That's it, they weren't *connected*. You know, not like, say, me, f'r instance. I mean, I'm connected to me wife and the nippers. People are connected to them they love, and who loves them back. You can feel it when you walk into a room, can't you, Miss?" Billy looked at Maisie for the first time since they had set out. "You know, you see photographs on the dresser, and all sorts of bits and bobs lying around that they've been given. And there's comfort, in't there? O' course, my wife would call it clutter, but you know what I mean."

"Yes, I do, Billy."

"Yeah, that's right. Now, like I said earlier when I spoke to my mate, you know, the one who works for the *Express*, well, he told me that the word is – and you know they can't print this sort of thing – that the Coulsden woman, Philippa Sedgewick, was seeing a gentleman who was married to someone else."

"Will your friend keep you in mind when he gets some more information?"

Billy gave a half-laugh. "Well, 'e's a bit of a new friend, ain't 'e, Miss. You remember, you said I 'ad to make me own connections wiv them what could give me information? This one only took a pint or two down the Prince of Wales on Wednesday after work, and 'e was singing like a nightingale."

"Wednesday night? Weren't you going to try to get home early before the children went to bed?"

"Got to strike while the iron's 'ot, 'aven't you, Miss? Saw 'im going in for a swift one as I was walkin' past, and thought I'd take advantage of the situation, as you might say. Certainly worked, didn't it?"

"Well, we'll talk about it all a bit more after meeting Waite. I can't say I'm looking forward to this."

"Me neither, Miss. Now then, mind you point your nose out!"

Harris, Waite's butler, had obviously recovered from his illness and welcomed them into the spacious hallway, whereupon he pulled a pocket watch from his waistcoat pocket.

"Four minutes to three. I will show you into the library, where Mr Waite will join you at three on the dot."

Harris led the way to the library, ensured that they were seated comfortably, and left the room. Maisie and Billy had been alone for barely a moment when the door swung open. Waite strode into the room, pulled out his chair before Billy could stand respectfully. He sat down with a heavy thud and checked his watch.

"Ten minutes, Miss Dobbs. Now then, it's been four days since I gave you the job of finding my daughter. Where's Charlotte?"

Maisie breathed deeply and spoke in a level tone. "I believe she may be in Kent, Mr Waite, though I cannot yet positively confirm the location of her refuge."

"*Refuge*? And what does my daughter need with a refuge?"

"May I speak frankly, Mr Waite?"

The heavy-set man leaned back, folding his arms in front of his chest. Maisie wondered if he knew how quickly he gave himself away. With that one move he was effectively telling her that her frankness was not welcome.

"I suspect that fear was at the heart of your daughter's departure from your house."

Waite moved forward in his chair. "Fear? What's she got to be —"

Maisie cut him off.

"I'm not sure at this stage, though my assistant and I are pursuing several lines of inquiry. Our first priority is to make contact with Charlotte."

"Well if you know where she is, just go and get her; that's what I'm paying you for."

"Mr Waite. Your daughter may be secure within the walls of a convent. If that is the case, without attention to certain protocols of communication I will not even be able to speak to Charlotte."

"I don't think I've ever heard such a load of nonsense in my life." Waite stood up and leaned on the table, resting his weight on his knuckles. "If you know where my daughter is, Miss Dobbs, then I want you to bring her back to this house at once. Is that understood?"

"Perfectly, Mr Waite." Maisie made no move, except to lean back just slightly. Her hands remained folded in her lap in a relaxed manner. Billy followed her lead.

"Is there something more, Miss Dobbs?"

Maisie consulted her watch. "We have almost five minutes left, Mr Waite, and I'd like to ask you some questions."

Waite stared at Maisie for a second, as if gauging how much power he would relinquish by reclaiming his seat. He reseated himself and folded his arms again.

"Can you tell me if you have ever met Philippa Sedgewick or Lydia Fisher?"

"Aye, I can. They were both acquaintances of my daughter, years ago. I think she's still in touch with Mrs Fisher but doesn't see her that often. I doubt if she's seen the other woman in years."

"What about other friends, Mr Waite? Surely your daughter had more than just two?"

Waite hesitated, frowning. He leaned forward and turned the ring on his little finger. "Aye, there was another friend." He sighed, continuing to twist the sparkling ring. "She's dead now. Killed herself a couple of months ago."

Maisie showed no surprise at Waite's revelation. "And what was her name?"

"Rosamund. Thorpe was her married name. She lived down on the coast somewhere. They were all at school together, years ago in Switzerland."

Maisie leaned forward. "Was Charlotte upset at the news of her friend's death?"

"Well, like I said, they hadn't spoken in years. Charlotte only found out when she saw Mrs Thorpe's name in the obituary columns, far as I know."

"Mr Waite, it would seem that Charlotte's engagement to Gerald Bartrup ended at approximately the same time as she learned of her friend's death."

"Oh, Bartrup. So you've seen him, have you?"

"Of course. And according to Bartrup, your daughter broke off their engagement. I have no reason to doubt his word."

Waite closed his eyes for a second and shook his head.

"Mr Waite. Why did you not tell me that Charlotte was your second child?"

Waite was visibly startled. He pursed his lips, then took a deep breath as if to compose himself before responding curtly to Maisie's question.

"Because it has nothing to do with Charlotte's behaviour, that's why. It has nothing to do with her running off. I've taken you on to investigate my daughter's disappearance, Miss Dobbs, not my life. Oh, I know, I know, you're thinking of some explanation based on her grief, or something like that. Well, they weren't close, though Joe was as soft as they come and looked after his sister, but she had all the false airs and graces of her mother."

Waite leaned forward but Maisie remained calm while Billy scribbled notes on an index card.

"He was one of the best, Miss Dobbs, the apple of my eye. Always there to help. I started him off in the shops, at the bottom so he'd earn the respect he'd need as he moved up in the company. Took to it like a duck to water, he did. Never complained that a job was beneath him. But to answer your question, I didn't tell you because she was nobbut a girl when her brother died, and she's a woman now. This nonsense of hers has nothing to do with my Joe!"

Maisie checked her watch. She had one minute. "And when did your son die, Mr Waite?"

Joseph Waite stared down at the table, and when he looked up his eyes were filled with tears. "Joe was killed in 1916. In July, Miss Dobbs, during the Battle of the Somme."

Maisie nodded in understanding. There was no need to acknowledge his loss with words: grief from the war cast a shadow that at times was dense and at others seemed as pale as a length of gauze. But it was never gone.

Joseph Waite looked at his watch and shook hands with Maisie and Billy; then, as he turned to leave, asked, "Miss Dobbs, why the interest in Charlotte's three old friends?"

Maisie picked up her document case. "Because they are all dead, Mr Waite. I thought you might have seen news of the deaths of Mrs Sedgewick and Mrs Fisher in the newspapers. Something of a coincidence, isn't it?"

"I must have read straight past those items. I tend to be more interested in overseas commerce and the business of the country, aspects of current affairs that directly affect Waite's International Stores. Which is what details of my daughter's disappearance will do if she is not brought back to this house soon. That's up to you, Miss Dobbs."

"I hope to communicate with her directly very soon. Of course you realize, Mr Waite, that while Charlotte might be persuaded to return to your home, she cannot be forced."

Waite said nothing but gave a loud *hmmph!* before opening the door. He turned to claim the last word. "I want her back in this house, Miss Dobbs. If she won't find a suitable husband to share a house with, then she'll live under my roof!" Glaring at Maisie, he gave an ultimatum: "I'm off to visit some of my shops for a few days, back next Tuesday. I expect to see you with my daughter upon my return. Tuesday, Miss Dobbs. You've got until Tuesday."

The door slammed, to be quickly opened by Harris, who escorted Maisie and Billy out. Billy was holding the driver's door of the MG open for Maisie when they were both startled by the sound of furiously flapping wings overhead as a flight of doves rose from an old-fashioned dovecote in the corner of the gardens.

"Lawd, would you look at that!" said Billy.

"Oh, my, they are beautiful!" said Maisie.

Billy shuddered. "Can't see it meself. Rather look at a mangy old dog."

The doves returned in ones and twos, landing on the dovecote and entering it through tiny doorways.

"Look at that, 'noses out,' Miss!" said Billy, joking again.

"Come on, we'd better be off."

Neither of them said a word as they drove steadily towards the main gate, which was opened by the young man who had let them in on their first visit. Each breathed a sigh of relief upon leaving the Waite residence behind.

"I tell you, Miss, that Joseph Waite really is a study, i'n't 'e?"

"No doubt about that."

"'Ere, do you think 'e was tellin' the truth, y'know, when 'e said that 'e never knew about them two women bein' murdered?"

Maisie accelerated the car confidently and replied, "Not in a million years, Billy. Not in a million years."

—⁓—

As soon as they returned to the office, Maisie and Billy set to work, adding new information to the Charlotte Waite case map as well as reviewing other cases in hand. While Maisie was away from London, Billy would complete reports for two clients, in addition to his other duties. Issuance of a final report also meant submission of an invoice, and with clients tending not to pay "on the button", as Billy observed, timely presentation of a final account was vital.

They worked together until six o'clock, when Maisie sent Billy home. For her part, Maisie would return to Ebury Place to prepare for the short visit to Kent. She had planned to leave early Saturday morning for the drive down to Chelstone. The next few days would be busy indeed: a letter had arrived from Dame Constance in the afternoon post informing Maisie that, despite nursing a heavy cold, she would be delighted to see her again, and there was time to be spent with Maurice and with Lady Rowan before leaving for Camden Abbey. As she made her way back to Belgravia, Maisie added another task to her trip: Chelstone was only an hour or so from Hastings on the Sussex coast, and she had ascertained that Rosamund Thorpe had lived in Hastings.

Traffic was mercifully light as Maisie made her way to Ebury Place. As rain spattered across her windscreen, compounding the dregs of a yellowish-green smog, Maisie thought not of the work ahead, but of her father, Frankie Dobbs. Whenever she visited him, he assured her, "Me? Don't you worry about me, love. I'm alright, like a sheep in clover down 'ere." But Maisie did worry, yet was ashamed that her concern had not led her to visit him more often.

She entered the house by the kitchen door. When the Comptons arrived back in town she would resume using the front door, which would once again be opened by Carter, the Comptons' long-serving butler. And once again Mrs Crawford, who had put off retirement for just one more year – to add to last year and the year before's "one more year" – would be mistress of all she surveyed in the kitchen. Maisie would straddle two levels of household life and knew only too well that her good standing both upstairs and downstairs was terrain to be negotiated with great care.

She placed her document case on the writing table in her sitting room and slumped down into the armchair by the fire, which was already burning brightly. Home. Was this home? Had she been too easily persuaded by Lady Rowan to reside at Ebury Place because she did not want to refuse the woman who had given her so much? When had she last felt truly *at home*?

Sighing, Maisie moved to draw back the long curtains and looked out at fog swirling around a streetlight. Soon the days would be longer and, she hoped, warmer. London's smog would dissipate as coal fires were extinguished and hearths cleaned out for the summer. As she looked at the streetlight illuminating the twists and curls of fog in front of her, Maisie remembered the small soot-blackened terraced house in Lambeth where she had lived with her parents. With both parents, that is, until she was thirteen, when her mother died in Frankie Dobbs's arms, her last words instructing him to do right by their girl. Her last true home, she remembered, had been with her father, until he had done his best for her by finding a place in service at the Ebury Place mansion of Lord and Lady Compton.

There was a knock at her door. Maisie called out, "Come in."

Sandra opened the door quietly and smiled. "Good evening, Ma'am. Would you like supper in your rooms or in the dining room, Ma'am?"

Maisie smiled. She was Ma'am again, upstairs. Maisie checked her watch. Seven o'clock. A plan was forming in her mind, inspired by the prospect of an evening alone in her rooms. Though she could not identify a place that was now home, there was a person who was home, and Maisie acknowledged her yearning to be with him.

"Sandra, I wonder if you could pack me up something to eat in the car, perhaps a piece of pork pie, or a cheese sandwich – and a bottle of Vimto or something like that?"

"Oh, Ma'am, you aren't going out in this, are you?" Sandra nodded towards the fog, which seemed to be growing thicker outside.

"I don't think it will be any better first thing in the morning, do you? I'll collect my supper on my way to the motor car. I just have to pack a few things, then I'll come straight down to the kitchen."

"Right you are, Ma'am. I'll have it all ready when you come down."

"Thank you, Sandra."

Maisie edged the MG out of the mews behind Ebury Place and into the damp London night. She drove through south London carefully, making her way along the Old Kent Road, and on towards Sevenoaks, Tonbridge, and from there along narrow country lanes to Chelstone.

As Maisie left London behind the smog gradually dispersed, leaving only a light rain to contend with. She uncovered the small wicker basket positioned on the passenger seat beside her, and reached for a sandwich. There was something soothing in this journey through the night, with only the flash of headlights as an occasional car passed. The engine rumbled confidently, and Maisie considered not only aspects of her own life that lately seemed to claim attention when she least expected such interruption, but the lives of Charlotte Waite and her women friends.

Keeping her right hand on the steering wheel and her attention on the road, Maisie reached out with her left hand to the basket again, took out a linen cloth, and wiped her hands and mouth. She reached for the bottle of Vimto and pulled the cork out with her teeth. Sandra had already removed the cork and replaced it halfway to make it easier for Maisie. She took just a few sips, then set the open bottle carefully in the basket, using one hand to tuck a table napkin around it, to keep the bottle upright and within easy reach. She slowed down as rabbits scurried across the open road, requiring that she swerve around them as they froze in the beam of the headlamps.

At last she reached Chelstone. She drove first through the village, where the lights were still on at the Fox and Hounds, probably for the landlord to see by as he pushed a heavy broom across the flagstone floor, for it was well past last orders. Finally, she turned into the carriage sweep leading to Chelstone Manor, the gravel spitting and crackling under the weight of the MG's tyres. A few lights were on at the manor house. The Comptons – especially Lady Rowan – kept late hours. Maisie passed the Dower House, where Maurice lived, and turned left several yards along. The lane narrowed where she parked outside the Groom's Cottage, and quietly took her bags from the car before tiptoeing along the path. And as she looked in through the latticed window Maisie saw her father, illuminated by the mellow light cast by a single oil lamp, staring into the fire.

As flames reflected on the folds and furrows of his face, Maisie realized there was another reason at the heart of her reticence to visit Frankie as often as she might. Though still vital, he was now an old man, and she did not want to confront the truth of the matter: that the person who was home to her was in his twilight years and might be taken from her at any time.

"Oh, Dad," whispered Maisie, as she ran to the back door and let herself into her father's house.

———

She awoke the next morning to the smell of bacon cooking on the wood-fired stove in the kitchen below. As splinters of sunlight cast a morning glow across her counterpane, she leapt out of bed, took her old woollen dressing gown from behind the door and, ducking her head so as to avoid the low beams, ran downstairs into the kitchen.

"Morning, Dad."

"And a very good mornin' to you, love." Frankie Dobbs stood at the stove and turned two thick rashers of back bacon. "Two eggs or one? Collected them myself this mornin', so they're nice and fresh. None of your shop-bought nonsense, sittin' in a warehouse for days before it gets to your plate."

"One egg'll be lovely, Dad." Maisie poured tea for Frankie and herself from a brown earthenware teapot.

"I expect you'll be off to see Dr Blanche as soon as you've 'ad your breakfast, eh, love?"

Maisie looked up at Frankie, knowing that he expected her to leave, to go immediately to the house of her teacher and mentor. How many times had she spent a moment with Frankie only to seek Maurice's company and counsel for hours? Though she had little time to spare, Maisie sat back in her chair.

"No, I don't have to hurry, Dad. I thought we could chat until you go out to the horses."

Frankie beamed at his daughter.

"Well, I've already been out once this morning," Frankie looked the clock. "But I'd best go to check on the mare again after I've 'ad a bit of bacon and egg. I don't like to leave 'er for long, not with the little 'un due any minute. I'm a bit tired this mornin', to tell you the truth, love."

"I've missed you, Dad," said Maisie.

Frankie smiled, and slid a slice of bacon and *two* perfect fried eggs onto a warm plate, which he put in front of Maisie. "There you are, get that down you, love. That'll set you up for the day."

Maisie waited for her father to depart before she in turn left the cottage, taking the narrow path that led from the bottom of her father's garden to the Dower House grounds. At the edge of Maurice's garden, where the man who had been fêted by the governments of France, Belgium and Britain for his services during the Great War now grew prizewinning roses, another gate led to apple orchards and paddocks beyond.

"Ah, Maisie, so very good to see you." Maurice Blanche, now well into his seventies, clasped Maisie's hands with his own veined and bony ones.

"And you, Maurice, and you." Maisie held his hands tightly.

"Come, child, let us sit, and you can tell me why it is that you have come to see your old teacher." Maurice led Maisie to the drawing room, took a pipe from a stand next to the inglenook fireplace, and pressed tobacco from a leather pouch into the bowl of the pipe. Maisie relaxed into a wing chair, and watched as he held a match next to the rim at just the right angle to the tobacco, and drew several times on the pipe.

"Now then, what is the case?" He threw the extinguished match into the cold fireplace and settled into his favourite leather chair.

Maisie told Maurice about being summoned to see Joseph Waite, and the search for his daughter Charlotte. She referred to the murders of Philippa Sedgewick and Lydia Fisher, and the suicide of Rosamund Thorpe, which she intended to look into. She immediately noticed the almost imperceptible response in Maurice's eyes when Waite's name was mentioned.

"Maurice, I have to ask —"

"You have no doubt seen my notes on Waite from so long ago."

"I have. Can you tell me what happened? What caused you to break off communication? I couldn't help but think that it wasn't like you."

Maurice drew several more times on his pipe, then looked at Maisie intently. "Joseph Waite, as you can probably tell, is a natural

103

and decisive leader. He is essentially a good man but at times a hard man, a difficult man. He is generous with those in straightened circumstances whom he believes genuinely cannot help themselves. He is no stranger to hard work and demands hard work from others, which is then repaid accordingly. He is, in fact, the epitome of the self-made man."

Maisie waited as Maurice drew again on his pipe. A "but" was imminent.

"As you will have seen from the notes, Waite was an interested and generous benefactor of my clinics in the poorer areas of east and south-east London. He gave immediately and unstintingly, but . . ." Maurice drew breath deeply and cupped the pipe in both hands, his elbows resting on the arms of the chair. "But he is a man who likes to be in control, or to at least *believe* that he is in control."

"What happened, Maurice?"

"In short, he began to instruct me in the finer points of doing my job. That may seem harmless enough. However, his instructions revealed deep prejudices. He began to make demands regarding the type of people my staff could or could not serve at the clinics. He tried to stipulate the nature of illnesses or indispositions that we could and could not treat. The people who came to the clinics were human beings, and as a doctor I could not turn away one who was sick, whether a felon or a drunkard, though certainly those who abused their health were subjected to strong words of advice."

Maisie was thoughtful as Maurice carefully composed the next part of his story.

"As with his shops, Waite had the habit of turning up at the clinics unannounced. I had always allowed access to benefactors. After all, seeing the work done on behalf of the poor encouraged further contributions from them. Few came. However, Waite was one of those who wanted to see his money at work. On the occasion in question – I was not there at the time – one of my staff was interviewing a girl. She was very young and with child herself, though at an early stage." Maurice brushed some ash from his sleeve. "Those who helped at the clinic were instructed by me personally that our concern was for the health of the mother and her unborn child. We'd given refuge to young women in similar situations, or placed them where they would be cared for. They were never to be put in a position of having to give up a child." Blanche shook his head. "The clinics are not large affairs, usually just two or three rooms, then a little extra space to store supplies. Though we do all we can to ensure confidentiality, Waite heard part of the conversation, rushed to judgment and gave the nurse and the young girl – already emotionally unstable – a piece of his mind. The girl ran away. I was alerted at the earliest opportunity and left Waite in no doubt that his money was no longer welcome."

Relations between Maurice and Waite at the time must have been incendiary, thought Maisie. "What happened to the girl?"

Maurice sighed. "By the time my staff located her, she had already taken her problem to a back alley. She was rushed to the clinic again. It was too late. I did all I could to save her life, but she died clutching my hand."

"Oh!" Maisie brought her hands to her mouth.

Maurice stood up and tapped tobacco from his pipe against the brick of the fireplace, emptying it into the grate. "Even from Chelstone, I am still very involved in the work of my clinics. All the more reason to ensure that the health of women and children is provided for and protected by those who are qualified for such a task. I also now ensure that no benefactor visits a clinic without my express permission. A gift is unconditional by its very nature. Waite brought his tendency to dominate, along with prejudices rooted in experience, into my clinic and, I believe, killed an innocent child. No – two innocent children. I refused later requests to accept funds from him. A difficult man, Maisie."

They were both silent for several moments. Maurice suggested a walk to the orchard. Fortunately Maisie had dressed with such an excursion in mind, knowing Maurice's maxim: "To solve a problem, take it for a walk." Her dark brown trousers, fashionably wide, were complemented by brown walking shoes, an ivory linen blouse and a light-brown-and-cream Harris tweed jacket with a shawl collar and large square pockets at the hips.

They strolled through still-damp grass and trees laden with blossom buds that gave a promise of summer's bounty, and they spoke of Maisie's work, her challenges, and how she had fared in the year since Maurice formally retired and she had set up in business on her own. Finally, Maisie spoke of her worries about Billy.

"My dear, I believe you already know what is at the root of Mr Beale's erratic behaviour."

"I have my suspicions," she confessed.

"How might you confirm them in such a way as to protect Billy?"

"First of all, I think I should visit All Saints' Convalescent Hospital in Hastings. It's where Billy was sent after being discharged from hospital in London. They should still have his medical records. The problem will be gaining access to them."

"I think I can help, my dear. The physician in charge is known to me: he was one of my students at King's College in London."

"Maurice, I do believe you know everyone!" Maisie moved a low bough aside as they walked through an avenue of trees.

"Not quite, but my contacts are useful. I will telephone him prior to your arrival – when will you go?"

"This afternoon. I know they are open for visitors on a Saturday."

"Good."

"Of course, what I really need to do is find a way to get him to a doctor to do something about the continued pain in his leg."

Maurice stopped. "Maisie, I sense that Billy has had enough of doctors. Sometimes people who have endured a chronic illness cannot face even a discussion with a doctor. And though I am a doctor, I can say that often there is good reason for such a reaction. We don't have all the answers."

"What do you suggest?"

"First, you must find out whether your suspicions are grounded. Then you must confront Billy. You know this already. But a confrontation of this sort is best followed by a plan, an idea, a lens through which the future can be viewed once the secret has been revealed. May I make a suggestion?"

"Oh, please."

"I suggest that you bring Mr Beale to the Dower House, where I would like him to meet a new acquaintance of mine."

Maisie inclined her head. "He's a German by birth, though he came to this country as a child. While he was interned during the war, he met a very interesting man, also a German. The man had developed a means of exercise and movement that helped maintain health in the camp: even during the first 'flu epidemic in 1917, not one of those interned was lost. In fact most of those in the camp were released in a healthier state than before the war, despite being poorly nourished. The physical movements incorporated in the regimen have been used to rehabilitate the severely wounded with great success. My friend is a practitioner of the regimen."

"Who is he?"

"Gideon Brown. After the war he changed his surname from Braun, and his Christian name from Günther to Gideon. It made life a little less difficult for him, given the manner in which those of German extraction were treated at the time. The man whose work he has followed now lives in America. His name is Joseph Pilates."

Maisie smiled. "I'm glad that at least I have the bare bones of a plan now . . . But my first step is All Saints'. In fact, I may be able to kill two birds with one stone, as Rosamund Thorpe lived in the same area." Maisie checked her watch. "Eleven o'clock. If I leave by noon, I should be there by half past one."

"You'd better get along then, hadn't you Maisie? Remember to ask for Dr Andrew Dene. I will have spoken to him by telephone before you arrive."

9

MAISIE REVERSED the MG out of the narrow lane onto the carriage sweep that led from the main gate to the manor house. As she drove slowly along the gravel road, Lady Rowan waved from the edge of the lawn where she was walking with Nutmeg and Raven, her two black Labradors, and a Welsh springer spaniel who answered to the name of Morgan. Though Lady Rowan walked with the aid of a silver-tipped cane, her posture gave the impression of youthfulness. She wore a tweed walking skirt, a brown corduroy jacket and a small fur tippet around her neck. Her ensemble was topped off by a jaunty brown felt hat, a single feather pinned to the band with an amethyst brooch. She waved again at Maisie, who slowed the car to a halt.

Maisie stepped from the MG. "Lady Rowan, how are you?"

"Hello, Maisie dear. So lovely to see you. How is the motor car running? Serving you well, I hope."

"Oh, yes, very well indeed." Maisie smiled warmly. "It's never broken down, and goes very smoothly. I'm off to Hastings this afternoon."

"Anything exciting, Maisie?" Before Maisie could respond, Lady Rowan held her hand up. "I know, I know, you can't divulge the nature of your work. I never learn, do I? It's just that you always seem to be involved with something so very intriguing!" Lady Rowan's eyes crinkled to emphasize not a little envy at Maisie's employment. "Mind you, I've had my day, Maisie, I've had my day."

"No you haven't, Lady Rowan. What's all this I hear about breeding racehorses?"

"It's most thrilling. Your good father and I have pored over breeding records. He is a most knowledgeable man when it comes to horses, so we expect to see the will to win in the eyes of this one! I confess I am beside myself with anticipation, which is why I am pacing back and forth across the lawn. Otherwise I would make a nuisance of myself in the stable."

"Dad's keeping an eye on the mare, but he said it could be a day or two yet."

"When do you leave, Maisie? Will you come to see me before you go back to London?" Lady Rowan refrained from displaying the affection that would embarrass them both, but in truth she viewed Maisie almost as a daughter.

"I am here until tomorrow, Lady Rowan. Aren't you coming back to London at the end of this week?"

"Hmmm. I confess, I'm tempted to stay at Chelstone until after Merriweather foals."

"Shall I call on you when I get back from Hastings?"

"Yes, that would be lovely. Don't let me detain you a moment longer. Come along, Nutmeg. Morgan, come here! Oh dear, it seems I've lost Raven again."

Maisie laughed, took her seat in the MG, and continued down the driveway, then along the country lanes until she joined the main road to Tonbridge. The journey to Hastings was an easy one. She saw few vehicles as she cruised through the Weald of Kent, crossing into Sussex near Bodiam, where she could see parts of the old castle beyond the hop gardens.

She entered Hastings from the east, negotiating the narrow streets of the Old Town, which was still so much like a fishing village, in stark contrast to the development along the promenade towards St Leonards, expanded during Queen Victoria's reign to cater for the town's increase in popularity with day-trippers.

Her first stop would be a visit to All Saints' Convalescent Hospital, a red-brick mansion on the Old Town's East Hill. It commanded sunfilled views over the channel on a good day, only to be battered by wind and rain when the weather turned. It was just after one o'clock, she had estimated the journey exactly. Because it was such a fine day Maisie decided to park the car along Rock-a-Nore, then take the path that led alongside tall wooden net shops where fishermen hung out their nets to dry. She would make her way to the East Hill via the Old Town's small funicular railway that took passengers from sea level to the upper lift station with its castellated towers, each containing an iron tank filled with more than one thousand gallons of water to operate the water-balance lift. Once outside the station, visitors would set off along the cliffs, where they could enjoy the fresh, if sometimes biting, sea air. At the top Maisie would have just a short walk to All Saints'.

Having made her way past the shacks with counters where day-trippers bought small bowls of tasty jellied eels, whelks or winkles, or strolled while lunching on fish and chips wrapped in newspaper, Maisie bought her ticket, and found that her companions on the ascent were four women clad in walking skirts, leather boots, and heavy pullovers; they were clearly prepared for a day's hiking. She felt her stomach turn when the funicular began to move. As the carriage made its way up the cliff, Maisie wondered if Billy had used this means of coming down into the town when he had reached a point in his convalescence at which short excursions were allowed. She knew that he had met Doreen in Hastings. Had it been on her day off, perhaps, when each had gone with friends to the pier to listen to the band and drink sarsaparilla? She imagined Billy cracking jokes as Doreen blushed and turned away towards her group, then back again to smile in a way that was just a little coy. The carriage lurched again, and Maisie waited while the four women alighted first, maps flapping in the wind, one pointing towards the Firehills at Fairlight where out-of-work Welsh miners had been brought in to create a series of walking paths along the cliffs.

Seagulls whooped and called below her as she walked along the edge of the East Hill. From her vantage point she could see the rooftops below. The architecture revealed the history of the town, from beamed medieval hall houses with huts and fish smokers in the back, to Regency mansions, and brick two-up-two-down cottages built perhaps only sixty years earlier.

Maisie stopped once to look at All Saints' Convalescent Hospital before setting out along the path lined with low trees and shrubs before it turned towards the broad front entrance to the house. The route she had taken was infinitely more enjoyable than driving along the ancient streets that spiralled precariously up the hill. The building was laid out in an exact square and had been constructed of red brick and wood at the turn of the century. Its architecture was of the new style, with clean lines and a shallow roof. Some outbuildings had been added during the war when it was requisitioned for use as a military convalescent home. The owner had eventually sold the property to the local authorities, possibly to pre-empt compulsory purchase at a reduced price, and it was now used for all manner of convalescent cases though many of the patients were still old soldiers.

The door, constructed from a single substantial piece of wood, moved easily after Maisie turned the brass handle, revealing a large entrance hall with wooden floors and plain white walls. There were arched wooden beams above the staircase before her. A lift had been added to assist those who were unable to move themselves. Rubber strips ran along the floor in strategic places, minimizing slippage for invalids learning to walk again with calipers, crutches, or new artificial limbs. Despite vases of flowers and a lingering aroma of lavender furniture polish, if one turned quickly or took a deep breath, there was the unmistakable hospital smell of disinfectant and urine.

Maisie knocked on the frosted glass window of the porter's office and was asked to wait while Dr Dene was summoned.

"Miss Dobbs, delighted to meet you." Andrew Dene began reaching out his hand when he was still three steps from the bottom of the staircase. "Maurice said to expect you here around one-thirty. Please." They shook hands, and he indicated another door which led to a long corridor. Though he had been one of the students who attended Maurice's medical school tutorials, Maisie had expected someone far older. He seemed to be only four or five years her senior. If she was right, then he had certainly made his mark early. Dene's light brown hair fell into his eyes repeatedly as they made their way towards his office. Maisie had to walk quickly to keep up with his athletic gait. She noticed with pleasure his ease of manner, as well as his obvious respect for Maurice and, by default, herself.

"You know," said Dene, "I always wondered what it must be like to work with Maurice, at his side. He said something once about his assistant, but you could have knocked me down with a feather when I found out that the accomplished assistant was a woman."

"Really, Dr Dene?" Maisie's tone caused Dene to rephrase his remark "Oh dear, that's not what I meant." Dene opened the door of his office and allowed Maisie to enter before him. "That's me all over: open mouth, insert foot. What I meant was . . . well . . . sometimes the work sounded so, you know, so tricky that . . ."

Maisie raised an eyebrow.

"I think I'd better just take it all back and get on with the business at hand before I have to show you out on my hands and knees."

"Indeed, Dr Dene, I can think of no better punishment at this moment." She removed her gloves and took the seat indicated. Despite his faux pas, Maisie thought Andrew Dene was rather fun. "Perhaps we can get down to business."

"Oh yes, quite." Dene checked his watch and reached for a manila folder with frayed edges that was already set aside from the other stacks on his desk. "I have a meeting in twenty minutes. Mind you, I can be late." He smiled at Maisie. "I understand you want to know more about the convalescent history of one William Beale, Corporal."

"Yes, please."

"Well, I've already looked at the file. I had to rescue it from what we refer to as the Dungeon down in the cellars. Unfortunately, the attending doctor has passed on now but the notes are all here. Looks like he's lucky to have kept that leg. Amazing what those doctors were able to do over there, isn't it?"

"I thought you . . ."

"Oh no. I was in medical school when I enlisted, but I was not qualified. They pushed me into the Medical Corps anyway, though not as a surgeon. As an assistant. Not quite a nurse, not quite a doctor. I ended up in Malta finding out more about surgical procedures on the job than I ever learned when I returned to medical school. By that time I had become more interested in what happened to soldiers when they came back, their recuperation, their post-operative care, and how I could best help them."

"I see. So what can you tell me about Mr Beale's recovery?"

Dene looked through the notes once again, sometimes turning the file to one side the better to see a chart or diagram; then he closed the folder. He looked up at Maisie. "It would be less like finding a needle in a haystack if you were to tell me why you are interested – the medical aspects, that is."

Maisie was taken aback by Dene's manner but understood the need, given the array of procedures and therapies that would have been noted in the file. Maisie described her observations of Billy's behaviour, adding that his family life was also disturbed by his mood swings.

"Is this is a recent development?"

"Over the past few months, along with the increased pain in his legs."

"Ah. Yes." Dene reached for the file again. "Miss Dobbs, you were a nurse in France, weren't you?"

"Yes, I –"

"And later, according to what I know, you worked with shell-shocked patients before returning to Cambridge. I understand from Maurice that you spent some time at the Department of Legal Medicine in Edinburgh."

"That's all correct."

"So you don't need me to tell you what's going on, do you?"

Maisie looked at Dene intently, her deep blue eyes sparking. "I thought it best to confer with the attending doctor, or his successor, before jumping to conclusions."

"A wise and very professional decision. Oh, and by the way, I'm *her* successor. Mr Beale's attending physician here was Dr *Mrs* Hilda Benton."

Maisie's cheeks reddened.

Dene leaned back in his chair and made a church-and-steeple with his fingers. It was the same way Maurice sat when considering a problem.

"Here's what I suspect is at the root of Mr Beale's behaviour, and I would add that it is not uncommon, though a terror to address. According to the notes," Dene opened the file and passed two pages to Maisie, "he was initially treated for pain with massive doses of morphine. I would imagine he was hard to medicate, probably one of those who can soak up medication and still feel everything."

Maisie remembered Billy being brought in to the casualty clearing station in June, 1917, his eyes wide even as the surgeon's knife cut into his flesh, and his promise that he would never forget the doctor and nurse who saved him.

"Of course, we didn't know as much about dosage then as we do now. In fact, the military was rather slap-happy with morphine, cocaine, and various other narcotics. You must remember that people could buy heroin kits from the corner chemist's, even from Savory & Moore, to send to their soldier loved ones in France, just in case. Then everyone cheerfully expected the need for medication to go away along with the pain as soon as the men were out of uniform. Boom-boom, good-bye soldier, you're on your way! Unfortunately in many cases the pain and the craving lingered. And even when both went away, recurrence of pain naturally re-creates that craving for medication. Doctors are a bit more careful now but there's a healthy black market in cocaine, especially among old soldiers. I don't want to cast aspersions, but to be candid, Miss Dobbs, I believe that Mr Beale is struggling with a dependence upon narcotics. Though from what you say, I would imagine he's not in too deeply. Yet."

Maisie nodded. "Dr Dene, I wonder if you could advise me on how I might go about initiating Mr Beale's withdrawal from the use of such a substance?"

"I think we can assume that increased physical discomfort was at the root of his initial self-medication. Now we have the addiction itself to cure, and I'm afraid that there is precious little to draw upon. I'm sure there are psychiatrists who would speak of their successes, but frankly I take such claims with a pinch of salt."

Dene leaned forward on the desk and looked up at Maisie. "If you want to help Mr Beale I would suggest the following: get him away from the source of supply, that's the first step. Then ensure that the pain is acknowledged and experiment with physical therapies. If necessary we can admit him here as an outpatient and I can prescribe controlled doses of painkillers. Finally, fresh air and something to do that he truly feels is of importance while he recovers. I do not hold with cures for such conditions while the mind and body are idle, it only gives the patient time to consider the desirable effects of the substance that is now no longer available."

Dene watched as Maisie nodded her head in agreement.

"Thank you, Dr Dene, for your advice and your time. You have been most kind."

"Not at all, Miss Dobbs. A summons from our friend Dr Maurice Blanche is as good as a call to arms."

"Before I leave, Dr Dene, I wonder if by any slight chance you might have known a Mrs Rosamund Thorpe? I understand she lived locally before her death in February."

"How extraordinary that you should ask! Mrs Thorpe was a visitor to the hospital. There's a group of women in the town who visit regularly, to read to the patients, talk with them, you know, make the long stay here a little easier to bear. She was widowed not that long before she died, but she never stopped coming here. Mrs Thorpe was especially good with the old soldiers. Of course she was the same age as most of them, but we do insist upon calling them old, don't we?" Dene shook his head, and continued. "It was such a shock when we heard. I'd spoken to her many times in the course of my work here, and would never have believed she would take her own life." He looked again at Maisie. "May I ask why you inquire about her?"

"I am engaged in work that has brought me into contact with one of her friends. I can say no more. I want to know about Mrs Thorpe's life, and her death. Is there anything you can tell me, Dr Dene?"

Dene seemed to consider whether to voice his observations, then continued. "Of course, she had been very sad at the passing of her husband, but I think the death was not unexpected as he was a good deal older than Mrs Thorpe and towards the end was heavily medicated. In fact they had moved here because of his health, hoping the sea air would effect a cure." Dene shook his head. "The behaviour of the younger Thorpes – her stepchildren, who were closer to her in age – over her late husband's will was reprehensible, but she seemed to evince none of the gloom one might expect to see in one at risk of suicide."

"I see." Maisie hoped that Dene might add more depth and colour to the picture he was painting of Rosamund Thorpe. He did not disappoint her.

"I will say, though, that she seemed different from the other volunteers." Dene allowed his gaze to wander to a view of the sea beyond the pile of books and notes on the sill above the cast-iron radiators. "She was very intense in her work here, always wanting to do more. If visiting ended at four, most of the women were on their way home at one minute after the hour, but Mrs Thorpe would spend extra time, perhaps to complete a letter or read to the end of a chapter for some poor soul who couldn't hold a book. In fact, she once said to me, 'I owe it to them.' But it was the way that she said it that caused me to remember. After all, we all *feel* that we owe so much."

Dene turned to Maisie and looked at his watch. "Crikey! I'd better be on my way." He pushed back his chair, and placed the file to one side, having scribbled on the front: "Return to archives."

"Thank you so much for your time, Dr Dene. Your advice is sound. I appreciate your counsel."

"Not at all, Miss Dobbs, not at all. One caution, though: I need not remind you that in taking on the responsibility of helping Mr Beale, you are also becoming involved, technically, in a crime."

"Yes, I am aware of the implication, Dr Dene. Though I hope – no, *expect* – Mr Beale to destroy any illicit substances soon after we speak."

Dene raised an eyebrow as he opened the door for Maisie. "Don't underestimate the task. Fortunately, Dr Blanche can assist you."

As they continued along the corridor, Andrew Dene gave Maisie directions to Rosamund Thorpe's house and the name of her housekeeper. Clearly everyone knew everyone else in the Old Town.

When they reached the door, Maisie had one more question for Andrew Dene. "Dr Dene, I hope you don't mind me asking, but you seem to know Dr Blanche very well, more than one might expect from someone who was simply one of many students in a lecture hall or tutorial. And your assessment of the situation with Mr Beale and your subsequent advice are very much what I might expect to hear from him."

Dene affected an accent he had lost long ago, explaining, "I'm a Bermondsey boy, ain't I?" Then he continued, reverting to his previous Home Counties diction, "My father died when I was young – he was a steeplejack – and then, when I was barely fifteen and out at work at the brewery myself, my mother became ill. There was no money for doctors. I made my way to Dr Blanche's clinic and begged him to come to the house. He visited each week and instructed me in her care, so I was able to administer medicine and make her comfortable even at the end. I paid him back by helping him. At first he trusted me with errands, then I helped at the clinics – obviously not with patients, as I was just a boy. If it hadn't been for Dr Blanche, I might never have known what I wanted to be, or what I could be. He helped me to apply to Guy's, which I attended on a scholarship. Mind you, I had to work night shifts at the brewery to earn my keep. Then the war broke out, and I think you know the rest."

Maisie smiled. "Yes I do, Dr Dene. I know the rest very well."

10

MAISIE PARKED the MG on the West Hill and looked across towards the East Hill, where she had strolled just thirty-five minutes earlier. She had walked down the 158 steps from the top of the cliffs onto Tackleway Street, then through a narrow alleyway known to locals as a "twitten," one of the many almost-secret paths that crisscrossed the Old Town of Hastings. It led out onto Rock-a-Nore, where she had parked the motor car. No wonder smugglers loved this place, thought Maisie.

It was a fine Spring afternoon. The sun and a light breeze conspired to glance light off whitecaps in such a way that the view across the Channel seemed to be repeatedly punctured by shards of crystal. Maisie shielded her eyes from the prismatic flashes of light as she looked out over the water before making her way to the four-storey Regency house that had been the home of Rosamund Thorpe. She was anxious to interview the housekeeper and be on her way back to Chelstone, to plan the next part of her visit to Kent. She was abundantly aware that the initial meeting with Joseph Waite had taken place almost a week ago, and she was not yet certain she had located her client's daughter.

A short woman answered the door and smiled warmly at Maisie. "You must be Miss Dobbs."

Maisie returned the smile. She thought the housekeeper resembled the quintessential grandmother, with her tight white curls, a plain dress in wool the colour of heather, and stout black shoes.

"Young Dr Dene from the convalescent hospital telephoned me and said to expect you. Very nice man, isn't he? Surprised he's not married, after all, it's not as if there's a shortage of young women. Mind you, he was walking out with that one girl last – Oh, excuse me, Miss Dobbs, I do go on at times! Now then –" Mrs Hicks showed Maisie into a drawing room with bow windows that commanded a view across the West Hill. "Dr Dene said that you were a friend of a friend of Mrs Thorpe's and wanted to know more about her passing on." The housekeeper regarded Maisie intently. "Normally, I wouldn't be talking to anyone outside the family, but Dr Dene said it was important."

"Yes it is, Mrs Hicks, though I can't really say much about it at the moment."

Mrs Hicks nodded and wrung her hands together in her lap, revealing her discomfort and, Maisie suspected, the fact that she wanted to speak of her employer very much. Maisie would give her that opportunity.

"Tell me, Mrs Hicks, is the house for sale? Mrs Thorpe passed on some two months ago now, didn't she?"

"They – Mr Thorpe's children by his first marriage, that is – have asked me to stay on and keep the place up until it's sold. It has only just gone up for sale, as there was a lot of legal to-ing and fro-ing and paperwork and so on to go through after . . ." Mrs Hicks's bottom lip wobbled, and she hurriedly pulled an embroidered handkerchief from her pocket. "I'm sorry, Miss, but it was so very hard, finding her there . . ."

"You found Mrs Thorpe?"

Mrs Hicks nodded. "I went up in the morning because she was late rising. Since Mr Thorpe passed away, the house has been so quiet. Even though he was that much older, they were always laughing together. I tell you, if they saw two raindrops running down the window, they'd bet on which one would reach the bottom first and have a giggle over who'd won." Mrs Hicks kneaded the handkerchief between her hands. "Anyway, Mrs Thorpe had trouble sleeping and was an early riser, so it was a change not to see her up and about."

"Was she in bed when you found her?"

"No, she was . . ." Mrs Hicks rubbed her eyes with the handkerchief. "She was lying there, on the floor in her sitting room. It's a small area that connects to the bedroom. She liked to sit there to have tea, for the view. The tea tray was still out from the day before, and there she was."

"When had you served tea?"

Mrs Hicks looked up at Maisie. "Well, she must've made it, because it had been my afternoon off. She often made herself a cup, especially if she thought I was busy with something else. They didn't keep a big staff here, the cleaning's done by Mrs Singleton and Mrs Acres who come up from the Old Town every morning, and if they were entertaining they called in a cook and maids. There was only the two of them for me to keep for."

"Mrs Hicks, I know this is difficult for you, but did you notice anything that made you think twice when you went into the room, or when you looked at it later?"

"It was all such a shock, but I suppose there was one thing that I thought about, you know, afterwards."

Maisie sat forward to listen.

"The tea tray was set for two: two pieces of malt loaf, watercress sandwiches for two, two scones and some biscuits. But only one teacup had been used. So I wondered if she was expecting someone who hadn't arrived. Mind you, she hadn't said anything to me in the morning. Apparently she'd taken it, the poison, and washed it down with a cup of tea and a biscuit. But, I don't know . . ."

"What don't you know, Mrs Hicks?"

"She was a funny little thing at times. She would spend hours up at All Saints' with the soldiers. I used to tell her that she did too much, but she'd say to me, 'Mrs Hicks, I have to make things right.' Anybody would have thought she was responsible for their suffering, the way she said it. She was well-liked in the town, would always stop to talk to folk if she was out walking, not one of those uppity types." Mrs Hicks bit her lip. "I know she was sad, very sad, when Mr Thorpe passed on, but I never, never knew that she was in such a state as to take her own life."

"Mrs Hicks, I know this is a strange question, but – do you really think she committed suicide?"

Mrs Hicks sniffed and dabbed at her nose; then, emboldened by loyalty to her employer, she sat up. "No, Miss Dobbs. I do not."

"Do you know of anyone who might have wanted her gone?"

"The younger Thorpes were jealous of her, no doubt about that, but to do away with her? No, they haven't got it in them. No gumption at the best of times, that pair. Still, they did want the money and property that was left to her by her husband, even though they were very well taken care of. They quite enjoyed all the back-and-forth with solicitors. Made them feel important. Otherwise I don't think she had an enemy. Though she must have, if her life was taken by someone else. I don't think she'd 've done it by accident, either. Very careful, she was, very careful. Wouldn't even take a powder if she had a cold. Of course, there were still medicines in the house from when Mr Thorpe was ill. For the pain. That's what the doctor said she'd taken. An overdose of the painkillers. But I just can't see her doing it." Mrs Hicks rubbed the handkerchief across her eyelids and dabbed at her nose again.

Maisie reached out and touched the housekeeper's arm. "Would you show me where you found Mrs Thorpe?"

❧

Maisie stood in the light and airy room, a gentle breeze blowing curtains through sash windows that were half open. She was sorry that the death was so far in the past, for the room had doubtless been cleaned several times since Mrs Hicks found the body of Rosamund Thorpe, as she had shown Maisie, lying between the small table set for tea and the settee placed at an angle to the window, offering views across the rooftops to the East Hill and out towards the Channel.

"Mrs Hicks, I know this may sound a little unusual, but would you mind if I spent a few moments in the room alone?"

"Of course, Miss Dobbs. Has a funny feel about it, this room, doesn't it? Can't put a finger on it myself, but it was always there, even before she died." Mrs Hicks dabbed at her eyes. "I'll just be outside if you need me."

Maisie closed her eyes. She stood perfectly still and allowed her senses to mingle with the aura of Rosamund Thorpe that still lingered in her room. Her skin prickled with sensation, as if someone had stood next to her and touched her lightly on the arm, to share a confidence, to say, "I am here, and this is my confession." She opened her mind to the secrets held within the walls and recognized the familiar presence of a troubled soul, kindred spirit to the veils of emotion left behind by Charlotte Waite and Lydia Fisher. She suspected already that Philippa Sedgewick had been equally troubled. Four unsettled women. But what could be at the heart of their disquiet?

As she breathed deeply and silently, Maisie framed a question in her mind: *What can you tell me?* It was immediately answered with a picture in Maisie's mind's eye, an image that began as a simple outline, gaining form and texture as if it were a photograph set in a tray of developing solution. Yes, she could see it. She hoped Mrs Hicks might be able to offer an explanation, and summoned the housekeeper.

Mrs Hicks poked her head around the door before entering. "All done, Miss?"

"Yes, thank you."

The housekeeper led the way downstairs, and opened the front door for Maisie.

"I wonder, Mrs Hicks, if I might ask one more question."

"Of course, Miss. Anything I can do to help."

"Do you know what medicines Mr Thorpe was prescribed by his doctor?" asked Maisie.

"Well, I do know that there were different mixtures and tablets. Mrs Thorpe was most particular to measure them out in the morning, putting them in little saucers. He had pills breakfast, lunch, supper, and bedtime. But at the end, you know, the doctor prescribed morphine. Mrs Thorpe was very upset about it. She said you know there's no hope when they start giving a patient morphine, because it means there's nothing more they can do to save a life. All they can do is stop the pain."

———◆———

Maisie loved to drive the motor car, whether weaving in and out of traffic in London – which was always a challenge given the noisy mixture of motor lorries, cars large and small, and horse-drawn delivery vans carrying groceries and beer – or meandering along country roads with only her thoughts for company. She found it easy to think in the car, turning over facts and ideas as she changed gear, or slowed down for a farmer moving sheep from one field to another.

Conversations were replayed, possibilities for action assessed and considered, and all manner of outcomes pictured in her mind's eye. Sometimes another driver might stop alongside the MG in slow traffic, look across at the young woman in the fast car with the cloth top down, and see her speaking to herself, her mouth opening and closing as she asked a question. Then, hearing the words aloud, she would nod.

She was driving across Kent to Romney Marsh. Dame Constance Charteris, Abbess of Camden Abbey, expected her at ten o'clock on the dot. She had left her father's cottage at Chelstone just after eight, allowing more time than was required for the journey because she wanted to think, to run through yesterday evening's conversations with Maurice and Lady Rowan, as well as to recollect the time spent with her father.

Maurice had quickly stepped forward to help Billy Beale, assisted by Dr Andrew Dene who, it seems, had been busy with his telephone again, speaking to Maurice after his meeting with Maisie to offer support in Billy's recovery. Billy could not be admitted as an in-patient at All Saints' Convalescent Hospital, but Andrew Dene offered to monitor his health along with his progress in overcoming a dependence on narcotics – *if* Billy was agreeable to leaving London. By the time Maisie had arrived back at Chelstone, it seemed that Maurice had already devised a skeleton plan, with the help of Frankie Dobbs. Billy would come to Chelstone, stay at the Groom's Cottage with Frankie, and meet Maurice each day to "talk".

Maisie knew well the healing power of Maurice's skills as a listener, when he would encourage confession with perhaps just one word, question, or comment. One word that could unlock memories and shine a bright light on a person's soul. Maisie had learned much from Maurice, but she knew that she was too close to Billy for such conversation. In addition to his time with Maurice, Billy would become a "patient" of Gideon Brown, who would instruct Billy in new methods of moving his wounded limbs so that he might free himself of the pain that dragged at his spirit. There was only one obstacle to overcome: Billy had to agree to the plan carefully laid out without his foreknowledge. Billy had to *want* to end his reliance on narcotics.

"Getting Billy to Chelstone is the hardest job, Maisie. And it falls to you," said Maurice as he tapped ash from his pipe into the fireplace.

Maisie repeated his words out loud as she drove through Brenchley and Horsmonden. As she drove on, the sun came from behind a cloud and shone across morning-bright green fields where newborn lambs ran on still-unsteady legs, and she knew that, whatever it took, she would get Billy on the road to Chelstone and recovery.

Clumps of primroses lined the hedgerows as she made her way slowly through Cranbrook and on towards Tenterden, winding through country lanes to the picture-postcard village of Appledore with its medieval cottages, thatched roofs, and climbing roses on trellises and porches. The promise of a perfect Sunday diminished as the hills flattened out and the soft undulating Weald of Kent gave way to land reclaimed from the sea, a jigsaw puzzle of fields for arable farming divided by hedges and stone walls. Maisie followed the Royal Military Canal while under a dark thunderous cloud that threatened to do its worst. She had a panoramic view across marsh-land where trees had grown leaning away from the wind, and small cottages and churches were dotted forlornly in an unforgiving landscape.

Maisie did not stop to pull up the roof of the MG but instead carefully wound a red woollen scarf around her neck and pulled on her black leather gloves. Frankie had insisted on filling a flask with hot tea "just in case". It seemed to Maisie that the Romney Marshes were living up to the description penned by William Lambarde in the sixteenth century: "Evil in winter, grievous in summer, and never good." But Maisie knew there was something to be found in this forlorn wasteland. She was close to Camden Abbey.

Long before she reached the end of the gravel road leading to the mansion that was now the home of twenty-four Benedictine nuns, Maisie saw the abbey in the distance. The abbey was E-shaped, with a long, two-storey north-south spine and three wings extending out. The centre wing held the main entrance. The end of each wing had an unusual bell-shaped gable, inspired by the houses of Holland, where the first owner had grown up. In her letter Dame Constance had written that the nuns had lost their home in Cambridgeshire when it was requisitioned by the War Office for officer accommodation. Sir Edward Welch, owner of Camden House, which was fortunately ill-situated for military use, bequeathed his property to the Order upon hearing of their distressing circumstances. He died shortly thereafter, and Camden House became Camden Abbey.

Maisie parked the MG, ensured that its roof was properly secured in case of rain while she was inside, and proceeded through the main door to what had once been a substantial entrance hall. To her left an iron grille at face height covered a small door. Maisie took the brass handle of the bell-pull next to the grille, drew it back and immediately heard the deep resonant clang of a large bell. She shivered in the cold, dark hall and waited.

The small door opened, and a nun nodded at her. Maisie smiled automatically, and as she did so she noticed the corners of the nun's mouth twitch before she looked down piously.

"I am here to see Dame Constance. My name is Maisie Dobbs."

The nun nodded and closed the door. Maisie shivered again, waiting alone. She heard another door open and footsteps grow louder as someone came to meet her. It was the same woman. She wore the habit of a postulant, and as she had not yet taken orders, she could meet Maisie without a barrier between them.

"Please follow me, Miss Dobbs." The postulant seemed to swirl around as if practising for the day when she would wear a full-length habit instead of a calf-length dress, and a cowl would replace the white collar buttoned tightly at her neck. The end of her veil flapped as she walked, reminding Maisie of the wings of a seagull slowing down for a landing on water. She opened an oak door with pointed iron hinges that stretched out into the centre of the wood, and allowed Maisie to enter. The nun left her alone in the room, closing the door behind her with an echoing thud.

It was a small room, with a fireplace at one end and a window onto the gardens at the other. Coal and wood crackled and sputtered in the grate, and the red carpet on the floor and heavy red curtains at the window made the room warm and welcoming. The plain wall bore no ornamentation but a crucifix. A comfortable wing chair had been placed in front of the grille that covered a small door situated next to the crucifix. A side table held a tray, and Maisie could see steam rising from the spout of a teapot covered with a plain white cosy. Upon closer inspection she found a plate of homemade oatmeal biscuits next to a milk jug, sugar, and a cup upturned on its saucer. The crockery was plain.

Each week for one term, when she had been at Girton, Maisie had walked to the order's former abbey after lunch on a Wednesday, along with her fellow students. At half past one exactly, the small door leading to Dame Constance's room would open, and she would greet them from behind the grille, ready to fire questions, question assumptions, and prod for opinions. Dame Constance had blended compassion with pragmatism. With the hindsight of the worldly experience she had since acquired, it was clear to Maisie that Dame Constance had suffered fools if not gladly, then with gracious ease.

The door clattered back, and the warm smile she had known so well greeted her from beyond the iron grille once more.

"Maisie Dobbs! How lovely to see you. No, mind you keep well back, I'm still getting over this wretched cold you know, so do keep your distance from my bars." Her demeanour did not give away her age. The timbre of her voice seemed that of a much younger woman. In fact, it had occurred to Maisie that she didn't know how old Dame Constance actually was.

"Do not let me see a biscuit left on that plate at the end of our talk, Maisie. You young women of today do not know how to eat. Why, in my day, that plate would have been nothing but a few crumbs by now, and I'd be licking my fingers and dabbing at them so as not to miss a thing!"

From her seat next to the grille, Maisie leaned towards the iron bars, the warning of germs notwithstanding. "I can assure you, Dame Constance, I eat very well."

Dame Constance was silent for a few seconds before continuing. "Tell me, dear girl, why have you come to me today? What can an old nun do for a young sleuth? It must be serious for you to come on a Sunday."

"I know of the guiding mission of the Benedictine order, and your solemn oaths of confidence. However, I believe that a young woman I am searching for may be within the walls of Camden Abbey." She stopped. Dame Constance held Maisie's eyes with her own and did not speak. Maisie continued. "Charlotte Waite is missing from home, and her father is concerned for her safety. I believe she has sought refuge here at the abbey. Can you confirm my suspicions?"

Dame Constance responded with a simple, "I see." Maisie waited.

"You know, Maisie, that in his Rule, Saint Benedict bade his disciples to show special care and compassion towards those seeking refuge, the poor and pilgrims, and he did so because 'in them is Christ more truly welcomed'. There are those who knock at the door daily for food and drink, yet sometimes a hunger is deeper, a yearning for sustenance that cannot be named, but one that is always fed at our table."

Maisie nodded.

"One of our pledges, when souls come to us seeking supersubstantial bread to assuage the poverty of the spirit, is the confidence of the cloister."

Dame Constance paused, as if expecting Maisie to counter her words.

"I seek not to . . . interrupt the sacred path of one making her way to the abbey's table for sustenance. I only seek confirmation that Charlotte Waite is here. That she is safe."

"Ah, *only*. An interesting word, don't you think? *Only*." This was the Dame Constance Maisie had expected.

"Yes, and we use it too easily, I'm sure."

Dame Constance nodded. "Only. *Only*. In the sharing of such information – and please do not take this as a confirmation or denial – I would be breaking a trust, a sacred trust. Where is the 'only' in that, Maisie? Come now, what say you?"

It was Maisie's turn to smile. The Abbess had put on the gloves and was ready to spar.

"In this context the *only* is a request for truth. I am here simply to gain information to put the mind of her father at rest."

"Simply and only, *simply and only*. Everything and nothing are simple, as you know."

Dame Constance reached for a cup of water, sipped, replaced the earthenware vessel, and thought for a moment in silence, her hands tucked together inside the copious sleeves of her habit. She looked up and nodded. "Do you know one of the most common questions I am asked? 'Why is an enclosed nun kept behind bars?' My response is always the same: 'The bars are there to keep you out, not us in!'" There was silence again, and Maisie waited for a final decision. "Your request must be considered by the Order, and to do that,

128

Maisie, I must have the whole story. Yes, I know – with this comment I have given you the answer you require. However, we both know that your *only* goes further, doesn't it?"

"Yes, it does. Let me tell you what has happened."

———❦———

Maisie was served an early lunch alone in the sitting room. She excused herself to use the lavatory and washbasin facilities provided for visitors. Upon her return, her shoes clattering on the flagstone floors, a fresh tray awaited her, bearing a hearty bowl of pearl barley-and-vegetable soup, a flask of cider with an upturned glass on top, and three slices of still-warm, crusty brown bread. She was just scooping up the final spoonful of soup when the small door was drawn back and Dame Constance smiled at her through the grille.

"No, do finish. You can carry on eating."

"It's all right. I'm all but finished." Maisie poured a glass of cider, took one sip, and quickly put down the glass. The beverage was clearly homemade and a strong brew.

"The order has decided that, on this occasion, we can confirm that Miss Waite is within the walls of Camden Abbey. She is tired and needs to rest and recuperate. I cannot allow her to be assailed with questions. Give her time."

"But –"

"There may be another life taken? The order has considered, and we have concluded that we must continue to offer refuge to Miss Waite." Dame Constance looked at Maisie intently. "We will pray, Maisie. We will petition God for His strength and His hand in this matter."

Thank heavens Stratton isn't here, thought Maisie. If he thought the order was offering succour to a murderer, he'd have something to say. Then Dame Constance surprised her.

"If you can return to Camden Abbey next week, you might be able to meet Miss Waite then. I will have had several conversations with her in the interim, so expect my letter."

"Thank you, Dame Constance."

"And perhaps you can stay longer next time. I sometimes miss the debate my students challenged me with when they stopped being scared of me, and before they were mature enough to realize that those who are older may know something after all." Dame Constance paused. "And perhaps you can tell me something, then, that I am curious about."

Maisie inclined her head to demonstrate her own curiosity.

"I'd like to know, Maisie, where do *you* find refuge? And who offers *you* close counsel and companionship?"

Maisie nodded. "I'll see you next week."

"Very well. Until then, dear child, until then." The small grille door closed with a click.

Maisie pulled up the collar of her jacket against the large raindrops that were beginning their assault on Romney Marsh. She opened the door of the MG and looked once again at the imposing buildings. Yes, it looked safe. Very safe. Charlotte Waite had found herself a fortress and an army of knights to protect her. The knights were women, and the arms they bore were prayers. But whom were they protecting? A murderer or another potential victim?

I I

LADY ROWAN chose to wait at Chelstone until after the new foal
was born. Lord Julian had decided to travel to Lancashire to visit
the site of a bankrupt factory he was considering for purchase. The
economic slump could not last forever, and he wanted to be well-
placed to boost the manufacturing arm of his investment interests
when the time was right. Upon her return to London, Maisie
would be alone in Belgravia for several more weeks with only the
servants for company.

Once again the drive back into London gave Maisie time to consider her next steps in light of the past few days' revelations. The
task she had been retained to perform in the Waite case was almost
complete. She knew where Charlotte Waite had taken refuge,
though it remained for her to persuade the woman to return to her
father's home. In the normal course of events Maisie would not
consider the case *completely* closed until personal conversations with
Charlotte and Joseph Waite had taken place individually and jointly,
with commitments from each to fashion a new relationship with
the other. But could the completion of her assignment conclude
this case, when there were the deaths of three other women to be
considered? Maisie detoured. Instead of driving directly into
London, she made her way west into Surrey, then north to
Richmond. It was time for her to make her monthly pilgrimage
to visit Simon, the former love who had sustained such serious
injuries during the Great War that he was now in a convalescent
hospital where he could be cared for along with other men who
had suffered profound injury to the mind. Though he would not

know that Maisie sat opposite him, taking his hands in hers as she spoke, Maisie would feel the warmth in his fingers, sense the blood coursing through his veins, and she would continue to tell him of her days. She would describe the gardens that lay beyond the windows, the leaves turning to brown, red and gold before falling, then, later, she would tell of snow on branches and Jack Frost leaving icicles where leaves would sprout in spring. Today she would describe the new leaves unfolding, the fresh green shoots of daffodils and crocuses, the sun higher in the sky, and the springtime nip in the air. Above all, as Simon's head nodded along with his breathing, his eyes focusing on a place in the distance only he could see, Maisie would share with him her deepest thoughts and secrets.

She parked the MG and, as was her habit, walked to the lower perimeter of the gardens before approaching the main entrance. Maisie watched the Thames snaking through Richmond, and consciously took four deep breaths, placing the fingers of her right hand against the cloth of her aubergine jacket at the point she knew to be the centre of her body. She closed her eyes and took one more deep breath. She was ready.

"Good morning, Miss Dobbs, very nice to see you again, but then it is your time, isn't it? First week of the month, right on the nail."

"And good morning to you, Mrs Holt. Do you know if Captain Lynch is in the Winter Garden, as usual?"

"Yes, I believe he is, but drop in to see Staff Nurse on the way, won't you."

"Oh yes, of course. I'll see you on my way out, Mrs Holt."

"Right you are, Miss Dobbs, right you are."

Maisie turned left and made her way down the corridor that led from the reception desk to the office where the Staff Nurse would be completing medication reports. Though she had only been visiting Simon regularly for six months, Maisie was known to the nurses.

Staff Nurse welcomed her with a broad smile, and Maisie smiled in turn as an almost identical dialogue to that with Mrs Holt followed. The Staff Nurse commented that Maisie could probably find her own way to the "Winter Garden" conservatory, by now.

"He's in there, all wrapped up and looking out at the gardens," said Staff Nurse, as she pulled a heavy chain from her apron pocket, selected a key and locked the medicine cabinet. "Never can be too careful." Ensuring the cabinet was secure, she turned to Maisie, "I'll have one of the nurses pop along in a while, to check on the captain."

Maisie found Simon seated in a wheelchair by a window in the conservatory, shaded by tall tropical trees that would surely die if planted outside in England's ever-changing climate. He was dressed in deep-blue-striped pyjamas and a thick blue tartan dressing gown. Matching blue slippers covered his feet, and a blanket had been placed across his knees. Doubtless his mother still shopped for him, ensuring a certain dignity in the clothing carefully chosen for an invalid who would never again consciously distinguish shade, hue, light, or dark. Maisie wondered how Simon's parents must feel, in their twilight years, knowing that their son would likely outlive them, and that the only farewell for them to remember was the one that took place in 1917, when he said good-bye after his last leave.

"Hello, Simon," said Maisie. Pulling up a chair, she sat beside him and took his hands in hers. "It's been an interesting month, Simon. Let me tell you about it."

In speaking aloud to one who could not comprehend, Maisie was aware that she was using this time to re-examine details of the Waite case and that of the murdered women.

The door that led in from the corridor swung open and a young nurse entered, nodded, and smiled. She quickly checked to ensure that her patient was showing no distress in the presence of his visitor, and then left silently.

And as the nurse departed, Maisie wondered what she was thinking as she observed a woman in her early thirties with the broken man who had once been her true love. Did she see futility – she who would later place food in the man's mouth and watch as muscles moved in physical response to the stimulus, without any obvious recognition of taste or texture? Or did the young nurse, probably a girl at the close of the Great War, see Maisie as one unwilling to open her heart to another, while her beloved was still there in body, if not in mind?

Maisie looked out at the gardens. How to remain loyal, but still open her heart anew? It was as if she was required to be in two places at once, one part of her in the past, one in the future. She sighed deeply and allowed her gaze to wander. She watched as two nurses walked along a path, each pushing a veteran of war in a wheelchair. In the distance, an older woman supported a man who walked in an ungainly fashion, his head lolling to one side. As they came closer, Maisie saw that the man was gazing into space, his mouth open, his tongue rolling back and forth between his lips. They moved towards the patio in front of the glass-paned conservatory.

The woman was as plainly dressed as she had been at their first meeting, when she opened the door to greet Maisie and Billy at Joseph Waite's home in Dulwich. In fact she had been so plainly dressed and pedestrian in manner that Maisie had not thought twice about her. Yet here she was again, with this man whose mind was clearly as lost in the wilderness of his past as Simon's. Who was he? A son? A nephew?

As she steered her charge towards a door to the side of the conservatory, a nurse came to her aid, taking the young man's weight on his other side while Mrs Willis kept her arm around his waist, her hand clutching his.

Maisie remained for a while longer, then bade Simon a solitary farewell. She stopped at the reception desk on the way out.

"Lovely day to visit, eh, Miss Dobbs?"

"Yes, it has been nice, especially to see the tulips coming up."

"See you in about a month, then?"

"Yes, of course, but I wonder, may I ask you a question about another visitor today?"

The receptionist frowned slightly, and pressed her lips together. "Another visitor? Well, let's see who was in today." She consulted the visitors' book on the desk in front of her and tapped a red finger along the names. "Whom were you interested in?"

"I thought I saw an acquaintance of mine, a Mrs Willis. Could she have been visiting a family member, perhaps?"

"Oh, Mrs Willis. Very nice woman. Quiet, doesn't say much, but very nice indeed. She's here to see Will, her son. Will, short for Wilfred, Wilfred Willis."

"Her son? Does she come once a month?"

"Oh my goodness, no! Once or twice a week. Never fails, always on a Sunday and, more likely than not, on a Wednesday or Thursday as well. She comes as often as she can."

"And she's been coming since the war, since he was admitted?"

The receptionist looked at Maisie and frowned again before speaking. "Well, yes, she has. But then, it's not surprising. She's his mother."

"Of course, of course. I'd better be off."

"We'll see you in a month then, Miss Dobbs?"

"Yes. A month. See you then." Maisie turned to leave, but the receptionist spoke again.

"Oh, Miss Dobbs, you might see Mrs Willis waiting down at the bus stop. I don't know if Dulwich is on your way, but I thought you'd like to know. It's a long journey for her by bus."

"Of course, Mrs Holt. If she's still there, I'll give her a lift home."

"Blast!" said Maisie, as she left by the main gates of the hospital. Mrs Willis was not at the bus stop, nor was there a queue waiting.

It was still only two o'clock in the afternoon, so Maisie decided to back-track. She was well aware that her curiosity regarding the murders of two women, and the suspected murder of another, had surpassed her interest in the Charlotte Waite "missing person" case. In truth, she was excited that she had discovered a link and that she had reason to investigate further. Maisie had a sense of who Lydia Fisher was, and how she lived, but she wondered about Philippa Sedgewick, the woman murdered in Coulsden. Detective Inspector Stratton had pronounced Lydia Fisher's murder "identical" to Sedgewick's. Were they unlucky victims of coincidence? Evidence suggested that her killer had been known to Lydia Fisher. Had Philippa Sedgewick known *her* killer? And if *her* death was murder rather than suicide, then Rosamund Thorpe had taken tea with her murderer as well. Yet in her case, there had been no vicious post-mortem knife attack. While steering with one hand, Maisie nibbled at the nail on the little finger of the other. Charlotte was the key.

In the meantime, while Maisie waited for an audience with Charlotte at Camden Abbey, she would see what she could find out about Philippa Sedgewick. Nothing could take the place of collecting information and impressions personally.

Maisie drove towards Kingston-upon-Thames, following a route that took her through Ewell as she made her way to Coulsden. A stop on her way from Kent to Richmond would have been a more judicious use of time and petrol but she hadn't planned to visit Coulsden when she set out this morning. Now she felt more anxiety than she had since the death of Lydia Fisher. The killer might strike again soon. If the deaths were random, with the killer soft-talking his way into victims' homes, then no woman on her own was safe. But if the killer was known to his victims, there might be more links in the chain that connected them.

As she entered Coulsden, Maisie pulled over to the side of the road and reached into her document case. She quickly turned to the second page of last week's *Times* until she found what she was looking for. COULSDEN WOMAN MURDER INVESTIGATION, followed by a subheading POLICE SEARCH FOR KILLER. Her eyes scanned the columns, the work of reporters feeding the story. As the words "merciless," "plunged," and finally "butcher" leapt out at her, Maisie finally found what she was looking for: "The dead woman, Mrs Philippa Sedgewick of 14 Bluebell Avenue . . ."

Maisie parked the car in the road opposite Number 14 and shut off the engine. The houses were not old, built perhaps in about 1925 for the new commuter class, the men who travelled into the City each day on the train, and the women who waved them goodbye in the morning and greeted them with dinner on the table when they returned. Children would be in pyjamas, bathed, and ready for bed as soon as father had placed his hat and coat on the stand by the door, kissed each girl on the head, and squeezed each boy on the arm along with the words, "Good man."

Young sycamores grew on each side of the street, planted with the intention of creating an opulent canopy to shade the family homes. Each house was identical, with a broad bow window at the front, an asymmetrical roof with a long sweep on one side, and a small turreted bedroom under the eaves of the other. The front door had a stained-glass window, and the same glass had been used in a border that ran along the upper edge of every other window at the front of the house. But this house was special. This was the house where Philippa Sedgewick had spent her days waiting for her husband to return from his job in the City. This was the house where a woman of thirty-two had been murdered. Maisie took out a small pack of index cards from her document case. She did not alight from the car, but simply described the house on a card, and pencilled questions to herself: *Why have I assumed husband worked in the City? Find out about husband. Job for Billy?*

The curtains were closed in mourning. The house seemed dark and cold, shadowy against the low sun of a spring afternoon. Yes, thought Maisie, death has passed over this house and will linger until the woman's spirit is at rest. She sighed, allowed her gaze to settle on the house again and slipped into a deliberately relaxed observation of the property. It appeared a very sad house, set in a street of homes for families with children. Already she could imagine them walking home from school, girls with satchels banging against hips, boys holding their caps in one hand, with arms out to balance as they returned a football or ran to tease the girls, pulling hair so that screams drew a mother into the street to admonish every one of them. According to the newspaper, there had been no children in the Sedgewick marriage, though perhaps children were hoped for, otherwise why live in such a place? Yes, a sad house.

The curtain moved almost imperceptibly. At first it was just a sensation at the corner of her eye. Maisie focused on the curved window of the turreted small bedroom to the left. The curtain moved again. She was being watched. Maisie stepped out of the MG and set off briskly across the road, unlatched the waist-high gate, and continued along the path to the front door. Grasping the brass door knocker, she rapped loudly, ensuring that anyone inside the house would hear her summons. She waited. No answer. *Rat-tat-tat* again. She waited, listening.

The door opened.

"Can't you people leave me alone?! Haven't you got enough stories? You're vultures, all of you. Vultures!"

A man of medium height stood before Maisie. His brown hair was in need of a comb, his face sported a rough salt-and-pepper shadow of beard, and he was dressed in baggy tweed trousers, a grey flannel shirt topped with a knitted sleeveless pullover in a pale grey with flecks of green and purple woven into the yarn. He wore neither shoes, socks, nor tie, and looked, thought Maisie, as if he could do with a good meal.

"I do beg your pardon, Mr Sedgewick —"

"Don't 'pardon, Mr Sedgewick' me, you nasty little piece of —"

"Mr Sedgewick, I am not a member of the press!" Maisie stood to her full height, and looked him in the eyes.

The man shuffled his feet, looked down, rubbed his chin, then looked again at Maisie. His shoulders, which had been drawn up tensely, almost touching his earlobes, now drooped, making him look as broken in body as he was in spirit. He was exhausted. "I'm sorry. Please forgive me, but I just want to be left alone." He began to close the door.

"But please . . . I need to speak to you." Maisie reminded herself that Philippa Sedgewick's husband might also be her killer. While she doubted that this man was a murderer, she had to proceed with caution.

"Be quick, and tell me what you want, though I doubt I can help anyone. I can't even help myself!" said Sedgewick.

"My name is Maisie Dobbs." Maisie opened the flap of her case and pulled a card from an inner compartment, not breaking eye contact with Sedgewick. "I'm a private investigator, and I think there is a connection between a case I am working on and your wife's murder."

For a few seconds, silent incredulity was visible on the man's face: his lips seemed frozen open, his eyes did not even blink. Then Sedgewick began to laugh almost hysterically. He laughed and laughed and laughed, bending over, his hands on his knees before raising his head as he attempted to speak. The thin line between emotions was being breached. This man, who had so recently lost his wife, was indeed in crisis. Maisie was aware that a neighbour was standing on her front doorstep looking across at the house. Then, as she turned again to Sedgewick, she realized he was crying. She quickly helped him inside his home and closed the door behind her.

Maisie illuminated the hallway with electric light and, still holding Sedgewick's arm, directed him to the back of the house, to the kitchen. Maisie connected a kitchen with warmth, but as she turned on another light she felt her heart sink at the sight that confronted her. Helping Sedgewick to a chair, Maisie opened the curtains, unlocked and opened the back door to the garden, and looked back at the cups and saucers piled on the draining board, along with dirty saucepans and one or two plates. The dregs of stale brandy and half-smoked cigarettes swirled against one another in crystal glasses, perhaps originally given to celebrate the marriage of the young couple years earlier.

"Oh, I'm sorry, I'm sorry, you must think me –"

"I don't think anything, Mr Sedgewick. You've been through a horrible time."

"Tell me again who you are and why you are here."

Maisie identified herself again and explained the purpose of her visit to the house of – as far as the authorities knew – the first victim of the "Heartless, Bloodless Killer," named for his use of poison before the knife.

"I can't see how I can help. I've spent hours, literally hours, with the police. I have spent every second of every day since my wife was murdered asking myself why and who. And, as you can imagine, for some time the police thought that I was the 'who'. They probably still do."

"They have to explore all avenues, Mr Sedgewick."

"Oh yes, the police line, I know it." Sedgewick rubbed his neck and as he did so, Maisie heard bones crack in his shoulder and back.

"Will you help me?" she asked.

Sedgewick sighed. "Yes, yes. If helping you ends up helping me, I'll do what I can to answer your questions."

Maisie smiled and, feeling once more like the nurse she had been so long ago, she reached out and squeezed Sedgewick's hand. "I appreciate it, Mr Sedgewick."

The man seemed to falter, then continued. "Miss Dobbs, would you mind using my Christian name? I know it's rather a cheek to ask . . . and I perfectly understand if you decline my request, but . . . I have been nothing but Sedgewick or Mr Sedgewick for weeks now. My neighbours are avoiding me, and I have been given leave from my work until the killer" – he seemed about to double over again – "until the case is closed. My name is John. And I am a man who has lost his wife."

They moved into the drawing room. Maisie watched John Sedgewick as he eased himself into an armchair beside the fireplace. She opened the curtains just enough to allow some natural illumination to enter. Sudden light might startle Sedgewick, who would feel a needle of sunshine to be piercing and painful. The room was untidy, with unread newspapers in a pile, cigarette ends mounting in ashtrays, and dust layered on the mantelpiece, the small writing desk, and the side tables. Spent coals in the cold grate made the room even less inviting. As if pressed inward by his discomfort, Sedgewick sat forward on the edge of the chair, hunching his shoulders and gripping his elbows. Maisie shivered, remembering Maurice in the early days of her apprenticeship: "Watch the body, Maisie; see how the posture reflects the state of mind." John Sedgewick was clutching his body as if to save himself from falling apart.

Maisie allowed a silence to envelop them, a time in which she composed her body, cleared her thoughts and saw in her mind's eye a connection forming between herself and the man opposite her. She imagined a stream of light emanating from the centre of her forehead just above her nose, a bright thread that flowed towards her subject and bathed him with a luminous glow. Slowly the man who wanted to be addressed informally as John relaxed his shoulders and released his arms. He leaned back.

Maisie knew better than to breach his trust by commencing with a fusillade of questions that must have already been put to him by the police.

"John, would you like to tell me about your wife?" she asked softly.

Sedgewick exhaled and gave a sharp, ironic half laugh. "You know, Miss Dobbs, you are the first person to ask me that question in that manner. The police are more direct."

Maisie inclined her head but did not speak, inviting him to continue.

"She was lovely, Miss Dobbs. A lovely girl. Funny, I always think of her as a girl. She wasn't tall, not like you. No, Pippin – that's what I called her, Pippin." Sedgewick closed his eyes again and wrinkled his face against tears that welled up behind his eyelids. Recovering, he continued, "She was slight, not a big girl. And I know she wasn't a girl any more, but she was a girl to me. We married in 1920. I met her at my parents' house, would you believe? She was visiting with her widowed mother, who knew my mother through the Women's Institute, or the church Flowers Committee, something of that order."

Sedgewick looked towards the garden, as if imagining that his dead wife would walk along the front path at any moment. Maisie knew that he held a vision of Philippa before him. An image began to form in her mind of a young woman in a plain, pale sea-green summer dress. She was wearing green cotton gloves to protect her fine hands while cutting roses in a myriad of colours, placing the blooms in a basket at her feet before looking up when she heard her husband's footfall as he opened the gate and came towards her.

"I think our meeting was arranged by the mothers, actually."
Sedgewick smiled, a narrow smile of remembrance. "And we got
on famously. She was shy at first – apparently she had been somewhat dark of mood since the war – but soon became quite buoyant.
People said it was having a sweetheart that did it."

Maisie made a mental note to delve a little deeper into the source
of Philippa Sedgewick's disquiet, but for now she wanted
Sedgewick to be at ease with her as his confidante. She did not
interrupt.

"We lived with her mother for a while after the wedding. It was
a small affair in the village, nothing grand. Then we rented a flat for
a couple of years, and when these houses were built in 1923, we
snapped one up straightaway. Philippa had a small legacy from her
father and I had my savings and some funds in a trust, so it wasn't a
stretch." Sedgewick became silent and breathed deeply before continuing. "Of course, you buy a house like this for a family, but we
were not to be blessed with children." He stopped to address Maisie
directly. "Heavens above, this must be far from what you want to
hear, Miss Dobbs! I'm sorry."

"Please continue Mr . . . John. Please tell me about your wife."

"Well, she was barren. Not her fault, of course. And the doctors
weren't much help, said there was nothing they could do. The first
one, a grey-haired doddery old duffer, said that it was nothing that
a couple of glasses of sherry each wouldn't cure. The blithering
idiot!"

"I am so sorry, John."

"Anyway, we just sort of accepted that we were to remain a
family of two. In fact, just before . . . just before the end . . ."
Sedgewick closed his eyes against images that now rushed forth,
images that Maisie knew to be of his dead wife. Again he breathed
deeply to combat his emotions. "Just before the end, we had
planned to buy a puppy. Thought it would be company for her
while I was at work. Mind you, she kept busy – reading to children
at the local school one afternoon a week, that sort of thing – and
she loved her garden. Trouble was, she blamed herself."

"Blamed herself?" Maisie watched him closely.

"Yes. For being barren. Said that you reap what you sow."

"Did she ever say what she meant?"

"Never. I just thought that she had dredged up every bad thing she'd ever done and heaped it on herself." Sedgewick shrugged. "She was a good girl, my Pippin."

Maisie leaned towards Sedgewick, just close enough for him to feel warmer and, subconsciously, more at ease.

"Can you tell me if your wife was troubled about anything else? Had there been any discord between her and any other person?"

"Pippin was not one to gush all over other people, or rush over to natter with the neighbours. But she was kind and thoughtful, knew if someone needed help and always passed the time of day if she saw someone she knew on the street. But . . . did you say 'ever,' Miss Dobbs?"

"I know that might be a tall assignment, John."

"You know, I think she only ever walked out with one man before we met. She was shy with men. It was during the war, and she was quite young really, only seventeen or so, if that. If I remember correctly, she'd met him when she was in Switzerland. He was one of several young men paying attention to Pippin and her group, in fact, he courted all of them at some point. He ended up marrying one of her friends, who I think, had nothing but trouble with him. Bit of a ladies' man, he was." Suddenly Sedgewick frowned, "You know, funny that should come to mind, because he was back in touch with her, I don't know, must have been towards the end of last year. I'd all but forgotten about it."

"Who was the man, and why had he made contact again? Do you know?"

"I have a terrible memory for names, but his was quite unusual. Not like your average 'John,' you know!" Sedgewick smiled faintly. "Apparently his wife, who, as I said, was an old friend of Pippin's, was drinking heavily. He tracked down Pippin and telephoned to see if she could help at all, speak to the wife, try to get her on the straight and narrow. But they hadn't been in touch for years and I don't think

Pippin wanted anything to do with it. She said no, and that was that. At least as far as I know. She told me that her friend probably drank to forget. Didn't think much about it at the time. She said, 'Everyone's got something to help them forget things, haven't they? She's got the bottle, I've got my garden.' Sounds a bit harsh, but I wouldn't have wanted her to get involved with a woman like that."

Maisie did not want to influence Sedgewick with her suspicions. "And you are sure you can't recall his name? What letter did it begin with?"

"Oh dear, Miss Dobbs . . . it was, um . . ." Sedgewick rubbed his brow. "Um . . . I think it was *M*— yes, that's it. *Muh, mih, mah* . . . *mah* . . . yes, *mah* . . . *mag* . . . Magnus! Yes, Magnus Fisher. Now I remember."

"And his wife's name was Lydia?"

"Yes, yes! Miss Dobbs, I do believe you knew all the time!"

"John, have you read the newspapers recently?"

"No, I can't stand it! They always point the finger, and while Pippin is still somewhere on the front page, the finger is pointed at me."

Maisie delved further. "The police haven't returned since last week?"

"No. Of course they come to the house to check that I'm still here, and I'm not supposed to leave the area, pending the closure of inquiries, or whatever the official line is."

Maisie was surprised that Stratton had not revisited Sedgewick since Lydia Fisher's body was discovered. "John, Lydia Fisher was found dead – murdered – last week. A subsequent post-mortem examination suggested that there were similarities between your wife's murder and Mrs Fisher's. I suspect the police have not spoken to you yet, pending further investigation. The press was rather too forthcoming with details of your wife's murder and as there are those who will copy infamy, the police might not want to draw attention to similarities at this very early stage. I have no doubt, though, that the police – and the press – will be on your doorstep again soon."

Sedgewick clutched his shoulders, rocking himself back and forth, then stood up, and began to pace. "They'll think it was me, they'll think it was me. . ."

"Calm down, John, calm down. They will not think it's you. I suspect that their conclusions will be quite the opposite."

"Oh, that poor woman, that poor woman . . . and my poor Pippin." John Sedgewick began to weep as he sat heavily in the armchair, and Maisie knelt so that he could lean upon her shoulder. All formalities of polite interaction between a woman and a man she did not know fell away as Maisie allowed her strength of spirit to seep into Sedgewick. Once again he fought for composure.

"I don't understand; what does this mean?"

"I don't know yet, but I intend to find out. Can you face more questions, John?"

John Sedgewick took an already soiled handkerchief from his pocket and wiped his eyes and nose. "Yes.Yes, I'll try, Miss Dobbs. And I am so sorry . . ."

Maisie took her seat and raised her hand. "Don't apologize. Grief should be aired, not buried. Do you know if your wife was also acquainted with a woman called Charlotte Waite?"

Sedgewick looked up at Maisie. "The Waite girl? Why, yes she was. Again, it was a long time ago, long before we met. I say, what is all this about, Miss Dobbs?"

"I'm not sure, John, I am simply picking up loose threads."

"Charlotte and Lydia were part of the same − coterie, I think you'd call them.You know, a group of young girls who spend time together on Saturdays, have tea together, and then spend their allowances on trifles, that sort of thing."

Maisie nodded, though as a young girl there had been no coterie for her, no trifles, only more errands to run and her chores below stairs to perform as efficiently and quickly as possible, leaving her more time to study.

"But they grew apart, you know, as people do. Charlotte was very wealthy, as was Lydia. Pippin was part of a certain social circle that, frankly, she did not choose to belong to as they matured. I think they all had a falling out, but as I said, this was long before Pippin and I began courting."

"Was a woman called Rosamund part of the group?"

Sedgewick sighed, and pressed his hands to his eyes. "The name rings a bell. I might have heard the name 'Rosie' – I don't think I heard 'Rosamund' . . . no . . . not 'Rosamund'."

Maisie prepared to ask her next question, when he spoke first. "You know, I have just remembered something odd. Mind you, I don't know if it's of any use to you."

"Go on."

"Well, it's about the Waite girl; her father, really. It must have been before we were married." Sedgewick scratched his head, "I'm as bad with time as I am with names. Yes, it was before we were married, because I remember being in Pippin's mother's parlour. Now it's coming back to me. I arrived at the house on my bicycle just as a rather large motor car was leaving. Too fast if you ask me, I remember the gravel spitting up and hitting me in the face. Anyway, the housekeeper let me in, said that Pippin was in the drawing room. As I walked in she was there, drying her eyes: she'd been crying. I pleaded with her to tell me what was the matter, but she would only say that she had had some sort of crossed words with Mr Waite, Charlotte's father. I threatened to go after him, but she wouldn't allow it and said that if I did, then she would never see me again. That it would never happen again, or something like that."

"And she never revealed the cause of the discord?"

"Never. I suspected it might have to do with Charlotte. I thought perhaps that Pippin had told a lie on her behalf – you know, saying that Charlotte was with her, when she was really somewhere else. Apparently Charlotte was quite rebellious as a young girl. See, my memory's warming up now!"

"Did your wife ever see Joseph Waite again? Or hear from him?"

"No, I don't think she did. She never mentioned it. After we were married we settled into a very ordinary life, especially here on Bluebell Avenue."

Sedgewick looked drawn, almost overcome with fatigue.

"I will leave you in peace soon, John. But first, I understand that your housekeeper found Mrs Sedgewick?"

"Yes, Mrs Noakes. She comes in daily to clean and dust, prepare supper, that sort of thing. She had gone out for a couple of hours, to the shops, and when she came home, she found Pippin in the dining room. It appears she'd had someone to tea, which was unusual, because she hadn't said that she was expecting a visitor or mentioned it to Mrs Noakes."

"And you were at work?"

"Yes, in the City. I'm a civil engineer, Miss Dobbs, so I was out at a site all afternoon. Plenty of people saw me, but of course, I was also travelling between places, which interests the police enormously. They sit there with their maps and train timetables trying to work out if I could have come home, murdered my wife, and been back on a building site in time for my next alibi."

"I see. Would you show me the dining room?"

In contrast to the untidy kitchen and drawing room, the dining room was immaculate, though evidence of a police presence was everywhere throughout the house. It was clear that a thorough investigation had taken place in the room where Philippa Sedgewick had met her death.

"There wasn't any blood to speak of." The tendons in Sedgewick's throat became taut as he spoke of his wife's murder. "Apparently the murderer drugged her with something first, before . . . before using the knife."

"Yes." Maisie walked around the room, observing but not touching. All surfaces were clean, with only a thin layer of dust. She walked to the window and opened the curtains to allow natural light to augment the grainy electric illumination. Fingerprinting was used widely now and Maisie could see residues of powder where police had tested for prints left by the murderer. Yes, Stratton's men had done a thorough job.

As if reading her mind, Sedgewick spoke. "Inspector Stratton isn't such a bad chap. No, not too bad. It's that sergeant of his that makes my skin crawl, Caldwell. He was a nasty piece of work. Have you met him?"

Maisie was preoccupied with scanning the nooks and crannies of the dining room, but an image of the small, brisk man with a pointed nose and a cold stare came to mind. "Only once or twice."

"Just as well. He all but accused me when they took me in for questioning. Stratton was kinder. Mind you, I've heard that they do that, you know, play nice and nasty so that the suspect either gets unsettled or too relaxed before the other goes for the jugular."

Maisie looked on each surface and under each piece of furniture. Sedgewick, who was now very much at ease in her company, seemed to ramble in conversation. Maisie touched a place on the floor, then brought her fingers close to her nose.

"I heard two of the constables speaking. Apparently Stratton lost his wife in childbirth five years ago. Got a little boy at home and is bringing him up alone. It would make him more understanding, I suppose."

Maisie had been kneeling. She stood so quickly that her head spun.

"I didn't mean to startle you, Miss Dobbs. Yes, he's a widower. Just like me."

Maisie quickly completed her investigation, taking care not to let her desire to be alone, to gather her thoughts, distract her from the job at hand. She might not have another opportunity. But there seemed to be nothing that spoke to her here except John Sedgewick's grief.

"It's time for me to go, John. Will you be all right?"

"Yes, I will. Speaking about Pippin seems to have fortified me. I should *do* something, I suppose. Tidy the house, that sort of thing. Mrs Noakes has been too upset to come back, though she did write to say that she believes me innocent. Which is heartwarming, considering that my own sister and mother are keeping well away, and Pippin's mother is too full of grief to visit."

"Perhaps if you open the curtains you'll feel even better. Let the light in, John."

Sedgewick smiled. "I could probably do with getting out into the garden. It was always Pippin's domain, you know, the garden. Since she was a child she loved to grow things."

"Enjoy the garden. After all, she planted it for both of you."

As Maisie turned to leave, she felt a pressure in the middle of her back, as if she was being restrained. She gasped at the sensation, and realized that she had missed something, something she should not have overlooked.

"John, is there a place here, a part of the garden, perhaps, that your wife particularly liked? Did she have a potting shed or greenhouse, that sort of thing?"

"Yes, at the side of the house here. In fact, Mrs Noakes said that Pippin was in there when she left to go shopping. She loved the greenhouse. I designed it for her. You'll see, it has three parts: a traditional glass section for bringing on seedlings; a shed with windows so that she would have a shaded area for potting; then the third part is a sort of conservatory, where she had her exotics, and where she would sit in her armchair with a gardening book. I don't think I ever saw her with another type of book. Let me show you."

Sedgewick led the way to the side of the house, where a willow tree obscured Philippa Sedgewick's horticultural sanctuary from street view. Maisie entered, and immediately felt the humid warmth of a well-tended greenhouse, along with the pungent salty aroma of young geraniums growing in terracotta pots. She walked slowly along an inner path to a stable door of wood and glass. Opening top and bottom, Maisie entered the musky potting shed, then walked through to the small conservatory-cum-sitting-room on the other side: the dead woman's own special domain.

It reminded her of the winter garden where Simon sat with his blanket and his secrets. A wicker chair with green and rose cushions was still indented, as if the owner had only just risen. It seemed so warm that a cat would have immediately claimed the place. Once again Maisie paced, and was immediately drawn to a gardening book set on a table beside the chair. She opened the front cover and leafed through until the book seemed to fall open at the point where Philippa Sedgewick had set her bookmark, perhaps when the killer had come to call. She imagined Philippa hearing the sharp rap of the door knocker in the distance, quickly marking her place and jumping up to answer the door. Or had the killer come to look for her when his knock was not answered? If he was an acquaintance, she would have marked her place and offered tea.

Geranium. *Pelargonium*. Maisie ran her finger down the spine of the book, and as she did so, she felt a faint prickle. Looking more closely, she reached in and carefully took out the spiny yet smooth source of the sensation. *Yes, yes, yes.*

Maisie placed her find within a handkerchief while John Sedgewick was looking at a rather large waxy green plant in the corner. "Of course, I couldn't tell one from the other, though Pippin could name every one, and in Latin. I think that's the only reason she studied Latin in school, to learn more about plants."

"I learned Latin once myself, simply to better understand another subject. I'd better be going, John. Thank you so much for your help, you have been most kind."

Sedgewick held out his hand to Maisie. "Well, it was a dodgy start, wasn't it? But I think you have helped me more than I've assisted you."

"Oh, you have helped, John. Enormously. I am sure that you'll be seeing Detective Inspector Stratton soon, and I'd appreciate it if no mention is made of my visit here today."

"Not a word, Miss Dobbs, not a word. But, before you go; what case are you working on, if I may ask?"

"It has to do with a missing person." She left at once, to avoid further questions. She needed to think. Starting the MG as quickly as she could, Maisie pushed the motor car into gear. She turned to look at Number 14 Bluebell Avenue one last time before speeding off, and saw John Sedgewick walk slowly towards his wife's roses, then reach down to pull out some weeds. Later, as she moved into traffic to return to London, Maisie thought not of Sedgewick but of Richard Stratton. A man who had lost his wife, too. And she thought of the chance discovery she had made, which she would now take back to her rooms and place with the twin that she had carefully wrapped in another linen handkerchief while standing in Lydia Fisher's drawing room.

12

THE GAS fire was turned off, so the room was cold by the time Maisie arrived back at the office on Sunday evening. On the desk in front of her she saw a single sheet of paper filled with Billy's large, primary school handwriting, along with several unopened envelopes placed separately on the desk so that Maisie could view each one individually before slicing it open. Billy had had a productive Saturday morning.

"Brrr. Let's see: Cantwell bill sent out, good. Lady Rowan telephoned, no message. Andrew Dene . . . Andrew Dene? Hmmm." Maisie raised her eyebrows and continued. "Returned folders to solicitors –" The telephone rang.

"Fitzroy five six double O."

"Miss Dobbs?"

"Yes."

"It's John Sedgewick here. Glad I caught you."

"Do you have some news, Mr Sedgewick?" Maisie deliberately reverted to a more formal address.

"Yes I do. I thought you'd like to know that Detective Inspector Stratton and the obnoxious Caldwell came to the house after you left. They were asking about that Magnus Fisher."

"Really? What did they want to know?"

"Well, more about his contact with Pippin. I told them what I told you. There wasn't more to tell. Don't worry, I did not breathe a word about your being here. But Stratton gave me something to think about."

"And that is?"

"It turns out that Pippin *did* see Fisher. He'd returned from one of his expeditions about two months ago, and it was during that time that they met. He went off again for a couple of weeks, then came back again. Apparently the dates of his return trips almost mirror the dates of Pippin and Mrs Fisher's murders, so the police are interested in him."

"Did they say anything about motive?"

"No. Stratton gave me the 'all avenues' line again, and asked if *I* knew Lydia Fisher. They also asked me – again, I might add – the most intimate details about my marital happiness."

"All in the line of duty, Mr Sedgewick. No doubt they asked you to speculate as to why Mrs Sedgewick met Fisher."

"Yes, and I said that I thought she might have been trying to help in some way, given Mrs Fisher's problems. I thought they were suggesting that there was something, you know, 'going on' between Pippin and Fisher, especially as they had walked out together in earlier years. It really is most distressing, Miss Dobbs."

"Of course it is, and I sympathize, Mr Sedgewick. However, the police really are just trying to do their job. They want to find the killer before he strikes again."

"It's very difficult for me, yet I know you're right."

"Thank you, Mr Sedgewick. You were most kind to telephone. Are you feeling better now?"

"Yes. Yes, I am. And you know, this evening one of my neighbours came to the house with some shepherd's pie, said she hadn't wanted to come around while the curtains were closed, and that they were so very sorry about Pippin. Mind you, she did bring her husband with her; she wasn't *that* sure about me."

"It's a start, though. Goodnight, Mr Sedgewick."

"Yes, goodnight, Miss Dobbs."

Magnus Fisher. Possible, thought Maisie, always possible. He had pursued Philippa and each of her friends. And he'd married Lydia. Had there been other, deeper relationships between Fisher and Rosamund and Charlotte? Had an earlier interest in these women lingered and faded, only to reignite and flare out of control later? She looked down and read on through Billy's notes.

"Lady Rowan again . . . definitely not returning to Ebury Place for another fortnight at least."

Maisie smiled at the next note, which was from Billy.

Dear Miss,

It's nice to have you back here in London. I will be in sharp, nice and early tomorrow morning. Hope you had a nice time in Kent.

Yours sincerely,
Billy Beale

Maisie could almost see Billy Beale as a boy, his wheaten hair dishevelled and matted, freckles speckling his nose, his tongue clamped tightly between his teeth as he concentrated on sweeping his dipping pen up and down, up and down, as he constructed a letter. No doubt his teacher had emphasized use of the word *nice*.

Maisie perused each sealed envelope in turn until she came to a hand she knew so well, an unmistakable fine copperplate in blue-black ink. She turned the envelope over to reveal the Camden Abbey wax seal. Underneath the address were the words "By Hand," so the letter had obviously been delivered by a later visitor to the abbey who had returned immediately to London, arriving before Maisie. Taking her Victorinox knife, Maisie slit the envelope open to reveal a folded sheet of crisp cream linen paper, so heavy it was almost card, upon which Dame Constance had written her letter:

Dear Maisie,

How lovely it was to see you at Camden Abbey. A visit from one of my most memorable students is always an event of great joy, but I confess I would like to see a little more weight on your bones!

I will not fill my communiqué with more pleasantries, dear

Maisie, but instead will come straight to the point as I must take advantage of delivery of this letter by a visitor from London who will be leaving shortly. I have counselled Miss Waite to see you, and she has agreed. Her confidence is due to the safety and refuge offered her by the community, so I must request that you honour my trust in you to proceed with integrity. Dame Judith has said that Miss Waite should rest for two or three days as she has caught that terrible cold we've all had. I suggest you come on Thursday morning.

Yours sincerely,
Dame Constance Charteris

"Good." Maisie sat at her desk, leaned back and smiled. She had no doubt that Dame Constance's powers of persuasion had been brought to bear on Charlotte, though she wished they had resulted in a more timely interview. She would have to choose her words carefully when meeting with Joseph Waite on Tuesday.

When she left the office a heavy smog seemed, once again, to be spiralling around the trees on the square, and she could barely see the streetlamps. In the distance, she could hear both the clip-clop of hooves and the pop and chug of motor cars ferrying people – better-off people – home from a Sunday excursion, or out to supper. Sound was distorted not only by the darkness but by the smog. She wished she were in Kent, to see the stars at night and silent fields illuminated by a full moon.

Had she already met the killer? Had they passed in the street outside Lydia Fisher's home? Was Charlotte Waite involved, or was her flight from her father's house simply the action of a woman who could no longer be treated as a girl? Could she *be* the killer? Or was she afraid of becoming the next victim? What of Magnus Fisher? What motive could he have for killing his wife and two of her acquaintances? Had something happened in Switzerland years ago? Something the women knew about that was so serious that he would kill to ensure their silence? What could Charlotte tell her about Fisher? And what of her tiny shreds of evidence, carefully preserved? Or were they nothing at all, just household detritus?

Once again her thoughts centred on the Waite household, and she examined her feelings towards both Charlotte and her father. She admitted some confusion where Joseph Waite was concerned: she found his arrogance distasteful, his controlling attitude toward his grown daughter appalling. Yet at the same time she respected his accomplishments and recognized his generosity. He was a man of extremes. A man who worked hard, who indulged himself, yet who gave help freely, with kindness, if he approved of the recipient.

Could he be the killer? She remembered the dexterity with which he wielded his array of butcher's knives. Did he have a motive? If he did, then did it explain Charlotte's flight?

What did she really know of Charlotte, except that she was not at peace? Her father's view of her was biased. If *only* she could meet Charlotte Waite sooner. She needed to form her own opinion of the woman's character. In the meantime, could she interview Fisher?

Maisie started the MG. It was time to return to her rooms at Ebury Place. She had much to consider, to plan. Tomorrow would be a long day, a day that had to begin with a difficult encounter. She must confront Billy about his behaviour.

The front door of the Belgravia mansion was opened even before she reached the bottom step.

"We heard your motor car turn into the mews, Ma'am."

"Oh, lovely. It's a cold evening isn't it, Sandra, and a foggy one."

"It is, Ma'am, and that old green stuff out there going down into your lungs doesn't help, neither. Never mind, soon be summer."

Sandra closed the door behind Maisie and took her coat, hat, and gloves.

"Will you have supper in the dining room tonight, Ma'am, or on a tray upstairs?"

Maisie stopped for a moment, then turned to Sandra. "I think

I'd like a nice bowl of vegetable soup on a tray. Not too soon – about half past eight."

"Right you are, Ma'am. Teresa went upstairs the minute she heard your car and she's running you a good hot bath, what with you driving up from Chelstone today."

Maisie went immediately to her rooms, placed her now-full document case on the writing table, and undressed, quickly replacing her day clothes with a dressing gown and slippers. Was it only on Friday night that she had left for Chelstone? She had departed again early this morning, indeed, she had risen as soon as she heard her father's footfall on the stairs at four o'clock; washed, dressed and quickly joined him for a strong mug of tea before he went to attend to the mare.

"I've added some lavender salts to the bath for you, Ma'am. Helps you relax before bedtime, does lavender." Teresa had set two large fluffy white towels on the rail by the bathtub, now full of steaming aromatic water.

"Thank you, Teresa."

"Right you are Ma'am. Will you be needing anything else, Ma'am?"

"No, thank you."

Teresa bobbed a curtsey and left the bathroom.

Maisie steeped her body, reaching forward with her foot to twist the hot tap whenever it seemed that the water was cooling. How strange to be living in the upstairs part of the Ebury Place mansion, to be addressed as "Ma'am" by girls doing the same job that had brought her to this house, and this life. She leaned back to allow the scented steam to rise up into her hair, and remembered the once-a-week bath that was all she had been allowed when she herself had been a tweeny maid. Enid would bang on the door as soon as she thought that Maisie had been in too long. Maisie could hear her now. *Come on, Mais. Let us in. It's brassy out here on the landing.*

And she remembered France, the cold mud that seeped into her bones, a cold that she could feel to this day. "You're a chilly mortal, my girl." Maisie smiled as she saw Mrs Crawford in her mind's eye, and almost felt the old woman's arms around her, comforting her, as she enveloped Maisie with her warmth when she returned, injured, from France. "Let's be having you, my girl. There, there, you're home now, you're home." And she had held Maisie to her with one hand, and rubbed her back with the other, just as a mother would soothe a baby.

There was a knock on the bathroom door.

"Goodness!" Maisie gasped when she realized how long she had soaked in the bath. "Coming! I'll be in right away!"

She quickly stepped out of the bath, dried herself, and pulled the dressing gown around her. She set her hair free, shook her head, and rushed into her sitting room. A supper tray had been placed on a small table set in front of her chair by the fire, which was glowing as flames curled around fresh coals being heaped on by Sandra.

"Better stoke it up a bit for you, Ma'am. We don't want you catching cold, do we?"

"Thank you, Sandra. A cold is the last thing I want!"

Sandra replaced the tongs in a brass coal scuttle, stood up, and smiled at Maisie. "Looks like Mr Carter will be returning next week, to get everything in its place for Her Ladyship coming back."

"Ah, then we'll know all about it, eh, Sandra?" Maisie smiled at the maid, taking her table napkin and setting it on her lap. "Mmm, this soup smells delicious!"

Sandra bobbed and nodded her head. "Thank you Ma'am." But instead of leaving, she seemed to waver. "Not as many staff as there used to be, are there?"

"Certainly not as many as before the war, Sandra." Instead of taking up her soup spoon, Maisie leaned back in the chair and looked into the fire. "No, definitely not. And if you asked Mrs Crawford, she'd tell you that there were even more before His Lordship bought the motor cars, when there were horses in the mews, and grooms."

Sandra pursed her lips and looked at her feet. "S'all changing, isn't it, Ma'am? I mean, you know, we wonder why they keep this place on, now that they spend more time down at Chelstone."

Maisie thought for a while and replied. "Oh, I think they'll keep Ebury Place for a few years yet, at least until Master James comes back to England. After all, it is part of his inheritance. Are you worried about your job, Sandra?"

"Well, we all are, Ma'am. I mean, I hope you don't mind me saying this, and all, but things are changing. Not so many girls are going into service these days. But you know, it's funny, like, when you can see change right before your eyes."

"Yes. Yes, you're right. We've seen a lot of changes since the war."

"I think people are trying to forget the war, don't you, Miss? I mean, who wants to be reminded? My cousin – not the one what died over there, but the one who came home wounded from Loos – he said that it was one thing to be remembered, and quite another to be reminded every day. He didn't mind people remembering what he'd done, you know, over there. But he didn't want to be *reminded* of it. He said that it was hard, because something happened to remind him every day."

Maisie thought of her bath, and how the sheer pleasure of it was a reminder of the past. Even if the reminder was of the opposite sensation, that of cold, of discomfort.

"Well, I'd better be getting along, Ma'am, let you eat your supper. Goodnight."

"Goodnight, Sandra. And Sandra, don't worry about things changing. It usually turns out for the best."

Maisie finished her soup and leaned back in the chair again to watch the hot coals turn to embers. She would make up the fire just a little before going into her bedroom, knowing that as she drifted into slumber, the tray would silently be taken from her rooms in the same way that a breakfast tray would silently appear as she was pinning up her hair in the morning. The conversation with Sandra had sparked her thoughts in another direction. Perhaps *she* was ready for change. Not outwardly, though she knew that exterior transformation was a signal of inner change, but in what she envisioned for her future. Yes, perhaps that was a subject worthy of consideration.

As Maisie settled back into the pillows, she thought of the fine line between remembrance and reminder, and how a constant reminder could drive a person to the edge of sanity. Could drive a person to drugs or drink, to anything that took away the past's sharp edges. But what if the reminder was another human being? Then what might happen?

13

MAISIE ROSE early. She washed quickly and dressed in her blue suit, with the collar and cuffs of a white linen blouse just visible underneath. Anticipating a chilly morning, Maisie remembered her navy blue coat, along with her old cloche and black gloves. She grabbed the black document case and left the room quickly.

She was about to open the disguised landing door that led to the back stairs and down to the kitchen, when she thought better of it. The girls downstairs might be embarrassed. She would use the main staircase. Then she could knock at the door in fair warning. Straddling the line of her position in the household required some thought.

Maisie knocked, waited a second or two, then poked her head around the kitchen door without waiting for a reply. "Good morning everyone!"

There was a collective gasp from Sandra, Teresa and Valerie. "Oh, Miss, you gave us a fright!" said Sandra. "I was just about to start your breakfast."

"Sorry to scare you. I thought I'd have breakfast in the kitchen, if that's all right."

"Of course it is, Miss. Of course. At least your hair's nice and dry this morning!"

"Your usual, Miss? Porridge, toast and marmalade? You'll need to stoke up the fires this morning, it's cold out there. They reckon we could be in for a wintry Easter this year."

Maisie smiled, noting the change of address again, from

161

"Ma'am" to "Miss." Maisie felt like a citizen of two countries, neither here nor there, but always somewhere in the middle.

"Easter's still a fortnight away and I need to be quick today. I'll have just a slice of toast and a nice cup of tea, thank you."

"Right you are, Miss. Cup of tea coming up, and toast to follow. Are you sure you don't want a nice boiled egg?"

Maisie shook her head. "Tea and toast will be plenty for me this morning, Teresa."

Maisie took some letters from her document case and began to read. She was aware that the girls had exchanged glances, and were mouthing messages to each other. Sandra cleared her throat and came over to the table.

"Miss?"

"Yes, Sandra?"

"Well, we was thinking, you know, and wondered if, you know, you'd like to come to the pictures with us, next Saturday evening. We don't usually go out together, the three of us girls – we like to make sure that one of us is always in the kitchen, even if there's no one upstairs – but it's not as if we're leaving the house unattended, what with the other staff being here."

"What's the picture?"

"It's a talkie, and a bit scary, I've heard. It's got Donald Calthrop in it. Called *Blackmail*. It's about this girl, and she's courting a feller in the police, a detective, and he –"

"I don't think so, Sandra."

"Hmmm, I s'pose anything to do with the police would be like going on a busman's holiday for you, wouldn't it, Miss?"

"It's lovely of you to ask, Sandra. Thank you very much for thinking of me. The funny thing is, I don't really like the scary ones, they keep me awake."

Sandra laughed. "Now that *is* funny, Miss."

Having barely touched her breakfast, Maisie left the Ebury Place mansion via the stone steps that led from the back door into the street, then made her way to the mews to collect the motor car. George, the Compton's chauffeur, was in Kent, but a young footman had been assigned to keep the garage spick and span, ready for the return of the Comptons' Rolls-Royce. The old Lanchester was kept in London, and though now used only occasionally, was cleaned, polished and tended to regularly. Maisie's MG gave the footman a more substantial daily job.

"I could've brought 'er round to the front for you, Miss. Anyway, there she is, all cleaned and polished ready for London. Got 'er in plenty of mud down there, didn't you?"

"The weather has no respect for the motor car, Eric, any more than it has for the horse. Thank you for shining her up again. Did you check my oil?"

"All done, Miss. Everything given the once over. She'd take you from John O'Groats to Land's End if you felt like the drive, and that's a fact. Lovely little runner, lovely."

"Thank you, Eric."

Maisie parked once again in Fitzroy Street, in exactly the same spot as the evening before. Few people had motor vehicles, so Maisie was regarded as a subject of some interest as she climbed from the gleaming crimson vehicle.

She walked slowly towards the office, knowing that this morning would be a difficult one. Her feet were heavy on the stairs and she knew that to have the energy for the next part of her day, she must bring her body into alignment with her intentions, that her sagging shoulders would not support her spirit for the task ahead.

Unlocking the door to the first-floor office, Maisie was surprised to note that Billy had not arrived yet. She looked at her watch. Half-past eight. Despite his message, Billy was late. She walked to the window, rubbing the back of her neck where her scar had begun to throb.

Placing her hands on her chest, with her right hand over the left, Maisie breathed deeply. As her tension eased, she began to envisage the conversation with Billy, concentrating on the closing words of a dialogue that had yet to happen. Pressing her hands even more firmly against her body, Maisie deliberately slowed her breathing to settle her pounding heart, and felt the nagging ache of her scar abate. That's a reminder, she thought, every single day, just as Billy's wounded leg is a reminder. And as she stilled her heart and mind, it occurred to Maisie to question herself: if Lydia Fisher chose alcohol, and Billy narcotics to beat back the tide of daily reminder, then what did *she* do to dull the pain? And as she considered her question, the terrible thought came to her that perhaps she worked hard at her own isolation, along with the demands of her business. Perhaps she worked so hard that she was not only able to ignore physical discomfort, but had rendered herself an island adrift from deeper human connection. She shivered.

"Mornin', Miss, and what a nice mornin' it is, too. Thought I'd need me overcoat this mornin', I did, but 'ad to run from the bus stop and ended up carryin' the thing."

Maisie looked at her silver watch, pinned to the lapel of her jacket.

"Sorry I'm a bit late today, Miss, but there was a bit of an 'oldup. I caught the bus this mornin', and 'alfway along the Mile End Road, I wished I 'adn't bothered. Would've been quicker to walk – and me with this leg and all. Big mess, it was. Motor car – and you don't see many of 'em down there – 'ad gone right into the back of a dray. Thank Gawd 'e weren't goin' too quick. Mind you, you should've 'eard them drivers goin' at 'im. Thought they'd whop 'im one with the whip, I did. One of 'em was shoutin', 'Put the traces on 'im and give the bleedin' 'orses a rest, the lunatic!' Oops, sorry, Miss, I was just sayin' what I 'eard them say. It's a poor old state of affairs, when motor cars –" Billy fussed as he spoke, avoiding eye contact, taking time to shake out his coat and cap, placing them on the coat stand, then riffling through the newspaper as if looking for something in particular.

"Now then, saw something 'ere this mornin' I thought you'd –"

"Billy."

"Got to do with that –"

"Billy!" Maisie raised her voice, then spoke more quietly.

"There's a matter I would like to discuss with you. Let's sit together by the gas fire here. Pull up a chair."

His face flushed, Billy put the newspaper on his desk, dragged his chair out, and set it next to Maisie's.

"Am I getting the sack, Miss?"

"No, Billy, you are not getting the sack. However, I'd like to see a bit more in the way of timekeeping on your part."

"Yes, Miss. I'm sorry, Miss. Won't 'appen again."

"Billy . . ."

"Yes, Miss?"

"I'll get straight to the point," said Maisie, realizing this was a prevarication, and that she was far from getting to the point. She took another deep breath, and began to speak. "I have been concerned for some time about your – let's say moods and –"

"I can exp –"

"Let me finish, Billy. I have been concerned about your moods and, of course, about the obvious pain you have been suffering with your war wounds. I have been worried about you."

Billy rubbed his knees back and forth, back and forth, his eyes on the flickering, hissing flame of the gas fire.

"You know only too well that I was a nurse and that I have some knowledge of the substances administered to the wounded during the war. I saw doctors working in terrible conditions, barely able to practise their profession. When it came to administering morphine and other drugs, they didn't always know what they were giving, in the way of strength of medication." Maisie watched Billy, choosing her words carefully as if she were navigating a minefield, trying to keep his attention yet not ignite a rush to defence or the explosive outburst that she feared. Billy's jaw worked back and forth as he listened and continued to gaze into the fire.

"Billy, I believe you were overdosed on morphine, though you probably didn't know it at the time. Even when we had wounded men being brought into the casualty clearing station by the hundreds, sometimes people stood out and, as you know, I remembered you. You were one of those it was almost impossible to medicate.

You were immediately released to the general hospital, where you were given more medication, then to convalescent care, where more morphine was prescribed to assist you with the pain."

Billy nodded, but still he did not speak.

"And when the prescriptions ended, like so many, you found that access to a substance with similar qualities was easy, especially in London. Cocaine, wasn't it? You probably gave it up for years, didn't you? But when the leg started nagging at you again, you had a bit more money coming in and a local source." Maisie paused.

Finally Billy nodded, then spoke, his eyes never leaving the hot gas jets that warmed their feet, but did nothing to dent the cold around their shoulders and heads.

"You amaze me sometimes, Miss." Billy's upper body seemed to give way as he resigned himself to the truth. "Of course you're spot-on right, as usual. No use me sayin' otherwise." His voice was uncharacteristically low, his speech slow. "When I was first out of convalescence, after I'd come back to London and before I went back down there and married Doreen and brought 'er 'ome, it was easy to get 'old of it. The Canadians on leave were the ones to see, called it 'snow,' they did. Good blokes, them Canadians. Lost a lot of their own. Anyway, just like you said, I stopped it. Then, oh, must've been four months ago, round Christmas when it was really nippy, me leg started on at me again, this time badly. There were days I thought I'd never get down the old stairs. And it just wore me out, just wore on me . . ."

Maisie allowed Billy to speak. He stared as if mesmerized, into the fire.

"Then this feller, who I'd known over there, saw me in the Prince of Wales. Just 'aving a swift 'alf one night before going 'ome, I was, when up 'e comes. 'Eh, is that you, Billy-boy?' 'e says, full of it. Next thing you know, 'e was tellin' me where 'e could get some." Billy put his hands over his eyes as if trying to erase the image from his mind, then lowered them once more to his knees and began rubbing his thighs. "And so I said alright. Just a bit would take the edge off. And, Miss, it was like before the war, with all the pain

166

taken away. I felt like a boy again, and let me tell you, I'd been feelin' like an old man."

Billy paused. Maisie reached out to the knob at the side of the fire and turned up the flame. Still she was silent, allowing Billy to tell his story in his own time.

"And to tell you the truth, I wish I'd never seen 'im or 'is stash. But I wish I could feel like that all the time. I just wish . . ."

Billy slumped forward and began to sob. Maisie leaned toward him; then she remembered Mrs Crawford and simply rubbed his back, calming Billy as if he were a small boy. Eventually Billy's tears subsided and he sat back. He blew his nose.

"Sound like a bleedin' elephant, don't I, Miss?" Billy folded the handkerchief and blew again. "Look, Miss. I'll go. I've no business workin' for you, and that's a fact. I can look for another job."

"Billy, before you do that, think about the lines of men looking for work. Anyway, business is good and I need you. But I also need you healthy and free of this burden, and I have a plan."

Billy looked up at Maisie, dabbing his nose, which had begun to bleed. He held the handkerchief tightly to his face to stem the flow and leaned back slightly.

"Sorry, Miss."

"I've seen worse, Billy. Now then, here's my plan. It will help you, but it will need an enormous effort on your part."

Maisie began to outline the plan of action that she had designed with Maurice.

"Oh, *Dr* Andrew Dene, the feller what called 'ere for you," said Billy. "There's me thinking that 'e might be someone you'd met down there."

"Well, he *was* someone I met down there," replied Maisie.

"No, Miss, I meant met, as in, you know, *met*."

"Billy, I met him to see if he could give me some advice. I wanted to see what could be arranged for you."

"Well, it's good of you to take the trouble and all, but I don't think I want to leave London." Billy dabbed at his nose, checked to see that the bleeding had stopped, then replaced the soiled handkerchief in his pocket. "I'd miss me nippers and Doreen. And I can't see me sitting around on me backside all day with nothing to do but wait to do some special moving of me legs, and to see a doctor."

Maisie sighed. She had been warned by Maurice that Billy would probably object initially, either mildly or more firmly. At this stage she should be grateful that he had not shown anger when she revealed knowledge of his dependence upon cocaine. Perhaps another means of helping Billy could be found, one that would keep him closer to London. In the meantime she needed a commitment from him. "Billy, I want you to promise that you will not procure any more of this substance."

"I never did let myself get too much of a likin' for it, Miss, not like some. I tried to take it only when I was in that much pain. Frightened me, to tell you the truth, to know that somethin' you took, y'know, could change you that much. Scared the bloomin' life out of me. But then when I felt bad again, 'avin' a bit didn't seem such an 'orrible thing t'do."

"All right. Let's not talk about it any more today. But I do insist that you speak to Doreen." She was careful to honour the confidence shared with Billy's wife. "If I have noticed changes in you, then I am sure she has. I urge you to speak to her and see what she says about what I've suggested."

"Aw, blimey, Miss, you don't know my Doreen. She's one of the best, but she can be as tough as old boots."

"Tough with a heart of gold, I suspect, Billy. Speak to her, please."

"Awright, I will, Miss."

Maisie felt a weight lifted from her shoulders. Her first challenge of the day was over.

Remembering Maurice's advice, she knew that Billy should be allowed time to regain his balance, now that his burden of secrecy had been lifted.

Now she had to concentrate on the Waite case. "I've quite a lot to tell you about my visit to Kent," said Maisie. "We'll need to get cracking with the pencils today. Charlotte *is* at Camden Abbey. At least I have performed the most important part of the Waite assignment. She has been located and she is safe."

Maisie wondered if she should show Billy what she had collected from the homes of Lydia Fisher and Philippa Sedgewick. Though she would never have asked him, she was sure that when she was an apprentice, Maurice had kept certain things to himself, as if in sharing a find before he felt that the time for revelation had come, he diminished its power. Maisie did not want to share what she had found until she could be sure of its significance.

"I want to speak to Magnus Fisher," said Maisie. "The police are sniffing around, looking into his past, who he's been seen with, and when. I believe he's a suspect in the murder of his wife, Lydia, so if I am to see him, then it must be soon."

"Won't D. I. Stratton wonder what you're up to? I mean, 'e's bound to find out that you've spoken to Fisher."

"That's true, but he also knows that I have been working on a missing-person case, and that Lydia Fisher may have had relevant information." Maisie was thoughtful. "Yes, I'll telephone Fisher now. Billy, what's the number at the Cheyne Mews house?"

Billy passed his notebook to Maisie, who placed the call.

The maid answered the telephone. "The Fisher residence."

Maisie smiled upon identifying the young maid's voice. "Oh good morning. It's Miss Dobbs here. How are you now?"

The maid warmed. "Oh, Ma'am. Thank you very much for asking, I'm sure. I'm getting over it all, though there've been a lot of people coming and going."

"I'm sure there have. Now then, may I speak to Mr Magnus Fisher, please?"

"I'm afraid he is not in residence, Ma'am. I could take a message."

"Do you know where he is? I haven't had a chance to convey my condolences yet."

"Oh, yes, of course, Ma'am. Mr Fisher is at the Savoy."

"The Savoy? Thank you."

"My, my, that was a little too easy," Maisie remarked to Billy as she replaced the receiver. "He's at the the Savoy Hotel, if you please."

"Well, 'e's not wastin' any time, is 'e?"

"It's a strange choice if he wants a measure of privacy, but on the other hand, the staff at the Savoy can keep the press at bay, which they'll need to do if the maid keeps giving out his whereabouts."

Maisie picked up the receiver again and placed a call to the hotel. She was surprised when she was connected.

"Magnus Fisher."

"Oh, Mr Fisher, I am surprised you were located so promptly."

"I was at the desk. Who is this?"

"My name is Maisie Dobbs. First of all, please accept my condolences for your loss."

"What's this about?"

"Mr Fisher, I am an investigator. I can say little until we meet in person. However, I am currently working on a case that may involve your late wife. I wonder if you might be able to meet me this morning?"

"Are you working with the police?"

"No."

"Well, you've aroused my curiosity. However, the police are keeping me very much in their sights. I'm currently unable to travel outside London. Where and when do you want to meet?"

"Let's say" – Maisie consulted her watch – "in about an hour. Meet me on the Embankment, by Cleopatra's Needle. I'll be wearing a navy blue coat and a blue hat. Oh, and I wear spectacles, Mr Fisher."

"See you in an hour, Miss Dobbs."

"Thank you, Mr Fisher."

"Putting on the fake specs again, Miss?"

Maisie reached into the top drawer of her desk and brought out a pewter case, which she opened, and then placed a pair of tortoiseshell spectacles on her nose.

"Yes, Billy. I've always found this one small change in appearance to be a useful tool. If a policeman follows Fisher and then makes a note of my description, he will most definitely remember the spectacles. And Stratton knows I do not require help with my vision."

"You sure Fisher is safe? I mean, look 'ow the weather's turned again, and if it's miserable, there won't be many people walking along by the water. That man could push you in, and no one would be any the wiser. After all, 'e could be –"

"The killer? Don't worry, Billy. You just continue working on the case map. Here are my index cards from this past two days." Maisie reached for her coat. "I'll take the underground – should be back by twelve."

"Right you are, Miss."

Maisie walked towards Warren Street station, thinking that the time alone in the office, and the task of adding more depth of information to the case map, would allow Billy to compose himself, now that his secret was out in the open. Though he might feel apprehensive, he was also free from the burden of guilt that had dragged at his spirit.

Maisie waved briefly to Jack Barker, the newspaper vendor, before going down to the trains. She travelled on the Northern Line to Embankment. The air was damp and cold as she left the station and walked down towards the Thames. A drizzle that was not quite rain, yet more than a mist, dulled the day, forcing some passers-by to use umbrellas. Maisie pulled up her collar, quickly rubbed a handkerchief across the spectacles and turned left to walk along the Embankment towards Cleopatra's Needle. The pavement beneath her feet was wet and slippery and the Thames was a dirty grey. The river air smelled of smoke and rotting tidal debris.

She reached the meeting place and consulted her watch. It was ten o'clock, exactly forty-five minutes since she had ended her telephone conversation with Fisher.

"Miss Dobbs?"

Maisie swung around. The man before her was about five feet eleven inches tall, broad shouldered and heavyset, though he did not appear to carry excess weight. He wore black trousers, a tan mackintosh and a brown hat with a beige band. She could see that under the mackintosh he wore a shirt and woollen pullover, but no tie. His face was partially obscured by an umbrella.

"Yes. Mr Fisher?"

Magnus Fisher moved the umbrella slightly to one side. He nodded.

"So where do you suggest we talk? Hardly a day for sitting on a bench on the Embankment and watching the dirty old river go by, is it?"

"Let's walk towards Temple station, Mr Fisher. We can speak as we go. Were you followed?"

Magnus Fisher looked around. They were quite alone.

"No. I slipped out of the staff entrance and then came down Villiers Street. The police know where I am and that I always come back. It's been like a game of cat and mouse, only we tip hats to each other." He turned to Maisie. "What's this all about?"

Maisie set a pace that was businesslike and deliberate. "I am investigating the case of a missing woman on behalf of her family. I believe she was a friend of your wife."

"And how can I help you? I spend most of my time out of the country, so I am not well acquainted with my wife's friends."

"May I assume we can speak in confidence, Mr Fisher?"

The man shrugged. "Of course. At least this chat of ours will take my mind off whatever the police are cooking up for me."

"Were you acquainted with Charlotte Waite?"

Fisher began to laugh. "Oh, the Waite woman. Yes, I knew Charlotte years ago, and yes, she and Lydia kept in touch."

"Where and when did you meet?"

"Just before the war broke out I was in Switzerland, mountain-eering with some chums. Lydia and Charlotte, being the daughters of poor boys made good, were at a second-rank finishing school there. We met at one of those yodel-odel-odel matinee social events."

"So you knew Lydia, Charlotte, and their other friends as well?"

172

"Yes. There were four of them in their little group. Lydia, Charlotte, Philippa, and wispy little Rosamund. I expect you know that Philippa is also dead. That's why they think it's me. Because I met up with Philippa on a couple of occasions when I was back in the country."

"I see." Maisie would return to Philippa Sedgewick later. First she wanted to learn how well Fisher had known each woman. "Did you see the girls in this group often in those days, Mr Fisher?"

Fisher held the umbrella between them, but put out his hand to feel the air.

"Might as well put this away." He put down the umbrella, and continued. "All right, I confess, my friends and I wooed all of them." Fisher sighed. "Look, Miss Dobbs, we were three young men in Europe, unchaperoned, meeting four young women who, it seemed, managed to lose *their* chaperone at every opportunity. What do you think? I courted every one of them. Charlotte was a bit too spoiled for me, frankly. Too many airs and graces. Rosie – not my type, I'm afraid. She was the one who always feared they'd be caught." Fisher laughed again in a manner that Maisie found distasteful. "Philippa fell in love with me, but she got on my nerves. I was twenty-two with the world at my feet – literally – so the last thing I wanted was a weeping willow at my door. I'm afraid I broke her heart."

Maisie remembered the weeping willow at the side of the Sedgewick house, and Philippa's almost secret haven behind the fronds of yellow leaves.

"And Lydia?"

"Lydia was the most fun. A good time was always had by all when Lydia was around, in those days anyway."

"When did you marry?"

"We met again after the war."

"Had you been in France?"

Fisher laughed. "Oh God, no. I joined an expedition to South America in May 1914. I'd tried to join Shackleton's little joy ride to Antarctica. Just as well I didn't, isn't it? They went through hell in the ice, then when they got back no one wanted to know about them. While they were trying to keep warm, I was poking around in ruined temples and swatting at flies. I came back in 1919 with no money, but I did have some good stories that didn't include trenches."

Maisie checked herself. Though the conversation was necessary, and Fisher was clearly enjoying her attention, she detested his attitude.

"I engineered contact with Lydia again; by that time she had come into her inheritance. We were married within the year." Fisher was silent and suddenly thoughtful. "Look, Miss Dobbs, I'll be honest with you: having a wife with money was attractive to me. I knew that if we were married, I could travel and enjoy a certain freedom that would be impossible otherwise. But I also thought it would be more fun than it turned out to be."

"What do you mean?"

Fisher kicked at a pebble on the pavement. "By the time I returned, it was clear that Lydia enjoyed a drink. I couldn't remember her touching any more than a half glass of glühwein in Switzerland, but in the interim she had obviously taken to wine by the bottle. I didn't realize how serious it was at first, but later it was a relief when a new expedition came along. Off I went at a dash. As time went on she acquired a taste for those fashionable new cocktails. Now, I like a drink myself, but this was beyond the pale. I tried to get in contact with her old friends for advice and help, but they'd lost touch. Lydia never said anything definite, but I think they had argued before the end of the war. Probably about Lydia's drinking. I did meet Philippa a couple of times in the weeks before she was murdered, as I said, but, frankly, she wasn't very helpful. I wanted her to speak to Lydia, try to get her to dry out."

"And did they meet?"

"No. Philippa said she would, then bagged out. I have to admit, I all but lost my temper. I mean, to let a silly little row get in the way. Women!" He shook his head. "Anyway, my pleas were met with a very cowardly 'You don't understand.' By that time, of course, our marriage had fallen apart completely. If you must know, I clung to the money, and Lydia clung to the nearest bottle. Apparently she even invited some Cockney tyke up to the house for a drink the evening she was killed. I've heard he's off the hook, though. Probably the man I saw when I went in to get my luggage. By the way – I'm not telling you anything I haven't already told the police."

Maisie nodded and continued. "You were at the house on the day your wife died?"

"For about five minutes. Lydia was in her cups, so I left again pretty sharpish, taking my belongings with me. The marriage was over."

"I see." Maisie gave nothing away about Billy's visit, and paused before her next question to Fisher. "And you are sure you never saw Charlotte Waite after Switzerland?"

"No. The others didn't even come to our wedding. Mind you, I don't actually know if they were invited. I just smiled and said 'Thank you' throughout the whole thing."

"And did your wife ever say anything about Charlotte?"

"Oh, I think she might have come to the house, and Lydia mentioned that she was kept on a close rein by her father. Absurd situation, if ever there was one. I cannot wait until they find the murderer and I can get back to Africa – or anywhere else as far away from this freezing miserable place as possible!"

They crossed the road to Temple station. "And you're sure there's nothing more you can tell me about Charlotte Waite, Mr Fisher?"

Magnus Fisher shook his head. "No. Nothing. With Stratton and his bulldog, the slobbering Caldwell, at my heels, my concern is self-preservation at the moment, Miss Dobbs."

"Thank you, Mr Fisher."

"Mind you, there is one thing."

"Yes, Mr Fisher?"

"Won't you have supper with me, as soon as the police are off my back?"

Maisie's eyes opened wide, so that even behind her spectacles her indignation was obvious. "Thank you for the invitation, but I think *not*, Mr Fisher. In fact, some time spent in mourning might not do you any harm at all."

And though he had just given Maisie a considerable amount of information to contemplate, she inclined her head curtly and left Magnus Fisher standing outside Temple underground.

To cool her temper Maisie walked briskly towards the Strand, where she turned left, making her way to Southam Street and Covent Garden.

"The cheek of it!" she muttered under her breath. "And his wife's body isn't yet cold!" But though she found him to be quite detestable, Fisher had not emanated an air of menace. She doubted if he cared enough about anything, even money, to kill for it.

Walking through the market, which was less frenetic now that the morning's business was done, soothed Maisie. It reminded her of her father, who would sometimes bring her to the market with him early in the morning when she was a child. She would laugh at porters moving to and fro with six, seven, eight, or ten round baskets of fruit and vegetables perched on their heads, and the air was always sweetly salty with the smell of sweating horses pulling heavy carts.

She descended into the depths of Covent Garden underground, taking the Piccadilly Line to Leicester Square, then the Northern Line to Warren Street, where she emerged.

"Morning, Miss Dobbs. In a rush today?" Jack Barker doffed his cap as Maisie walked quickly past him.

"Always busy, Mr Barker."

Maisie slammed the door behind her, causing Billy to jump.

"Blimey, Miss! Gawd, you scared the daylights out of me."

"I'm sorry, Billy. I've just met Magnus Fisher. Not the most savoury person in the world though he was useful." Maisie removed her coat and walked over to the table where Billy was working. She placed several more index cards on the table.

"I jotted these down while I was on the train."

Billy began to read. "Oh, so –"

A sudden thud on the window made Maisie and Billy start. Maisie gasped and held her hand to her chest.

"What the –"

"Stupid bloomin' pigeon!"

"Pigeon?"

Billy walked over to the window. "Not to worry. 'E didn't top 'is self. Probably flyin' around with a bit of a bump on 'is 'ead though. Stupid bird."

"Was it a pigeon, then, Billy?"

"Certainly was, Miss. They do that sometimes, fly into windows."

"Well, I hope that doesn't happen too often."

"My old Mum would've been goin' to pieces if she'd been 'ere. Always said that a bird in the 'ouse, or tryin' to get inside, came with a message from the dead."

"Oh, just what I wanted to hear!"

"Nah, Miss, nothing to worry about. Old wives' tale, it is. Me, well I can't stand birds. Hate the bloomin' things, ever since the war."

The telephone began to ring, and Billy walked over to Maisie's desk.

"Billy – why since the –" Maisie stopped speaking as Billy picked up the receiver.

"Fitzroy f –" Billy was interrupted while trying to give the telephone number. "Yes, sir. Oh, that is good news, sir. Yes, I'll put her on." Billy cupped his hand over the receiver.

"Who is it, Billy?"

"It's that Detective Inspector Stratton. All pleased with 'imself. They've just arrested the feller who murdered them women."

Maisie took the receiver, greeted Stratton, and listened carefully, punctuating his news with "Really?" and "I see" along with "Very good!" and "But –" before endeavouring to deliver her final comment.

"Well, Inspector, I must offer congratulations, however, I do feel —"

There was an interruption, during which Maisie ran her fingers through tendrils of black hair that had once again escaped the pins securing her tresses in an otherwise neat chignon. Billy leaned over the case map while listening to Maisie's half of the conversation.

"That would be lovely, Inspector. Tomorrow? Yes. All right. Schmidt's at noon. Of course. Yes. I look forward to it."

Maisie replaced the receiver and returned to the table near the window. She took up a pencil, which she tapped on the paper.

"So, good news, eh, Miss?"

"I suppose you could call it that."

"Is there anything wrong?"

Maisie turned to Billy. "Nothing wrong, really."

"Phew. I bet a few women will answer their doors a little easier for that news, don't you?"

"Perhaps, Billy."

"Well, who is it? Anyone we know?"

"They have just arrested Magnus Fisher at his hotel. I only left him just over an hour ago. Stratton could not disclose details of the evidence. And by the way, Billy, keep quiet about this, as news hasn't reached the press yet. Stratton said that there was a witness to Fisher entering the Cheyne Mews house on the evening of his wife's death, and that he'd been having an affair with Philippa Sedgewick." Maisie clasped her hands and rested her lips against her knuckles.

"Whew, would you believe it?" Billy noticed Maisie's furrowed brow. "It sounded like you 'ad a few 'ard words with ol' Stratton."

"I wouldn't say 'hard,' Billy, but I did try to caution him."

"Caution 'im? Why?"

Maisie looked at Billy, her midnight blue eyes piercing through his puzzlement.

"Because, Billy, in my opinion Detective Inspector Stratton has arrested a man who is innocent of the crime of murder."

14

MAISIE MADE her way along Charlotte Street towards Schmidt's. The day was once again changeable and brisk, so she wore her mackintosh over the new black dress. She had changed three times before leaving the house this morning, considering not only lunch with Detective Inspector Stratton but the meeting that afternoon with Joseph Waite. As she dressed she was aware of a feeling in her stomach and legs that she attributed to anxiety. Though she looked forward to seeing Stratton, she was disappointed at the peremptory way in which he had brought the case of the murdered women to a close. She felt that a grave error had been made. Was this the source of the physical sensations that seemed to render her temporarily dizzy on two occasions before she left the house?

Now, as she walked along the grey flagstones, heat seemed to rise up through her body. She felt faint. She quickly turned into a side street and leaned against a brick wall for support. As she breathed deeply, her eyes closed, Maisie hoped that no one would attempt to inquire after her health, or to assist her. *I feel as if my foundations have been rocked*, thought Maisie. She opened her eyes and gasped, for it seemed that her surroundings *had* changed, although they remained the same. As she tried to focus her gaze, it was as if she were looking at a picture that had been hung incorrectly, a picture that she could not quite set straight. Up a bit . . . no, down a bit . . . to the left . . . too much, just a fraction right . . . And as she continued to look, the picture changed, and now she saw the Groom's Cottage at Chelstone. Then it vanished.

Regaining her composure, Maisie stood away from the wall,

keeping one hand outstretched, touching the bricks. As confidence in her stability returned, she walked slowly into Charlotte Street. Maisie brushed off the episode, telling herself that it served her right for skipping breakfast. Frankie Dobbs would have had something to say about that! "Breakfast, my girl, is the most important meal of the day. You know what they say, Maisie: 'Breakfast like a king, lunch like a lord, and dine like a pauper.' Key to bein' as fit as a fiddle, is that." But as she saw Stratton in the distance, waiting for her outside Schmidt's, Maisie decided to telephone Chelstone after luncheon. Perhaps the foal had been born by now. Perhaps . . .

<hr />

Maisie poked a fork into the rich German sausage, which was served with cabbage and potatoes.

"Miss Dobbs, I'm glad to be away from the Yard this afternoon, if only for an hour," said Stratton. "Since news of the arrest appeared in the newspapers, we've been deluged. Of course, I give Caldwell credit for inserting the final piece of the jigsaw puzzle."

Maisie continued to clutch her knife and fork, but she could not eat. "Inspector Stratton, I think you – and Sergeant Caldwell – are mistaken."

Stratton leaned back in his chair. "Miss Dobbs, I know that you have certain skills in this field."

"Thank you Inspector. It's just that" – Maisie set down her cutlery on her plate – "I think there has been a rush to judgment."

Stratton straightened his tie. "Look, if you've evidence that I am not aware of . . . ?"

Maisie considered the white linen handkerchief and asked herself whether the delicate items held within could be termed "evidence". But evidence of what? She had made an assessment of Fisher's character based on a single interview, of Philippa Sedgewick's on the word of her husband. The police case against Fisher was based on concrete fact.

"No, Inspector. I have nothing tangible."

Stratton sighed. "I respect your work, Miss Dobbs. But we are all wrong at times, and this time the evidence points to Fisher. Even if he were not having an affair with the Sedgewick woman, and his communication with her *was* regarding his wife as he claims, he had been seen with her on several occasions. We believe that the Sedgewick woman knew he was after his wife's money so she represented a risk to him. And we know, Miss Dobbs, that the mind of the killer may not be rooted in reality. They think they can get away with it. In Fisher's case he knew what he wanted — ultimately the money — and he thought he could take it once his wife was dead, and then leave the country."

"But the method —"

Stratton raised his right hand before taking up his knife again.

"Fisher has no shortage of tools, in view of his work, which seems to be something between archaeologist, raconteur and inveterate gambler. He was always in debt to someone somewhere, and Mrs Fisher was an heiress. He stood to inherit the lot at her death."

"Has Spilsbury positively identified the weapon?"

Stratton cut into the thick sausage on his plate and speared a piece on his fork, along with some red cabbage.

"Yes. The bayonet from a short-barrel Lee Enfield rifle. Standard issue in the war. And — surprise, surprise — something that Fisher kept among the tools I just mentioned. Bit of a cheek, considering he was nowhere near the battlefield. Of course his story is that he has several items that are not usually employed by archaeologists, but he uses them for the *ooh-ahh* effect from the audience of fearless travellers that accompany him. According to Fisher, poking around a pile of old bones in the sand with the tip of a bayonet keeps the intrepid followers happy and gives them something to talk about at the dinner table when they get back to Britain. The evidence against him is strong. I'm sure we will have a confession soon."

Maisie, who had barely touched her food, could not face another bite. "Inspector, I have the impression that you are more than usually intent on securing a conviction."

Stratton tried not to reveal his exasperation.

"The man killed his wife, Miss Dobbs. And he killed another man's wife. He is a murderer, and he should hang for it!"

Maisie wondered if he was allowing his personal history to affect the outcome of this case. After all, Stratton, like John Sedgewick, was a man who had lost his wife.

Stratton settled the bill.

"Thank you for lunch, Inspector Stratton."

"You are most welcome, Miss Dobbs. Indeed, I hope you are successful, though I do wish you would try to avoid becoming involved in investigations that should have been referred to the police."

"That is my client's choice. It seems to me that such involvement would have represented a waste of police time."

Stratton ran his fingers around the brim of his hat before placing it on his head. "Perhaps we could meet again for lunch, or supper?"

"When we have both completed work on our respective cases, Inspector, certainly."

Stratton tipped his hat. "Until then, Miss Dobbs."

Maisie smiled and inclined her head. "Until then, Inspector." She made one last effort. "Inspector, I urge you to go back over the evidence that has led to Fisher's arrest. You know better than to be pressured by the public's wish to see a suspect behind bars. More time is needed, Inspector."

"We must agree to disagree, Miss Dobbs. Good-bye."

As she made her way back to Fitzroy Square, Maisie admonished herself for alienating Stratton. Then, reconsidering, she drew back her shoulders and set forth at a brisk walk. No, she thought. He's wrong. They've got the wrong man. And I'll prove it!

As Maisie lifted her head, she saw a flash of gold in the distance, over the heads that bobbed to and fro past her. It was Billy's familiar shock of hair. He was walking – no, running – in her direction.

"Billy," she yelled, "Walk! Don't run! Walk!"

Still he came towards her in an ungainly stumbling lope that was more than a walk but not quite a run, as if one side of his body were intent on speed that the other simply could not match. Maisie in turn ran to him so that those observing the scene might have thought them lovers who had been separated by distance and time.

"Billy, Billy, what is it? Take a deep breath, calm down, calm down."

Billy gasped for breath. "Down 'ere, Miss. Let's get off the street." Billy jerked his head to the right, towards a side street.

"Right. A deep breath, Billy, a deep breath."

Billy fought for air, his gas-damaged lungs heaving against his ribcage so that Maisie could see the steep rise and fall of his chest. He brought his chin down as if to retain more of the life-giving air that his body craved. "Miss . . . I thought I'd never find you . . . that you might've gone off with Stratton."

"What's happened, Billy? What's happened?" As she clutched at the cloth of Billy's overcoat, knowledge flooded Maisie. "It's my father, isn't it, Billy? It's Dad?"

"Yes, Miss. Got to get you to Chelstone. 'E's alright, comfortable, apparently."

"What's *happened*?"

"Miss, stop. It's alright, alright. Listen to me. It was an accident, with the 'orse this mornin'. Word just came from Mr Carter. The mare was 'avin' trouble, so Mr Dobbs 'ad set up the ropes, you know."

"I know what they do, Billy." Maisie was thinking clearly now, and began to walk into Charlotte Street, Billy limping behind her.

"Well, anyway, something 'appened and 'e slipped, then something else 'appened and 'e got knocked out cold. Rushed to the 'ospital in Pembury, 'e was, for X-rays. Bad old do at 'is age."

"I want you to telephone the Waite residence. Cancel our appointment."

"Miss, you ain't thinkin' of goin' on yer own, are yer? Not drivin' all that way, bein' as you're not —"

"Not what, Billy?" Maisie stopped, her eyes flashing at Billy. Yet

183

as she looked at him, rivulets of perspiration oozing from his forehead and running across his cheekbones, tears sprang into the corners of her eyes. "I'm sorry. Thank you."

"'E'll be alright, you'll see. Strong as 'ouses, your dad is, Miss. But I reckon I'd better come with you, Miss."

"No, I haven't the time to wait while you go to Whitechapel, and you can't leave without letting your wife know."

"She'll be alright, Miss. I can get on the dog'n'bone to the shop up the street. They just 'ad one put in. They'll run along to 'er wiv a message."

Maisie shook her head. "I'm going alone. I need you here. There's business to take care of. Have a rest, a cup of tea, and look after my business for me, Billy."

"Yes, Miss."

Maisie started the motor car as he closed the door for her.

"Oh, and Billy, your nose is bleeding again. And I'll tell you now Billy Beale, that if I ever learn that you are at that stuff again, I will box your ears for you!"

Billy watched Maisie screech into Warren Street on her way to Kent, knowing that she would push the MG to maximum speed whether on a London street or along a country lane.

> Faster than fairies, faster than witches,
> Bridges and houses, hedges and ditches;
> And charging along like troops in a battle . . .

It had been Maisie's favourite poem as a child, when her mother would set the small, dark-haired girl on her knee, then rhythmically recite the verse, tapping her foot so that Maisie felt propelled forward by the momentum of movement, imagining that she really was in a railway carriage.

> All of the sights of the hill and the plain
> Fly as thick as the driving rain . . .

Pressing the MG as fast as it would go, Maisie sped towards Pembury. Rain was now coming down in thick icicle-like slants across the windscreen. As she moved closer to see the road, wiping condensation from the glass with the back of her hand, her heart was beating furiously against her chest. And still the poem echoed in her mind.

> Here is a child who clambers and scrambles,
> All by himself and gathering brambles . . .

And in her mind's eye Maisie saw the small kitchen at the terraced house in Lambeth where she had spent the years before her mother's passing. She looked again into the kind, sparkling eyes, then over to the stove, where her father leaned against the wall while listening to his wife and his girl laughing together. So long ago; it was so long ago.

> Here is a cart run away in the road
> Lumping along with a man and a load;
> And here is a mill and there is a river;
> Each a glimpse and gone forever!

Her mother was gone forever, Simon was gone forever. What if her father was lost too? Maisie cried out as she whirled through Tonbridge and on towards her destination.

Swinging in along the broad driveway, Maisie saw the large brick-built hospital in front of her, the tall chimney at the far side belching smoke. She remembered passing the hospital in an earlier time, when her companion had told her that if the chimney was smoking it meant that amputated limbs were being burned. Maisie had rolled her eyes, sure that she was being teased. But now the chimney loomed over the hospital like an evil genie who would grant no wishes. She parked the motor car quickly and ran towards the main building.

"I'm looking for Mr Francis Dobbs. He was brought in this morning, injured. Where is he?"

The uniformed porter was clearly used to dealing with the emotions of breathless relatives, but at the same time he would not be rushed.

"Let me see." He ran his finger down a list of names. But Maisie could not wait, and snatched the clipboard, scanning the names for her father.

"Ward 2B. Where is that? Where can I find him?"

"Easy up, Miss. Visiting time's over, you know." The porter reclaimed his clipboard.

"Just tell me where to find him!"

"All right, all right. Keep your hair on! Now then, here you go."

The porter stepped from his office and directed Maisie with his hand. She thanked him, then ran towards the staircase.

They must have made all these hospitals the same. Maisie recognized the building though she had never set foot within its walls before. The tiled corridors, disinfectant-smelling staircase, long wards and iron-framed beds were all so reminiscent of the London Hospital in Whitechapel, where she had enlisted for VAD service in 1915.

She entered the cloister-like ward, with two lines of beds facing one another, not even one eighth of an inch out of place. She knew that each day the nurses would go along the ward with a length of string and a yardstick, ensuring that all beds were positioned precisely, so that during her rounds Matron would see a ward that completely adhered to her high standards of order. Not one patient, nurse, bed or bottle would be anywhere but where Matron expected them to be. Amid this order, as the slowly setting late-afternoon sun glanced off the ward's cream-painted walls, Maisie searched for her father.

"Follow me, Miss Dobbs," instructed the Staff Nurse, who checked the watch pinned to her uniform in the same way that Maisie still consulted her own watch every day. "He's comfortable, though not yet recognizing anyone."

"You mean he's in a coma?"

"Doctor expects him to be much better tomorrow. The other

gentleman hasn't left his side. Allowed to stay on doctor's orders."
The nurse whispered as they moved along the ward, to a bed set
apart from the others, with screens pulled around to ensure privacy
so that other patients would not see the man who lay unconscious.

"What other gentleman?"

"The older gentleman. The doctor."

"Ah, I see," replied Maisie, relieved that Maurice Blanche was
here.

The nurse pulled back the screens. Tears welled up in Maisie's
eyes as she quickly went to her father's bedside and took his hand
in hers. She nodded at Maurice, who smiled but did not move
towards her.

Leaning over her father's body, which was covered with a sheet
and standard-issue green hospital blanket, Maisie rubbed her father's
veined hands as if the warmth she generated might cause him to
wake. She reached across to touch his forehead, then his cheek. A
thick white bandage had been bound around his head, and Maisie
could see dried blood where a deep wound had been tended.
Looking down at his body, she saw a small frame over his legs.
Fracture? Remembering the smoking chimney, she hoped so.

"I'm glad you're here, Maurice. How did you manage to be
allowed to stay?"

"I informed the ward sister that I was a doctor, so I was allowed
to remain. Apparently, they are a bit short staffed and we both
thought it best that your father be attended at all times."

"You must be tired, but thank you, thank you so much." Maisie
continued to massage her father's hands.

"Those of us who have reached our more mature years know the
value of a nap, Maisie, and we can indulge ourselves without the
comfort of pillow or bed."

"Tell me what happened, Maurice."

"The mare was experiencing some difficulty. According to your
father, she was presenting incorrectly. Your father instructed Lady
Rowan to summon the vet. Of course he was out on a farm somewhere. It's lambing season, as you know. In the meantime your

187

father was following all recognized procedures and had requested a length of rope to manoeuvre the foal into a better position for the birth. Lady Rowan was there, as were two of the farmworkers. From what I understand, your father lost his footing on hay that had become damp and soiled, and fell awkwardly. His head connected with the stone floor, which is bad enough, but a heavy implement that one of the farmworkers had left standing against the stall fell and struck your father."

"When did this happen?"

"This morning, about half past nine or so. I came as soon as I was summoned, tended his immediate wounds, then deferred to Dr Miles from the village, who arrived straightaway, followed by the vet. Your father was brought here immediately."

Maisie watched the rise and fall of her father's chest beneath the white and blue stripes of hospital-issue pyjamas. She had only ever seen her father in his old corduroy trousers, a collarless shirt, waist-coat, and somewhat flamboyant neckerchief. Though a country groom since the war, on a working day he still looked more like a London costermonger, ready to sell vegetables from his horse and cart. But now he was pale and silent.

"Will he be all right?"

"The doctor thinks that the loss of consciousness is temporary, that he'll be with us soon enough."

"Oh God, I hope he's right." Maisie looked at her hands, now entwined with her father's. Silence seeped into the space between Maisie and her former teacher and mentor. She knew that he was watching her, that he was asking questions silently, questions that no doubt he was waiting to put to her in words.

"Maisie?"

"Yes, Maurice? I think you want to ask me something, don't you?"

"Indeed, yes." Maurice leaned forward. "Tell me, what is at the heart of the division between yourself and your father? You visit rarely, though when you do you are pleased to see him. And though there is conversation between father and daughter, I see none of the old camaraderie, the old 'connection' in your relationship. You were once so very close."

Maisie nodded. "He's always been so strong, never ill. I thought nothing could stop him, ever."

"Not like illness stopped your mother, or injury stopped Simon?"

"Yes." Maisie brought her attention back to her father's hands. "I don't know how it started, but it's not all my fault, you know!"

Blanche looked up intently. "Since our very early days together, when you were barely out of childhood, I can safely say that I do not think I have ever heard you *sound* like a child until now. You sound quite petulant, my dear."

Maisie sighed. "It's Dad, too. He seems to be drawing back from me. I don't know what came first, my work keeping me in London, even at weekends, or my father always finding jobs to do. He's pre-occupied with other things when I visit. Of course he loves me, and there's always a warm welcome, but then there's . . . nothing. It's as if seeing me is troublesome to him. As if I'm not part of him anymore."

Maurice said nothing for a while, then asked, "Have you given it much thought?"

"Of course I've thought about it, but then I just put it out of my mind. I suppose I keep hoping that I'm imagining it, that he's just immersed in Lady Rowan's ambition to raise a Derby winner, or that I'm too caught up in a case."

"But if you had to guess, if you brought your intuition into play, what would you say – truly – is causing the change?"

"I . . . I don't really know."

"Oh, Maisie, I think you do know. Come on, my dear, we have worked together for too long, you and I. I have seen you grow, seen you strive, seen you wounded, seen you in love, and I have seen you grieve. I know when you are evading the truth. Tell me what you *think*."

Kneading her father's hands, she spoke quietly. "I think it has to do with my mother. I remind him of her, you see. I have her eyes,

189

her hair – even these." She pulled at a tendril of hair, then pushed it back into the chignon. "In just a few years I'll be the same age as she was when she first became ill, and I look just like her. He adored her, Maurice. I think he only kept going because of me. The fact is that he can't see me without seeing her, though I'm not her. I'm different."

Maurice nodded. "The pain of being reminded is a sharp sword. But there's more, isn't there?"

"Yes. Yes, I suppose there is." Maisie swallowed deeply. "He sent me away, didn't he? To Ebury Place. And I know, I know, it all worked out for the best, and I wouldn't be where I am today if he hadn't, but –"

"But you can't forget."

"No."

"And what of forgiveness?"

"I love my father, Maurice."

"No one is questioning your love. I ask again: what of forgiveness?"

"I suppose . . . yes, I suppose some resentment still lingers. When I think about it, even though we made up and he would do anything for me. I . . . I suppose I am still upset, in a deep part of me, right in here." Maisie placed her hand against her ribs.

Silence filtered into the air around them once again, drowning out the echoes of Maisie's whispered confession until Maurice spoke again.

"May I make a suggestion, Maisie?"

She nodded and replied quietly, "Yes."

"You must speak with your father. Not *to* him, but *with* him. You must create a new path. You do not need me to tell you that, strong as he is, your father is not getting any younger. This accident will have weakened him, though I expect he will enjoy a full recovery. I observed you enter this ward dragging your guilt, regret, and – yes – fear with you, fear that you might have lost your chance. But you haven't lost it at all. Use your training, Maisie, your heart, your intuition and your love for your father to forge a new, even stronger, bond."

Maisie watched Maurice as he spoke.

"I feel so . . . weak, Maurice. I should have known better than to allow the situation to continue."

"*Should* have? *Should*, Maisie? Fortunately you are a human being, and it is recognizing our own fallibility that enables us to do our work." Blanche stood up from his chair and rubbed his back and neck. "Now then, it's getting late."

"Oh I'm sorry. I shouldn't have kept you."

Blanche held up his hand to silence her. "No, I wanted to remain here until you arrived. But now, I must report back to Lady Rowan. I suspect that our patient will improve with your presence."

"Thank you, Maurice."

Blanche inclined his head, and took up his coat and hat, which had been placed on the back of the chair.

"Maurice, I wonder if I might speak with you tomorrow about a case."

"Waite?"

"It's gone a bit further than that, really. I'm now convinced that the Coulsden and Cheyne Mews murders, and perhaps one more, are connected with the Waite case."

"You will need to return to Chelstone later, perhaps after doctor's rounds tomorrow morning, or before if Matron learns that you are here. Come to the Dower House when you are ready."

"Thank you." Maisie looked at her father again, then turned back to Maurice. "You know, it's strange, but I believe the murders have to do with being reminded, and remembering . . . and, now that I think about it, with forgiveness, too."

Blanche smiled and drew back the screen to leave. "I am not at all surprised. As I have said many times, my dear, each case has a way of shining a light on something we need to know about ourselves. Until tomorrow."

Maisie took Maurice's seat at her father's bedside, ready to continue the vigil until he regained consciousness. In the distance she heard a receding footfall as her mentor left the ward. She was alone with her thoughts, and though she held on to her father's hands firmly, and made a commitment to better times together in the future, she was wondering about the murdered women, and about Charlotte.

15

MAISIE OPENED her eyes as dawn was just visible through the tops of rectangular paned windows beyond the screens. How long had she slept? She moved her head to look at her father and sat up carefully so that she would not disturb him.

"Dad! Dad – you're awake!"

Frankie Dobbs forced a smile. "Been awake for a while, love. Just didn't want to unsettle you."

"Oh, Dad, I'm so glad." Maisie leaned across the bed to embrace her father, then sat back.

"And I'm glad you came, love."

"Straightaway, as soon as I heard."

Frankie squeezed his daughter's hand in his own broad palm. "To tell you the truth, for a moment I thought you were your mother. Fair took my breath away, it did, seeing you there. Thought I'd been taken, I did, and was with 'er again."

Maisie checked her father's pulse and touched his forehead with her slender fingers.

"Always checking something, my girl. Always making sure, eh?"

Father and daughter were silent for a while. Maisie knew she must use the door that Maurice had opened, in speaking of her mother.

"We don't seem to talk of Mum any more do we, Dad?"

Frankie tried to move towards Maisie, and grimaced. "No, love, we don't. Kept my memories to myself, and I s'pose you did, too."

"Oh, Dad –"

"And I was thinking, as I was watching you 'ave a kip, that we've let a few things get between us, 'aven't we?"

"I know –"

With a low screech the metal feet of the screen were pulled across the floor, and the nighttime Staff Nurse interrupted their conversation.

"I thought I heard voices. Good to see you awake, Mr Dobbs. Had us all worried there. Doctor will be along to see you soon, and Matron will have a fit if she finds you here, Miss Dobbs. I'll be going off duty directly Doctor has finished, but you'd better be off, Miss."

"Yes, I'd better. Dad, I'll be back later today, during visiting hours." Maisie reached down to kiss her father, then left the enclosure to step out into the ward. Morning sunlight was filtering in, warming patients and nurses alike.

Walking towards the exit, Maisie turned to the nurse.

"What's the prognosis?"

"Well, Miss –"

"I was a nurse myself, so I have some understanding of the situation."

"I'm not supposed to say, but I can tell you this – of course, we'll know more after Doctor sees him this morning – but he sustained a serious concussion, plus he's cracked both tibia. Not complete fractures, but something to watch all the same. I suspect he will need at least two or three months of rest, considering his age, and they will probably advise convalescence where he can receive adequate care."

"I see."

"But we'll be able to say more when you come back this afternoon. Go home, have a nice cup of tea and a good sleep. Your father needs you in tip-top health!"

━━━━

As Maisie drove, she thanked any unseen entity or power that might have had a hand in the events of the past hours, for openings that seemed to have materialized in several directions. It occurred to her that helping out with the horses in her father's absence would be a real job for Billy. He would be close enough to be guided by

Maurice, to receive instruction from Gideon Brown, and to be monitored by Andrew Dene. Her father wouldn't rest until he knew the horses were being cared for by someone he knew, and who better than another London man? If her father needed to enter a convalescent home for a month or so, perhaps All Saints' would be a good choice. Dr Andrew Dene would understand a man who spoke his own language.

Her brain was in top gear as she sped along the country lanes to Chelstone, a list of things to do growing in her mind.

> Faster than fairies, faster than witches,
> Bridges and houses, hedges and ditches;
> And charging along like troops in a battle . . .

But before she did anything, before she bathed, took nourishment, or slept, she must go to Maurice. Maisie leaned sideways towards the passenger seat and, keeping her eyes on the road, reached inside the document case to feel the linen handkerchief in which she had carefully placed the tiny items she had taken from the homes of Lydia Fisher and Philippa Sedgewick. She wanted to share her delicate clues with Maurice. She wanted his counsel.

Maisie slowed as she drove along the gravel carriage sweep leading to Chelstone Manor. As grit began to spit and crackle under the tyres, she rubbed her eyes against the onslaught of spring sunshine rising at a low angle into a clearing sky. It would be a bright but cold day. Frost-dusted daffodil heads bobbed in columns along the driveway, interspersed with bluebells and primroses. Yes, it would be a good day. Frankie Dobbs was out of the woods.

The upstairs curtains at the Dower House were still closed; Maurice was not yet up and about. Maisie felt a tinge of frustration, but she checked herself. Perhaps it was fortunate that she would have more time alone to marshal her thoughts and to anticipate questions. She missed working with Maurice, though awareness of the chasm left by his retirement was fading as she grew in skill and confidence. She manoeuvred the car into the courtyard behind the manor house, the domain of George, the Comptons' chauffeur.

"Mornin', Miss." George wiped his hands on a clean white cloth and walked across the flagstones towards Maisie. "Blimey O'Reilly, what've you been doin' with that little motor of yours? Racin' 'er at Brooklands? I'd better get the full kit out this mornin'. You'll need oil, a good cleaning under the bonnet, to say nothing of 'er paintwork. And look at them tyres!"

"You're the man for the job, George!"

"Actually, Miss, it'll be nice to 'ave something to get me teeth into." George lifted the bonnet, then turned to Maisie again. "How's Mr Dobbs this mornin'? Better?"

"Much better, thank you. He's awake, though it might be a while before he's up on his feet."

"Fair gave us all a shock, did that. Everyone's waitin' for news."

"I'll see that the household is kept posted. Can I leave Lily with you then? I'll need her by three this afternoon – to be at Pembury by visiting time."

"*Lily*? You call a car like this 'Lily'?"

Maisie smiled, then laughed. "By three, thank you George."

"Right you are Miss. By the way, I saw 'er Ladyship walking over to the stables a little while ago."

"Oh, good. I'd better give her the latest news."

Lady Rowan was leaning on a fence surrounding the paddock adjacent to the stable where Frankie Dobbs had fallen. She seemed thoughtful as Maisie approached. The older woman's three canine companions, investigating bushes alongside, lifted their heads and greeted her with tails wagging.

"My dear girl, how is your father? I have been beside myself with worry."

"He is better Lady Rowan, much better, though I will know more this afternoon when I see his doctor."

"Your father, Maisie, may well surprise us all. I think he'll live until he's one hundred years old!" Lady Rowan looked at Maisie with more gravity as she, too, leaned on the fence to watch mare and foal together. "You will not have to worry about convalescence, Maisie. Your father's recovery is in my interests, and the costs of any necessary procedures or care –"

"Thank you, Lady Rowan."

"Good." Lady Rowan turned to the paddock. "So what do you think of him?"

Maisie watched the foal standing under the protection of his mother's head and neck. His chestnut coat shone with newborn softness, the tufted promise of a rich, thick mane standing up like a shoebrush on his long and delicate neck. The foal's legs were surprisingly straight, and as the two women watched him, Maisie could swear she detected a certain defiance in his manner.

"He's quite . . . quite the little man, isn't he?"

"Oh yes, he certainly is, and only a day old, mind you." Lady Rowan continued to regard her new project closely. "Thought I'd call him 'Francis Dobbs' Dilemma'. But no, he'll be named Chelstone Dream. Apt, don't you think? I'll call him 'Dreamer' for short."

The foal stared at them intently in return.

"You see that look, Maisie? The way he's standing?"

Maisie nodded. "Yes."

"They call that 'the look of champions', Maisie. He's the one; he'll do it for me. In three years he'll bring home the Derby for me – I know it! Can't you just see Gordon Richards atop Chelstone Dream, flying past the post at Epsom?" Lady Rowan became pensive again. "But in the meantime, what will I do without your father?"

"Ah," said Maisie. "Don't worry. I have a plan."

Lady Rowan laughed, her voice cutting through the morning quiet in such a way that the mare started, and moved her foal to the back of the paddock. "I would have put money on your having a plan, Maisie. What is it?"

"I'll tell you this evening, Lady Rowan, when I've sorted out a few details." She looked at her watch. "But I have to telephone my assistant, then I must see Maurice. May I use the telephone at the manor?"

"Of course. I shall expect to see you for supper this evening, when you can give me news of your father's progress. And I cannot wait to hear your plan!"

Maisie looked back at the foal as she made her way towards the manor house. And she could have sworn that Dreamer, the foal with the look of champions, had watched her every move.

"Billy, I'm glad I've caught you!"

"'Oldin' the fort, Miss. 'Oldin' the fort. How's Mr Dobbs?"

"Much better, thank you. Out of the woods. What happened when you cancelled our appointment with Waite?"

"Well, at the beginnin' I 'ad to give a message to 'is secretary, who then 'ad to speak to 'im. Poor woman, you'd 've thought I'd asked 'er to tell 'im that 'is shops'd all burned down. Scared of 'im, she is, scared silly."

"Billy —"

"Anyway, she went off; then Waite 'imself comes on the blower, boomin' down the line 'e was, boomin' about how 'e was Joseph Waite and that no one does this to 'im."

"Oh dear."

"Then I told 'im what the reason for you not bein' available was, and I must say, 'e drew 'is neck in a bit sharpish. Funny that, innit? Says somethin' about family comin' first, and that it was nice to know that a daughter 'onoured 'er father, and all that."

"Can he see me soon?"

"Made an appointment for Friday, sayin' that I just 'ad to let 'im know if there were any difficulties, and that you was to let 'im know if 'e could be of service. Very strange man, Miss. Very odd, that about-turn."

"He's certainly odd where family are concerned, I'll give you that." Maisie paused as she noted the details. "With a bit of luck I'll have good news for Waite. I'm going to Camden Abbey tomorrow, to talk to Charlotte."

"Sounds to me like you've got your plate full."

"My father's not allowed any visitors until late this afternoon, and probably only once a day until the doctor says anything to the contrary, so I'll be able to work on the case while I'm here."

"Right then. Dr Dene telephoned again."

"Really?"

"Yep. And it's interestin' because 'e wanted to leave a message for you about your visit to see – let me look 'ere. I tell you, Miss, I can't even read me own writin' sometimes – Mrs Thorpe's 'ousekeeper."

"What was the message?"

"Didn't say, except 'e wanted to pass on a message from 'er, that she'd like to see you again. She remembered something that might be useful."

Maisie wrote notes on an index card as she spoke to Billy, and checked her watch.

"I'll *make* time."

"Awright, Miss. Anythin' else?"

"Actually, there is. You know we spoke about your coming down to Chelstone, for a while, perhaps a month or so? And you didn't want to 'sit on your backside', I think you said?" Without pausing to allow Billy to reply, Maisie said, "Well, I've got something for you to do that's vital to me and to Lady Rowan. Billy, it's to do with Chelstone Dream, the odds-on favourite to win the Derby in 1933."

Before she was able to retreat to the Groom's Cottage, Maisie fielded inquiries about her father's health from Carter and Mrs Crawford. As she walked into her father's home, Maisie shivered. Never before had she felt a chill in the house, yet today the heavy dew outside seemed to permeate the stone walls and storm windows, creeping into each nook and cranny to claim a place.

Well, this won't do! thought Maisie as she looked around the cottage.

Her father had obviously left in a hurry to tend to the mare. An enamel teapot three-quarters filled with old cold tea sat on the table; a loaf of bread, now crusty and hard around the edges, had been roughly cut and not returned to the bread bin. The butter dish and a jar of Mrs Crawford's homemade three-fruit marmalade were open on the table, with a sticky knife set on a plate. Maisie smiled, imagining her father hurriedly drinking scalding tea, quickly spreading a doorstep-like slice of bread with marmalade, then running out to get to the stable. She set about cleaning the room before seeking the comfort of a hot bath.

She lit the fire and set two large kettles of water on the hotplate, along with a cauldron usually used for soup. She dragged a tin bathtub from a hook in the scullery and placed it on the floor in front of the stove, ready to receive the scalding water, which she would cool to stepping-in temperature with cold water from the tap. She closed the curtains, locked the doors and went to the small box-like bedroom that had once been her own. Opening a wardrobe, she wondered if she would find anything to wear. She touched garments that should have been given to the rag-and-bone man years ago. There were her clothes from university years, the cast-offs from Lady Rowan so expertly fitted for her by Mrs Crawford's dexterous needlewoman's fingers. There was the blue ball gown given her by Priscilla, her friend at Girton. As she touched the cool blue silk, she thought of Simon, of the party where they had danced the night away. Shaking off the memories, Maisie pulled out a pair of rather baggy brown trousers that had also been given her by Priscilla, at a time when women who wore trousers were considered "fast".

As soon as she had found an old pair of leather walking shoes, Maisie took a clean white collarless shirt from her father's chest of drawers, along with a pair of socks to complete her ensemble for the day. She would find an old corduroy jacket hanging up in the scullery, or she would simply wear her mackintosh while waiting for her clothes to be cleaned up at the manor. She'd not had time to pack a bag before leaving for Kent, but she could make do.

Maisie prepared her bath, opened the stove door and settled down to soak before embarking on the rest of her day. She began to soap her body, wondering what Rosamund Thorpe's housekeeper might want to speak to her about. The Old Town in Hastings housed a small community, and Maisie imagined the grieving woman remembering something, some vital piece of information, after her visit. Then, not knowing how she might contact Maisie – for she would not readily have used her former employer's telephone – Mrs Hicks would have sought out Dr Andrew Dene hoping that he might pass on a message for Maisie to see her when next in Hastings. But why did she not simply tell Dene what it was that she had remembered? Maisie suspected that the loyal housekeeper probably would consider such a disclosure tantamount to gossip. *And that would never do.* She soaped her shoulders and with a cloth allowed hot water to run across her neck. Rosamund Thorpe, Lydia Fisher and Philippa Sedgewick. Maisie saw each woman in her mind's eye. *What have you in common? Charlotte Waite, why did you run?* Four women. Four women who had known each other years ago. A coterie. A coterie of young girls on the cusp of womanhood. *What did that feel like?* Maisie closed her eyes, plunging her thoughts once again into the past. The library at Ebury Place, Girton, old clothes from Lady Rowan, the blue ball gown, Priscilla laughing as she pressed another cigarette into an ivory holder, the London Hospital . . . *France.* When she had been little more than a girl, she had served almost at the battle-front herself. Still sitting in the cooling water, Maisie allowed her thoughts to wander further. *What did you do during the war, you sheltered young women cocooned in your world of privilege, your safe little circle?*

A sharp knock at the door jolted Maisie from her reflections. Unwilling to interrupt her train of thought, she did not move, did not reach for a towel hanging over the back of a chair, did not call out 'Just a minute!' Instead, she silently waited until she heard the rustle of paper being poked under the door, and footsteps receding along the garden path. She settled back into the water for just a few more minutes, the now-blazing fire keeping her warm. *Rosamund,*

Lydia, Philippa and . . . Charlotte. What did you do in the war? And if Charlotte, too, is in danger, why does someone want you all dead?

A note had been delivered by Maurice Blanche's housekeeper, inviting Maisie to join him for breakfast. She dressed quickly, pulling on trousers, white shirt and the pair of brown leather walking shoes which, she thought, were set off quite nicely by her father's best Argyll socks. Before leaving the Groom's Cottage, Maisie took her folded linen handkerchief from the document case and slipped it into the pocket of the old jacket she had found, as predicted, hanging up in the scullery. Instead of drawing her hair back into a tidy chignon, Maisie plaited her long tresses into a loose braid so that, walking towards the manor house with her clothes folded under one arm, she caused Mrs Crawford – who was on an expedition into the far reaches of the kitchen garden – to exclaim, "Maisie Dobbs, you look five and ten all over again!"

Seeing Maisie approach, Maurice opened the door as she made her way along the path leading from the Groom's Cottage to the Dower House.

"He came round, Maurice, he came round as I was sleeping!"

Maisie ran to his side, and in the same way that Mrs Crawford was taken aback, so Maurice was reminded of the years when Maisie was his pupil, drinking eagerly from the well of knowledge he provided.

"I am so glad, so very glad. Now he will be on the mend. It's amazing how the body and mind are connected. Even when conscious thought has slipped away, the patient is aware of the healing presence of love."

"If I had that much power, Maurice, he'd walk out of there today. But, listen, there's more. We began to talk . . . together."

Maurice stood aside, holding out his arm to allow Maisie to enter his home.

"It is indeed a wondrous universal alchemy, is it not? When one's heartfelt intentions cause mountains to move."

"Well, whatever it is, I'm glad, very glad. And if it's not too selfish of me, I'd like a mite more alchemy in my work on this case. The conservatory?"

"Yes. There's eggs and bacon, if you like, and some quite delight-ful fresh rolls. They quite remind me of my childhood in Paris."

Maisie smiled, looking forward to the strong black coffee that Maurice favoured.

Teacher and pupil, master and apprentice, Maurice Blanche and Maisie Dobbs sat together in the warm, light-filled conservatory which commanded a flower-filled view across the garden to the fields beyond, as Maisie gave Maurice a full account of her work on the Charlotte Waite case, and how it had expanded to encompass the murders.

"Yes, your investigation thus far does seem to indicate that the Thorpe woman's death should be looked at more closely." Blanche leaned back in the Lloyd Loom wicker chair, watching a flight of sparrows descend on the bird table freshly laden with breadcrumbs. Maisie waited.

"An overdose for Thorpe? Followed by morphine *and* the bayonet of a Lee Enfield rifle for the other two women, you say?"

She sipped the soothing coffee but hardly touched her crusty roll, despite her realization that she hadn't eaten anything since yes-terday's lunch with Detective Inspector Stratton. She was beginning to wish she had a glass of Maurice's elderflower wine clasped in her hand. Her interrogation was beginning.

"It's as if the murderer was not satisfied with the poison alone, as if a deeper . . . emotion — yes, I think that's the right word, *emotion* — needed to be vented. Vindicated."

"Have you spoken to Mrs Thorpe's physician regarding her mental well-being? Have you completely ruled out suicide?"

"No . . . not completely. Her physician is the one who issued the death certificate. He'd concluded it was suicide. I spoke to the housekeeper, who knew her very well, and to others in the town."

"I don't doubt your instinct, but intuition must be supported by footwork. Now then, about the Sedgewick woman. You say that Fisher has been arrested on the basis of evidence linking him to Mrs Sedgewick, suggesting that they were romantically involved?"

"According to John Sedgewick, her husband, Fisher had been in touch regarding his wife's drinking, which was beyond his power to control. He also said that his wife did not want to meet Fisher, but acquiesced out of some sort of loyalty to her old friend. It's a very different relationship to the one the police have posited. I get the impression, Maurice, that – with the exception of a level of communication between Lydia and Charlotte – these women, who had once been good friends, kept well away from one another."

"And why do you think there was a division among them?"

Maisie allowed her eyes to rest on the bird table and the flurry of excitement, beaks peck-pecking for a crumb of food, peck-pecking at one another as they pressed tiny, fragile bodies onto the wooden platform.

"What do you *think*, Maisie?"

"I think that *something* happened, years ago." Maisie spoke slowly and deliberately while watching the frenzied feeding at the bird table. "Something . . . I'm not sure, but I feel . . . very much, that it's something of which they want no reminder. And seeing each other, keeping in touch, brings back the . . . *shame*."

Silence enveloped the room. Then Blanche said, "Do you have something to show me."

"Yes, I have." Maisie reached into her pocket, taking out the folded handkerchief and setting it on the table between them. "Shall I get your spectacles, Maurice? I think you'll need them."

Blanche nodded.

"Here you are." Maisie handed the lizard-skin case to Maurice, who opened it, so carefully that she could hear the almost imperceptible whine of its hinges. He took out the wire-rimmed half-moon spectacles, placed them on his nose and leaned forward to watch as Maisie unfolded the handkerchief, his chin tilted upward just slightly to improve his view.

With the tips of the thumb and forefinger of each hand, Maisie spread out the handkerchief to reveal her evidence.

Maurice looked at the opened fine linen square, then back into Maisie's eyes. They had moved into such proximity that they could feel each other's breath.

"Ah, so delicate. Nature is by far the most talented artist."

"Yes, she is, isn't she?"

"And you found one at the Fisher house and the other at the Sedgewick house?"

"I entered Lydia Fisher's house soon after her murder, and was drawn to the first, although it was almost concealed. The one at the Sedgewick house was hidden inside a book."

"Which you just happened to open, no doubt?"

"Yes."

"And the woman in Hastings? Mrs Thorpe?"

"Many weeks have passed since her death, Maurice, and Mrs Hicks has ensured that the house is immaculate for a potential buyer. I fear that if there was one, it would have been swept away by now."

"So, Maisie, what are your thoughts? What does this mean?"

"I'm not sure, but I feel that they are significant."

Like marionettes operated by the same puppeteer, Maisie and Maurice reached forward at the same time to touch the delicate perfection that lay before them: two small, white, downy feathers.

16

AFTER BREAKFAST Maisie reclaimed the MG from George – who protested that he had barely started on the paintwork – and left for Hastings, planning to be there in plenty of time to allow her to return to her father's side that afternoon. As she came over the hill into the Old Town, the sea sparkled on the horizon with sunlight reflecting on the water, making it seem as if diamonds had been sprinkled liberally on the surface. Parking outside All Saints' Convalescent Hospital, Maisie stopped for a while to admire the view and to look down at the lilliputian Old Town itself. In the distance she could hear the clinker-built fishing boats being drawn up onto the pebble beach with heavy winches, and seagulls wheeling overhead. The morning catch was late coming in.

"That sea air does you a power of good, you know!"

"Oh, Dr Dene! I didn't see you walking as I drove up the hill."

"No, you wouldn't have, I took a short-cut. The Old Town's full of nooks, crannies, twitters and secret places that only the locals know and I'm a fully fledged local now."

Andrew Dene reached to open the door for her. She saw that he had noticed her informal attire.

"I just have to let the office know I'm here; then let's go to my lair where we can discuss the two things on your mind." Dene poked his head around the door to the office. She heard his voice, then laughter among the staff before he retracted his head and led Maisie along the corridor to his "lair", which was still just as untidy.

"So: your father's convalescence and Rosamund Thorpe?"

Maisie removed her gloves. "How do you know about my father?"

Dene raised an eyebrow. "The jungle drums have been beating. *And* I had cause to speak with Maurice this morning. I know Dr Simms at Pembury who attended your father when he was brought in. Good man. All his patients make an excellent recovery. I've worked with him on several cases."

"I see."

As if reading her mind, Dene continued. "We have a first-class accident recuperation record here, Miss Dobbs. I'd be delighted to arrange for your father to be admitted upon his discharge from Pembury. I can start –" Dene leaned towards a pile of folders that wobbled precariously at his touch. Maisie instinctively reached to steady the pile.

"Don't worry, Miss Dobbs, haven't lost a file yet." He pulled a buff-coloured folder from the mountain of paperwork. "That'll tell you how much work I have to do. As I was saying, I can start the file right now and contact Dr Simms to let him know we've spoken."

"Thank you. That will be a weight off my mind."

"Good, good. It's settled, then. We can go over the admission details with the administrator as you leave." Dene made several notations on a sheet of paper, closed the folder and set it on the desk. "Now to Mrs Thorpe."

"Yes. I wonder if you could tell me something more about her, especially her demeanour in the days leading up to her death. I know she spent a good deal of time here."

"Frankly I thought she was doing quite well, especially as she was so recently a widow. But she was clearly still in mourning." Dene leaned to one side, moved another pile of folders, and looked out at the sea before turning to Maisie again. "You think she was murdered, don't you?"

Maisie's eyes registered her surprise. She had not expected to hear such speculation from Andrew Dene. "Well, actually –"

"Oh, come on, Miss Dobbs. I know Maurice, remember. I

207

know very well what you do. And Rosamund Thorpe was well liked and respected in the Old Town, even though she was an outsider."

"Do you think she killed herself, Dr Dene? Wouldn't you recognize the symptoms of the despair that precedes such an action?"

Dene was thoughtful.

"Does your silence mean there is doubt?"

"My thoughtfulness is simply that, Miss Dobbs: thoughtfulness. You see, though I think it *unlikely* that a woman such as Mrs Thorpe would take her own life, I noticed her sadness on several occasions, particularly when she was reading to veterans. Now it's a subjective observation, completely lacking in the protocols of diagnosis, but – her sadness seemed more poignant than anything I observed with other volunteers. You have to understand that among volunteers there are differing emotional responses to what they see. For example, we all know a veteran of the war when we see one on the street, whether he's an amputee, blinded, or disfigured, but when we are close to that person, in a setting like this, filled with others who are equally disabled – it's a reminder, a terrible reminder. I believe it can make people recall events and feelings that they would rather forget. Most quickly get over it and before they know where they are, they're singing 'I Don't Want To Go Into The Army' with the patients at the hospital Christmas party."

"But Mrs Thorpe?"

"She wasn't like that. Though she had a broad smile for every patient – and she particularly asked to be of assistance to those who were soldiers – she was grieving as she left after each visit. It was as if coming here, doing this volunteer work, was a sort of self-flagellation."

"Do you think she killed herself?"

"Put it like this: because of what I saw, I think she had it *in* her to reach certain depths of despair, but at the end of the day, I just can't see her actually taking her own life."

"Why?" asked Maisie.

Andrew Dene sighed. "I'm trained as a doctor of medicine. I

specialize in accidents and rehabilitation. I deal in the specifics of what is happening to the body, though I am interested in what motivates a person to become well again. I am used to fine lines, but only have a passing familiarity with the type of speculation that is clearly your bailiwick. But if I were to hazard a guess . . ."

"Yes?"

"I would say that she . . ." Andrew Dene faltered. As Maisie said nothing, Dene exhaled, and continued, "I think she felt she had a debt that had not yet been repaid. So coming here was part of that repayment, wasn't it? Don't get me wrong —" For just a moment, Maisie detected Dene's original accent breaking through. "I don't want to stick my neck out and have you take it as fact. It's just my opinion."

"Thank you, Dr Dene. I appreciate your honesty, which will be kept in absolute confidence. Now, you said that Mrs Hicks wants to see me again?"

Dene looked at his pocket watch. "She'll be at the house now. I'll telephone her to tell her you're on your way."

Andrew Dene moved several books and papers to reveal the telephone. He quickly placed a call to the Thorpe house and informed Mrs Hicks that Miss Maisie Dobbs was just leaving the hospital. Then he set down the receiver and pushed the books and papers back on top of the telephone. Maisie's eyes widened at such disarray.

"Dr Dene, please forgive me for saying this, but wouldn't it behoove you to invest in a cabinet for your files?"

"Oh no. I'd never find a thing!" he replied with an impish grin. "Look, would you be free for a spot of lunch after you've seen Mrs Hicks?"

"Well . . . visiting time at Pembury is at four, so . . . as long as I'm on my way again by one-thirtyish. I like to leave plenty of time."

"Yes, I'm sure you do. We can walk along by the net shops and perhaps have some fish and chips. There are no posh restaurants down there, it's all a bit spit and sawdust. But you'll never taste fish like it anywhere else in the world."

As Maisie parked the MG outside Rosamund Thorpe's house on the West Hill, Mrs Hicks opened the front door to greet her.

"Thank you for getting in touch, Mrs Hicks, I do appreciate it."

"Oh, Miss Dobbs, I'm only too glad to help. I had the feeling that you were acting in Mrs Thorpe's best interests, so when I remembered, I thought I'd better get in touch. Hope you don't mind me asking Dr Dene. Such a nice man." She closed the door behind Maisie and led her into the drawing room, where a teapot and two cups were set on a tray with some biscuits.

Maisie took a seat on the settee and once again removed her gloves. Despite extra clothing she still felt the cold, in her hands as much as in her feet.

Mrs Hicks poured tea for Maisie, passed her cup, then offered biscuits which Maisie declined. She would need to leave space for a hearty helping of fish and chips. "Right. I expect you'll want me to get straight to the point."

"Yes, please. It really is important that I understand why Mrs Thorpe might have taken her own life or, on the other hand, who might have wanted her dead."

"Well, as you know, I've racked my brains trying to answer the first question, and haven't had much luck with the second. Everyone thought well of Mrs Thorpe. Then I remembered a visit; years ago, it was, not long after she was married. Probably not long after the war, either. Joseph Waite –"

Maisie set her cup down on the saucer with a clatter.

"Is that tea cold, Miss?"

"No . . . no, not at all. Please continue Mrs Hicks." Reaching into her document case, she took out an index card and began to make notes.

"Well, anyway, Joseph Waite – he's the father of one of her old friends. Mind you, they hadn't seen each other for years and years, not since the war. Anyway, Mr Waite came here, big motor car and a chauffeur and all, and asked to see Mrs Thorpe. Perhaps he didn't know her married name, because he took liberties. What he actually said was, 'I'd like to see Rosie.' It was the first I knew that she used to be called Rosie, and I thought it was a bit of a cheek, calling a respectable married woman by her Christian name – in fact, *any* woman, when I come to think of it."

"Go on."

"Well, I showed him into the drawing room, then informed Mrs Thorpe that she had a caller and who he was. She was shaken, I know that. Didn't like it at all. Said, 'Thank heavens Mr Thorpe isn't here'; then,'You will keep this to yourself, won't you, Mrs Hicks?' And I never told anyone, until now."

"What happened?"

"Well, she goes into the drawing room to greet him, like the lady she was, and he was all huffy. Didn't want tea or any refreshment. Just says he wants to speak to her in private, looking across at me. So I was dismissed."

"Do you know what he came to see her about?"

"No; sorry, Miss, I don't. But he was angry, and he got her all upset, he did."

"Did you hear anything?"

Mrs Hicks sighed and tried to gather her thoughts. "Of course, at my age you forget things, but him I remember. These houses are built like fortresses on account of the wind and storms. Built for Admiral Nelson's lieutenants, they were, originally. You can't hear much through these walls. But he upset her, I do know that. And as he was leaving the room – he'd opened the door, so I heard everything – he said something . . . well, threatening, I suppose you'd call it."

"What was it?"

"He said 'You'll pay. You'll all pay one day. Mark my words, my girl, you will pay.' Then he left, slamming the front door behind him so hard I thought the house would fall down. Mind you, as it's been here this long, the likes of Joseph Waite won't hurt it now!"

Mrs Hicks was quiet for a while before speaking again, this time with less forcefulness.

"But you know what was the strangest thing?"

"What was that, Mrs Hicks?" Maisie's voice was so low it was almost a whisper.

"I came out of the dining room, where I had been arranging some flowers, when I heard the drawing room door open. I wanted to be ready to show him out. Well, he held up his hand to me, like this" – Mrs Hicks held her arm out as a London bobby might when stopping traffic – "when he'd finished speaking, to stop me from coming towards him. Then he turned away quickly. You see, Miss, he was crying. That man had tears streaming down his face. I don't know whether it was anger or sadness, or what it was. But . . . very confusing it was, what with Mrs Thorpe so upset, too."

That the control-obsessed Joseph Waite had lost his composure did not surprise Maisie, for she knew that when such people cross an emotional boundary it often leads to a breakdown. She remembered Billy's despair, and those times when she, too, had known such sadness, and as she did so, her heart ached not only for Rosamund but, strangely, for Joseph Waite. Whatever else he might have done, this was a man who had truly known sorrow.

"Did he come here again?"

"Never. And I would have known about it if he had."

"And she never took you into her confidence, about the reason for his visit?"

"No. Seemed to me like he wanted to make her as miserable as he was."

"Hmmm. Mrs Hicks, I know I've already asked you this, but I must be sure: do you really think that Mrs Thorpe's death was caused by someone else?"

The housekeeper hesitated, turning her wedding ring around on her finger repeatedly before replying.

"Yes, I do. There is some wavering in my heart. And I can't be sure because I wasn't here. But to take her own life? I do doubt it very much, very much indeed. She seemed to be on a mission to help people, especially those men who'd been to war, the ones who were just boys, wounded boys."

The clock on the mantelpiece began to strike a quarter to twelve.

"Thank you so much for your time, Mrs Hicks. You have been very helpful once again."

Mrs Hicks took a handkerchief from her pocket and dabbed her moist eyes.

Maisie stood and placed an arm around the housekeeper's shoulder. "Oh, Mrs Hicks, you must miss her very much."

"Oh, I do, Miss Dobbs. I do miss her very much. Mrs Thorpe was a lovely, kind woman, and too young to die. I haven't even had the heart to send her clothes away, like Mr Thorpe's children told me to do."

Maisie felt a sensation of touch, as if another hand had gently been placed upon her own as it lay on Mrs Hicks' shoulder. A picture of Rosamund had formed in her mind.

"Mrs Hicks, was Mrs Thorpe in mourning attire when she died?"

"Well, yes, as a matter of fact she was. Her nice black dress, very proper, yet fashionable. She wasn't a dowdy one, Mrs Thorpe, always beautifully turned out."

"Was she buried in –"

"The dress? Oh no, I couldn't allow that, not going into the cold ground in her widow's weeds. No, I made sure she was in her lovely silk dressing gown. Like a sleeping beauty, she was. No, the dress she was wearing is in the wardrobe. I put it away as soon as I'd dressed her. Didn't want strangers putting clothes on her so I dressed her myself. I thought I should throw it out, the black dress, but I couldn't bring myself to."

"May I see the garment, please?"

Mrs Hicks seemed surprised at the request, but nodded. "Well, of course, Miss Dobbs. Through here."

Mrs Hicks led the way into the bedroom, where she opened a mahogany wardrobe and took out a black low-waisted dress in fine wool with a silk sash that matched silk binding at the neckline and cuffs. There were two elegant patch pockets on the bodice, each rimmed with black silk.

Maisie held up the dress by the hanger, then walked to the bed and laid the garment out in front of her.

"And the dress has not been cleaned since?"

"No, I put it straight in the wardrobe, with mothballs of course."

Maisie nodded and turned to the dress again. As Mrs Hicks moved to open the window to "let some air in here", Maisie reached into the left pocket and searched inside carefully. Nothing. She leaned over and looked down into the right pocket and again reached inside. Something pricked at the pillowed skin on the underside of her fingertips. Maintaining contact, with her other hand Maisie reached into her own pocket for a clean handkerchief, which she opened before carefully pulling out the object that had so lightly grazed her fingertips. The soft white feather of a fledgling. She inspected her catch briefly before placing it in the waiting handkerchief which she quickly returned to her jacket pocket.

"Everything all right, Miss Dobbs?"

"Yes, it's lovely. Such a shame to waste a beautiful dress, yet it's tinged with so much grief."

"I thought the same myself. I should've burned it, really I should. Perhaps that's what I'll do."

The dress might be evidence, and must not be lost. Maisie cautioned the housekeeper, careful not to cause alarm. "Oh no, don't do that. Please keep it – look, I think I know someone who could make good use of the dress. Shall I let you know?"

The housekeeper nodded. "Well, it is too good to destroy. I'll keep it until I hear from you."

"Thank you, Mrs Hicks. You've been most kind, especially as I came unannounced and at short notice."

"Oh, but you weren't unannounced. Dr Dene said to help you in any way I could. That you were completely trustworthy and acting in Mrs Thorpe's best interests. You'd better hurry or you'll be late for your lunch."

"How did you know?"

"It was just a good guess, Miss Dobbs. Dr Dene seemed a bit too sparky when I told him I had some information for you, as if he quite liked the idea of speaking to you again himself. Now, it's none of my business, and it's not how it would have been done in my day, not when Mr Hicks and I were walking out together. But I thought he might invite you to have a spot of lunch with him today. He had that sound in his voice."

Maisie blushed. "And what sound is that, Mrs Hicks?"

"Oh, you know. That sound. The one that a gentleman has when he's pleased with himself."

Maisie suppressed a smile and said good-bye to Mrs Hicks. Though she was looking forward to lunch with Andrew Dene, she was also anxious to be alone, to spread out the index cards that she had made notes on, to assess what this morning's gathering of information meant. The picture was becoming clearer, as if each conversation were a series of brushstrokes adding colour and depth to a story that was now unfolding quite rapidly. She had three feathers, evidence that the three deaths were linked, and that Rosamund Thorpe, too, had most definitely been murdered.

She drove down the hill to meet Andrew Dene by the fishing boats, at the place where the old horse turned the winch that brought the boats ashore, wishing she could get back to London, yet feeling guilty for wishing because of her father's need for her. She was anxious to sit with Billy at the incident table with all their clues, suspicions, evidence, hunches, and scribbles laid out in front of them. She wanted to find the key, the answer to her question: what was the connection between three small white feathers, three dead women and their murderer? And how was Joseph Waite involved? She felt for the handkerchief in her pocket and patted it.

"Thank you, Rosamund," she said, as she placed her hand on the steering wheel again.

Maisie parked the car at the bottom of the High Street, to much attention from passersby. As she walked along the seafront, where seagulls and pigeons followed pedestrians in the hope that a breadcrumb or two would be dropped, she made a mental note to ask Billy why he couldn't stand pigeons.

The weather was crisp, but fine enough for Andrew Dene and Maisie to walk to the pier after a quick fish-and-chips lunch. The sun was higher in the sky and had it been warmer one might have thought it summer.

"I cannot believe you removed all that lovely batter before eating the fish!" Andrew Dene teased Maisie.

"I love the fish, but don't really care for batter. Mind you, the chips were tasty."

"But you fed most of them to the seagulls, and they're fat enough already!"

They walked in silence. Maisie looked at her watch once again.

"Do you know how many times in one minute you've looked at your watch? I know you can't find my company *that* tedious. You should break yourself of the habit."

"I beg your pardon?" Maisie's eyes widened. She had never met a man of such impertinence. "I was going to say that I ought to be turning around, to get to my motor by —"

"Half past one? Ish? Yes, I haven't forgotten. Have you made any headway today, Miss Dobbs?"

"I've certainly gleaned more information, Doctor. It's putting the pieces together in a logical form that's the challenge. Sometimes it's guesswork all the way."

"Anything more I can do to help?" They were strolling back to the car, Maisie consciously keeping her hands deep in the pockets of her raincoat, holding tight to the linen handkerchief that held the third feather. She would not look at her watch again until she was well away from Andrew Dene.

"No . . . yes, yes there is, actually. Tell me, Dr Dene, if you were to name one thing that made the difference between those who get well quickly and those who don't, what would it be?"

"Phew. Another simple question from Maisie Dobbs!"

"I'm serious."

"And so am I. It's a tricky one, and one that you are probably more qualified to answer than I. You were a nurse and, more important, you have training in psychological matters."

"I'd like your opinion. Please, take a stab at it." Maisie turned towards him as she walked, challenging Dene to respond.

"Well, if I were to name one thing, it would be acceptance."

"Acceptance? But doesn't that stop the injured or wounded from trying to get better?"

"Ah, now you're playing devil's advocate, aren't you? In my opinion acceptance has to come first. Some people don't accept what has happened. They think, 'Oh, if only I hadn't walked up that street when I did,' or in a case like your father's: 'if only I'd known the ground was that wet and that Fred, or whatever his name was, had left his tools in the way.' They are stuck at the point of the event that caused the injury."

"Yes, I think I know what you mean."

"So, in the case of the soldiers who find it difficult to move on – and of course, some have had terrible injuries that all the therapeutic assistance in the world can't help – but those who find it difficult to accept are stuck in time, they keep thinking back to when it happened. And it's not so much, 'Oh, I wish I'd never enlisted.' In fact most say, 'At least I went,' but instead it's a case of 'If only I'd ducked, jumped when I could have, run a bit faster, gone back for my friend.' And of course, it all gets mixed up with the guilt of actually surviving when their pals didn't."

"So what's the answer?"

Dene stopped as they came alongside the MG, and Maisie leaned on her car, facing the Channel, her face warmed by the sun.

"I wish I had *one*, but, I would say that it's threefold: one is accepting what has happened. Three is having a picture, an idea of what they will do when they are better, or improved. Then in the middle, number two is a path to follow. For example, from what I've heard about your father, he'll make a good recovery: he's accepted that the accident happened, he has a picture of what the future holds for him when he's better – ensuring that the colt is in tip-top condition ready for training at Newmarket – and in the middle he's already aware of the steps that he'll take. At first he'll only be able to stand for a minute or two, then he'll use crutches, move on to walking sticks, and then the casts will come off. Dr Simms will give him instructions as to what not to do, and the sort of activities that will set him back."

"I see."

"There are grey areas," Maisie resisted the urge to look at her watch again as Andrew Dene went on. "For example, if we take Mr Beale – oops, you had better get going, hadn't you, Miss Dobbs?" Andrew Dene opened the door of the MG for Maisie.

"Thank you, Dr Dene. I enjoyed our lunch."

"Yes, I did too. I look forward to seeing your father at All Saints' soon."

"I'll be in touch with the administrator as soon as I can confirm the arrangements."

"Right you are, Miss Dobbs."

Phew! What a character he is! Still, Maisie found Dene interesting, engaging, challenging – and fun. He was able to laugh at himself. But there was something else about him, something that nagged at her, that she both liked and found confusing at the same time: he seemed to know who *she* was. Not by name. Not by accomplishment or by profession. No. There was more than that to her identity. Andrew Dene understood her roots. Even if he had never been privy to her story, Maisie knew that he understood her.

Following her father's accident, and the talks at the hospital with Maurice and later her father, Maisie had been able to recollect more of the times spent with her mother. She remembered being in the kitchen, a girl of about nine. Her mother had been telling her the story of how she'd met Maisie's father and known straight away that Frankie Dobbs was the one for her. "I set my hat for him there and then, Maisie, there and then." And she'd laughed, wiping the back of her sudsy hand across her forehead to brush back ringlets of black hair that had fallen into her eyes.

Maisie wondered about the business of setting one's hat for a man, and how a woman of her age might go about doing such a thing.

As she drove along, up over the ridge towards Sedlescombe, her thoughts shifted to Joseph Waite and the many tragic events that had befallen him. A father and brother killed in mining accidents, a wife dead in childbirth, a son lost to war, and an estranged daughter whom he tried to control without success. Hadn't Lydia Fisher indicated to Billy that Charlotte had been something of a social butterfly? But as she passed into Kent at the boundary near Hawkhurst, Maisie checked herself, and the certain pity she had begun to feel for Joseph Waite. Yes, she felt pity. But was it pity for a man who had stabbed three women, quite literally, in cold blood?

Perhaps Charlotte Waite had the answer. Tomorrow she would be able to judge Charlotte for herself. Was she, as her father believed, a 'wilting lily'? Or, was she, as Lydia Fisher had intimated to Billy, a habitual bolter? Magnus Fisher's account did not help. But each narrator's story revealed only one perspective, one representation of the person that Charlotte revealed herself to be in their company. Where did the truth lie? Who was Charlotte, really?

17

THURSDAY GREETED Kent with driving rain and howling winds. Maisie looked out at the weather from the cozy comfort of the Groom's Cottage, shivering but not at all surprised.

"Typical! Bring in the clouds for a drive to the marshes!"

Today she would make her way across Kent again and on through the relentless grey of the marshlands, where people — if she saw any — would be rushing along with heads bent, anxious to get to and fro from work or errands. It was a day when locals tried not to venture outside and even farmworkers found jobs to do in the barn rather than out in the fields. Today she would finally meet Charlotte Waite.

"Ugh," uttered Maisie as she ran to the MG.

George joined her, wearing the sort of foul-weather clothing one usually associated with fishermen.

"Going to catch a trout for tea, George?"

"No, Miss. I'd've thought catching things was more in your line of work."

"I deserved that, George," Maisie laughed as George lifted the bonnet to turn on the petrol pump, the first of five steps to start the MG. "Thank you for coming out."

"Saw you running across in this rain, Miss, and wanted to make sure you got off safely. Pity you've got to go somewhere today, so you mind how you go, Miss. Take them corners nice and easy."

"Don't worry, George."

"Know what time you'll be back? Just so's I know?"

"I won't be back to Chelstone today. After Romney Marsh, I'm off to Pembury to visit Mr Dobbs, and afterwards straight on to London. I expect to return to Kent as soon as I can to see my father." Maisie waved good-bye to George, who patted the back of the MG with his hand before running into the garage and out of the rain.

Apple orchards that were filled with blossom only yesterday were now sodden and sorry. Tall cherry trees bent over and the branches of roadside elder laden with bloom seemed almost to ache with the task of standing tall. Maisie hoped that the storm would pass, that the trees and land would dry quickly, and that spring, her favourite season in Kent, would be restored to its resplendent richness soon.

As she manoeuvred the MG, Maisie reflected upon her visit to see her father the day before. She had entered the ward to see Frankie at the far end of the column of beds, straining forward in his sitting-up position to greet her as she approached.

"How are you, Dad?"

"Better every day, expect to be up and about soon."

"Oh, I don't know about that. I've just spoken to Dr Simms, and he says that you should have two weeks convalescence by the sea before returning home, and even then you shouldn't be putting any weight on your right leg at all."

Frankie was about to protest, then looked at his daughter. "You've got a bit more colour in your cheeks, my girl, and you're looking more rested."

It was true, even Maisie had noticed that the grey rings usually etched under her eyes had diminished, her hair seemed more lustrous, and she felt much better, though she'd had so much on her mind that she hadn't even noticed feeling below par in the first place. It was Maurice who pinpointed a possible reason for Maisie's fatigue. "You've taken something on, Maisie. You've absorbed something of whatever was held inside the three women. And though being a sponge can aid your work, it can also hinder, for becoming one with the subjects of your investigation does not necessarily help you."

During her visit more was revealed to Maisie, more wounds were healed, more firm footing added to the ground as father and daughter tentatively made their way forward. As her reflections became illuminated by the light of understanding, so she felt a certain resentment lift, enabling her to look back on the past more kindly, with a little more compassion. And as she made her way towards Camden Abbey, she thought of Lydia, Philippa, and Rosamund, her thoughts coming back time and time again to who might not have been able to forgive them, and what it was they might have done to warrant such deep, unrelenting anger. An anger laced with a passion that led to murder.

She was close to Camden Abbey when the rain seemed to become lighter and for a moment it seemed as if the sun might manage to push its way through leaden clouds scudding across an already purplish grey sky. But that was the way of the marshes. The promise of light made it seem as if the elements were holding their collective breath. Then the observer realized that such a breath was only a minute's respite before it started blowing again even harder, a biting wind with a volley of more stinging rain.

Parking in front of the abbey, Maisie secured the car and ran inside, where she was immersed in silence, broken only by the drip-dripping of water that came from her mackintosh.

"Dame Constance has instructed me to escort you directly to the sitting room, where you can dry off." The young postulant avoided eye contact as she reached out to take Maisie's outer clothing. "Your coat, hat, and gloves will be ready for you by the time you leave."

"Thank you." Maisie inclined her head, and followed her guide, who walked close to the wall as she made her way to the room where Maisie had met Dame Constance previously.

Once again a fire crackled in the grate, though this time two wing chairs had been positioned alongside the grille. Maisie sat down and leaned back with an audible sigh. The door behind the grille slid open to reveal Dame Constance. Her eyes sparkled as she spoke.

"Good morning, Maisie."

"Good morning, Dame Constance. You have been most kind to encourage Miss Waite to agree to this meeting."

"I know it's important for you, Maisie, and the work you must do. However, my concern is primarily for Miss Waite. We have to consider how we can best be of service in her healing and recovery."

Maisie understood that this preamble to the meeting with Charlotte was important.

"You see, when a young woman makes a petition to join the community . . ." Dame Constance looked at Maisie intently. "You are surprised? Ah, Maisie, I would have thought that you had intuited by now that Miss Waite wishes to remain here, to join us. It is an attractive option for a woman who has found a measure of solace within these walls. However, I should add that there is no instant acceptance. Ever."

Dame Constance waited for a comment from Maisie. Then she went on. "There is a misconception that a religious community is a place of escape, that the refuge offered on a temporary basis can easily become more permanent. But that is not so. Our novices are women who are at peace with the world outside. They have enjoyed society in its broadest sense; they have had the support of loving families and in some cases no shortage of suitors. I have advised Miss Waite that her foundations must be solid before she can commit to a relationship with God. She cannot come out of fear, to hide."

"What do you mean, Dame Constance?"

"Joining a religious order is not a means of escape. It is a positive undertaking. One's foundation is the relationship one has with family, with one's first love, so to speak. Charlotte Waite has had difficulties with familial interactions, especially with her father. Such difficulty represents a crack in the foundation. The house of her future cannot be built if her very foundations are compromised."

Maisie frowned, thinking of her own situation rather than Charlotte's. Was that why she had felt such loneliness? Had it been the rupture in her relationship with Frankie that had prevented her from making other associations, so that she felt that she was always missing the mark in some way? Never quite able to join in, and surprised when she did? Never able to open her heart to another? Perhaps. After all, hadn't she noticed, now she came to think of it, a greater ease in her more personal interactions of late? She thought of Andrew Dene.

"Ah, I see you understand, Maisie."

"Yes, I think I do, Dame Constance."

The nun smiled, then continued. "I believe that Charlotte Waite might reveal to you what is at the heart of the discord between her father and herself. I will summon Miss Waite to meet you, but I will remain during your interview, at her request, though she will join you here in the sitting room."

"Thank you, Dame Constance."

The small door closed and Maisie was left alone with her thoughts. She would rather have seen Charlotte alone, but was grateful for any meeting. She had undertaken to urge Charlotte to return to Dulwich, to her father's home. But in so doing, would she be persuading Charlotte to risk her life? Might she be putting the lives of others in harm's way? Was it even possible that Charlotte was now seeking a religious life to expiate the crime of murder?

The sitting room door opened quietly and a woman of average height entered the room at the same time as the sliding door behind the iron grille that separated Dame Constance from visitors opened again with a thud.

Maisie studied Charlotte quickly. She wore a grey skirt, a long woollen cardigan knitted in a fine gauge, a plain white blouse, black shoes and opaque stockings. Her mousy hair, parted in the centre and drawn back into a loose bun, seemed to form a pair of curtains framing her face. Her only colour came from her bright, pale blue eyes. So presented, she was unremarkable and completely forgettable. And as she opened her mouth to greet Charlotte, Maisie remembered Andrew Dene's remark about Rosamund Thorpe: "It was as if coming here . . . was a sort of self-flagellation."

Maisie rose from her chair. "Good morning, Miss Waite." She

held out her hand, quickly trying to take the measure of her subject in the mood and emotions revealed by her stance. "I am so pleased that you agreed to see me," Maisie assured the still figure before her.

Charlotte Waite seemed to be frozen to the spot. Only her eyes betrayed a certain dislike of Maisie, based in all likelihood upon her hostility toward the person whom she represented.

"Let's sit down," offered Maisie.

Charlotte moved silently towards the other wing chair set opposite, smoothed the back of her skirt and was seated, her knees together with her legs slanted to one side, as she had been taught at her finishing school in Switzerland.

Maisie cleared her throat. "Charlotte, your father is very worried about you."

Charlotte looked up, then shrugged, giving the impression of a spoiled girl rather than a grown woman.

Maisie persisted. "I realize that there may be some miscommunication between yourself and your father. Please help me to understand what has come between you. Perhaps I can be of service in some way."

Charlotte Waite appeared to consider the question. Eventually she spoke in a voice that seemed to Maisie very much like her father's. It was a strong voice, a voice that didn't belong in the grey-clad, slender, almost frail body.

"Miss Dobbs, I appreciate your efforts. However, Joseph Waite wants only to have what he considers his property collected nicely together with all the rest of his possessions. I am exercising my choice to belong not to him but to myself."

"I understand your position, Miss Waite. But surely this cannot be attained by flight?" Maisie stole a glance at Dame Constance through the grille.

"I have tried to speak to my father. I have lived in his house for a long time. He wants me to be dependent upon him for my every thought, for me to remain in his sight, under his control."

"And what is the reason, in your estimation, for such behaviour?"

Maisie knew she must suspend all judgment. But she had begun to dislike and mistrust Charlotte Waite and her rationalizations. Had her earlier feeling of pity for Joseph Waite biased her?

"Well, you're certainly different from the last investigator he sent after me."

"Indeed. But my question remains."

Charlotte Waite took a handkerchief from her pocket and blew her nose. "I've tried, Miss Dobbs, all my life, to make up for the fact that I am not my brother. I am not Joseph the Second. All the things I was good at were so different from all the things that he was good at, and he excelled at being my father's favourite." Charlotte Waite blurted out her words.

Maisie suspected that she had never confided her true thoughts before. "And what were your feelings towards your brother, Miss Waite?"

Charlotte Waite began to cry.

"Speak to me, Charlotte." Maisie deliberately addressed her by her first name.

"I loved Joe. I adored him and looked up to him. He was always there, always. He protected me, but . . ."

"Yes?"

"I was torn, too."

"Torn?"

"Yes, I . . . I was sort of . . . envious of him, especially as I grew older. I wondered why he was the favourite and not me. He could work for my father, while I was treated as if I didn't have a brain at all. I was pushed to one side and ignored."

Maisie was silent. How fortunate, by contrast, she had been in her growing up and in her opportunities, though Charlotte was a rich man's daughter. How very lucky she had been. She took a deep breath. Maisie wanted to move on, to the day that Charlotte left her father's house. She must balance her undertaking to bring back Joseph Waite's daughter to him with her need to solve the murders of three women. The other members of Charlotte's coterie.

"Miss Waite. Charlotte, if I may. Perhaps you could explain to me the connection between the feelings you describe, and what happened on the day you left your father's house."

Charlotte sniffed, and dabbed at her nose. Maisie watched her carefully, mistrusting the volatility of the other woman's emotional state. *She's on her guard again.*

"Frankly, I was fed up with being in my father's house. I had wanted to leave for years, but he wouldn't support me unless I remained under his roof."

Maisie bristled at the assumption behind Charlotte's words. *Remain dispassionate.* Maurice's teaching echoed in her mind. This case was challenging Maisie at every turn.

"Support you, Miss Waite?"

"Well, it would never do, would it? The daughter of Joseph Waite living alone and working."

"Hmmm. Yes," said Maisie, in a manner she hoped would encourage Charlotte to continue. She could feel Dame Constance watching her now, and suspected that she had intuited her thoughts and understood her dilemma.

"Anyway, life had become difficult. Breakfast was the last straw."

"Did you have an argument with your father?"

"No, we didn't say a word to each other, except 'Good morning.' Perhaps it would have been better if we'd argued. At least it would have meant he noticed me."

"Go on, Charlotte."

Charlotte breathed in deeply. "I sat down, opened the newspaper and read that an old friend had . . ."

"Been murdered."

"How did you know?"

"It's my job, Miss Waite."

"You knew that I had been upset by reading of Philippa's death?"

"I suspected it. But why did you leave your father's home? What did you fear?"

Charlotte swallowed. "I hadn't actually seen her for a long time, not since the war. If I had told my father about her death, he would have thought my distress unwarranted."

"Is that all?"

"Yes."

She's lying, thought Maisie, who continued to press her subject, as far as she dare. "Was there another reason for your departure? You said that relations between you and your father had been troublesome for a while."

"All my life!" Charlotte was vehement.

"Yes, I realize that. It must have been very difficult for you. But you seemed to suggest that relations with your father had been more difficult than usual."

Charlotte stared at Maisie, as if trying to guess how much she already knew, then relented. "Another friend had died several weeks earlier. She . . . had taken her own life. We hadn't been in touch since the war either, and I only knew because I read about it in the obituary column of *The Times*. In fact, I didn't know at first that she'd . . . done it herself. I found out later when I telephoned the family to offer my condolences."

"I see. And your father?"

"Wouldn't let me attend the memorial service. Forbade it. Of course, she didn't have a funeral, not a proper one, because the church doesn't permit funerals for suicides."

"And why do you think he forbade you to attend?"

"Oh, probably because I had known her so long ago, and I . . . I get upset."

"Is there anything else, Charlotte? Any other reason?"

"No."

Too quick. Too quick to answer.

"How did you first become acquainted with these two friends, Philippa and . . .?"

"Rosamund." Charlotte picked at a hangnail. "We knew each other ages ago, first at school, then during the war," she replied, dismissively.

Her manner was not lost on Maisie, who pushed for a more concrete answer.

"What did you do during the war, together?"

"I can't remember now. It was so long ago."

Maisie watched as Charlotte Waite rubbed her hands together, in an effort to disguise their shaking.

"So, your father disliked two of your friends. And what did he think of Lydia Fisher."

Charlotte jumped up from her chair. "How do you know Lydia? Oh, my God, you knew all the time, didn't you?"

"Sit down, Miss Waite. Take a deep breath and be calm. I am not here to antagonize you or to harm you. I am simply searching for the truth." Maisie turned briefly to the grille and saw Dame Constance raise an eyebrow. *I'm on shaky ground, but she'll let me press on. For now.*

Charlotte took a seat once again.

"What's Lydia got to do with this?"

"You won't have seen the papers, Charlotte, but Lydia Fisher is dead."

"Oh, no! *No!*" It seemed to be an outcry of genuine surprise.

"And her husband, Magnus, has been arrested for the murders of both Philippa and Lydia."

"Magnus?"

"You seem surprised."

Charlotte Waite's throat muscles were taut. "But he hadn't seen Rosamund since school!"

"Rosamund? I thought she took her own life?"

Charlotte hid her face in her hands. Dame Constance cleared her throat, but Maisie tried for one last answer.

"Charlotte!" The tone of Maisie's voice made her look up. Tears were running down her face. "Charlotte, tell me – why was a white feather left close to each of the victims?"

Charlotte Waite broke down completely.

"Stop! This must stop now!" said Dame Constance, her voice raised. The door to the sitting room opened, and two novices helped Charlotte from the room.

Maisie closed her eyes and breathed deeply to steady her heartbeat.

"So, that is how you work, Maisie Dobbs?"

"When I have to. Yes, it is, Dame Constance."

Dame Constance tapped the desk in front of her and thought for a moment. Then she surprised Maisie.

"She'll get over this interlude," she sighed. "And it is evident even to me that she is withholding information. That, however, is her prerogative."

"But –"

"No buts, Maisie. Your questioning was not what I had expected."

"Perhaps I could have been kinder."

"Yes, perhaps you could." Dame Constance was thoughtful. "However, you might have rendered me a service, not that it excuses your manner with Charlotte." She sighed again and explained. "To rebuild a relationship means first confession, which is best spoken aloud to one who hears. There is a confession to be spoken here and you managed to lead her to the edge of the fire, though Charlotte is clearly afraid of the heat."

"That's one way of putting it, Dame Constance." Maisie thought for a minute. "Look, I know I pushed rather hard, but three women have been murdered, and an innocent man has been arrested. And Charlotte . . ."

"Holds the key."

"Yes."

"I will advise her to speak to you again, but not before she has recovered. Maisie, I must have your word that you will not conduct your next interview in such a hostile manner. I remain deeply disappointed in you."

"Dame Constance, I would be most grateful if you would urge Miss Waite to speak to me again. I give my word that I will be more considerate of Miss Waite's sensibility when we meet. But . . . time is of the essence."

Dame Constance nodded, and when the sliding door behind the grille closed, Maisie stood to leave.

A postulant entered the room with Maisie's dry mackintosh, hat, and gloves, which she donned before returning to the MG. As the engine stuttered into life, Maisie hit the steering wheel with her hand. "Damn!" she said.

18

M AISIE WAS already at her desk when Billy arrived on Friday morning. Much work had to be completed on several cases, and two potential new clients who had come to the office during her absence had to be discussed.

"You've been working long hours, Billy."

"Takes my mind off it."

"Leg been bad this week?"

"Just nags away at me all the time now. And I've bin good, Miss. On the straight and narrow."

Billy's eyes seemed to be framed with circles as dark as her own. If only he would go to Chelstone soon.

"Have you given thought to my proposal?"

"Well, Doreen and me 'ave talked about it and all. Of course we're worried about the money."

"I've given you my assurance, Billy."

"I know, I know, Miss. But, I feel sort of, oh, I dunno . . ."

"Vulnerable?"

"Sounds about right."

"Billy, that's to be expected. I cannot tell you how much your help with my father means to me. Having someone I trust to be with him, and to assist with the horses – he'll make himself ill worrying about them otherwise. And I know your leg bothers you, so one of the farmworkers will take on the really heavy work. Dad's doing very well. He'll be out of the wheelchair by the time he comes back to Chelstone, and we'll set up a bed downstairs at the cottage. You won't have to do any lifting."

"Be like two old peg legs together, won't we?"

"Oh, come on now, you'll see — you'll come back with all fires blazing. I've heard that Maurice's friend, Gideon Brown, is an amazing man and has worked wonders with wounded and injured people. Plus you'll be outdoors, in the fresh air . . ."

"And well away from temptation, eh Miss?"

Maisie sighed. "Yes, Billy. That's another thing."

Billy nodded. "Awright, then. Awright, I'll go, but not until this business with Miss Waite and them women is closed. I can't leave work 'alf done."

"Right you are, Billy." Maisie acquiesced. "And is there anything else?"

Billy looked at Maisie in earnest. "Can Doreen and the nippers come down?"

"Of course they can. It isn't prison, you know. In fact, if she wants, I think Doreen could get work from Lady Rowan."

"Oh, she'd like that."

"Yes, apparently Lady Rowan has been so preoccupied with the mare and foal, that she is 'behind' — as she puts it — with preparing for her return to London. She wants to have several gowns altered rather than buy new ones, so I told her about Doreen."

"You should get a job down the labour exchange, Miss. You'd 'ave everyone in work and off them lines in next to no time."

Maisie laughed. "Come on, let's get cracking. I want to see where we are with everything that's happened while I've been away. We should leave here by ten. And we'll continue this afternoon as soon as we're back. Also, I'll need to speak to Detective Inspector Stratton later today."

"T' see whether Fisher has spilled the beans?"

"Yes, in a way. Though I think the only beans Fisher has to spill concern his wife's drinking and his gambling debts. But the newspapers are having a field day with him."

"All over him like a rash, Miss. Feel a bit sorry for him, I do."

"You should. I would bet my business on his innocence."

233

Quite deliberately, Maisie had not discussed her latest news on the Waite case in detail with Billy. Though she wanted to work on the case map as an artist would an unfinished canvas, she also knew the value of letting facts, thoughts, observations and feelings simmer. In the hours of driving that followed her meeting with Charlotte Waite, Maisie had concluded that the only person who was at risk now was Charlotte. A plan had begun to form in Maisie's mind. Execution of that plan would depend upon Charlotte.

At ten o'clock on the dot, just as they were about to leave for the appointment with Joseph Waite, the telephone rang.

"Always the way, innit?"

"You can say that again." Maisie reached for the receiver and gave the number.

"May I speak to Miss Maisie Dobbs?"

"Speaking."

"Ah, Miss Dobbs. This is the Reverend Sneath, from the village of Lower Camden. I have an important message for you from Dame Constance at Camden Abbey. I visited her earlier today, and she asked me to telephone you as a matter of some urgency as soon as I returned to the vicarage."

"What is the message, Reverend Sneath?" Maisie was filled with dread. Seeing her complexion change, Billy moved closer to the desk.

"I'll read it out to you, so I don't miss anything."

Maisie bit her lip as she listened to the rustle of paper, the message being unfolded. The vicar cleared his throat. "Dear Maisie. Miss Waite has left Camden Abbey. She went to her cell immediately after your meeting with her yesterday, and did not join us for our meals or for our devotions as is her practice. I gave instructions for a food tray to be left for her, and when it was discovered untouched this morning we searched the abbey to no avail. I fear that yesterday's distressing events have weighed heavily on her. I have not informed the authorities as Miss Waite is not a member of the community. However, I am concerned for her wellbeing. Do all that you can to find her, Maisie. I need not remind you that her safety is your responsibility. We will hold you and Miss Waite in our prayers."

"Oh God." Maisie slumped into her chair.

"Yes, quite."

"Thank you, Reverend Sneath. Please destroy the message. And would you be so kind as to get word to Dame Constance that I will be in touch as soon as I have located Miss Waite."

"Of course. Good day to you, Miss Dobbs." The line clicked.

"She's run away again, Billy." Maisie's hand was still on the receiver, as if willing the telephone to ring with news of Charlotte.

"Oh blimey! Now what're we goin' t' tell ol' Waite?"

"Nothing. I don't want to alarm Waite until we've made inquiries. For now we'll carry on as if we know where she is. But we have to find her – and pretty sharpish. Come on, let's get going. We can talk about it in the car."

Maisie and Billy exchanged ideas throughout the journey to Dulwich, until Maisie put a stop to their speculation. "Let's give this problem some air. Now we've speculated back and forth, let's allow some room for inspiration."

"Awright, Miss. Let the ideas come to us instead of chasing them."

"Exactly." Maisie spoke as forcefully as she could but was unable to escape the dread that pulled at her stomach. Where was Charlotte Waite now?

***

Once again, Maisie was required to park "nose out" at the Waite mansion and, once again, after a most cordial greeting from Harris, the calm was broken by the entrance of Miss Arthur, Joseph Waite's secretary, clutching her files.

"Oh, Miss Dobbs, Miss Dobbs, Miss Dobbs. I tried to telephone you, but your line was engaged, and then when I telephoned a second time there was no answer. I'm sorry, I'm sorry, I'm sorry."

Miss Arthur reminded Maisie of a startled hen, with her arms flapping. Maisie raised her hand as if to smooth the other woman's ruffled feathers.

"What is wrong, Miss Arthur?"

"It's Mr Waite." Miss Arthur ushered Maisie and Billy into her wood-panelled office next to the entrance hall. "Of course, he sends apologies, many apologies, but he has been . . . called away urgently . . . on a business matter."

Miss Arthur was not a practised liar, Maisie noted. She frowned. "I see."

"I tried to reach you, but I expect you had already left," the flustered secretary continued.

"Not to worry, Miss Arthur. Of course I have much to report to him."

"Yes, yes, he expected that. He asked me to attend immediately to any interim bills you may wish to submit. For your services."

"That is very kind." Maisie turned to Billy, who handed her a brown envelope which she in turn handed to Miss Arthur. "Perhaps I can make an appointment for next week?"

"Indeed, Miss Dobbs." Miss Arthur stepped quickly to the other side of her desk, reached into a drawer and pulled out a cheque-book and ledger. She glanced briefly at the bill, and commenced writing a cheque, while still speaking to Maisie. "In fact Mr Waite said to let you know that he's reviewed your previous conversations and he's satisfied with your progress. He trusts that you will be bringing Miss Waite back to the house in the fullness of time."

"A bit of an about-turn, Miss Arthur?" Maisie was suspicious of the fact that both Charlotte *and* her father were eluding further confrontation with her. A coincidence? Or by design?

Miss Arthur did not respond as she continued to sign the cheque in her small, rounded hand. She slipped the cheque into an envelope that she passed to Maisie; then she looked down to complete the ledger entry before reaching for a substantial desk diary. "Let me look at his diary. How about next Wednesday? At noon?"

Maisie nodded at Billy, who noted the time on an index card.

"Perhaps you would be so kind as to inform Mr Waite that I expect to be in a position to make arrangements for Miss Waite's return very soon."

"I understand, Miss Dobbs. We are all very anxious to see her back home."

"Yes." Maisie looked sharply at Miss Arthur, who seemed intent on shuffling the papers on her desk. She had always thought that Miss Arthur, along with the other members of Joseph Waite's household, dreaded Charlotte's return. What was the secretary keeping from her? Was Charlotte already in the house? Had Waite located his daughter and dragged her home? But, if so, why conceal her whereabouts from Maisie?

"I'll summon Harris to show you out."

"Thank you, Miss Arthur."

Maisie and Billy were almost at the door when Maisie turned to the butler. "Is Mrs Willis available? I just want to see her for a moment."

"She's taken an afternoon off, Miss. Mind you, she may still be in her quarters. Shall I summon her?"

"Oh no, I'll quickly knock on her door, if that's all right. I saw her at the bus stop in Richmond recently and wanted to offer her the occasional lift." Maisie began to move as she spoke, which she knew would subtly pressure the butler into acquiescing.

"Of course, Madam. Follow me."

"Billy, wait for me in the car, won't you?"

Billy hid his surprise. "Right you are, Miss."

Maisie was escorted along a corridor that led first to a staircase giving access to the lower floor, then, once downstairs, continued to the side of the house. The property's design, though intended to give the impression of an older architectural style, was actually modern. The staircase leading to the kitchens was wide and airy, the quarters for senior staff spacious. This house had been designed to give owner and servants alike a measure of comfort unknown in times past.

Harris knocked on an eggshell-gloss-painted door. "Mrs Willis? Visitor for you."

Maisie could hear movement inside; then the door opened to reveal the housekeeper, who was patting the sides of her head to calm any stray locks of hair. She wore a light amethyst wool day dress, with a narrow white collar and cuffs, and was still kneading the leather of one of her black shoes with her heel in an attempt to get it on her foot without having to stoop in front of her visitor.

"Oh, this is a surprise."

"I'm sorry to disturb you, Mrs Willis." Maisie turned to Harris. "Thank you for showing me the way." He bowed and left, as Maisie turned again to Mrs Willis.

"May I come in?"

"Of course, of course. I am sorry. I don't get visitors, so do pardon me not being ready to receive a guest." Mrs Willis beckoned Maisie to follow her into the immaculate sitting room. A small settee and matching armchair were positioned to face the fireplace and a gateleg table, one flap folded to fit neatly into the limited space, was placed near the wall, the highly polished wood reflecting a vase full of daffodils that stood on a lace doily. A series of photographs sat on the sideboard by the window, which offered a pleasing view to the gardens at the side of the house.

"May I offer you refreshment, Miss Dobbs?"

"No, thank you, Mrs Willis."

"Do sit down. I expect you've come to make arrangements for Miss Waite coming home."

"Actually, Mrs Willis, I came to to see you."

The woman looked across at Maisie, her eyes wide. "Me, Miss Dobbs?"

"Yes. I hope this isn't a cheek, but I saw you in Richmond last time I visited a dear friend. He's being cared for in the same home as your son."

"Oh, I am sorry, Miss Dobbs. Was he your sweetheart?"

Maisie was a little surprised by the forthright question. But such an observation might be expected, as there were many women of Maisie's age who had remained spinsters, their loved ones lost to war. "Well, yes. Yes, he was, but it was a long time ago, now."

"Hard to forget though, isn't it?" Mrs Willis sat opposite Maisie.

Maisie cleared her throat. "Yes, sometimes. But look, Mrs Willis, I just wanted to say that if I can give you a lift, you must let me know."

"That's very kind of you, but –"

"I don't go there every week, but I can telephone first to see if you would like a lift when I am planning to visit, if you like."

"Well, Miss, I can't put you to any trouble. Really I can't."

"It's no trouble at all. And if you should see my motor car outside when you're visiting, do wait for me to bring you home."

"All right, Miss Dobbs. I'll do that." The housekeeper smiled at Maisie.

She won't ask for help. Ever, thought Maisie.

Suddenly, a clatter at the window caused Maisie to gasp. Mrs Willis stood. "Here they come, after their lunch!"

"What on earth is that noise? It frightened the life out of me."

"It's just the doves, Miss Dobbs. Always after a bit extra, always. It's lunchtime; they know who's a soft touch and where they can get a titbit or two." The housekeeper took the lid off a brown-striped earthenware biscuit barrel set on the mantelpiece, selected a biscuit, and walked to the window. Maisie followed, and watched as she leaned over the sideboard and lifted the sash window to reveal a dozen or more doves sitting on the windowsill.

"There you are, you little beggars. Eat up, because that's all you're getting today!" Mrs Willis crumbled the biscuit onto the window-sill.

Maisie laughed to see the birds jostle for position, pushing and shoving in an effort to get more.

"You watch, they'll try upstairs next."

"Why, who else feeds them?"

"Oh. Mr Waite. He's a soft one, if ever there was. He pays all the bills for my son's care, you know. His bark is far worse than his bite, as they say."

As if drawn by the unheard signal of a mystical piper, the doves swept up and away from the windowsill, taking to the air in a cloud of wings. Maisie watched as they flew up, while Mrs Willis closed the window very slowly. And for a moment it seemed to Maisie as if time were faltering yet still moving forward, for in their wake the doves discarded dozens and dozens of tiny, perfect white feathers, each one zigzagging down, borne on a light breeze, until it fell onto the freshly cut lawn, or fluttered against the windowpane like snow.

"Oh dear, are you one of those people who doesn't like birds?" asked Mrs Willis.

"No, not at all." Maisie turned back into the room, and regained her composure. "Mind you, my assistant doesn't care for them."

"Why ever not? They're so beautiful."

"Yes, they are, aren't they? I don't know why he doesn't like them. I must make a point of asking him." Maisie looked at her watch. "I really should be going now, Mrs Willis. Don't forget to ask if you need a lift."

"That's very kind of you, Miss Dobbs." Mrs Willis walked Maisie to the door, which she opened for her. "Will we be seeing Miss Waite home soon?"

"Yes you will. Probably in the next week."

"That's very good news, very good. The sooner she's back home, the better. Let me show you the way."

Maisie allowed Mrs Willis to escort her to the front door. It would not have been correct for a guest to be left to find her own way out, especially in the mansion of Joseph Waite. At the door, she bade farewell to Mrs Willis again. Then, as she reached the bottom of the front steps and heard the door close behind her, Maisie set a course for the corner of the house where the front garden looped around. She heard Billy rushing to catch up.

"Don't run, Billy! For goodness' sake, spare your leg and your lungs!"

Billy came alongside. "What was all that about, Miss? The little chat with Mrs Willis?"

"Initially just doing a favour. But now I don't know."

"Not followin' yer, Miss."

"I'll explain later." Maisie reached the corner of the house and looked first towards the outer windowsill of Mrs Willis's rooms, then up to the windows above.

"Aw, them bleedin' birds!"

"Don't worry, Billy, they're not interested in you," said Maisie, her attention on the window as she watched a hand reach out to sprinkle more crumbs for the hungry doves. It was a broad hand, a hand that Maisie could easily recognize from the ground, helped by the sun which broke through the clouds at just the right moment to catch the light reflected by a gold ring encrusted with diamonds.

"See anything interestin', Miss?"

"Oh yes, Billy. Very interesting. Very interesting indeed."

Billy seemed relieved to be inside the car again and on his way back to London.

"Shall we talk about Charlotte Waite's possible whereabouts?"

"No. Wait until we get back to the office. We need to get our heads really clear. First, tell me why you don't like doves or pigeons. Does your dislike extend to all birds?" Maisie pulled out into the middle of the road to pass a rag-and-bone man, his horse clip-clopping along as if it knew instinctively that it had been a bad day for business.

"Aw, Miss, it don't make sense, not really. I mean, it ain't the bird's fault, is it?"

"What isn't the bird's fault?"

"Nah, Miss. Can't tell yer. It'll make you think I'm a few coals shy of a load, it will. S'all a bit silly, all a bit in me 'ead, as you would say."

"I don't think I'd say anything of the sort." Maisie pulled over to the side of the road and stopped, allowing the engine to idle as she turned to him. "Spill the beans, Billy. Why do you hate birds?" She had a distinct feeling that, with his "silly" feelings, Billy might have something for her to consider.

He sighed. "S'pose I'm gonna 'ave to tell you, ain't I?"

"I suppose you are."

"And you ain't gonna move this motor till I do, are yer?"

"Absolutely right."

He sighed again. "Well, it in't all that stupid, now I know a bit more about what goes on up 'ere, from working wiv you." Billy tapped the side of his head. "But . . . I don't like 'em because of the war, and even thinkin' about it makes me leg get bad again." Billy rubbed his leg.

"What's your leg got to do with it?"

"Well, y'see, I didn't enlist straightaway. There was only me and me brother, both workin' for me dad. Not like we came from one of them big families, not like there was ten of us and if one went there was always a few left. Anyway, I was going to join up, but me mum didn't like it, though I thought I should do my bit. But you know what it's like when you keep meanin' t' do something . . ."

Maisie nodded. *You're rambling, Billy.*

"Then one day, I decided that there was no time like the present, so I went down and got meself enlisted. Me mum, when I told 'er, aw you should've 'eard 'er go on, and on, and on. At least me brother was too young to go, so she'd still 'ave 'im at 'ome. Anyway, I 'ad a few days at 'ome before I 'ad to report for duty, so me and me little brother, fifteen at the time 'e was, went out for a bit of a laugh one afternoon. I didn't 'ave a uniform yet, in fact, let me tell you, even after I was at the barracks in Colchester, I never 'ad a uniform for three weeks. They was enlistin' so many at once, they'd run out of uniforms. Run out of uniforms? I tell you, it's no wonder we 'ad trouble over there. No wonder."

Billy shook his head, while Maisie waited for his story to unfold.

"Gawd, seems I was like an old man already, but I was only eighteen. Anyway, there we were, walkin' down the street, when this young lady comes up to us, all smiles. Then she 'ands me and 'im a feather each, and tells us we should be in uniform, and —"

"Oh my God!" Maisie gasped. "It was there all the time, only I couldn't see it!"

Maisie pushed the car into gear, looked over her shoulder, and pulled out onto the road.

"See what, Miss?"

"I'll tell you later, Billy. Keep on with your story."

Billy was silent.

"It's all right, Billy, I'm still listening." Maisie pressed down on the accelerator to gain speed.

"Well, it's them feathers. Sign of cowardice, ain't they? I mean, I was signed on anyway, so it didn't bother me, did it? Water off a duck's back. But not Bobby, oh no, 'e was only a youngster. Couldn't wait to be a man. And o' course, nice young woman comes along, calls 'im a coward, what does 'e do, eh? Goes an' enlists on the sly, just after I left."

Maisie blushed, remembering the lies she told about her age in order to enlist for nursing service, and her father's furious frustration at her actions.

"Me mum does 'er pieces, me father went mad, and all the time, I'm runnin' around takin' orders from 'igher-ups who didn't know much more than I did."

Suddenly Maisie slowed the car, her speed checked by the cold chill of realization. "What happened to your brother, Billy?" She looked sideways at him, her hands clutching the steering wheel.

Billy looked out of the passenger window.

"Copped it, didn't 'e. Silly little bugger. Sixteen years of age, and pushin' up daisies in a place where 'e couldn't even talk the lingo. All because of a bleedin' feather."

"Why ever didn't you tell me all this?"

"S'long time ago, innit, Miss? Mind you, it seems that every time I see a bird, you know, *look* at a bird, well, the stupid animal seems to drop a feather or two, just as they're flappin' their wings t' get away, and every time I see a feather, I see our Bobby with the feather between 'is fingers, runnin' after me, sayin, 'She called me a coward. Did you 'ear that? Eh, Billy? She called me a *coward*! Now everyone'll think I'm not up to it!' But 'e weren't no coward. Sixteen, and gave 'is life."

Billy rubbed at his legs again. Maisie let the silence linger. *I must get him to Chelstone as soon as I can.*

"Billy, Billy, I am so very sorry."

"Named my boy after 'im, I did. Just 'ope there won't be any more wars in case I lose 'im. My biggest fear, that is, Miss. That there'll be another war, when 'e's enlistin' age."

Maisie nodded, fearfully.

"So what's all this about, then? Y'know, what you couldn't see when it was there all the time."

19

MAISIE PICKED up the telephone to place a call to Scotland
Yard as soon as she and Billy returned to the office.

"My old mum always used to say that the best place to 'ide a
thing was in plain view. She'd say that when I gave up me wage
packet of a Friday night. She'd take the money, stick it in a pot on
the table, and then give me a couple o' bob back for meself. P'raps
Miss Waite is 'iding somewhere in plain view?"

Maisie held up her hand for silence as her call was answered.

"Inspector, I wonder if we might meet to discuss the Sedgewick-
Fisher case? I have some information that might be of interest to
you."

Maisie heard an audible sigh.

"Is it regarding Mr Fisher?"

"Well . . . no, no, not directly."

"Miss Dobbs, we are convinced we have the right man."

Maisie closed her eyes. She must tread carefully. "I've made some
observations that may be useful to you."

Another sigh, augmented by the sound of voices in the background. Would this telephone call to Stratton be fodder for mirth
among the men of Scotland Yard's Murder Squad? It was a risk she
would have to take. She could not withhold evidence from them
once she was convinced of its importance. If the police refused to
listen, that was quite another matter.

"Look, Miss Dobbs, I am grateful for any and all information.
Obviously in my position I can hardly say otherwise, and if your
information concerns Fisher I would be more than delighted to

have it. But the point is that we find that investigating many so-called leads wastes valuable time when we already have the killer."

"You've taken an innocent man into custody, and you should hear me out!"

"I say, Miss Dobbs, now just you wait a minute!"

"But Inspector, another perspective might –"

"All right, Miss Dobbs." Stratton sounded exasperated, but Maisie knew she had appealed to his sense of duty. "Meet me at the caff on the corner of Oxford Street and Tottenham Court Road in – let me see – half-an-hour."

"Thank you, Inspector Stratton. I know exactly where you mean – diagonally opposite Waite's International Stores."

"That's it. See you in half-an-hour."

"Until then."

Maisie replaced the receiver and blew a gust of breath between lips rounded into an O.

"Bit frosty, was 'e, eh, Miss?"

"More than a bit. And I've got to be careful too. In providing Stratton with information, I risk undermining him or antagonising him further. After all, if he chooses to listen, he's the one who has to return to the Yard and retract the accusations against Magnus Fisher. I need to keep him as an ally."

"What's wrong wiv 'im, then?"

Maisie took the folded linen handkerchief from her case and walked to the table where the case map had already been unfurled and pinned ready for work. She motioned for Billy to join her.

"He's let two things get in the way, I think: his personal history and his standing in the department. Of course, he has to be careful, because if I were to take a bet on it –"

"And we know you're not the bettin' type." Billy smiled at her.

"No, but if I were, I'd wager that Caldwell is after the Detective Inspector's job, and is making Stratton's life a misery while he's nipping at his heels. So Stratton has to be careful in terms of who he is seen taking information from."

"What's 'is personal history, then?"

Maisie leaned over the map, and unfolded the handkerchief. "Well, he's a widower. His wife died in childbirth about five years ago, leaving him to bring up his son alone."

Billy scrunched up his face, "Aw, blimey, Miss. Tha's terrible. Wish you 'adn't've told me that. Now I'm gonna think about it every time I see the man." He leaned forward. "What've you got there?"

"Feathers. Tiny white feathers. The ones I collected during my investigation. I found one feather for each woman. Two were close to where the victims had been sitting just prior to meeting the murderer. In Rosamund Thorpe's case, the feather was in the pocket of the dress she was wearing when she died."

"Ugh." Billy shuddered.

"They can't hurt you. The women who gave them out in the war are the ones who did the harm."

Billy watched as Maisie placed the feathers on the case map, using a smudge of paste to secure each one to the paper.

"Do you know who the killer is, Miss?"

"No Billy, I don't."

Billy looked sideways at Maisie and reflected for a moment. "But you've got an idea. I can see it there."

"Yes, yes, I have, Billy. I do have an idea. But it's just an idea. Right now we've got our work cut out for us. We must find Charlotte Waite. Here's what I want you to do —"

Billy flipped open his notebook ready to list his instructions as Maisie closed her eyes and ran though a catalogue of possibilities: "An animal will make for its lair if in fear or wounded. Mind you, Charlotte may have no reason to fear, she may just want to get away, to escape from being Joseph Waite's daughter. We have to consider that she may have fled to Europe, after all, she's familiar with Lucerne and Paris. See if you can check the passenger list for the boat-train. Charlotte might have travelled from Appledore station on the branch line to Ashford, or she may have come to London first. There are one hundred ways she could have travelled. Check with Croydon Aerodrome and Imperial Airways — oh, and there's an aerodrome in Kent, at Lympne. Check as many hotels in London as you can – but don't start with the big ones. Contact the hotels that are neither too posh nor too shabby. Telephone Gerald Bartrup. No, *visit* Bartrup. I want you to look at him when you ask him if he's seen Charlotte in the past twenty-four hours. Pay attention Billy, with your body as well as your eyes. You'll know if he's lying."

The list was long and Billy would be hard at work until late. Maisie wondered if Charlotte had funds that were known only to her, squirrelled away into a private account. Where had she gone? *Where was she now?*

Though their conversation was sometimes strained, Maisie looked forward to her meeting with Detective Inspector Stratton. She knew that he admired her and was taking tentative steps to further their acquaintance. But how prudent would it be to agree to such an outing? Would her work and her reputation be put at risk by a closer friendship?

Stratton stood outside the cafeteria where Maisie joined him after walking down Tottenham Court Road from Fitzroy Square. He lifted his hat and opened the door for Maisie.

"There's a seat over there. This place is definitely more *caff* than *café*, but it's quick. Tea, toast, and jam?"

"Lovely, Inspector Stratton." It was at that point that Maisie realized that she hadn't eaten since breakfast.

Maisie sat on a bench by a wall decorated with floral wallpaper that was now quite faded and stained in places. She unbuttoned her jacket and looked out of the window while she waited for Stratton, who was at the counter placing cups of tea and a plate of toast and jam on a tray. She craned her neck to watch customers going in and out of Joseph Waite's double-fronted grocery shop across the road. *And they say there's no money about!*

"Here we are." Stratton set the tray down on the table, pulled out the chair opposite Maisie, and sat down. "You could stand a spoon up in that tea. They make it strong here."

"Stewed tea, fresh from the urn – nothing like it, Inspector. It's what kept us going over in France."

"Yes, and there's been many a time when a flask of that stuff has sustained me when I've had to work all night, I can tell you. Let's get down to business. I didn't come here to discuss the tea. What have you come across, Miss Dobbs? I know you did some snooping around when you found Lydia Fisher's body."

"Lydia was a friend of Charlotte Waite. I had been asked by Joseph Waite to locate his daughter, who had left her father's home temporarily. He is my client." Maisie reached for a triangular wedge of toast. She was ravenous and quickly took a bite, then dabbed at the sides of her mouth with a handkerchief. This was not the kind of establishment where table napkins were supplied.

Stratton raised an eyebrow. "Not much to get your teeth into, a missing debutante, if you don't mind me saying so Miss Dobbs." Stratton reached for a slice of toast.

"But enough to pay for my own office, an assistant, and a nippy little motor car, Inspector," replied Maisie, her eyes flashing.

Stratton smiled. "I deserved that one, didn't I?"

Maisie inclined her head.

"So, let's get down to brass tacks. What have you got to tell me?"

"Lydia Fisher and Philippa Sedgewick were friends."

"I know that!"

"As was Rosamund Thorpe, of Hastings."

"Who is?"

"Dead. She is thought to have committed suicide some weeks before Mrs Sedgewick was murdered."

"And this has . . . what to do with your investigation or our murder inquiry?"

"They were all friends once, the three dead women and Charlotte Waite. A coterie, if you like."

"So?"

Maisie appraised Stratton before speaking again. *He's being deliberately obtuse.*

"Detective Inspector Stratton, people who knew Rosamund

Thorpe cannot believe she took her own life. Also, the four former friends seem to have made a point of avoiding one another. I think they were kept apart by shame. During the war, I believe they distributed white feathers to men who were not in uniform."

"Oh, those terrible women!"

"And . . ." Maisie halted. *Shall I tell him about the feathers I found? Will I be mocked?* "And . . . I believe that Magnus Fisher did not kill his wife or Philippa Sedgewick. The person you seek is someone –"

"We have our man!"

"Inspector, why are you so . . . so . . . quick to send Fisher down?"

"I'm not at liberty to say."

"The public wants a murderer behind bars, and you – you and Caldwell – have decided to give them one."

Stratton sighed. "And we are right. It's an open-and-shut case."

Maisie clenched her fists in frustration. "And you can't stand a man who abandoned his wife, and whom you believe deprived a loving husband of his."

"Look here Miss Dobbs, leave this sort of work to the professionals. I know you've had some luck in the past. You've helped us before when you worked for a man of some stature, but . . . do not interfere!" Stratton stood up. "I hope we can meet again under less strained circumstances."

Much as she wanted to have a last word, Maisie knew that she must not allow them to part with rancour. "Yes, indeed, Inspector. I am sorry if I have offended you. However, do expect to hear from me again soon."

Stratton left the cafeteria, as Maisie took her seat once again. *I should have known better. I shouldn't have lost control. I could see by the way he moved, the way he sat and the manner in which he spoke, that he was obdurate. I've told the police as much as they would hear. Should I have mentioned the feathers? No, he would have laughed.*

Maisie gathered her belongings and followed Stratton out.

She was ready to turn the corner into Tottenham Court Road,

when she stopped to look back at the blue and gold-fronted Waite's International Stores. She changed direction and walked instead towards the entrance of Joseph Waite's most prominently situated grocery store.

Once again, when Maisie entered the hubbub of the shop, she watched as assistants reached forward to point to a cheese and nod, or hold up a cut of meat for inspection. Dried fruits were weighed, biscuits counted, and all the time money passed back and forth and shop assistants constantly washed their hands. Maisie stood in the centre of the floor, near the round table with a display of the latest foods imported from overseas. Yes, there was money about, despite long lines at soup kitchens in other parts of London.

Maisie watched the busyness of business in Joseph Waite's domain. *Why have I come back? There is something here for me. What is it? What did I not see last time?* She looked up at the walls, at the intricate mosaics that must have cost a fortune. Then down at the polished wood floor and across at the boy whose job it was to walk back and forth with a broom, ensuring that Waite's customers never noticed so much as a crumb underfoot.

No one paid attention to the young, well-dressed woman who stood without a shopping bag, making no move towards a counter, and displaying no intention to purchase. Both shop assistants and customers were too preoccupied with their tasks and errands to see her close her eyes and place her hand where she could feel the beating of her heart. Just for a second, just for a fleeting moment, Maisie gave herself over to her inner guidance in this most public place. Then, as if responding to a command that only she could hear, she opened her eyes and looked up at the place above the door, at the tiled memorial to the employees of Waite's International Stores. She allowed her eyes to rest on the tile dedicated to Waite's son Joseph, beloved heir of a self-made man. A man known to be as hard as rock but at times also a man of compassion. A man of extremes. *Don't stop*, said a voice in her head. And Maisie obeyed. She read each name, starting from the beginning: Avery . . . Denman . . . Farnwell . . . Marchant . . . Nicholls . . . Peters . . . so many, oh, so *many* . . . Richards, Roberts . . . Simms, Simpson . . . Timmins . . . Unsworth . . . every letter in the alphabet was represented as she silently mouthed the names, like a teacher reviewing the class register. Then Maisie stopped reading. *Ah.* She closed her eyes. *Ah. Yes. Of course.*

Opening her eyes again, Maisie looked at each food counter until she saw one of the older members of staff. "Excuse me. I wonder if you could help me?"

"Yes, Madam, Of course. The sausages are fresh made this morning, by our very own butchers. Personally trained by Mr Waite, they are. These are the best sausages in London."

"Oh, lovely, I'm sure. But could you tell me where I can find someone who worked for Waite's during the war? Someone who might have known the boys up there?" Maisie pointed to the memorial.

"But Miss, there's names up there from all over. Mind you, old Mr Jempson in the warehouse knew just about all of the London boys. Joined up together you know, as pals. Most of the boys who enlisted came from the warehouse; it's where the apprentices start, and where the butchering is done before the carcasses go out to the shops. Waite's delivers to its own shops with special ice-packed lorries, you know."

"Could you tell me where the warehouse is?"

"Across the water. In Rotherhithe, the 'Larder of London,' where all the warehouses are. Let me get a piece of paper and write down the directions for you. It's easy to find, close to St Saviour's Docks, Madam. Relative, are you?"

"A friend."

"I see. Mr Waite's own son was down at the warehouse, before he went over there. Started him at the bottom, did Mr Waite. Said he had to work his way up like anyone else." The assistant left the counter and returned with a folded piece of paper which she handed to Maisie. "There you are, Madam. Now then, what about some sausages for your supper?"

Maisie was about to decline, then thought otherwise. Smiling at the assistant, she gave her order. "Lovely. A pound, please."

"Right you are." And with a flourish copied directly from Joseph Waite, the assistant swept up a string of bulbous pork sausages and laid them on the scale. The Beale family would eat well tonight.

"Stratton any easier to talk to this afternoon, Miss?"

"I wish I could say yes, Billy. It started out well enough, then became rather difficult."

"Funny, that. 'E always seemed such a reasonable bloke."

Maisie took off her mackintosh, hat, and gloves, and laid her document case and a brown carrier bag on her desk. "It'll settle down and we'll all be talking again after this case is closed, Billy. Men in Stratton's position can't close too many doors, especially those leading to people they've consulted with in the past. No, there are two struggles going on there: one in the department and one inside Stratton. As long as we are *seen* to be doing our part, I'm not going to worry." Maisie looked at her watch. "Oh, look at the time, Billy! It's almost half past four. Let's just go over some details on the Waite case and make plans for Monday. I'm driving down to Chelstone tomorrow morning first thing, and I must also visit my fath —"

Maisie was interrupted by the telephone.

"Fitzroy five — Miss Waite. Where are you? Are you all right?"

"Yes." The line crackled.

"Miss Waite? Miss Waite you may be in danger. Tell me where you are."

Silence.

"Miss Waite? Are you still there?"

"Yes, yes, I'm here."

"Well, can you speak up a bit, please? This is a terrible line."

"I'm in a telephone kiosk." Charlotte's voice was slightly louder.

"Why have you called me, Miss Waite?"

"I . . . I . . . need to speak to you."

"About what?" Maisie held her breath as she pushed Charlotte just a little.

"There's more to tell you. I didn't tell you . . . everything."

"Can you tell me now?"

Silence.

"Miss Waite?"

"I have to speak to you privately, in person."

"Where are you? I'll come right away."

Maisie thought she heard Charlotte crying; then there was silence but for the crackling telephone line.

"Miss Waite? Are we still connected?"

"Oh, it's no use. It's no use −"

There was a click and the line was dead. Maisie replaced the receiver.

"Damn!"

Billy's eyes widened. "What was all that about, Miss?"

"Charlotte Waite. She said she wanted to talk to me, then hung up saying it was 'no use'."

"Lost 'er bottle, did she?"

"She certainly did. It was a bad line. She could have been anywhere. Mind you, there was noise in the background." Maisie closed her eyes as if to hear the entire call again. "What was that sound?"

"D'you still want me to do all this?" Billy held up the list.

"Yes. She could have been in Paris for all I know. Or outside an hotel on the Edgware Road. But at least we know she's still alive. It's getting late, but you can make a start, and then get on with it again tomorrow morning."

"Right you are, Miss."

"I'll need to speak to Lady Rowan at Chelstone before I see my father, then I'll come back to London to continue the search for Charlotte Waite."

"How can 'er Ladyship help?"

Maisie turned to Billy. "She was involved in the suffrage movement before the war, and knows a lot about what different women's associations did. I could use more colour on the page."

"I know, Miss."

Maisie looked up at Billy, walked over to her desk, and sighed. "Billy, give it another half an hour or so and then get on your way. It's been a long day – in fact, it's been a long week, and you'll have to put in quite a few hours tomorrow."

"Aw, thanks, Miss. I want to see the nippers before they go to bed."

"Oh, and Billy – here's something for you." Maisie held out the brown paper carrier bag.

"What's all this, Miss?"

"A pound of Waite's sausages. Best in London, they say."

Shortly after Billy began his evening journey back to Whitechapel, Maisie climbed into the MG, started the engine, and pulled out of Fitzroy Square. A telephone call had confirmed that Waite's warehouse in Rotherhithe remained open until late in the evening, while lorries bound for the shops were packed with the next day's deliveries. Mr Jempson, the warehouse manager, was available and had kindly agreed to see Maisie as soon as she arrived.

Fog horns bellowed along the Thames as carriage drivers, motorists and barge captains alike made their way through the murky smog that once again began to shroud London. Maisie negotiated the MG along narrow roads that were almost lanes, byways that led from the docks to riverside warehouses. Following directions carefully, she eventually turned into a cobbled side street and drew up in front of a pair of open gates with a sign above in blue-and-gold lettering: WAITE'S INTERNATIONAL STORES. SOUTH-EASTERN WAREHOUSE. A guard in a blue-and-gold uniform waved from the gatehouse and came out to greet Maisie, a clipboard under his arm.

"Evening, Miss." He touched the peak of his blue cap. "Expected, are you?"

"Yes, I'm here to see Mr Jempson, in the offices."

"Ah, of course, he telephoned through to put you on the list not long ago." The guard leaned down towards Maisie and pointed ahead, to an extensive courtyard illuminated by a lamp in each corner. "Don't park by the lorries, otherwise you'll have them drivers givin' me a row. Go over to where it says 'Visitors' and put the motor there. And Miss, park nose out, if you don't mind."

Nose out at the warehouse, too? Maisie's countenance revealed her thoughts.

"It's the way Mr Waite likes it, Miss." He smiled at Maisie. "You see that door there, the big wooden one? You go through there, up the stairs, and one of the clerks will be there at the top to meet you. I'll telephone to let them know you're on your way."

Maisie thanked the guard, noting that no expense seemed to have been spared even in equipping the warehouse. Having parked the MG following the guard's instructions to the letter, Maisie entered the granite building through the wooden door and was greeted at the top of the stairs by a young man in dark grey trousers, polished brogues, a crisp white shirt and black tie, with armbands to keep his sleeves drawn away from his wrists. A freshly sharpened pencil protruded from behind his right ear.

"Evening, Miss Dobbs. My name's Smithers. Come this way to Mr Jempson's office."

"Thank you."

Maisie was led to an office surrounded by windows that looked down onto the warehouse floor, the rich cherrywood frames and panelling gleaming under the glow of several lamps that illuminated the room.

"Thank you, Mr Smithers."

Jempson held out his hand for Maisie to take a seat in the leather chair on the opposite side of the desk. It was obviously reserved for guests. A rather less comfortable chair was situated alongside.

"I am most grateful for your time, Mr Jempson."

"How may I be of service to you?"

Maisie had to tread carefully. She already knew that Mr Jempson's employer was held in great esteem by his staff.

"I wonder if you could help me with a most delicate matter."

"I'll try." Jempson, a tall, thin man wearing an ensemble almost identical to his assistant's, looked over half-moon glasses at Maisie, on his guard.

Maisie relaxed into her chair, an adjustment that was mirrored by Jempson. *Good.* Sensing that the conversation might now proceed, Maisie envisaged the tiled memorial of names in Waite's International Stores, and began to ask the questions that had plagued her since the visit to Dulwich this morning.

Maisie took her leave from the warehouse an hour later. Mr Jempson had indeed been most helpful. In fact, as he confessed while escorting her to the MG, "It's done me good to talk about it all. I saw them all go, and most of them never came back. Broke the boss's heart, it did. Couldn't do enough for the families either. Must be terrible for him. To be reminded of it every day, every day when you look into the eyes of your own daughter. It's a wonder he wants her back, if you ask me. Mind you, like I said upstairs, he had to keep her at home, after all that business with the windows being broken when he got her that flat on her own, after the war. Everyone loved Mr Waite, but there's no love lost on his daughter or them harpies she was with. I wouldn't blame anyone who, you know, had lost someone . . ."

Maisie placed a hand on his arm. "Thank you again, Mr Jempson. Take good care, and don't worry, this conversation is in absolute confidence."

The man touched his forehead as Maisie left him to drive away into the thick darkness pierced by foghorns. Maisie did not go far. Parking close to the water, she remained in the motor car for some moments to review her plans. She would telephone Lady Rowan that evening to ask if she might join her for a walk before breakfast. She knew that the older woman would have valuable insights to add to the evidence Maisie now had to hand. Her absolute priority was to find Charlotte. Was she ready to make a confession? Or was she in immediate danger? Maisie shook her head, pulled her collar up and stepped from the car. She walked along Bermondsey Wall and stopped to watch the thick smog which seemed to curdle above the water. A wall had originally been built to keep out floodwaters in the Middle Ages; as people walked on the wall to avoid the muddy ground, the wall became a road, but the name was never lost. Maisie stood in silence feeling as if she were caught in the mud, unable to move. Charlotte was lost, and it was her fault. The chain of foghorns up and down the Thames began their round of blasts again, and as they did so Maisie closed her eyes. *Of course!* What was it that Billy had said to her? Just after she'd received the call from Reverend Sneath? Something about being hidden in full view? While listening to Charlotte speaking from the telephone kiosk, she'd heard the foghorns from south of the river. Charlotte was somewhere right under her father's nose. She was close to the warehouse. But where?

The area was always teeming with people. It would be like finding a pebble lost on the beach. Sarson's Vinegar, Courage's Brewery, Crosse & Blackwell's tinned foods, the leatherworks, Peek Frean's biscuit factory, the docks, warehouses receiving foods from all over the world – she could be anywhere in Bermondsey. Maisie knew that the journey to Kent could not be delayed, but she would return to London quickly. Charlotte might have chosen to call from an identifiable area deliberately to send them in the wrong direction. She needed a source of information in Bermondsey. Maisie smiled. *A Bermondsey boy. That's what I need.*

20

LEAVING LONDON at the crack of dawn, Maisie arrived at Chelstone early. The interior of the small cottage was cold and not at all welcoming as it would have been if Frankie Dobbs were at home. Maisie began opening curtains and windows to let in shafts of early morning sunshine, and a breath of fresh air. The rooms were neat and tidy, revealing regular attention from staff up at the manor house. Frankie Dobbs was much loved at Chelstone. His house had been well kept in anticipation of his return, but it lacked the life that Frankie brought to his simple dwelling.

Maisie moved around the cottage, running her fingers across her father's belongings, as if touching the leather traces kept in the scullery awaiting repair, or his tools and brushes, brought him closer. She made a list of things that required attention. A bed must be moved into the small sitting room so that Frankie would not have to negotiate the stairs. A room must be prepared for Billy upstairs. She must speak again to Maurice about plans for Billy's rehabilitation, in body, mind, and soul. She knew her father's contribution to this part of Billy's recovery was just as important, for Frankie was above all else a father, and Billy would gain as much from him as he would from Maurice, Gideon Brown, or Dr Andrew Dene.

Her task complete, she left the cottage to join Lady Rowan, who was in the distance striding as purposefully as she could across the lawns at the front of the manor.

Lady Rowan waved to Maisie with her walking stick and called out. "Good morning, Maisie," followed by, "Nutmeg, drop it! Drop it now and come here!"

Maisie laughed to see the dog come to his owner, tail between his legs, head down, and filled with remorse.

"This dog will eat anything, absolutely anything. How lovely to see you, my dear." Lady Rowan reached out and squeezed Maisie's upper arm. Though she held Maisie in great affection, Lady Rowan, restrained by considerations of position and place, had only once demonstrated her feelings. When Maisie returned from France, Lady Rowan had taken her in her arms and said, "I am so relieved, so very relieved that you are home." On that occasion Maisie was silent in her embrace, not knowing quite what to say.

"And it's lovely to see you too, Lady Rowan," replied Maisie, placing her hand on top of Lady Rowan's for just a second.

"Now then, before we get down to business" – she glanced at Maisie as they began to walk together across the lawn – "because I know you're here on business, Maisie, what's the news about your dear father and the young man you're sending to help."

"Well, I'll see my father later, before I return to London. I've spoken to Dr Simms, who thinks it'll be another week before he's transferred to the convalescent hospital. I think he'll be there for about three or four weeks, according to Dr Dene, who says it might have been longer, but he's spoken to the doctors at Pembury, and my father is making excellent progress, even at this early stage. During that time Mr Beale will look after the horses. Then, when Dad comes home to Chelstone, Mr Beale will stay on at the cottage and work under his supervision."

"Which as we both know means that your father will be hobbling over to the stables each day even though he shouldn't."

"Probably, though I've told Mr Beale to keep an eye on him."

Lady Rowan nodded. "I'll be so relieved when he's back in charge. Then I'll feel I can leave for Town."

"Yes, of course. Thank you, L–"

Lady Rowan held up her hand to silence Maisie, as they leaned toward each other to avoid the low branch of a majestic beech tree.

"What can I do for you, Maisie Dobbs?" Lady Rowan smiled at Maisie, a gleam in her eye.

"I want you to tell me what you know about the different women's affiliations in the war. I'm particularly interested in those women who handed out white feathers."

Lady Rowan blinked rapidly, the sparkle vanishing instantly. "Oh, those harpies!"

"Harpies." It was the second time in two days that Maisie had heard the term in connection with the women. And in her mind's eye she saw the illustrated flyleaf of a book that Maurice had given her to read, years ago. A short note had accompanied her assignment: "In learning about the myths and legends of old, we learn something of ourselves. Stories, Maisie, are never just stories. They contain fundamental truths about the human condition." The black-and-white charcoal drawing depicted birds with women's faces, birds carrying humans in their beaks as they flew away into the darkness. Maisie was jolted back to the present by Lady Rowan.

"Of course, you were either engrossed in your studies at Girton or away overseas doing something worthwhile, so you would have missed the Order of the White Feather." Lady Rowan slowed her pace, as if to allow memories to catch up with the present. "This was before conscription, and it was all started by that man, Admiral Charles Fitzgerald. After the the initial rush to enlist had fallen off, they needed more men at the front, so he obviously thought the way to get them there was through the women. I remember seeing the handbills starting to pop up all over the place." Lady Rowan mimicked a stern masculine voice: "Is your best boy in uniform yet?"

"Oh yes, I think I saw one at a railway station before I went into nursing."

"The plan was to get young women to go around giving the white feather – a sign of cowardice – to young men not in uniform. And–" she raised a pointed finger in emphasis. "And those two women – the *Scarlet Pimpernel* woman – what was her name? Oh yes, Orczy, the Hungarian baroness, well, she was a great supporter of Fitzgerald, and so was Mary Ward – Mrs Humphrey Ward."

"You didn't care for her, did you?"

Lady Rowan pursed her lips. Maisie realized that she was so intent upon Lady Rowan's words that she had been ignoring the vista of the Weald of Kent around her. They had reached a gate and stile. If she had been alone, Maisie would have clambered over the stile with the same energy as the three dogs before her. Instead, she pulled back the rusty iron gate lock and allowed Lady Rowan to walk through first.

"Frankly, no, I didn't." Lady Rowan continued. "She did a lot of very commendable work in bringing education to those who might not otherwise have had the opportunity, organizing children's play groups for working women, that sort of thing. But she was an anti-suffragist, so we were like oil and water. Of course she's long gone now, but she supported recruiting men for the trenches by this most horrible means, through the accusations of women. And as for the women themselves –"

"Yes, I'm interested in the women, the ones who gave out the white feathers."

"Ah yes." She sighed. "You know, I wondered about them at the time. What made them do it? What made young women say, 'Oh, yes, I'll do that. I'll walk the streets with my bag of white feathers, and I'll give one to each boy I see not in uniform, even though I don't know one jot about him!'"

"And what do you think, now that time has passed?"

Lady Rowan sighed and stopped to lean on her walking stick. "Maisie, that question is more up your alley than mine, really. You know, the business of discovering why people do what they do."

"But?" Maisie encouraged Lady Rowan to speak her mind.

"When I think back, it's alarming, some of the things that came to pass. One minute the suffrage movement was seen as a tribe of marauding pariahs by the government, then, as soon as war was declared there was a division in our ranks. One lot became the darlings of Lloyd George, who persuaded women to release men to the battlefield by taking up their work until they returned home. The other half of our number went all out for peace, joining with women throughout Europe. Frankly, on an individual level, I think women needed to take part. We're all Boadiceas really." Lady Rowan's smile was sad. "But some women, some young women who perhaps didn't have a cause, found some level of belonging, of worthiness – possibly even of some sort of connection – in joining together to force young men to join the army. I wonder if they saw it as a game, one in which they scored points for each man intimidated into joining up."

The two women turned simultaneously and began to make their way back towards Chelstone Manor. They walked together in silence for some moments, until Lady Rowan spoke again.

"Aren't you going to tell me why you've come to me with these questions? Why the curiosity about the Order of the White Feather?"

Maisie took a deep breath. "I have reason to believe that the recent deaths of three young women are connected to the white feather movement." Maisie checked her watch.

Lady Rowan nodded, seeming somewhat weary now that the early walk was coming to an end. "That's one more thing that I detest about war. It's not over when it ends. Of course, it seems as if everyone's pally again, what with agreements, the international accords, and contracts and so on. But it still lives inside the living, doesn't it?" She turned to Maisie. "Heavens, I sound like Maurice now!"

They followed the path back to the manicured lawns of Chelstone Manor.

"Will you join me for breakfast, Maisie?"

"No, I'd better be on my way. Before I go, may I use your telephone?"

"You've no need to ask. Go on." Lady Rowan waved Maisie on her way. "And take good care, won't you? We expect to see your Mr Beale here by the end of the month!"

Only if I close this case quickly, thought Maisie as she ran towards the manor.

Miss Dobbs. Delightful to hear from you. I've had another word with Dr–"

"This isn't about my father, Dr Dene. Look, I must hurry. I wonder if you can help me. Do you still know Bermondsey well?"

"Of course. In fact, once a fortnight I work at Maurice's clinic for a day or two on a Saturday or Sunday."

"Oh, I see." Maisie was surprised that she didn't already know about Dene's continued connection with Maurice's work. "I need to find a person who may be hiding in Bermondsey. She may be in danger, and I have to locate her soon. Very soon. Do you know anyone who might be able to help me."

Dene laughed. "All very cloak-and-dagger isn't it, Miss Dobbs?"

"I am absolutely serious." Maisie felt herself become impatient with him. "If you can't help, then say so."

Dene's voice changed. "I'm sorry. Yes, I do know someone. He's called Smiley Rackham and he can usually be found outside the Bow & Arrow; it's just off Southwark Park Road, where they have the market. Just make your way along the market until you see a pie 'n' mash shop on the corner, turn into that side street and you'll see the Bow. Can't miss it. Smiley sells matches and you'll recognise him by the scar that runs from his mouth to his ear. It makes him look as if he's pulling a huge grin."

"Oh. Was he wounded in the war?"

"If he was ever in a war, it was probably the Crimean. No, Smiley worked on the barges as a boy. Got an unloading hook caught in the side of his mouth." He laughed, "Knowing Smiley, it was open too wide at the time. Anyway, even though there are lots of new people in Bermondsey now, he doesn't miss a trick. He's a good place to start. He'll cost you a bob or two though."

"Thank you, Dr Dene."

"Miss Dobbs –"

Maisie had already replaced the receiver. She had just enough time to drive to Pembury for morning visiting hours.

Maisie was filled with guilt from the time she left Pembury Hospital until she parked the car in Bermondsey. The conversation with her father had been stilted and halting, each searching for a subject that would engage the other, each trying to move beyond a series of questions. Maisie was too preoccupied to speak of her mother. Finally, sensing her discomfort, Frankie had said, "Your mind's on your work isn't it, love?" He insisted that she need not remain and, gratefully, she left the ward, promising that she'd stay longer next time. Next time . . . *He's not getting any younger.* With Maurice's words pounding in her head, Maisie sped towards London. Now she had to locate Smiley Rackham.

The market was a writhing mass of humanity by the time she arrived, and would be alive with people until late at night. Even the women stallholders were dressed like men, with flat caps, worn jackets, and pinafores made from old sacks. They called to one another, shouted out prices, and kept the throng noisy and moving. Maisie finally found the Bow & Arrow. Smiley Rackham was outside, just as Dene had predicted.

"Mr Rackham?"

Maisie leaned down to speak to the old man. Smiley's clothes, though dapper, as if they had once belonged to a gentleman, had seen much better days. His eyes sparkled below a flat cap and his stubbled chin dimpled as he smiled. It was a broad smile that accentuated the livid scar so well described by Dene.

"And who wants 'im?"

"My name's Maisie Dobbs," Maisie continued, deliberately slipping into the south London dialect of her childhood. "Andrew Dene said you'd 'elp me."

"Old Andeeee said to see me, eh?"

"Yes. *Andy* said you knew everyone hereabouts."

"Gettin' tricky, what wiv all these Oxford and Cambridge do-gooders comin' in."

Had the situation not been so urgent, Maisie might have grinned. Now she wanted to get down to business. She took out the photograph of Charlotte Waite and handed it to Rackham.

"Course, me old eyes ain't what they were. Probably need to get some glasses." He squinted at Maisie. "Mind you, cost of glasses today –"

She reached into her purse and handed Smiley a shining half-crown.

"Very nice pair of glasses, too. Now then let me see." Smiley tapped the side of his head. "This is where I've got to rack 'em, you know, the old brain cells." He looked at the photograph, brought it closer to his eyes, and squinted again. "Never forget a dial. Got a photographic memory, I've been told. Now then," – Smiley paused "she looks a bit different nah, don't she?"

"You've seen her?"

"I'm not one 'undred percent. It's me eyes again."

Maisie handed him a florin.

"Yeah. Dahn the soup kitchen. Only been there a coupl'a days, but I've seen 'er comin' and goin'. She weren't all dolled up like this though."

"Which soup kitchen? Where?"

"Not the one run by the Quakers, the other one, on Tanner Street, just along from the old workhouse –" Smiley gave directions.

"Thank you Mr Rackham."

Smiley's eye's sparkled. "O' course my name ain't Rackham."

"It isn't?"

"Nah! My surname's Pointer. They call me Smiley Rack'em cos that's what I do." He tapped the side of his head. "But now I won't 'ave to do anythin' for a day or two, thanks to you Miss Dobbs." Smiley rattled the coins as Maisie waved and went on her way.

She stood for a while just inside the door of the soup kitchen, in the shadows, where she would be able to observe without being seen. There was one large room lined with trestle tables, all covered with clean white cloths. The staff were working hard to maintain the dignity of people who had lost so much in a depression that was affecting every stratum of life. And at the lowest end there was little or no comfort. Men, women, and children queued for a bowl of soup and a crust of bread, then filed to the tables to find a place

266

among known faces, perhaps calling out to a friend, "Awright, then?" or making a joke, even starting a song going for others to join in. Maisie saw that there was something here that money could not buy: spirit. As she watched, one man at the front of the line began to shuffle his feet in a dance, then clapped out a tune. Everyone started to sing as they waited, so that even in her anxiety to find Charlotte, Maisie smiled.

> Boiled beef and carrots,
> Boiled beef and carrots,
> That's the stuff for your Darby Kel,
> Makes you fat and it keeps you well.
> Don't live like vegetarians,
> On food they give to parrots,
> From morn till night blow out your kite
> On boiled beef and carrots.

Then she saw Charlotte.

It was a different woman whom Maisie watched moving back and forth between the kitchen and the tables, talking to other workers, smiling at the children, leaning over to tousle the hair of a mischievous boy or stop a fight over a toy. *Two days. She's been here only two days and people are looking up to her.* Maisie shook her head as she watched Charlotte help another worker. *And no one knows who she is.* There was something in the way that Charlotte moved and spoke to the people that reminded Maisie of someone. *A natural and decisive leader.* Charlotte Waite was her father's daughter.

Maisie made her move. "Miss Waite." She touched Charlotte's sleeve as she was returning to the kitchen with an empty cauldron.

"Oh!"

Maisie reached for the pot just in time, and together they placed it safely on a table.

"How did you find me here?"

"That's not important. You wanted to speak to me?"

267

"Look –" Charlotte glanced around her. "I can't talk here, you know. Meet me when I've finished. I'm on duty until seven, then I go back to my digs."

Maisie shook her head. "No, Miss Waite. I'm not letting you out of my sight. I'll stay here until you finish. Find me an apron and I'll help out."

Charlotte's eyes grew wider.

"Oh, for goodness' sake, Miss Waite, I'm no stranger to a bit of elbow grease!"

Charlotte took Maisie's coat, and when she returned they began to work together while another refrain from the hungry Londoners echoed up into the rafters.

> I like pickled onions,
> I like piccalilli.
> Pickled cabbage is all right
> With a bit of cold meat on Sunday night.
> I can go termartoes,
> But what I do prefer,
> Is a little bit of cu-cum-cu-cum-cu-cum,
> A little bit of cucumber.

The women left the soup kitchen together at half past seven. Charlotte led the way through dusky streets to a decrepit three-storey house that was probably once the home of a wealthy merchant, but now, a couple of centuries on, had been divided into flats and bed-sitting rooms. Charlotte's room on the top floor was small, with angled ceilings so that both women had to stoop to avoid collision with the beams. Despite being confident in her soup kitchen role, Charlotte was now nervous and immediately excused herself to use the lavatory at the end of a damp and dreary landing. Maisie so mistrusted her charge that she waited on the landing, watching the lavatory door. In those few moments alone she prepared her mind for the conversation with Charlotte. She breathed deeply, and with eyes still closed she visualized a white light shining down on her head, flooding her body with compassion, with understanding, and with spoken words that would support Charlotte as she struggled to unburden herself. *May I not sit in judgment. May I be open to hearing and accepting the truth of what I am told. May my decisions be for the good of all concerned. May my work bring peace . . .*

Charlotte returned and, stooping, they entered her room again. It was then that Maisie saw a framed prayer on the wall, most probably brought from Camden Abbey to her Bermondsey refuge.

In your mercy, Lord, give them rest.
When you come to judge the living and the dead, give them rest.
Eternal rest grant to them, O Lord,
And let perpetual light shine upon them; in your mercy, Lord.
Give them rest.

Had Charlotte found any rest at Camden Abbey? Were Rosamund, Lydia, and Philippa now at rest? And the killer? Would there ever be rest for all of them?

Charlotte pulled up two ladderback chairs in front of a meagre gas fire, and they sat down, neither taking off her coat as the room was far too cold. They were silent for some minutes before Charlotte began to speak.

"I don't know where to begin, really . . ."

Maisie reached across with her now-warm hands and, taking Charlotte's hands in her own, spoke gently. "Start anywhere; we can go back and forth as we need."

Charlotte swallowed and pursed her lips before speaking.

"I . . . I think the beginning is when I first realized how much my father loved my brother, Joe. It wasn't that he didn't love me. No, it was just that he loved Joe so much more. I think I was quite young. Of course, my mother wasn't there very often. They weren't at all suited, I expect you know that already." Charlotte sat in silence for a few moments, her eyes closed, her hands trembling. Maisie noticed how her eyelids moved, as if conjuring up the past caused her pain.

"It wasn't obvious, it was little things, really. He'd come home from work and as soon as he saw Joe his eyes would light up. He'd ruffle his hair, that sort of thing. Then he'd see me. The smile he gave me wasn't so . . . so *alive*."

"Did you get along with your brother?" asked Maisie.

"Oh, yes, yes. Joe was my hero! He *knew*, I know he knew how I felt. He'd always think up a special game for us to play, or if my father wanted to play cricket with him or whatever, Joe would always say, 'Charlie has to come, too.' That's what he called me: Charlie."

Maisie was silent, then touched Charlotte's hand again for her to continue.

"I don't know when it started to *annoy* me. I think it was when I reached twelve or thirteen. I felt as if I were running a race I could never win and I was out of breath with trying. Of course my mother was firmly ensconced in Yorkshire by then, kept out of the way by my father, who was doing very well in business. New shops were opening, and Joe was always there with him. Joe was seven years older than I and being groomed to take over the business eventually. I remember at breakfast one day, I announced that I wanted to do what Joe was doing, start working for the business, at the bottom, like all the other apprentices. But my father simply laughed. Said that I wasn't cut out for hard work – graft he called it. 'Not got the 'ands for a bit o' 'ard graft.'" Charlotte mimicked her father's broad northern accent perfectly.

"Then he sent me off to Switzerland, to school. It was horrible. I missed Joe, my best friend. And I missed home. But . . . but something happened to me. I've thought about it a lot." She looked directly at Maisie for the first time. "I've really considered what might have happened. I became . . . very detached. I had been pushed away for so long you see." Charlotte began to stutter. "It *seemed* the best thing to do, to be. If I was going to be the one pushed to the outside, I might as well stay there. Do you understand?"

Maisie nodded. Yes, she understood.

"I made some friends, other girls from the school. Rosamund, Lydia, and Philippa. It was the sort of school where girls were 'finished' rather than educated. I felt humiliated, as if he thought me only good for arranging flowers, buying clothes and knowing how to correctly address servants. Then, when war was declared, we all came home to England. Of course, my father, the great man of commerce" – Maisie noticed the sarcasm in Charlotte's voice – "had already secured government contracts to supply army rations." Charlotte looked up thoughtfully. "It's amazing, when you think of it, the people who do well out of war. My clothing allowance came courtesy of soldiers being fed by Joseph Waite." She looked away and for a while they sat in silence until Charlotte was ready to take up her story again.

"After we'd returned home, the four of us were pretty much at a loose end. We tried knitting scarves, socks, that sort of thing. Rolling bandages. Joseph was working at the warehouse. He'd started off at the lowest rung and at that time was a receiving clerk. Mind you, he had been apprenticed with the butchers, taken the deliveries out, and he was the blue-eyed boy of the whole business. Everybody loved 'Young Joe'." She mimicked a south London accent, which made Maisie look up suddenly.

"How did you get along with Joe after your return?"

"Very well, actually. When I asked to work for the business and my father refused, Joe stuck up for me, said it would be a good idea, a good example." Once again she looked into the distance. "He was a wonderful young man, Joe."

Maisie said nothing while Charlotte paused to gather her thoughts.

"So, there we were, young girls with few skills, time on our hands and – for my part – nowhere I seemed to . . . to . . . *belong*." Charlotte exhaled deeply. "Then I found out about the Order of the White Feather. I saw a bill posted. So I persuaded the others. It didn't take much. We went along to a meeting." Charlotte held out her upturned hands helplessly. "And that was the beginning."

Maisie watched Charlotte. *A natural and decisive leader.*

"Then the game went on, and we were more than willing players. Each day we would venture forth with our little bags of white feathers, and we'd hand them out to young men not in uniform. We each took out an equal number of feathers and when we saw one another later, we'd see if all the feathers were gone. Of course, we thought we were doing the right thing. Sometimes . . . sometimes, I'd walk past an enlistment office and I'd see a young man standing there, or two together, still holding the feathers I'd given them. And I thought, *Oh, good*."

"No one at home knew what I was up to. My father was busy, always so busy, and Joe was working hard at the warehouse. No one wondered what I might be doing. Joe always asked for me as soon as he came home. I think he knew that I was unravelling. But inside me . . ." – she touched the plain belt buckle of her dress with the flat of her hand – "inside me, I was resentful towards Joe. It was as if I didn't know where to put all the *horribleness* that was festering inside me. It was like a disease, a lump." A single tear slid down her cheek. "Then, one day, I thought of a way to get back at him – my father – and to get Joe out of the way for a while. The trouble was, I didn't *think*. I didn't think that it would be forever."

Silence descended. Maisie rubbed her upper arms with hands that had become cold once again. *May I not sit in judgment.*

"Go on, Charlotte."

Charlotte Waite looked at her. Some might have thought the woman's posture arrogant, Maisie knew that she was searching for strength.

"I suggested to the girls, to Rosamund, Lydia, and Philippa, that we should try to place feathers in the hands of as many young men as we could. And I also suggested a means of accomplishing the task. The warehouse, which employed so many young men – the runners, the drivers, the packers, the butchers, clerks . . . an army, in fact – was run in shifts, with a bell sounding for the change between each shift. It was my plan for the four of us to wait outside the gates when the shifts changed, to hand out feathers." Charlotte put her hand to her lips, then plunged on. "We handed a feather to each and every man who walked from the warehouse, regardless of age or job. And when we had done that, we went to the main shops, as many as we could get to in a day, and did the same thing. By the time my father found us, I'd handed out all but one of my feathers." Charlotte's chin dipped. "He drew alongside us in the motor car, with another motor following. The door opened, and he was furious. He instructed the chauffeur in the other car to take Rosamund, Lydia, and Philippa to their homes, and he grabbed me by the arm and almost threw me into the motor." Opening her eyes, Charlotte looked again at Maisie. "You are no doubt familiar, Miss Dobbs, with the wartime practice of men enlisting as 'pals' – men who lived on the same street, worked with one another, that sort of thing?"

Maisie nodded.

"Well, Waite's lost a good three-quarters of its workforce when the men joined up as pals within a week of our handing out the feathers. Waite's Boys, they called themselves. Joe was one of them."

Maisie's attention was drawn to Charlotte's hands. The nails of one had dug into the soft flesh of the other. Her hand was bleeding. Charlotte covered the wound and began speaking again.

"My father is a quick thinker. He saw to it that the families knew that the men's jobs would be there for them upon their return. He offered wives and daughters jobs, with the promise that they would be paid a man's wages and he saw to it that each man who enlisted was sent a regular parcel from Waite's. He's good at taking care of the families, my father. The trouble is, none of that compassion extended to me. The workers thought he was marvellous, a real patriarch. There were always parties for the children, bonuses at Christmas. And all through the war Waite's kept going, doing very well."

Without thinking, Charlotte inspected her bloody hand and wiped it along the side of her coat. "And they were all lost. Oh, a few came home, wounded, but most of them were killed in action. Joe died. He's buried over there." She looked into Maisie's eyes again. "So, you see, we – I – killed them. Oh, I know, you might say that they would have been conscripted sooner or later, but really, I know that we sent them off to their deaths. Counting the parents, the sweethearts, the widows and the children, there must be a legion of people who would like to see the four of us dead."

In the silence that followed, Maisie took a fresh handkerchief from the pocket of her tweed jacket. She held it between Charlotte's hand and her own, pressed their palms together, and closed her eyes. *May I not sit in judgment. May my decisions be for the good of all concerned. May my work bring peace.*

21

MAISIE INSISTED that Charlotte accompany her back to Ebury Place. It was too dangerous for her to be left alone in Bermondsey. They said little on the drive across London, which included a detour to Whitechapel where Charlotte remained in the MG while Maisie called upon Billy briefly to ask him to meet her at the office the next morning. Sunday was to be another working day, and an important one.

Confident that Charlotte would not abscond now, Maisie settled her into a guest suite on the same floor as her own rooms before taking rest. It had been a very long day and would be a long night as her plan, which must be executed soon, took shape. It was past ten o'clock when she went to the library to telephone Maurice Blanche. She heard only one ring before her call was answered.

"Maisie!" Maurice greeted her without waiting to hear her voice. "I have expected your call."

Maisie smiled. "I thought you might."

They both knew that Maisie needed to speak with her mentor when a case was nearing closure. As if drawn by invisible threads, they each leaned closer to their respective telephone receivers.

"I was speaking with Andrew Dene this morning," Maurice continued.

"Oh – did he telephone to talk about my father?"

"No, actually, he came here this morning."

"Oh?" Maisie was startled.

Maurice grinned. "You are not the only pupil who comes to my house, Maisie."

"Well, yes, of course." Maisie was glad that Maurice could not see the blood rising to her cheeks.

"Anyway, Andrew came to see me about several things, including Mr Beale."

"And?"

"Nothing of great concern, simply a discussion of how we may best help the man."

"I see."

"I expect he'll be here shortly, in the next day or so?"

"Yes. When this case is closed."

"So, Maisie, I sense that as far as your assignment is concerned, the case is already closed. You have found Charlotte Waite?"

"Yes. Though Mr Waite insisted that her return to his home in Dulwich would be the point at which he would consider our work complete."

"And when will that be?"

"I will be meeting Billy at the office tomorrow morning. The three of us will take a taxicab to Dulwich."

"You have another plan, don't you, Maisie?"

"Yes. Yes, I do."

Maisie heard Maurice tap out his pipe and the rustle of a packet of sweet Old Holborn tobacco. Maisie closed her eyes and envisaged him preparing the bowl, pressing tobacco down, then striking a match, holding it to the tobacco and drawing on the stem to light the fragrant leaf. Maisie breathed in deeply, imagining the aroma. In that moment she was a girl again, sitting at the table in the library at Ebury Place, reading aloud from her notes while her teacher paced back and forth, back and forth, then holding the bowl of the pipe in his right hand, pointed at her and asked out loud, "Tell me what evidence you have upon which to base such conclusions."

"So, what else have you to tell me? And where, if I may ask, are the police?" asked Maurice.

"Charlotte has confessed her part in bringing about the enlistment of a good number of her father's employees, including her older half-brother, Joe, who was the apple of her father's eye."

Maisie drew breath deeply and told Maurice the story that she had first heard from the warehouse manager and then from Charlotte. "She believes herself guilty of a crime."

"I take it that you do not consider Charlotte capable of murder."

"I am sure she is not the killer, though she may be the next victim."

"And the man in custody, the man the police believe to be the murderer?"

"I believe him to be innocent of the crime of murder. He may not be a good man . . . but he did not kill Rosamund, Philippa, and Lydia."

"Stratton seemed a fair man in the past. Has he not heard your protests?"

As they spoke, Maisie felt, not for the first time, a sensation of oneness with the mind of her teacher, an intimacy of intellect and understanding, even as he quizzed her. "Detective Inspector Stratton has brought his prejudices to the case. He lost his wife in childbirth and was left with a son. His inner turmoil has clouded his usual sound judgment. The man he believes to be the killer – Magnus Fisher – is an unlikable character, one who has not treated women fairly. Indeed, he admits that he married Lydia Fisher for her money."

"Ah, I see."

"I've tried to communicate my suspicions to him on several occasions, to no avail. Stratton will not believe that Fisher is not the guilty man until I hand him the real murderer on a plate."

"Yes, yes indeed." Maurice drew deeply on his pipe. "And you plan to trap the killer, do you not?"

Maisie nodded. "Yes, I do."

Maurice began to speak once more. "Tell me about the means of death again, Maisie."

"Sir Bernard Spilsbury has concluded that poison was administered, which Cuthbert has identified as morphine. In two of the cases the victim's death was followed by a brutal stabbing."

"The weapon?"

"The bayonet from a short-barrel Lee Enfield rifle."

Maurice nodded. "The killer venting his fury after the death of his victim."

"Yes."

"Interesting."

"Anger, pain, suffering . . . loneliness," said Maisie. "There's quite a cocktail of motives there to be going on with."

"Charlotte is right, Maisie. It could be any one of a hundred people."

"One hundred people might have reason for vengeance, but not every one of those people would seek revenge in such a way. The killer is a person tormented day in and day out, one for whom there is no respite, not for one minute in twenty-four hours. And that person has discovered, tragically, that in meting out punishment there has been no escape from the terrible ache of loss. The killer isn't just anyone in that mass of grieving relatives, Maurice. No, it's one person in particular."

Maurice nodded. "And you know who it is, don't you?"

"Yes. I believe I do."

"You will take all necessary precautions, Maisie."

"Of course."

"Good."

They were silent for a moment, then Maurice spoke quietly. "Be wary of compassion, Maisie. Do not let it blind you to dangers. Never let pity gain the upper hand. I know this killer must be stopped, that he may not feel that his pain is assuaged even if he kills Charlotte. He may go on killing thereafter. We have together faced great dangers, Maisie. Remember all that you have learned. Now then – go. You must prepare for tomorrow. It will be a long day."

Maisie nodded. "I'll be in touch as soon as it's over, Maurice."

◆

Before finally seeking the comfort of her bed, Maisie once again put on her coat and hat and slipped out of the house, remembering her mentor's counsel when they first worked together: "When we walk, and when we look out at a view other than one we are used to every day, we are challenging ourselves to move freely in our work and to look at our conclusions from another perspective. Move the body, Maisie, and you will move the mind." As she walked the quiet night-time streets of Belgravia, Maisie realized that in his final words to her, Maurice had made an assumption, an assumption that was quite wrong.

She had spent hours in silent meditation and was now ready for what the next twenty-four hours might hold. Before taking a light breakfast in the kitchen, where Sandra confirmed that she had personally served breakfast on a tray to Miss Waite in the guest suite and had run a bath for her, Maisie placed a telephone call to the Waite residence. In the kitchen, she went over her other arrangements before knocking on the door of Charlotte's room.

"Good morning." Charlotte answered the door.

"Are you ready, Miss Waite?"

"Yes."

"Well, let's get on then, shall we? It's time we left. I will meet you by the front door in twenty minutes."

It was ten o'clock when they arrived at Fitzroy Square, which was Sunday quiet. As they drew up alongside the Georgian building that housed Maisie's office, Billy crossed the square.

"Oh, good timing," said Maisie. "My assistant has arrived. He is part of my plan, and will be going with us to Dulwich."

Maisie formally introduced them and, once in the office, Billy reached out to take Charlotte Waite's coat. Maisie removed her jacket and hung it on the back of the door.

"Let's get down to business. We should leave by one. That should give us enough time to be absolutely sure of each step." Maisie beckoned Charlotte to join her and Billy at the incident table. A large sheet of paper had been placed where a case map would usually have been unfurled and pinned. "Here's what we're going to do." Maisie took up a pen, and began to explain.

During the conversation that followed, Charlotte excused herself twice and each time Billy stood outside the office door until she returned, to ensure that she did not leave the building. These were the only interruptions until Maisie pushed back her chair and walked over to the telephone on her desk. She dialled the Waite residence in Dulwich.

"Hello. Maisie Dobbs here. I want to confirm that all necessary arrangements have been made for Miss Waite's arrival home this afternoon." Charlotte and Billy looked on as Maisie listened. "Indeed, yes, I spoke to Mr Waite early this morning and I know that he was just about to leave for Yorkshire. Back on Tuesday, isn't he? Yes, good. Do remember, though, Miss Waite does not wish to see anyone and no one must be informed of her arrival. Yes, she'll go straight to her rooms and I will remain there with her until she is settled. Quite. Yes. No, absolutely no one. Good. Right you are. Thank you." Maisie replaced the receiver and turned to Billy.

"Time to get us a cab, Billy."

Billy reached for his coat. "Back in two shakes, Miss."

As Billy closed the door behind him, Maisie turned to Charlotte. "Now then, you are clear on what you are to do?"

"Of course. It's simple really. You're the one taking all the risks."

"As long as you know that when you do your part, you must not be recognized. It's imperative."

"And you think it'll – you know – all be over in a few hours?"

"I believe the murderer will strike again quickly."

Billy returned, flushed with exertion.

"Billy, I've told you not to run!"

"Miss, the taxicab's outside. Better get going.'

They climbed into the cab but were silent throughout the journey, each mentally reviewing the part to be played as the evening unfolded. Upon arrival at Waite's Dulwich mansion, Billy took Charlotte's bag.

"All right?" Maisie put her arm around Charlotte's shoulders and led her towards the house. Charlotte's head was lowered, with only a few strands of hair visible beneath her close-fitting grey hat.

"Yes. I won't let you down."

"I know."

The door opened before they reached the steps leading up to the front door, and Maisie nodded acknowledgment to Harris as she hurried Charlotte inside.

"Thank you. We'll go straight to Miss Waite's rooms."

The butler bowed, inclined his head to Billy as he came through the doorway with Charlotte's bag, then followed the two women upstairs.

"Billy, wait outside this door until I come for you."

"Right you are, Miss." The door to Charlotte's rooms closed behind him as Billy took up his place.

Maisie took off her coat, then her hat, followed by her blouse. "Hurry, I want you to leave as soon as possible."

Charlotte began to undress. "I . . . I'm not used to . . ."

Maisie pointed to the bathroom. "Go in there, undress, leave your clothes behind and use your dressing gown."

Charlotte scurried into the bathroom while Maisie removed the rest of her clothing. After several moments, Charlotte opened the door and came into her small sitting room again. Maisie pointed to the pile of clothes on the chair.

"Now, put those on and pull some strands of hair free. I'll be out in a minute."

She dressed as swiftly as she could. Her hands were cold and she found it hard to do up the buttons at the front of Charlotte's dress. Perhaps she didn't really need to wear Charlotte's clothes, but in case someone looked up at the sitting room from the garden, she must be prepared. It would be Billy who had to take care not to be seen.

Returning to the sitting room, Maisie gasped. "Oh, my . . . if I didn't know better!"

"Your clothes fit me very well, Miss Dobbs."

"And the hat seems to be a good size for you, too."

Charlotte smiled. "I . . . I should thank you –"

Maisie held up her hand. "Don't say anything . . . not yet, anyway. This day is far from over. You know what to do next?"

"Yes. I have to return directly to Number 15 Ebury Place. Sandra is expecting me and will remain with me at all times until you return."

"And you must not leave your room. Is that understood? You must stay with Sandra!" Maisie spoke quietly but urgently.

"I understand, Miss Dobbs. But what about my father?"

"One step at a time. One step at a time. Right, are you ready?"

Charlotte nodded.

"Good." Maisie opened the door and beckoned Billy into the room.

Billy looked from Maisie to Charlotte Waite and back again. "So, this is it, then?"

"Ready, Billy?"

"I'm ready." Billy reached for the door handle. "You know, there's one question I've been meaning to ask you, Miss Waite?"

Charlotte looked first at Maisie, then back at Billy. "Yes, Mr Beale?"

"Did you 'ave two address books, you know, one what was old with all your addresses in, and another what you left behind?"

"Why . . . yes, yes I did. I took the old one with me because I never did get used to the new one. It was so empty, it made me feel as if I didn't really know anyone."

"Thought so. We'd better be on our way now." He turned to Maisie. "Take care, Miss."

⸻

The light was beginning to fade. Maisie watched from the window of Charlotte's sitting room as they left, noticing how Charlotte had straightened her spine. The small rear lights of the taxicab were extinguished as it drove towards the gatehouse. She knew that she had taken a chance with Billy; his weak leg rendered him a questionable asset. But she was forced to ask him to return surreptitiously to the Waite mansion. She needed a witness, someone on her side, and did not know how far the household could be trusted. If only Stratton had been open to another view – but he had not.

Maisie's eyes were drawn to the dovecote, where it seemed for just a second that she saw movement in the evening shadow. Something stirred again, and a few doves flew up. Maisie watched the ghost-like flapping of wings in the twilight sky as the doves circled before swooping down to return to their home for the night. When she looked at the dovecote again, the shadow was gone. She knew that, disguised as Charlotte Waite, she had cause to fear. Entering the bedroom, Maisie closed the curtains then walked across to the bed. Drawing back the counterpane and bedclothes, she pulled off the pillows and repositioned the long bolster so that it seemed as if the bed were occupied.

The oldest trick in the book – let's hope it works. She turned on the dressing-table lamp and scanned the room before reopening the curtains; then she surveyed her handiwork from the door. *Yes. Very good.*

In the sitting room, Maisie was reaching for the curtains when she heard a soft knock at the door. She did not answer. There was another gentle knock, then a woman's voice.

"Miss Waite? Miss Waite? I thought I'd come to see if you'd like a cup of tea. Miss Waite?"

Maisie breathed a sigh of relief. She sat in silence. A minute passed before she heard steps receding along the hallway. She checked her watch, the one accessory she had not relinquished. Billy should be back soon. She sat in the same chair she had occupied on her initial visit to the rooms, when she had first felt Charlotte's lingering fear and sorrow. And she waited.

Another knock at the door. She listened carefully, for if all had gone well, Billy should have returned by now.

"Miss Waite? Miss Waite? Can you hear me? What about a bowl of chicken-and-dumpling soup? You need to keep up your strength, Miss Waite."

Maisie was silent, listening. When at last footsteps receded along the hallway for a second time, Maisie realized that she was indeed in need of sustenance. Opening Charlotte's bag she took out a bottle of lemonade and a sandwich. To maintain absolute silence, she went into the tiled bathroom to eat and take a few sips of lemonade.

It was now completely dark outside. Had she been wrong to anticipate that the murderer would strike again quickly? Time passed slowly.

Ten o'clock. Another knock. Maisie tensed.

"Miss Waite? Miss Waite? You must be gasping for a nice cup of tea and something to eat by now. As you don't want to see anyone, I'm leaving a tray outside the door. There's a pot of tea and some macaroons. They're fresh from the oven, I made them especially for you."

The tray was set down. Retreating footsteps indicated that the corridor was now empty. Very slowly Maisie turned the key and handle and pulled the tray inside. She closed and locked the door behind her, then set the tray down on the table next to the wing chair.

Maisie lifted the lid of the teapot and sniffed the Earl Grey, strong with the smell of bergamot. *Yes.* Then she crumbled the fresh macaroon, still warm and filled with the aroma of almonds. Simple attempts to disguise a toxic feast. Taking up the pot, she poured a cup of tea, added milk and sugar, swirled the liquid around then went to the bathroom to pour all but a few dregs into the sink. She poured away half of the tea in the pot, so that the provider would think she had taken two or three cups. Then, leaving the door to the bedroom ajar, she dropped the cup and saucer to the floor, spilling what poison-laced tea was left across the carpet. She was so close to the window that her silhouette could be seen from the gardens so, knowing that there was an observer, she half-staggered across the bedroom and fell onto the bed. Once there, Maisie rolled sideways onto the floor and crawled to the corner, where she took up her hiding place behind the wardrobe. From this vantage point she could see the doorway and the bed. Her only concern now was for Billy's arrival.

She waited.

Just at the point when she thought a leg cramp was becoming unendurable, a key turned in the lock of the main door to Charlotte Waite's suite of rooms. Maisie held her breath. A light footfall stopped at the chair; then came a clinking sound as the intruder reached for the fallen china and set it on the tray. She heard the lid being taken off the teapot, then replaced. Another moment passed, footsteps came closer and Maisie crouched lower as a long shadow unfolded across the floor when the door opened wide.

She swallowed and, in the tension of the moment, feared that the person who had come to kill Charlotte Waite might have heard her. Once again she held her breath and watched as a hand was held high with blade ready. The killer moved towards the bed, then lost all control and screamed to the heavens. Doubling over, she keened so deeply and with such passion that even her shadow seemed to emit a deep guttural cry. She sobbed as only a mother can, her whole body given over to the grief and rage of one who has lost her children. Again and again she rammed the bayonet home into what she believed to be the already cold body of Charlotte Waite.

The killer slumped to the floor, her chest heaving, her lungs gasping for air. Maisie moved to her side, knelt and pulled the woman to her, holding her close while taking the bayonet from her limp, unresisting grasp.

"It's all over now, Mrs Willis. It's all over. It's over."

22

"MISS!" BILLY snapped on the light, kneeling awkwardly beside Maisie. He pulled a handkerchief from his pocket and carefully removed the bayonet from her hand.

"Miss, I couldn't get back in again. I tried, but there was too —"

"Never mind, Billy. Summon Stratton immediately. Go now, but first make sure that bayonet is somewhere safe!"

When Billy returned, Maisie had already helped Mrs Willis into the sitting room, seating her in Charlotte Waite's wing chair. She was calm, but her eyes were dull as she stared in front of her.

"He's coming right over. They telephoned 'im at 'is 'ome, Miss, and 'e's on 'is way."

There was time to sit with the woman who had taken three lives and would have taken a fourth. Billy stood by the door, Maisie kneeling beside Mrs Willis, who sat gazing into the fire Maisie had lit for her comfort. The scene might have reflected a young woman visiting a favourite aunt.

"I'll hang, won't I, Miss Dobbs?"

Maisie looked into the glazed eyes of the woman leaning forward in Charlotte's wing chair.

"I cannot second-guess a jury, Mrs Willis. When the whole story is told, they may find grounds for mercy. You may not even be considered fit to stand trial."

"Then they'll send me away."

"Yes. You will lose your freedom."

Mrs Willis nodded, her lips forming a crooked smile. She gazed into the flames. "I lost my freedom a long time ago, Miss Dobbs."

Maisie remained still. "I know."

"They *killed* my whole family. All except my youngest, and he's as good as lost to me."

"Yes." Maisie knew that now was not the time to raise the issue of nuances, of what might have happened anyway, after conscription.

"It seems as if it were yesterday." Mrs Willis looked up at Maisie. Billy came a little closer so that he, too, could hear.

"My Frederick was a master butcher. Had worked for Waite's for years. We were young when we got married. I fell for our eldest straight away; honeymoon baby, that's what they called him. Our Anthony. Oh, he was a love. Soft, was Tony. If that boy saw a bird in the street that couldn't fly, well, it would be in the kitchen with a saucer of bread and milk before you knew it. Then a year later came Ernest. Different kettle of fish altogether, that Ernest . . ." Mrs Willis smiled as she looked into the past.

"Ernest was a little tyke. If there was mischief, then you could bet Ernest was in the middle of it. But Tony was there to put him right, and as much as they were chalk and cheese, they were always together. Always. Then came Wilfred, Will, our youngest. Loved books, loved to read. And so thoughtful, you'd have supposed he was in a dream half the time. The neighbours said I was lucky, to have three boys who got on so well. Of course there were times that they had a bit of a dustup. Like puppies, tumbling all over each other until Frederick had to go out and take each of them by the scruff of the neck. He was a big man, my Frederick. He'd end up there with them, wrestling in the garden with them all over him. People said I was born under a lucky star, with my boys."

Billy had moved even closer. In the distance, Maisie heard the main gate open and the crunch of tyres as Stratton's Invicta motor car made its way to the front of the house. Another vehicle followed, presumably the van that would transport Mrs Willis. She motioned to Billy to stand by the door, ready to prevent a noisy entrance by the police.

"Well, first Tony went to work at Waite's, then Ernie went, and

Will last." Mrs Willis brought her gaze back to Maisie. "Mr Waite liked having families work for the company, said it was good for morale for sons to learn from their fathers. He was doing the same thing with young Joseph." She stared silently.

"Go on." Maisie could hear voices in the corridor, which then subsided as Billy met the police. When Billy, Stratton, and a newly-minted woman police constable stepped into the room, Maisie raised her hand to stop them. Mrs Willis continued her story, oblivious to the new arrivals.

"Then one day Tony came off his shift, very down at heart. Not like himself. Ernie and Will came home, didn't say much. Went straight upstairs. I could hear the three of them talking, but I thought something had happened in the warehouse, you know, a bit of trouble, something like that. Frederick wasn't there that day, he'd gone to the abattoir. Mr Waite liked one of his master butchers to go there, to check up, to make sure work was being done to the highest standards."

Mrs Willis paused. Maisie's eyes met Stratton's. He was prepared to wait.

"You know, I can't say as I know quite what happened next. It was as if one minute there we were, going along nicely, this lovely little family. We weren't well-off, not by any means, but we got by with a bit of room to spare, 'specially now that the boys were bringing something home. Then it all changed. Tony and Ernie came home the next day – they'd been very quiet – and they'd joined up. Enlisted! Their father and me, we just couldn't believe it. Everything crumbled, my house crumbled. Frederick said that he couldn't have his boys joining up without him to look after them. He was still a young man, really. Not even forty. He was too old on paper, but the enlisting office wasn't that picky, as long as you were a fit man. Joined up with them he did, and of course, they were together with all the other men and boys who'd enlisted from Waite's." Mrs Willis looked up into Maisie's eyes again. "And do you know, the thing was that I still didn't know then what had caused it all, what had made them run off and do it. Frederick said it was that being a soldier made them feel big, that they were still so wet behind the ears, they didn't know what it was really all about. I don't think any of us did."

Mrs Willis fell silent. The WPC moved towards Mrs Willis, but Stratton placed a hand on her arm.

"It was Will that told us. Mind you, word had already started to go around, about the Waite girl and those friends of hers with their little white feathers. Stupid, stupid, stupid girls." She balled her fists and pounded her knees. Tears began to flow again as she spoke. "Frederick told Will – I can see him now, standing in the doorway on the day they left, all in uniform, a little family army marching off to war – 'You look after your mother, my boy. You stay here and do the work for me and your brothers.'" She placed a hand on her chest. "But the silly little beggar wouldn't listen. Too young by half, he was, too young by half. He had to go and join up, didn't he? Said that no one called the Willis men cowards, that if his dad and brothers were over there, then he'd go too. Oh, I wish his father had been there to stop him. 'You'll be all right, Mum, Mr Waite will look after you, all the families will be all right. Then we'll all be home again before you know it.' But they weren't. Even Will, he might have come home in body, but he never came home to me again, not as my Will." Mrs Willis slumped forward, crying into her hands. Maisie moved to her side. "I lost them all, I lost them because of those wicked, wicked girls. And . . . and . . . I just couldn't bear it any more. I just couldn't bear the . . . the . . . ache. . ."

Maisie was aware of the silence of the group watching, but did not look back. She placed a comforting arm around Mrs Willis.

"It was like a knife through my heart," the woman sobbed. "The man came with the telegram, and at first I couldn't do a thing. I couldn't hear, couldn't even breathe. I just stood there like I'd been frozen." Mrs Willis pressed her hand to her heart. "The man said, 'I'm sorry, love' and there I was, completely alone. I was in a daze, a terrible daze, with this flimsy piece of paper in my hand, wondering, Which one? *Which one?* Then the knife went in, right there. And it happened three times; three times I was stabbed, and then again when I saw the state Will was brought home in. And the pain hasn't stopped since . . . right here, right here . . ." The woman pounded her chest and struggled for breath.

Maisie closed her eyes and remembered the last three names commemorated in handmade tiles above the door of Joseph Waite's shop in Oxford Street: Frederick Willis, Anthony Frederick Willis, Ernest James Willis. She spoke softly, yet took care to ensure that Stratton could hear all that was said.

"Is that why an overdose of morphine wasn't enough?"

Mrs Willis nodded. "I drugged them first. I wanted them to hear, before they died. I didn't want them to walk away or ask me to leave. I wanted them to die as they listened to me tell them about my boys. I wanted them to know *why*, and I wanted it to be the last thing they heard on this earth. God only knows what my boys heard."

"And then you left the white feathers behind?"

"Yes. I left them behind. If their spirits lingered, I wanted them to linger in torment. I wanted them to be reminded. I wanted them to suffer as my boys suffered, as all those boys suffered, and as their people at home suffered. I wanted them to be between this world and the next, never at peace. Never, ever at rest." Exhausted, Mrs Willis leaned into Maisie's arms and wept.

As Maisie held the grieving woman to her, she lifted her head and motioned for Stratton and the WPC. Passing the weight as gently as one would hand a new baby back to its mother, Maisie allowed the WPC and Stratton to help Mrs Willis to her feet. As Maisie joined Billy she noticed moisture in his eyes. She touched his arm.

"S'alright, Miss. I'm alright."

Mrs Willis mustered the strength to stand tall while Stratton formally cautioned her and as the three moved towards the door, she stopped in front of Maisie.

"Would you look in on my Will, Miss Dobbs? He won't even know I'm not there. I think my visiting is just for my sake, really. But I'd like to know that someone is looking out for him every now and again."

"Yes, of course I'll visit, Mrs Willis."

"Me, too. I'll go too," added Billy.

Two constables stationed outside the door accompanied Mrs Willis and the WPC to the idling vehicles. At the far end of the corridor, a cadre of staff waited, all of whom reached out to touch Mrs Willis as she passed. Two more constables waited for orders to secure the crime scene.

"I owe you an apology, Miss Dobbs," said Stratton.

"I think the apology must go to Magnus Fisher. And perhaps to John Sedgewick." Stratton nodded, and for a moment neither knew quite what to say.

"And once again, I must offer my congratulations. I'll also have to ask you to come down to the Yard to make a formal statement."

"Of course."

"And you too, Mr Beale."

"Right you are, Detective Inspector. Oh, and by the way . . ." Billy reached over to the fire irons and took out the bayonet. "Couldn't think of where else to put it. But like I mentioned to you before Miss, my old mum always said that it was 'ardest to find something 'idden in full view."

BILLY WAS loath to leave his family, and Maisie despaired of ever getting him to Chelstone. But he finally acquiesced, and on the first Monday in May Maisie parked the MG at Charing Cross station and accompanied him to the platform.

"Thanks for bringing me to the station, Miss. Don't think I would have left Doreen and the nippers if you 'adn't."

"It won't be long until you see them again, Billy. And it's for the best."

Billy pulled change from his pocket to buy a newspaper. "Look at this, Miss." Billy pointed to the front page, "I dunno, there's this young lady, Amy Johnson, flying off to Australia on 'er own – twenty-six she is – and goin' in a little aeroplane, if you please. And here I am, scared of going down to Kent on the train."

Maisie placed her hand on Billy's shoulder. "Never judge a journey by the distance, Billy. Your journey, from the time you went over to France, has demanded bravery of a different kind – and I admire you for it."

Maisie drove to Joseph Waite's house in Dulwich after seeing Billy off. It was a fine day, one that was welcome after the fiercely cold Easter. It seemed to presage another long hot summer, perhaps to rival the previous one. Maisie had dressed in summer clothes for the first time that year, and wore a new pale grey suit, with a hip-length jacket and mid-calf skirt with two small kick pleats at the front and back. Simple black shoes matched a new black hat made of tightly woven straw with a grey ribbon joined in a flat rosette at the side – at two guineas the hat had been an extravagant purchase from Harvey Nichols. The jacket had a shawl collar, a style that Maisie favoured, even though it had been more fashionable several seasons earlier.

She parked according to the usual instructions, and smiled as the door opened and Harris inclined his head in greeting.

"Good morning, Miss Dobbs. I trust that you are well?"

"Yes, very well, thank you very much Harris."

The butler smiled and a moment passed when neither knew quite what to say next. Maisie took the lead.

"Have you seen Will this week?"

"Oh yes, Miss Dobbs. Two of the maids went on Sunday afternoon, and I expect to go on Thursday, my afternoon off."

"How is he?"

"The usual, Miss. The usual. He seemed a little confused when new people turned up to take him into the gardens, but settled down again quickly. We can let his mother know that he's not been forgotten."

"Yes, of course."

"Will you visit him, Miss Dobbs?"

"I promised Mrs Willis that I would, so I'll see him when I next visit my . . ." Maisie stopped speaking for a second as an image of Simon came to her, not as he was now, but as a young man. "When I next visit my friend."

The butler indicated the library's open door.

"Mr Waite will be with you shortly."

"Thank you."

Maisie walked over to the library window which commanded a broad view of the gardens and the dovecote. The white birds flew to and from their home, cooing as they settled again, perched among their kind.

"Good morning, Miss Dobbs." Joseph Waite closed the door behind him and offered her one of the chairs by the fireplace. He waited until Maisie was seated, then settled into his own chair.

"How are you, Miss Dobbs?" he asked.

"I'm well, thank you. Is Charlotte settling in comfortably?"

"Yes, she seems to be."

"Have you spent much time with her, Mr Waite?"

Joseph Waite shifted uncomfortably in his chair.

"I know this is a difficult time for you, Mr Waite −"

"You think this is difficult? I lost my son, you know."

Maisie allowed a moment for Joseph Waite's still pent-up anger to settle, and watched as the tension he felt coursed through him. Unmoved, she was determined to continue.

"Mr Waite, why did you instruct your staff to tell me you were not at home when I came here for our previous appointment?"

Joseph Waite twisted the diamond ring on his little finger, the ring that had caught the sun so easily as he reached out to feed doves at his windowsill.

"I . . . I don't know what you're talking about."

Maisie settled into the chair, a move that caused Joseph Waite to look up.

"Yes, Mr Waite, you know very well what I'm talking about. So please answer my question."

"I don't have to take this! Just give me your account and −"

"With respect, Mr Waite, I risked my life in this house, so I will be heard."

Waite was silent, his face flushed.

"The truth is that you kept your daughter in this house because you feared for her life. Your grief and anger over what she had done when she was but a foolish young girl festered, but your love for her caused you to keep her close."

"*Hmmmph!*" Waite looked away.

"You thought that if she lived alone, she would be in danger." Maisie paused. "So you insisted that she, a grown woman, live at home. You didn't even trust a potential husband to keep her safe, did you? Yet though she was under your roof, you could not forgive her."

Waite was restless and again fidgeted in his chair. "You don't know what you're talking about. You have no idea what it's like −"

"You gave Mrs Willis a job as soon as her family went to war. You felt her predicament so keenly that you asked her to come to your home to work as your housekeeper. You paid for Will's care, so that she would never have to worry. And you watched her bitterness grow. But you thought that as long as she, too, was under your roof, you would be in control. When Rosamund and Philippa were murdered, you suspected Mrs Willis, but you didn't do anything about it. Was it because you felt as angry and aggrieved towards them as she did?"

Waite placed his head in his hands, but still he did not speak. Maisie continued.

"When Charlotte disappeared you wanted her back, for you believed that Mrs Willis would not strike at her in your home. It was only close to the end that you became unsure. Though the three deaths were terrible, you did not grieve for those families. Your all-consuming rage at what the women had done was still as sharp as a knife in your side. But if Charlotte was taken from you, too . . ."

Waite shook his head. "I couldn't go to the police. I had no evidence. How could I point the finger at a woman who was broken already, whose family had given their all for my business and for their country."

"That decision, Mr Waite, is subject to debate. You'd visited each woman a few years after the war, to give them a piece of your mind. But it didn't afford you much relief. Anger still gnawed at you, along with the terrible grief at losing Joe."

"Your final account please, Miss Dobbs. Then leave."

Maisie did not move. "What are you going to do about Charlotte, Mr Waite?"

"It'll all work out."

"It hasn't worked out in fifteen years, and it won't work out now unless both you – particularly you – and Charlotte embrace a different idea of what is possible."

"What do you mean? You come here with your fancy ideas –"

"What I mean is this: resentment must give way to possibility, anger to acceptance, grief to compassion, disdain to respect – on both sides. I mean change, Mr Waite. Change. You've remained a successful businessman by embracing change, by mastering it, even when circumstances were against you. You should know exactly what I mean."

Waite opened his mouth as if to argue but then fell silent, staring into the coals. Several minutes passed before he spoke again. "I respect you, Miss Dobbs, that's why I came to you. I don't believe in buying a dog and barking myself. I pay for the best, and I expect the best. So say your piece."

Maisie nodded and leaned forward, forcing Waite to look at her. "Talk *with* Charlotte, not *at* her. Ask her how *she* sees the past, how she feels about losing Joe. Tell her how you feel, not only about your son, but about her. Don't expect to do it all at once. Go for a walk every day in that big garden of yours where the grass is never disturbed by a footprint, talk a little every day, and be honest with each other."

"I don't know about all this talking business."

"That's quite evident, Mr Waite." Maisie continued while she had his ear. "And give her a job. Ask Charlotte to work for you. She needs a purpose, Mr Waite. She needs to stand tall, to do something, to gain some self-respect."

"What can she do? She's never done –"

"She's never had the chance. Which is why neither of you knows what she is capable of accomplishing, of becoming. The truth is that from the time she was a girl you knew which of your two children had it in them to succeed you, didn't you? Joe was a lovely young man, as everyone who knew him agrees, but he didn't quite have what it takes to be the leader your company needs, did he? And though you love Charlotte, you wanted Joe to be the leader so much that you stifled her spirit and she floundered."

"I don't know . . ." Waite struggled. "It's too late now."

"No, it isn't. Experiment, Mr Waite. If one of your grocery items doesn't sell in the front of the shop, you put it in another place, don't you? Try that with Charlotte. Try her in the offices, try her out on the shop floor, have her check quality. Start her at the bottom, where she can show her worth to the staff as much as to you – and to herself."

"I suppose I could."

"But if you really want to blaze a trail, Mr Waite, you'll put her where she can do some good."

"Whatever do you mean?"

"Joseph Waite is known for philanthropy. You give away surplus food to the poor, so why not put Charlotte to work on distribution? Make your contributions into a job and allow her work her way up. Let her prove her mettle, and give her a means to earn respect."

Joseph Waite nodded his head thoughtfully, and Maisie knew that the canny businessman was three steps ahead already, was envisaging capitalizing on her advice in ways that even she could not imagine. She fell silent. Joseph Waite looked at her directly. "Thank you for bringing Charlotte home. And for being frank. We might not always like what we hear but, where I'm from, folk value honest talk, plainly spoken."

"Good." Maisie stood up, reached into her document case and pulled out a manila envelope. "My final account, Mr Waite."

Over the summer months, Maisie travelled to Chelstone each weekend to spend time with Frankie and to see how Billy had progressed. A generous bonus from Joseph Waite allowed her the financial leeway to enjoy her father's company for longer periods of time. In addition, Waite retained Maisie's services for her continuing counsel in rebuilding the relationship between Charlotte and himself.

For his part, Billy regained strength and movement in both legs, each week meeting with the practitioner who instructed him in exercises and movements to counteract the lingering effects of battlefield injury.

"What 'e says, Miss, is that I'm increasing my core."

"Your core?" Maisie watched Billy brush out the mane of Lady

Rowan's latest purchase, a bay mare with an enviable track record, now out to grass and ready for breeding.

"Yep, me core. Makes me sound like a Cox's Orange Pippin, don't it?" Billy curried the horse's mane, continuing with his work as he spoke. "There are all these different exercises, some to stretch me legs, some me arms, and me middle, and some of 'em are really small movements right 'ere." Billy pointed to his stomach with the curry comb. "Which is me core."

"Well, it seems to be doing you a lot of good. I saw you walk across the stable yard with barely a limp."

"The main thing is that the pain ain't what it was. Of course I 'ave to go over for these little chats with Dr Blanche, and then there's Dr Dene who comes up to see me every now and again, you know. And of course, 'e sees yer dad as well."

Maisie felt her face flush, and she looked at the ground. "I would have thought that Dad didn't need any more checkups from Dr Dene, not with the doctor coming up from the village."

Billy secured a lead rein to the mare's halter and they walked outside into the sunshine.

"I think Dr Dene likes to see Dr Blanche, so 'e drops in on yer dad. Asks about you every now and again, 'e does."

"Asks about me?" Maisie shielded her eyes.

Billy grinned, then looked around as tyres crunched on the gravel and a new Austin Swallow came to an abrupt halt at the far end of the courtyard, close to the Groom's Cottage.

"Well, talk of the devil, there's Dr Dene now."

"Oh!"

"Miss Dobbs. How very nice to see you here. And Mr Beale, still making good progress I see."

"Yep, doing very nicely, thank you, Dr Dene. Wasn't expecting to see you today."

"No, I'm on a flying visit to see Maurice." He turned to Maisie. "Stroke of luck meeting you, Miss Dobbs. I've to come up to London soon, for a meeting at St Thomas's. I wondered if you would join me for supper, perhaps a visit to the theatre."

Maisie blushed again. "Um, yes, perhaps."

"Righty-o, I'll get on the dog-and-bone when I'm up there." Andrew Dene shook hands with Billy again, executed a short bow in front of Maisie, then turned and sprinted in the direction of the Dower House.

"Don't mind me sayin' so Miss, but 'e's a bit of a cheeky one, ain't 'e, what with the old rhymin' slang and all. Where did 'e learn that then?"

Maisie laughed. "Bermondsey, Billy. Dr Dene's a Bermondsey boy."

Now that her father was well on the way to a full recovery, and Billy's sojourn in Kent almost at an end, it was time for Maisie to complete the ritual of bringing a major case to a close in the way that she had learned from Maurice. In visiting places and people pertinent to the case she was honouring her teacher's practice of a "full accounting", so that work could move on with renewed energy and understanding. First she visited Hastings again, spending time with Rosamund Thorpe's housekeeper, who was busy packing belongings now that the house had been sold.

"I've found a very nice little cottage in Sedlescombe," said Mrs Hicks. Maisie had declined to come into the house, respectful of the task of packing up to begin a new life. Now she strained to hear the woman's soft voice which was drowned by the seagulls wheeling overhead. "Of course, I'll miss the sea, people always do when they leave the Old Town, not that many do."

Maisie smiled and turned to leave, but Mrs Hicks reached out to her.

"Thank you, Miss Dobbs. Thank you for what you did."

"Oh, please, don't –"

"You know, I always thought that I'd see Mrs Thorpe's killer hang and not feel a shred of pity about it. But I feel terrible for that woman. Terrible. They say she probably won't hang, that they'll send her away. Mind you, if it was me I'd *want* to be dead. I'd want to be with my family."

Later, when Maisie pulled up outside the Bluebell Avenue house in Coulsden, which John Sedgewick had shared with his wife Philippa, a 'For Sale' sign was flapping back and forth in the breeze and Sedgewick was working in the garden. He brushed off his hands and came to greet Maisie as soon as he saw her opening the gate.

"Miss Dobbs, I am so glad to see you!"

"Mr Sedgewick." Maisie held out her hand, which Sedgewick took in both of his.

"How can I ever thank you?"

"Please, there's no need."

"Well, thank you for finding out the truth." Sedgewick placed his hands in his pockets. "I know that what Pippin did was wrong, but I also know that she was a good person. She tried to make up for it."

"Of course she did, Mr Sedgewick. I see you're moving."

"Oh, yes. Time for a complete change, a very complete change. I've accepted a position in New Zealand. There's a lot of building going on there, so chaps like me are rather welcome."

"Congratulations. It's a long way, though."

"Yes, it is. But I had to do it, make a clean break. It's time to go, no good staying here and moping. In any case, this is a street for families, not widowers. They say that change is good for you."

"Good luck Mr Sedgewick. I'm sure you'll find happiness again."

"I hope so, Miss Dobbs. I do hope so."

Though she walked by the mews house owned by Lydia Fisher, she did not ring the bell. The upper windows were open, and she could hear a gramophone playing at a volume that showed no consideration for neighbours. A woman laughed aloud, and even from the street below Maisie could hear the clink of glasses. She thought of the vaporous loneliness that had seeped into every piece of furniture, every fabric in Lydia Fisher's home, and whispered, "May she rest in peace."

———

The red brick of Camden Abbey seemed almost aflame against a seldom-seen blue sky that graced the Romney Marshes, but a chill breeze whipped across the flat land to remind all who came that this was pasture reclaimed from the sea. Once again Maisie was led to the visitors' sitting room where, instead of tea, a small glass flagon had been placed on a tray with some milky white cheddar and warm bread. Dame Constance was waiting for her, smiling through the grille as she entered.

"Good afternoon, Maisie. It's lunchtime, so I thought a little of our blackberry wine with homemade bread and cheese might go down well."

Maisie sat down opposite. "I don't know about wine, not when I have to get behind the wheel again soon. I think I should beware of your Camden Abbey brews."

"In my day, Maisie —"

Maisie raised a hand. "Dame Constance, I confess I wonder how they ever let you in, what with the things you did in your day."

The nun laughed. "Now you know the secret of the cloister, Maisie, we only take people who know the world. Now then, tell me how you are. We are not so isolated that we know nothing of the news here, you know. I understand that your investigations met with success."

Maisie reached towards the flagon and poured a small measure of translucent deep red wine. "I find the word 'success' difficult to apply to this case, Dame Constance. Yes, the murderer has been brought to justice, but many questions linger."

Dame Constance nodded. "People assume that we have a head start on wisdom in a place such as this, where women gather in a life of contemplation, a life of prayer. But it isn't quite like that. Wisdom comes when we acknowledge what we can never know."

Maisie sipped her wine.

"I have come to wonder, Maisie, if our work really *is* so different. We are both concerned with questions, are we not? Investigation is part of both our lives, and we are witnesses to confession."

"When you put it like that, Dame Constance —"

"We both have to avoid making personal judgments and we are both faced with the challenge of doing and saying what is right when the burden of truth has been placed on our shoulders."

"My job is to look hard for the clues that evade me."

"And you have learned the lesson, no doubt, that while looking hard for clues in your work, you may be blind to the unanswered questions in your own life. Or you may be providing yourself with a convenient distraction from them."

Maisie smiled in acknowledgment as she sipped again from the glass.

Stratton was restrained as usual during their long-postponed lunch at Bertorelli's. He did not repeat his regret at failing to listen to her theory, though they could not help but discuss the case.

"Has Mrs Willis told you yet where she obtained the morphine?" asked Maisie.

Stratton rested his right forearm on the table and ran a finger around the rim of his water glass. "Various sources. There was an attempt to procure some from the hospital in Richmond, but she was disturbed by a nurse just as she was entering the nurses' office. Of course they couldn't prove anything, but they became rather more vigilant regarding the security of medicines. Some of her supply came from – you will never believe this – the belongings of a maiden aunt who had passed away earlier this year. Mrs Willis found several of those tins of morphine in phials that were once so fashionable among the ladies, and easily purchased. Though old, the substance had lost none of its strength. She bought some from a chemist, and also used the deceased Mr Thorpe's supply. Morphine can take a long time to do its work, but she was lucky – if you can call it that – in rendering her victims helpless enough to hear what she had to say before administering a fatal dose."

"And the bayonet."

"Street market."

Maisie shook her head.

They were quiet, and for a time Maisie wondered whether Stratton might talk about his son, but when he spoke again it was of a business matter, an offer that rather surprised her.

"Miss Dobbs. You must have read the news in the papers about two weeks ago, that there's a new Staff Officer in charge of the Women's Section at the Yard."

"Yes, of course. Dorothy Peto."

"Yes. Well, she's suggesting all sorts of changes, including women being posted to the Criminal Investigation Department. I was wondering if you might be interested. You know, I could put in a word –"

Maisie held up a hand. "Oh no, Inspector. Thank you all the same, but I prefer to work alone, with only Mr Beale to assist me."

Stratton smiled. "Just as I thought."

Conversation idled as lunch came to a close, though Stratton's demeanour had changed, becoming warmer.

"I wonder," he said, "If you would care to join me for supper, perhaps. I was thinking of next Wednesday evening, or Thursday."

Very clever, thought Maisie. Wednesday didn't have the significance of Friday, not when it came to a man asking a woman out to dine. "Thank you for the invitation, but I . . . I'll let you know. My assistant returns to work next week. He's been taking time for a special course of therapy to ease a troublesome war wound. I have much to do before he comes back."

Stratton rallied quickly. "Then may I telephone you on Tuesday afternoon?"

"Of course. I'll expect to hear from you, then."

Maisie heard the telephone in her office ringing even before she opened the front door, and hurried up the stairs before the caller lost patience.

"Fitzroy five —"

"Is that Miss Maisie Dobbs?"

"Speaking."

"Andrew Dene here."

"Good afternoon, Dr Dene."

"So glad to have reached you. I'll be up in London early next week. That meeting at St Thomas's? It was postponed, but now it's on again. Look, I wonder, would you care to have supper with me, say, Wednesday or Thursday?"

Maisie quickly ruffled some papers on her desk. "Let me see . . . I'm really quite busy at the moment. Could you give me a ring on, oh, Tuesday afternoon?"

"Right you are, Miss Dobbs. I'll telephone you on Tuesday. Until then."

"Yes, until then."

She replaced the receiver.

Maisie stood by the window on Wednesday morning waiting for Billy Beale to return to work. She rubbed the back of her neck and paced to the mirror, checked her appearance for the one hundredth time since her visit to Bond Street the previous afternoon. Time for a change. She thought of Simon. Yes, though she would continue to visit, probably forever, it was time to move on, to set her cap for . . . whatever fate might bring her way.

Turning to the window again, she saw Billy round the corner, walking briskly. *Yes.* With a spring in his step and barely any sign of a limp, Billy Beale made his way across Fitzroy Square, tipping his cap at a woman walking with her children, and – she was sure of this – whistling as he walked. *Yes.* He was the old Billy again. *Good.*

Just before he reached the front door, Billy stopped in front of a flight of pigeons that had gathered to pick at the paving stones. He shook his head, then carefully made his way around the birds before running up the steps and polishing the brass nameplate with the underside of his sleeve before entering.

Maisie listened. The door closed with a loud thump and Billy whistled his way up the stairs. She rubbed at her neck again as the door swung open.

"Mornin' Miss, and innit a lovely – blimey!"

"Good morning, Billy. It's good to have you back, even though you've brought some rich language with you."

"You've . . . you've changed."

"Thank you for being so observant, Billy. That's what you're paid for." Maisie touched her hair.

"I mean, Miss, well, it's a bit of a shock, innit? But it suits you, really it does."

Maisie looked at him anxiously. "Are you sure? You're not just saying that, are you Billy?"

"No, Miss. Even though my Dad always said that a woman's 'air is 'er crownin' glory. It suits you, makes you seem more . . . sort of modern."

Maisie walked to the mirror again, still surprised to see her reflection, with her hair cut into a sharp bob.

"I just couldn't stand all that hair any more, especially the bits that always flew out at the sides. I wanted a change."

Billy hung his coat on the hook at the back of the door and turned back to Maisie. "Now all you need is somewhere nice to go."

"Well, I *am* going out for supper tonight."

"Supper?" said Billy with a mischievous grin. "Now Miss, I thought you said you didn't dine out in the evenings because supper meant something more than lunch."

Maisie laughed. "I changed my mind."

"I 'spec it's with Dr Dene. 'E's up here this week for 'is meetin's."

"Yes, I believe he is."

"Or is it the Detective Inspector?"

"Now then, Billy."

"Go on, Miss, you can tell me."

"No, Billy, I can't. Let's just say that it's something for me to know and you to deduce. And talking of powers of deduction, I've just taken on an interesting new case."

Acknowledgements

M Y FRIEND and writing buddy, Holly Rose, was the first to read *Birds of a Feather* and I am ever-grateful for her support, honesty, insight and enthusiasm. My agent, Amy Rennert is a powerful blend of friend, mentor and coach – and is the best. Thanks must also go to my editor Laura Hruska and to everyone at Soho Press – a terrific publishing team.

I am indebted to my Cheef Resurcher (who knows who he is) for the hours spent among dusty old copies of *The Times* and for his invaluable counsel on the history of the inner workings of "The Yard." Any wide turns with fact and procedure may be attributed to the author who will gladly repay his hard work with a few bottles of the peaty stuff.

My parents, Albert and Joyce Winspear, have once again been wonderful resources regarding "old London" and have also entertained me with their renditions of Cockney ballads via long-distance 'phone calls.

Kenneth Leech, to whom this book is dedicated, was the foundation stone of my education. It was in his classroom, when I was ten, that I first heard the Great War story that inspired *Birds of a Feather*. He was a great teacher and a very dear person.

To my husband, John Morell: thank you for being my numero uno fan – and for scouring used bookstores for even more sources for me to draw upon in my quest to bring colour and depth to the life of Maisie Dobbs.

Every writer should have a dog and I have Sally, my constant companion while I'm working, along with her friend, Delderfield, a completely idle cat.

Read more ...

Jacqueline Winspear

MAISIE DOBBS

Maisie Dobbs takes on her first investigation in 1920s London

Young, feisty Maisie Dobbs has recently set herself up as a private detective. Such a move may not seem especially startling, but this is 1929 and Maisie is exceptional in many ways.

Having started as a maid to the London aristocracy, studied her way to Cambridge and served as a nurse in the Great War, Maisie has wisdom, experience and understanding beyond her years. Little does she realise the extent to which this strength of character is soon to be tested. For her first case forces her to uncover secrets long buried, and to confront ghosts from her own past.

'Jacqueline Winspear's Maisie Dobbs is a welcome addition to the sleuthing scene. Simultaneously self-reliant and vulnerable, Maisie isn't a character I'll easily forget' Elizabeth George

'Readers sensing a story-within-a-story won't be disappointed. But first, they must prepare to be astonished at the sensitivity and wisdom with which Maisie resolves her first professional assignment' *New York Times*

Order your copy now by calling Bookpoint on 01235 827716 or visit your local bookshop quoting ISBN 978-0-7195-6622-6 www.johnmurray.co.uk

Read more . . .

Jacqueline Winspear

PARDONABLE LIES

Much-loved Maisie Dobbs returns to investigate her third case, a thrilling story of family tensions and mysterious deaths in the First World War

London, 1930. Maisie Dobbs, the renowned psychologist and investigator, receives a most unusual request. She must prove that Sir Cedric Lawton's son Ralph really is dead.

This is a case that will challenge Maisie in unexpected ways, for Ralph Lawton was an aviator shot down by enemy fire in 1917. To get to the bottom of the mystery, Maisie must travel to the former battlefields of northern France, where she served as a nurse in the Great War. As her investigation moves closer to the truth, Maisie soon uncovers the secrets and lies that some people would prefer remain buried.

'Feisty, working-class heroine Maisie is a deliberate throwback to the sleuthettes of old-fashioned crime writing. The well-plotted story, its characters and the picture of London between the wars are decidedly romantic' *Guardian*

'For readers yearning for the calm and insightful intelligence of a main character like P. D. James's, Maisie Dobbs is spot on'
Boston Globe

*Order your copy now by calling Bookpoint on 01235 827716 or
visit your local bookshop quoting ISBN 978-0-7195-6736-0*
www.johnmurray.co.uk

Read more . . .

Jacqueline Winspear

MESSENGER OF TRUTH

Charming sleuth Maisie Dobbs returns in her fourth mystery, investigating a suspicious death in the art world of 1930s London

London, 1931. Nick Bassington-Hope, veteran of the Great War and controversial artist, is suddenly found dead. His death from a fall, the night before a much-anticipated exhibition of his work, is recorded as 'accidental' – but his sister is not convinced.

Despite overwhelming evidence to the contrary, Georgina Bassington-Hope believes that her brother was murdered, and she turns to Maisie Dobbs for help. Still fragile after her war-related breakdown, Maisie's immersion in her work could lead her to lose more than she bargained for, while a desperate family with strong ties to her heart urgently needs her help.

'A new Maisie Dobbs mystery is always a cause for celebration . . . *Messenger of Truth* is fiendishly entertaining' *Time Out*

'The British counterpart to Alexander McCall Smith's *The No. 1 Ladies' Detective Agency*' *Associated Press*

Order your copy now by calling Bookpoint on 01235 827716 or visit your local bookshop quoting ISBN 978-0-7195-6739-1
www.johnmurray.co.uk